HERE'S WHAT ~
TH

S~

"All the color and imagery of a film enliven this story…Rarely has a novel captured so authentically the enduring faith of the Irish peasant…"

EOIN MCKIERNAN, Founder,
Irish American Cultural Institute

Book 2
Heart of the Lonely Exile…

"…A brilliant picture of the excitement and drama of life in New York City
a century ago."

IRISH BOOKS AND MEDIA

"These are people to admire and care about, people who have struggled with
the demons of sickness, death, and despair, and have survived because of
their strong faith and trust in God."

OHIOANA QUARTERLY

"…A captivating, faith-filled saga as exuberant, lyrical, and spirited as the
Irish themselves…A historical saga so rich, so vivid, and so riveting you'll
feel like you've gone back in time."

GUIDEPOSTS BOOK CLUB

Book 3
Land of a Thousand Dreams…

"A big, colorful novel, full of the type of upbeat Christian values to be found
in much of Hoff's fiction."

IRISH ECHO

"…Captures the melodic vernacular of the Irish world through a myriad of
complex characters in a sweeping story of the battle to survive, on both the
peasant lands of the Emerald Isle and on the uncertain streets of New York."

WEST COAST REVIEW OF BOOKS

Book 4
Sons of an Ancient Glory...

"Hoff tells a number of striking stories, all involving characters we come to care about immediately. She clearly knows her history, her religion, and her audience, and does a fine job of presenting the first two to the third. This is a series that deserves a lengthy run."

WEST COAST REVIEW OF BOOKS

Recipient of Christianity Today's Critic's Choice Book Award, Fiction

Sons *of an* Ancient Glory

THE EMERALD BALLAD

BJ HOFF

HARVEST HOUSE PUBLISHERS

EUGENE, OREGON

Cover by Koechel Peterson & Associates, Inc., Minneapolis, Minnesota

BJ Hoff: Published in association with the Books & Such Literary Agency, 52 Mission Circle, Suite 122, PMB 170, Santa Rosa, CA 95409-5370, www.booksandsuch.biz.

Previously published in 1993 by Bethany House Publishers.

SONS OF AN ANCIENT GLORY
Copyright © 1993 by BJ Hoff
Published by Harvest House Publishers
Eugene, Oregon 97402
www.harvesthousepublishers.com

Library of Congress Cataloging-in-Publication Data
Hoff, BJ
    Sons of an ancient glory / BJ Hoff.
    p. cm.
    ISBN 978-0-7369-2795-6 (pbk.)
    1. Irish Americans—Fiction. 2. Immigrants—Fiction. 3. Ireland—Fiction I. Title.
PS3558.O34395S63 2011
813'.54—dc22

                                                                2010021580

            11 12 13 14 15 16 17 18 19 / LB-SK / 10 9 8 7 6 5 4 3 2 1

TO MY READERS:

This book is for you. You have overwhelmed me with your letters of encouragement, strengthened me with your prayers of support, and affirmed the value of the stories by opening your caring hearts to me with your *own* unique stories: stories of your struggles, your sorrows, and your victories.

Storytelling has always been of the utmost importance to the Irish. Because the Gaelic language was outlawed for generations, the ancient art of storytelling was crucial to the survival of Irish culture. For centuries in Ireland, the itinerant *Seanchai*—the Storyteller—was the person who kept the legends, the history, the traditions of the people alive.

I believe God has used my own passion for all things Irish to motivate me to take up the tradition of the *Seanchai* and tell the story of Ireland's tragedy—and the long-range effect of that tragedy on both the Emerald Isle and America. But because I also believe that the Irish represent a *universal* immigration experience (having endured bondage, religious persecution, genocide, displacement, and ethnic prejudice), I like to think that the Emerald Ballad novels are not only stories about Irish immigrants, but stories about *all* immigrants. Many of you have written to confirm that belief, and I thank you.

Above all else, I hope *Sons of an Ancient Glory* and all the other Emerald Ballads portray a compassionate God at work among His people, a God who understands our frailties and redeems our failures. Time and time again God charges us in His Word to tell our children and our grandchildren of His deeds. So, as I tell you these stories of the Children of Erin, it is my prayer that you will pass them on. May we all be faithful to tell our children...and *their* children...of "His deeds, His power, and the wonders He has done."

Dia linn...
God bless us.
BJ Hoff
2010

Acknowledgments

My warmest thanks and appreciation to Harvest House Publishers for publishing this new edition of *Sons of an Ancient Glory,* the fourth book of The Emerald Ballad series, and for their ongoing support and encouragement of my work.

About BJ Hoff

BJ Hoff's bestselling historical novels continue to cross the boundaries of religion, language, and culture to capture a worldwide reading audience. In addition to The Emerald Ballad series, her books include such popular titles as *Song of Erin* and *American Anthem* and bestselling series such as The Riverhaven Years and The Mountain Song Legacy. Her stories, although set in the past, are always relevant to the present. Whether her characters move about in Ireland or America, in small country towns or metropolitan areas, reside in Amish settlements  or in coal company houses, she creates *communities* where people can form relationships, raise families, pursue their faith, and experience the mountains and valleys of life.

A direct descendant of Irish ancestors who came to this country before the Revolutionary War, BJ brings a decade of historical research and strong personal involvement to The Emerald Ballad series. Her understanding of the Irish people—their history, their struggles, their music, their indomitable spirit—lends to her writing all the passion and power of her own Irish heritage. BJ and her husband make their home in Ohio.

For a complete listing of BJ's books published by
Harvest House Publishers, turn to page 377.

Contents

PART THREE
LIGHT OF HOPE • GLORIOUS GRACE

PRINCIPAL CHARACTERS

Ireland

Morgan Fitzgerald (the *Seanchai*): Poet, patriot, and schoolmaster. Grandson of British nobleman, Richard Nelson. Formerly of County Mayo. Dublin.

Finola: Mysterious beauty with no memory of her past. Dublin.

Annie (Aine) Fitzgerald: Belfast runaway adopted by Morgan Fitzgerald. Dublin.

Sandemon (the "West Indies Wonder"): Freed slave from Barbados. Hired companion and friend of Morgan Fitzgerald. Dublin.

Sister Louisa: Nun employed as teacher by Morgan Fitzgerald for his new Academy. Dublin.

Tierney Burke: Rebellious son of Michael Burke. Formerly of New York City. Dublin.

Jan Martova: Romany Gypsy who befriends Tierney Burke. Dublin.

Lucy Hoy: Friend and nurse to Finola. Dublin.

America

THE KAVANAGHS AND THE WHITTAKERS

Daniel Kavanagh: Irish immigrant, formerly of Killala, County Mayo. Son of Owen (deceased) and Nora. New York City.

Nora Kavanagh Whittaker: Irish immigrant, formerly of Killala, County Mayo. Wife of Evan Whittaker. Mother of Daniel Kavanagh. New York City.

Evan Whittaker: British immigrant, formerly of London. Assistant to Lewis Farmington. New York City.

Winifred Whittaker Coates: Evan Whittaker's widowed aunt, formerly of England. New York City.

Johanna and Thomas (Little Tom) Fitzgerald: Irish immigrants, orphaned children of Thomas (Morgan Fitzgerald's deceased brother). Adopted by Evan Whittaker and Nora. New York City.

THE BURKES AND THE FARMINGTONS

Michael Burke: Irish immigrant, New York City police captain, formerly of Killala, County Mayo.

Sara Farmington Burke: Daughter of shipbuilding magnate Lewis Farmington. Wife of Michael Burke. New York City.

Lewis Farmington: Shipbuilder, Christian philanthropist. New York City.

THE DALTONS

Jess Dalton: Mission pastor, author, and abolitionist, former West Point Chaplain. New York City.

Kerry Dalton: Irish immigrant, formerly of County Kerry. Wife of Jess. New York City.

Casey-Pitz Dalton: Irish immigrant orphan, adopted by the Daltons. New York City.

THE WALSHES

Patrick Walsh: Irish immigrant, formerly of County Cork. Crime boss. New York City.

Alice Walsh: Wife of Patrick. Mother of Isabel and Henry. New York City.

OTHERS

Billy Hogan: Fatherless Irish immigrant, formerly of County Sligo. New York City.

Quinn O'Shea: Newly arrived Irish immigrant with troubled past. Formerly of County Roscommon. New York City.

Denny Price: Irish immigrant, New York City police sergeant, formerly of County Donegal. New York City.

Nicholas Grafton: New York City physician.

Pronunciation Guide

Aine . . . . Än′ya

a gra . . . . (my love) a grä′

alannah. . . . . (my child) a län′uh

aroon . . . .(my dear, my love) a rōōn

Finola . . . . (from Fionnuala) Fi nō′ la

gorsoon. . . . . (boy) gor sun

Killala . . . . Kil lä′ lä

macushla . . . . (my darling) ma cush′ la

Sandemon . . . . .Sanda mōhn′

Seanchai . . . . (storyteller) Shan′ a kee

I have given them the glory that you gave me, that they may
be one as we are one: I in them and you in me. May they be
brought to complete unity to let the world know that you
sent me and have loved them even as you have loved me.

JOHN 17:22-23

Glory Renewed

And, long, a brave and haughty race
Honoured and sentinelled the place—
Sing oh! not even their sons' disgrace
Can quite destroy their glory's trace.

THOMAS DAVIS (1814–1845)

Killala, Western Ireland
January 1, 1801

Dan Kavanagh flew out of the cottage, little Barry in hand, the midwife's harsh words like grapeshot at his back.

"Ye'll be naught but a nuisance here, man!" shrilled Jane O'Dowd. "Take the tyke, and away with you! Go to McNally's, why not? O'Casey, the *Seanchai,* is there with his tales. I'll send word when it's time, never fear!"

Not a man in the village would argue with the flint-tempered Jane O'Dowd. Dan was off in a shake, little Barry at his heels. The older two boys, Niall and Tim, had gone gaming in the woods with Oran Browne early that morning, no doubt in anticipation of the ordeal to come. Dan did not blame them at all; his own eagerness to get away had been suppressed only with great effort. Though he doubted that even the Storyteller could take his mind off Peg and the babe trying to be born, he could not resist the chance to escape for a bit.

Despite the wind whipping the thatch on McNally's cottage, the door stood open. An entire gaggle of townspeople had gathered close-in, which, of course, meant the inside would be filled to overflowing. That was ever the case when a *Seanchai*—a Storyteller—passed through the village.

Hoisting wee Barry onto his shoulder, Dan wedged a place for them near the door. He caught just a glimpse of the silver-haired O'Casey inside, his spidery-frail bones perched on a stool near the turf fire. Ringed by what appeared to be the entire McNally clan and a remarkable number of villagers, the old traveling man might have been holding court; the cabin was hushed, the facial expressions rapt.

After a moment, Dan realized that O'Casey was giving forth the latest news from Dublin City, where on this very day—the momentous first day of a new century—the despised Act of Union between England and Ireland was to commence.

"But what of the Parliament?" Big Tommy Conlon was asking. "Our Irish Parliament?"

"Irish Parliament, *indeed*!" snorted O'Casey. "As of today, there *is* no Irish Parliament, not that it was ever more than a bad joke entirely." The Storyteller curled his lip. "From this time forth, Ireland and England are to be the same as one country. Our land belongs to the British Crown now, and that's the truth."

"As do our souls," muttered Frank Duggan, a heavy-shouldered farmer hunched near the fire.

A dull pain settled over Dan's chest at their words, though O'Casey's news merely confirmed what was already suspected. After today, there would be no more pretense of the people having any say in the running of their own country. In an obscene show of tyranny, bribery, and fraud, the Union between Ireland and Britain had been forged, and there was nothing for the Irish to do but live with it.

And, more than likely, die with it as well....

Like an ominous dark cloud, the reality of the Union hung over the day, threatening to spoil what should have otherwise been a grand occasion. For at any moment now, Peg would be delivering a new babe—the first which Dan had fathered.

The other three boys were his dead brother's sons. After Brian was hanged for treason in '98, Dan had taken Peg as his wife and the boys as his own. Today would mark the first fruit of their marriage, and by rights he should be thinking of nothing else.

But the ache for his country would not go away, not even for the thought of a new child. Hundreds of years of English oppression had finally come to this, Ireland's greatest humiliation. A paper union, unwanted, despised—a loathsome offspring of corruption, binding the people to an enemy who counted them as less than human.

An insistent nudge from young Emer Costello, next to him, jerked Dan back to his surroundings. He glanced up to see John McNally, inside, beckoning to him and the boy.

"'Tis bitter cold for the wee lad," said McNally, pointing to Barry, who stood shivering in the wind. "Bring him inside. We'll make room."

Parting the crowd, Dan squeezed himself and little Barry through the narrow doorway. Like his own cottage, McNally's place had two rooms, with rock from the hills for a floor. On one wall leaned a rough wooden box which held pieces of cracked pottery and plates. In the chimney corner stood a bed of straw, covered with a heavy gray blanket. The turf fire was low, but seemed to offer a great warmth after the harsh sting of the wind.

As he and Barry crowded in among the family, Dan nodded respectfully to O'Casey, who seemed to take no notice. Obviously intent on his own dark thoughts, the Storyteller's finely webbed face was set in a deep scowl, his hands clenched and anchored on one knee.

"Union!" he hissed, the venom in his tone making a curse of the word. "'Tis nothing short of a rape of the country, and that's the truth! The English have ravaged us again, this time with the help of our own politicians!"

"'Tis said the votes were all bought, every last one of them!" offered the eldest McNally son from the chimney corner.

"Bought, coerced, bribed!" shot back the Storyteller. "Every vile means known to the Crown was employed, and aren't we all well-acquainted with most of them?" Suddenly, the grizzled old man bent over the stool, as if exhausted.

Dan had witnessed O'Casey's long silences before and knew he might not speak again for hours.

No matter. What was there to say, after all? The foul deed was done, and would not be undone, at least not in the foreseeable future, God help them all.

Some claimed the Union would be a fine thing for Ireland, that she would share in the riches of the Crown and enjoy equal rights for all—even the Catholics and the tenant farmers. Others, however—and these

Dan knew to have a better understanding of such things—claimed the new agreement would serve only to bring Ireland more completely under the heel of the British oppressor, that indeed it would be the end of what small freedoms remained to the Irish.

Dan knew he was not as clever a man as some, but he could not help but believe that union with their centuries-old enemy would bring nothing but disaster for Ireland.

Before he could drift further into another fit of melancholy, the quiet of the cottage was pierced by the sound of shouting outside. His head snapped up when he heard his name called.

"Dan Kavanagh! Where's Dan Kavanagh?"

Dan hoisted Barry into his arms and shoved through the crowd. Charging out the door, he found young Joey Mahon barreling up the yard. The lad's thin face was flushed, his eyes fairly dancing with excitement.

The boy stumbled in his haste, then righted himself. "You're to come right away!" he croaked, shifting from one foot to another like a jittery chicken. "Jane O'Dowd said I was to fetch you home without delay!"

A blow of panic struck Dan. He hugged little Barry so tightly to his chest that the tyke let out a wail of protest. "'Tis the babe, then?" he choked out.

Joey Mahon's narrow face cracked to a wide grin. "Not the *babe,* Dan! Oh, not at all, at all! The *babes*! *Two* babes, says Jane O'Dowd!" The boy stopped, gasping for breath. "You've two new sons, Jane says, and you're to get movement under you and come at once!"

Dan stared at the boy. Dazed, he clutched Barry to still the trembling of his hands. "Two?" he said, convinced he had not heard him clearly.

Young Joey's head bounced as if it were on a hinge. "Aye, *two*!" he insisted, his chin bobbing up and down.

"Two," Dan repeated softly to himself. "Two sons."

It was beyond the power of his imagination. He stood like a great lump, staring numbly at the Mahon lad. The worried murmurs nearby now swelled to cries of amazement, then shouts of laughter and congratulations. Men crowded close in. A few crossed themselves, others slapped Dan on the back and pumped his hand.

Dan's head buzzed like a hive full of bees, but at last his legs found life. Twisting free of the well-wishers, he took off at a run, wee Barry chortling in his arms.

Joey Mahon trotted along beside them, his words spilling out in ragged gulps as they ran. "What will you be naming the both of them, Dan? Now you'll be needing two names instead of one!"

Not breaking his stride, Dan glanced at him. *Names?* They had already decided on a name: Brian, for his dead brother. Sure, they had given no thought to needing *two* names!

"And what of the harp, Dan?" Joey Mahon piped on. "Who will claim the Kavanagh harp, now that you've two new sons?"

Dan looked intently at the boy. That question, at least, required no decision on his part. "Why, the harp will belong to my firstborn, sure," he said, slowing his pace only slightly as they passed the Quigley cabin. "Eldest son of the eldest son. When my brother Brian died, the Kavanagh harp was passed to me. Now it will belong to the elder of the twins—Brian, his name shall be, after his uncle. 'Tis only fitting."

A fine, cold rain had begun to fall since they left McNally's place, and already the ground was turning slick with mud. Joey Mahon almost careened into Dan as they turned the corner and started up the road toward the cottage. Putting out a hand to steady the boy, Dan stopped, setting Barry to his feet. "Here, now, lad," he said to Joey Mahon. "Will you be seeing to Barry for a bit while I go inside?"

Taking Barry's chubby hand in his, the lad nodded. "Aye, Dan, I'll take him on home with me. You'll be wanting to visit with your new sons a spell, I expect."

Something in wee Barry's eyes made Dan hesitate. The tyke was staring up at him as if he felt himself abandoned. After another instant, Dan changed his mind and again lifted the boy to his shoulder.

"On the other hand," he said, looking at the child in his arms, "perhaps he'd best be staying with me. No doubt," he added with a smile, "Barry will be glad to meet his new brothers."

Joey Mahon looked a bit disappointed, but merely nodded and said politely, as was his way, "Aye, Dan. I'll just be going, then. But you can send for me later, if you've need of some help."

For a moment Dan stood watching him trudge down the road, a small, solitary lad whose mother had died giving birth to him. The thought made him squeeze Barry a bit closer to his heart, then take off at a near run toward the cottage.

It had turned out to be a fine day, after all. Let there be union with

England—what of it? A man should not be fretting over politics on such a day as this. There would be time another day to think on such solemn matters.

A man with a full quiver of sons had more important things to consider. "Isn't that so, lad?" he said, grinning at the round-faced wee boy in his arms as they approached the cottage door. "An Irishman with five lads under his roof has greater things than Union to study over. Greater things indeed, and God be thanked."

Ah, and weren't there some things that England could not steal from Ireland? The glory of the island's past and her hope for the future were renewed with every fine son born to a man.

That being the case, it did seem to Dan Kavanagh that he had done more than his part for his country.

PART ONE

LIGHT OF PROMISE

New Beginnings

*"For I know the plans I have for you," declares the Lord, "plans to prosper
you and not to harm you, plans to give you hope and a future."*

JEREMIAH 29:11

1

An Afternoon in the Park

But one little rebel there,
Watching all with laughter...
ALICE MILLIGAN (1886–1953)

Brooklyn
May 10, 1849

Little Tom Fitzgerald grinned when he spied the frog at the edge of the pond. It was just a little bullfrog, but big enough, sure, to bring some fun. Big enough to scare some *girls*.

Looking back over his shoulder, he saw that his sister, Johanna, and her friend, Dulcie, were still at the edge of the park where the woods began. They were looking for the nest of baby rabbits they'd discovered the day before.

The yellow-haired Dulcie was giggling. Dulcie was always giggling, because she was a girl and she was silly. Tom expected Johanna would giggle, too, if she could. But his big sister could neither hear nor speak; she merely gave forth with her funny, whispered laugh at Dulcie's foolishness.

Tom didn't think Dulcie was funny at all. In truth, he didn't even like their next-door neighbor very much. She treated him like a baby, teasing him and calling him "Little Tom," even though he had cautioned her not to.

Other than the bossy old Dulcie, most everyone else called him just plain "Tom" these days. He was four years old, after all, close on five, so it was time to be treated like the big boy he was. Aunt Nora and Uncle

Evan were trying, although they often forgot. Johanna still treated him like a wee wane, but somehow his sister's fussing didn't bother him quite so much.

Even so, she had provoked him more than a little in the park this afternoon. Too intent on finding the bunnies to pay Tom any heed, she hadn't even come to his defense, as she usually did, when Dulcie began to tease and order him about. Finally, he'd wandered off by himself, in search of something more interesting than silly girls or baby rabbits.

Then he had spotted the frog. The odd-looking creature had just been sitting there, on the bank of the pond. When Tom took a few steps toward him, he hadn't moved a bit. It was almost as if he were glad for the company.

Now, glancing again from the girls to the bullfrog, Tom stuffed his hands in the pockets of his breeches and started toward the pond. He walked with deliberate slowness, so the frog wouldn't catch on that he was after him. Here and there he kicked a stone, pretending to have nothing more on his mind than taking a stroll through the park.

He imagined himself an Indian brave, like the ones in some of Uncle Evan's bedtime stories. A warrior, that's what he would be today, a warrior on the way to the river, where he would launch his canoe and catch some fish for his family.

Tom wasn't quite sure whether Indian warriors actually went fishing or not. Glancing down over himself, he frowned at the boots Aunt Winnie had made him wear because of the mud in the park. One thing he was almost certain of: Indian warriors did *not* wear boots.

Sitting up in bed, feeling even more restless and bored than usual, Nora Whittaker watched Evan's Aunt Winnie attend to the household chores. Chores she should be doing herself.

The older woman was scurrying about the room like a ballerina, humming cheerfully and whisking a feather duster over the furniture with fluid motions. Despite her pique at feeling so worthless, Nora had to smile. Aunt Winnie was petite and lithe in a rose-colored morning frock, her blond coiffure fresh and neat. Indeed, she looked for all the world as if she should be presiding over a Fifth Avenue tea instead of cleaning house.

Evan's aunt returned Nora's smile, making a graceful pirouette as she gave the wardrobe a few hasty swipes. Standing off as if to admire her work, she nodded with satisfaction, then came back to the bed and sat down beside Nora.

"You're just lying there seething because you can't be up doing your own work," she said, taking Nora's hand. "I can tell."

Nora's smile gave way to a sigh. "That's the truth. I feel so—"

"Bored?"

"There's that," Nora admitted. "But mostly I'm feeling guilty. And entirely useless."

"But you're *not* useless, and you certainly have nothing to feel guilty about! Oh, I know you must be weary beyond imagining of just lying in, but taking care of your baby is much more important than housework, dear!"

"Aye, I know," Nora agreed. "It's just that I hadn't counted on having to stay in bed all this time. It seems the next two months will drag on forever."

"But they won't," Aunt Winnie said practically. "And in the meantime, you must remember that it will all be worthwhile in the end. And," she added, her tone allowing for no argument, "you must also remember that I don't mind helping out. Not in the least. To the contrary, I'm actually enjoying it. I've never kept house before, you know."

At Nora's startled look, Aunt Winnie went on to explain. "My first husband, George Mountjoy, was outrageously rich—didn't Evan tell you about him? Goodness, even George's *servants* had servants!" She put a hand to her cheek. "Dear George. We'd been married only seven years when he passed on."

She paused, giving her flawless coiffure a reassuring pat. "My next husband—Neville—wasn't exactly rich. But he was *Old Family*, you see. His servants were ancient, like the rest of the family, but he had an entire household of them, so I never got to do anything domestic there either. Except," she added with a deep sigh, "for pouring tea."

For the life of her, Nora couldn't decide whether to laugh or commiserate. Impulsively, she squeezed Aunt Winnie's hand—a small hand, delicate and exquisitely manicured. "I can't imagine how you managed. Being widowed twice, I mean. When Owen—my first husband—died, I wanted to die, too."

"I know," Evan's aunt said with another small sigh. "But one does one's best." She looked at Nora, her expression brightening. "And at the moment, you are to do your best to stay strong and cheerful. For the baby. And for Evan, too, of course. Just *see* how happy you've made him, Nora. You're very good for Evan, dear, you really are!"

Nora looked away. "Lately, I feel more burden than blessing to Evan," she confessed softly. "The man has little to look forward to each day when he comes home. An invalid wife who can do nothing at all but lie here like a great lump."

"Oh, pshaw!" Aunt Winnie retorted. "Such foolish talk! So long as Evan has *you* to come home to, you won't hear him complaining, I promise you! Goodness, his heart floods his eyes every time he looks at you. Why, if a man looked at me the way my nephew looks at *you*, I'd simply swoon! Really, I would."

Nora laughed. "You'd best have a caution about Mr. Farmington, then, I'm thinking."

"I'm sure I don't know what you mean," replied Evan's aunt, the faintest hint of pink flushing her cheeks.

Nora lifted one eyebrow, but Aunt Winnie merely smiled prettily, saying, "Lewis is a thoroughly charming man."

"He is, indeed," said Nora.

"Well," said the other, springing to her feet, "I must get on with the dusting. I'll start dinner in a few moments, dear, before Lewis and Evan arrive from the yards."

"Perhaps Mr. Farmington would stay for the meal if you'd ask," Nora suggested.

"Oh, we can't, dear! Lewis is taking me to see Macready at the Astor Place theater tonight. I'm going to change here before we leave so I won't have to stop at the flat on the way."

She started toward the door, then turned back. "As for *you*, my dear, I want you to do what *I* do when I'm tempted to feel sorry for myself."

Unaware until this instant that she *had* been feeling sorry for herself, Nora stared.

"I take pen and paper and make a detailed list of all the things I'm thankful for," explained Aunt Winnie, smiling. "Then, once I've written them all out plain to see, I read each one aloud. By the time I've finished reading the list, I've forgotten why I was feeling blue." She stopped. "Would you like me to get you some writing paper, dear?"

Again Nora burst into laughter. "Yes, please do, Aunt Winnie."

Evan's aunt beamed. "Wonderful! You'll head *your* list with Evan and those delightful children, of course. And the little one on the way."

"And *you,* Aunt Winnie," said Nora sincerely. "You will also be at the very top of my list. Sure, you are a special blessing to us all."

※

Approaching the bank of the pond, Tom glanced down over himself. He saw that his shirttail was out, and grinned. If Johanna could see, she would be wagging her finger. She was as bad as Aunt Nora when it came to shirttails tucked in and noses wiped clean.

With a backward glance, he reassured himself that the girls were still out of view. Then he turned back to the bullfrog.

If the creature knew he was being stalked, he seemed to be enjoying the game. Having leaped atop an old fallen tree trunk that lay across the narrow end of the pond, the bullfrog now sat studying Tom with fat, bulging eyes, as if waiting to see what came next.

Grinning at the frog, Tom trundled on, imagining the shrieks he would get from the girls when he shook that old frog in their faces. Or, better yet, slipped it up under Dulcie's petticoats.

His grin widened and he put on speed.

I'm going to get you, sure enough, you funny-looking old frog. Going to get you and scare those silly girls out of their wits!

Reaching the gnarled tree trunk, Tom looked at the pond. This part of the water was almost completely coated with big leafy plants and some other green, slimy stuff. Tom thought the pond looked a bit disgusting, with all those things growing out of it.

Turning back to the bullfrog, he watched as it flicked out its tongue to snatch a bug from the air. Tom imitated it with his own tongue, then grinned and stepped gingerly onto the log.

The frog's bulging eyes gave no hint of fear. Tom decided this was going to be easier than he'd thought.

Foot over foot, Tom began to pace off the distance between him and the bullfrog.

"I'm coming to get you, old Bull-Frog. You and me, we'll have ourselves the time of it, we will! Just don't you be moving, now. Stay…right… there…."

Suddenly, Tom's foot slipped on the log. His heart raced. He lurched forward, then weaved, finally righting himself.

The frog didn't so much as blink, just sat staring at him. Ignoring the pounding of his heart, Tom wondered if frogs could think, and if they could, what this one was thinking right now.

"Do you want to play, old Bull-Frog? Want to help scare those silly girls?"

A cloud passed over the sun, and all at once the afternoon seemed to go dark, as if the sky were sliding down to meet the pond. The wind that had been blowing most of the afternoon now turned sharper, slicing over the water and causing Tom to shiver in his shirtsleeves. He wished he'd worn his jacket, as Aunt Nora had cautioned.

He was close enough now that he could almost look right into the frog's eyes. When the creature still made no attempt to move, Tom slowly crouched down to his knees, then dropped to his belly. Hugging the log, he began to creep forward. He didn't take his eyes off the bullfrog.

But he hadn't counted on the rough, splintered bark of the tree trunk. "Blast!" He jerked when the bark raked the tender skin exposed by his loose shirttail.

Suddenly, as if Tom's sharp movement had set off a warning, the frog leaped from the tree trunk into the pond.

"Blast!" Tom cried again, louder this time, breaking his crawl to watch the frog disappear under the water.

Johanna let out a gasp of horror at the sight of the big black cat trotting into the woods at the far side of the park. With a tiny bundle of fur in its mouth, it fairly swaggered with feline satisfaction.

Grabbing the sleeve of Dulcie's dress, she gestured toward the cat. The younger girl opened her mouth to let out a shriek. Then they both took off running.

Johanna, with her long, thin legs, easily outdistanced Dulcie. As they ran, they flailed their arms and Dulcie screamed, hoping to frighten the cat into dropping the baby rabbit.

Johanna began to cry as they crashed through the trees, her heart wrenching at the sight of the tiny bunny in the clutches of the cat. Hiking her skirts up still more, she cleared decaying tree stumps and bramble bushes with ease, never taking her eyes off the cat.

With the baby rabbit still in its mouth, the cat continued to dash into the woods, but aimlessly now, lunging first in one direction, then another, as if uncertain which way led to escape.

Sprinting far out in front of Dulcie, Johanna managed to bring herself up almost even with the cat. The animal acted as though it didn't see her, veering off to the right, leaning into the wind as it ran. But Dulcie, shrieking and wildly waving a tree branch, cut around Johanna to close in on the cat.

Unexpectedly, the animal seemed to lose all sense of direction. It darted first one way, then another, whipping back and forth. Finally, it tossed its tiny prey on the ground and took off in a frenzied run into the heart of the woods.

Johanna dropped to her knees to retrieve the baby rabbit, wiping her eyes with the back of one hand. Cradling the pitiful little bunny against her, she got to her feet. She could feel the tiny heart racing beneath her hand and thought perhaps the rabbit was as frightened of her and Dulcie as it had been of the cat.

Suddenly, a flash of remembrance struck her. *How long had they been gone? Little Tom…he's been alone all this time….*

With her free hand, she motioned to Dulcie that they had to get back to the park right away!

Holding his breath, Tom hugged the log and waited. It seemed like a very long time since the frog had disappeared. The wind was blowing harder now, whipping up the pond and setting off a wailing in the trees.

Tom trembled all over, not only from the cold, but also with a fierce disappointment at losing the frog. Holding on tight, he peered down into the pond. He could see nothing beneath the big lily pads and vines growing up out of the water.

"Come back here, you old Bull-Frog!" he demanded. He was angry at the frog, even angrier with himself for letting it get away.

Now he had nothing to show for all his effort but a skinned belly and a bad case of the shivers. Once more, but with no real hope, he rippled the

water with one hand, trying to catch a glimpse of the creature that had out-
witted him. Seeing nothing, he finally began to creep backward on the log.

It hurt even worse than before, the splintered bark tearing at his
stomach and scratching the palms of his hands. Stopping, Tom carefully
pushed up on his knees, then, bracing both hands on the log, pulled himself upright.

At a splash in the water close by, just off to his left, followed by a strong
burst of wind at his other side, Tom jerked around. He teetered, one foot
going out from under him. Thrashing his arms, he grabbed nothing but
air. With a sharp cry, he pitched off the log into the pond.

Tom sank fast. His heavy boots felt like stones pulling him down,
down into the darkness. He tried to scream, but only managed to pull in
huge gulps of the rancid pond water.

Pushing and kicking, he bobbed up once, then again, flailing his hands
in a desperate search for the tree trunk, for something to grab onto. He
found only ropelike vines, his vision totally obscured by the dense covering of lily pads and vegetation.

Tom thought he heard someone shouting and opened his mouth to
cry out. Instead, he strangled on the rush of bitter water that flooded his
lungs.

Pain squeezed his heart, his lungs, his throat. Tears of terror mingled
with the pond water as he tried to scream. Panic engulfed him. He kicked
wildly, beating the water as hard as he could. Once more, he bobbed up,
smacking his head on something hard.

Just before they reached the clearing, the girls stopped long enough to
tuck the baby rabbit safely into its nest.

As they broke free of the woods, Dulcie indicated to Johanna that
someone was shouting in the park. Johanna lifted her head, staring across
the distance toward the pond.

A chill wind had blown up, and the sun had gone behind the clouds,
leaving the afternoon pewter-gray and bitter. Johanna's eyes locked on
a woman standing on the bank of the pond. Across from her stood two
elderly men.

Johanna began to walk, her eyes fixed on the woman in the bonnet and flounced dress. After a few steps she could see that the woman was holding what appeared to be a man's coat.

A chill washed over Johanna. For an instant she stopped, feeling as if her legs were weighted to the ground. Dulcie touched her arm, and Johanna looked at her, then turned back to the pond.

Desperately, she looked around for a glimpse of Little Tom, but he was nowhere in sight. Her breath caught in her throat as she saw the young woman drop the coat on the ground, then put her hands to her face in a gesture of dismay. At the same time, the two elderly men on the opposite bank moved even closer to the water.

Only then did Johanna see the man in the pond, standing chest-high in the water, holding something in his arms.

She was vaguely aware that she had begun walking again, moving as if in a dream toward the scene across the park. Fear, cold and painful, hammered against her chest, and she suddenly took off at a dead run.

The wind blew across her face, whipping her hair against her skin. Her legs cramped, and the bottoms of her feet burned through the soles of her shoes. Her pulse thundered faster as she ran.

As they drew near the pond, Dulcie grabbed her arm as if to hold her back. Johanna whipped around to look at her, throwing off her hand and running the rest of the way to the pond.

She came to a dead halt at the water's edge. For the first time she saw clearly what the man in the pond was holding in his arms.

Johanna's anguished scream found no voice except in the breaking of her heart.

2

A Gray, Chill Day

Far off is a spark
From the lamp-lit town,
And the grey, chill day
Slips away with a frown.

JAMES STEPHENS (1882–1950)

New York City

Michael Burke was only one of over three hundred city police officers assigned to the Astor Place Opera House late that afternoon. Most were to be deployed later in the evening, but even now several star badges could be seen in the vicinity.

It was a damp, unseasonably cool day for May. The wind held a threat of rain, but the weather hadn't deterred the crowd. Already, hundreds were milling about outside, shoving toward the theater entrance.

After walking the perimeter of the building, Michael stood surveying his surroundings. The theater, often described by the press as resembling a Greek temple, occupied a far too vulnerable position to his way of thinking. In its triangular location with Astor Place on the south, Eighth Street on the north, and the Bowery and Broadway running east and west, it presented a number of defense problems.

His men had been busy for some time boarding up windows, but Michael couldn't see how the boards would provide much protection, should the rocks start flying. And there was every likelihood they would. A great deal of pavement had been broken up for the purpose of laying sewer pipes, leaving loose rock lying all about the building. A handy arsenal for a mob.

And a mob was exactly what the mayor and the police were expecting this night. Michael shook his head in disgust at the foolishness of men. It seemed the height of absurdity that an ongoing feud between two actors—one a silk-stockinged Englishman and the other a stage star from Philadelphia—could bring an entire community under siege.

To the genteel, kid-gloved audiences who frequented the Opera House, the English-born William Macready was a "gentleman" and an "aristocrat," while Forrest, the popular American actor, was "common," even "vulgar." According to the press, there had been bad blood between the two for years, resulting in a number of questionable incidents and, more recently, an all-out feud.

The American, Forrest, had been hissed and reviled while performing *Macbeth* in London. He blamed the insults on Macready and got even by hissing the English actor in the same role in Edinburgh. Ever since, they had been at each other like a hound and a tomcat, the result being that the press adored them both, for there was no denying that their antics sold newspapers.

Michael was rapidly becoming convinced that both men were fools. Macready's opening at the Astor House on Monday night had provoked a nasty disturbance just short of a major riot, with the English actor being pelted on stage with eggs and old shoes. The irate Macready had vowed to end his engagement then and there, but an appeal from a number of influential New Yorkers apparently convinced him to stay on.

Tonight, the city officials were expecting an even rowdier crowd than Monday night's. Michael had it from two of his best informants that the notorious crime boss, Isaiah Rynders, was plotting some sort of row with his bully-boys at the theater during the performance.

If anyone could mix up trouble, it was Rynders, Michael thought sourly. A knife fighter, a gambler, and a Tammany politician, "Captain Rynders" controlled most of the gangs in the Five Points. He was a known English-hater and would set his hoodlums on Macready with no other provocation than a whim.

As if Rynders and his thugs weren't enough to contend with, another hothead, a writer of dime novels who called himself "Ned Buntline," was said to be planning a fracas with his own bunch of hoodlums. Buntline, the head of a swaggering nativist group who claimed "America for Americans," had declared his intention to put all "aliens" out of the country, and had been agitating against Macready for days.

Michael sighed. Some of his men thought it ridiculous that most of the police force had been dispatched to Astor Place. Even the militia was mustered, awaiting orders at the Parade Ground.

Michael, however, thought it only good judgment on the part of the mayor and Chief Matsell. Of late, the entire city seemed to be simmering with excitement and a growing lust for trouble.

Well, trouble was coming, Michael could feel it. After all these years on the force, he could sense the approach of trouble the way a hound sensed a storm moving in. And on this chill and dreary afternoon, every nerve in his body was tensed in anticipation of a calamity.

Evening was almost upon them. The late afternoon light had faded into a weak mist of gray, leaving the room dim and shadowed. On a small stand beside the examining table, an oil lamp flickered, providing just enough light for the doctor to work by.

Jess Dalton glanced across the room at Nicholas Grafton and his young assistant, Daniel Kavanagh. Dr. Grafton was bent over a little girl, one of the city's numerous children who worked in a tenement crowded with other family members. No more than nine, the child had open sores on her lips, her cheeks, and all over her fingers.

Nicotine poisoning. Jess had watched the physician treat enough cases, that he recognized it now when he saw it. Frequently seen among those who worked stripping tobacco and rolling cigars, it was no respecter of age. Dr. Grafton claimed to have treated children as young as five or six years for it.

Jess was standing by the door when a message from Brooklyn arrived—a scrawled note from Lewis Farmington, brought over on the ferry by one of the boys from the shipyards.

Daniel was needed at home right away, the note urged. There has been an accident, a serious one. Could Pastor Dalton and Dr. Grafton come, too?

Jess glanced up at the doctor, read the note once more, then turned to the youth who had delivered it. "What sort of accident, son, do you know?"

Clutching his cap in his hands, the boy replied in a thick brogue, "I don't, sir. I was only sent with the message, you see. But I did hear someone make mention of a drowning."

A sick feeling of dread settled over Jess. With another glance at the scene on the other side of the room, he lowered his voice. "A drowning?" he repeated softly.

"Aye, sir," the boy replied with a quick nod. "That seemed to be the word about the yards."

Jess stared with dismay at the lean-faced boy. After another moment, his gaze again went to rest on young Daniel. Finally, with heavy steps and an even heavier heart, he started across the room.

By half past six that evening, most of the city's police force had been dispatched to the Astor Place theater. The majority of the men were posted inside, with fifty at the rear of the building, along Eighth Street, and another seventy-five at Astor Place.

Michael remained inside with most of his men, receiving periodic updates from the streets. Finally, he decided to have a look for himself and made his way to the main entrance at Astor Place.

He groaned aloud when he looked outside. Some of the men had thought the threatening skies and cold temperatures would discourage a large theater crowd. To the contrary, from Broadway to the Bowery, the streets swarmed with a wave of human flesh.

If the military were indeed mustering, as reported, he fervently hoped they would not delay their arrival. From the looks of the crowd converging on the theater, the police were going to need all the help they could get.

He stood watching for another minute, then ducked back inside. Turning around, he nearly collided with Chief Matsell himself. "Sorry, sir!" he blurted out, embarrassed to be caught lurking in the doorway.

The chief gave a grim smile and waved off Michael's apology. A young man for his position, Chief Matsell had from the beginning made himself approachable to his officers. At the same time, he managed to inspire a formerly unknown sense of discipline and respect throughout the force. He treated his men with courtesy and fairness, his captains with unmistakable regard.

"We've got trouble tonight, Captain," he said, meeting Michael's eyes. "Bad trouble."

"Aye, sir, so it would appear. We'll be needing the militia soon, I'll warrant."

The chief nodded. "General Sanford is to send word when they're ready. After that, the mayor has only to issue the orders."

Michael hoped the guardsmen would not delay their preparation. He had the sick sense that they would soon need every man available.

The curtain went up at 7:40, ten minutes late. By then the word had been passed that more tickets had been sold than the building could accommodate, which meant that in excess of eighteen hundred people now crammed the theater.

The chief had positioned himself in the Astor House box on the right of the stage, making sure he was readily visible to his men and to the patrons. To Michael's great relief, Denny Price came round with the news that the militia was formed and would move the minute they received their orders.

Despite the troublemakers in the audience, the first two scenes went off without event. In the third scene, however, Macready swaggered onto the stage attired as Macbeth.

"So foul and fair a day I have not seen." The first line he spoke fired the bullies in the crowd like a torch tossed into a pan of gunpowder. Michael saw Isaiah Rynders himself jump to his feet to lead his cronies in a roar of boos and hisses. At the same time, Macready's champions broke into cheers and applause, tossing their hats and waving handkerchiefs in the air.

For a full fifteen minutes, all movement on the stage came to a dead halt as the noisy factions in the house did their best to outshout one another. Michael and the men lining the back of the aisles stood, tense and waiting. Finally the play resumed, although the dialogue of the actors was barely audible.

Only then did Michael remember that Sara's father and the Widow Coates were planning to be in attendance this evening. He snapped his gaze up to the left, toward Lewis Farmington's box. Seeing it empty, he gave a sigh of relief. Perhaps they'd gotten wind of the expected trouble

and changed their plans. In any event, they were well out of this pande-
monium.

The moment the second act began, chaos broke out. The barricaded
windows rattled, some shattering, as the rowdies outside began to hurl
rocks against the building. Soon the police had all they could do to keep
replacement boards going up. As the noise in the street swelled, the launching of stones began in earnest.

The dull ache that had lodged itself at the back of Michael's neck earlier in the day now moved up his head, drumming fresh pain into his
skull with every rock heaved against the building. When a deafening crash
sounded at one of the upper windows, he thought his head would explode
in agony. Looking up, he watched in horror as a stone went sailing into the
magnificent chandelier in the center of the theater, smashing it to ruins.

He ran to the window and peered out between the missing shards of
glass upon a cursing, snarling mob that seemed to have gone entirely ber-
serk. Someone had opened a water hydrant, flooding the pavement. Every
streetlamp within view had been shattered. Glass from the lamps and the
windows formed a treacherous moat about the building.

Michael saw in an instant that the police were greatly outnumbered.
They had gone on the counterattack with their clubs, but their numbers
were pathetically few against a mob that had to range in the thousands.

Most of the rabble-rousers appeared young, little more than boys. To
his astonishment, Michael saw that some wore firemen's uniforms. Carrying ladders, they rushed the building, yelling, "BURN THE DEN OF
ARISTOCRACY!" There were more than a few Irish faces in the crowd,
spewing their invective against the English as they flung their stones and
other missiles at the theater.

Whipping around, Michael found himself face-to-face with the sheriff.

"Rally your best men to the Eighth Street door, Captain! There's a
bunch of roughnecks over there trying to break through!"

With the help of Denny Price, Michael mustered a platoon of men. As
he and Price rushed the door, the officers poured out behind them, driving back the front ranks of the mob.

His blackthorn club raised, Price drove through the crowd like a
stampeding bull. Michael had abandoned his club and drawn his gun
before charging out the door. He took off after Price, shouldering his
way through the red-faced attackers, leveling the pistol on one angry face

after another as he went. They had been instructed against firing into the crowd, but there had been nothing said about firing a warning shot or two into the air.

Once they'd pushed the mob back and managed to secure the door, Michael left Price in charge and hurried off to the main entrance at Astor Place. For a moment he could only stand and stare at the scene in front of him. The mob here was denser, and clearly more violent. The young participants, mere boys, had gotten the best of the police. From all appearances, they were about to break through the main doors.

Even as he watched, a policeman trying to force them back fell, crumpling under a volley of stones. Rage rose up in Michael, and he took off running after the officer's assailant. Shooting once in the air, he caught up with the youth, grabbing him hard from behind and shoving him down onto the street. He had no orders to make arrests, but arrest the little thug he did, sending him stumbling into the theater under the strong arm of a young patrolman.

The officer who had fallen was unconscious. Pocketing his gun, Michael hooked his hands under the man's arms and hurriedly dragged him inside. When a fiery-eyed youth and his companion tried to block the policemen from the entrance, Michael flung out his leg, booting one a hard blow to the kneecaps, the other a kick in the groin.

Once inside, he shouted at nobody in particular, *"We need a doctor for the injured!"* then took off toward the house doors to see if he could muster some additional men to hold the main entrance.

Behind him, someone called his name. Michael whipped around to see Benjamin Fairchild, captain of the Eighth Ward Precinct, rushing toward him.

Fairchild's face was a thundercloud. "We're to order our men inside right away!"

"Inside?" Michael stared at him in amazement.

The other precinct captain nodded shortly. "We're to rally every man inside in order to hold the building. The military is on the way."

Michael's anger quickly gave way to mere frustration. He knew it was the only sensible call.

"We can't hold them off any longer, Mike," Fairchild reasoned. "We're but a few against their thousands. And they're altogether out of control. The chief says it would be meaningless slaughter to leave the men out there any longer. The best we can do is secure the building—if we can—until the guardsmen arrive."

Michael gave a curt shrug. "Aye, well, let us hope, then, they don't arrive too late for us all. I'm thinking the slaughter will be worse if that rabble storms the building."

Fairchild left him, and Michael turned to glance inside, toward the stage. Incredibly, the play was still going on. Furious noise battered the building, the chandelier hung in ruins, shards of broken window glass lay everywhere, and the crowd was screaming. But the English actor, Macready, still raced through his part, looking entirely foolish in his attempt to make himself heard.

It was dark by the time Daniel and the others hurried off the ferry at Brooklyn and made for home. When he saw Mr. Farmington waiting at the docks beside his carriage, Daniel's stomach wrenched with fear. Whatever had happened must be bad. Bad, indeed.

Mr. Farmington's face was grave, his eyes tired. He shook hands briefly with each of them, then took Daniel by the arm. "Daniel...a moment, son."

A heavy weight of dread settled over Daniel's chest. He saw Mr. Farmington dart a look to Pastor Dalton, then Dr. Grafton. "A sad thing has happened," he said quietly, returning his gaze to Daniel. "A tragic thing, I'm afraid."

He hesitated, and something in Daniel suddenly flung up a protest. He did not want to hear another word. He didn't want to know about this latest tragedy, whatever it was. He had thought they were finished with tragedy. At least for a time. There had been enough of it in their lives. More than enough.

Daniel looked at Mr. Farmington. Slowly he shook his head, denying what was to come before he even heard the words.

3

A More Recent Sorrow

*For the world's more full of weeping
than you can understand.*

W.B. YEATS (1865–1939)

By nine o'clock the militia had arrived at Astor Place, but as yet the soldiers had refrained from firing.

The mayor had also made his presence known, along with a number of news-hungry reporters. When the curtain finally came down on *Macbeth*, Michael and some of his men ushered the audience out through the door on the Astor Place side. They passed without incident through a detachment of infantry who stood with fixed bayonets.

After another forty-five minutes, both the police and the militia were pleading for orders to fire on the mob, but the mayor—a politician to the end—resisted and subsequently disappeared. Michael was standing nearby when a young officer, blood streaming down his face, virtually begged for permission for the police to defend themselves. Finally, in the mayor's absence, Sheriff Westervelt gave the militia orders to fire.

By this time, the actor, Macready, had retreated to his dressing room. Rumor had it that he'd been given protection by a number of leading citizens, including one Robert Emmett, under whose roof he would shortly be secured.

Michael knew who Emmett was: a nephew and namesake of one of the great Irish patriots from the failed rising at Dublin Castle in the early 1800s—Emmett of the Unmarked Grave. "Let no man write my epitaph," the hero had declared before his execution. "When my country takes her place among the nations of the earth, then and not till then, let my epitaph be written."

It occurred to Michael that the great patriot would turn over in his unmarked grave were he to learn of his nephew's alliance with an English stage actor. For another moment, he watched the furtive flight of Macready and his protectors from the Eighth Street entrance, then started back inside.

His hopes that the trouble might ebb before the bullets started to fly were rudely dashed by the explosion of musket fire. Whirling around, he bolted through the door and hit the street at a run, crouching low as he went, to avoid making himself a target.

As if in a dream, Daniel entered the house, stopping just over the threshold. There was a hush throughout, except in one of the back rooms, where someone was quietly weeping. The sound tore at his heart.

His mother...once again, his mother was weeping....

Abruptly, he thought of Johanna and looked about the parlor, but there was no sign of her. He felt Pastor Dalton put an arm around his shoulders, and he allowed himself to be led to the rear of the house, to his mother's bedroom.

His knees felt stiff and wooden as he entered. He stopped just inside, caught by a sudden sense of his surroundings going dark. Everything seemed submerged in shadows except for the scene in front of him. For a moment, it was as if the rest of the world had faded away and left him only this one small corner of reality.

In the carriage on the way home, Mr. Farmington had related the little he knew about the accident, repeating the witness's explanation of what he had seen before pulling Little Tom out of the pond. But in spite of the painful pictures that assailed his mind, Daniel somehow could not comprehend it all. On the way up the walk to the house, he had shaken his head to clear it, to prove to himself he was awake and not dreaming.

Now he stood staring across the bedroom, still numb even as he beheld his mother. She was sitting up in bed, clinging to a white-faced Evan as she sobbed against his shoulder. At the foot of the bed, Dr. Grafton was already opening his medical bag and searching its contents.

Daniel caught a deep breath as Evan, then his mother, turned toward him. Her face in the candle glow was ashen and tear-streaked, her eyes enormous and frighteningly bleak. At the sight of Daniel, she gave a choked sob and opened her arms.

In her trembling embrace, Daniel's own sense of loss nearly overwhelmed him. A terrible grief…grief for them all wracked his entire body as he felt her weight collapse against him. He was aware of Evan's hand on his back, as if he sought both to comfort and be comforted.

For a time the three of them had no words. They could only vent their sorrow, while feebly attempting to console one another.

At last Daniel managed to speak. "Where is Johanna?"

His mother's weeping began anew as she gestured toward the hall, in the direction of Johanna's bedroom. Gently Daniel released himself from her embrace, making way for Dr. Grafton to examine her.

Daniel would have thought that the ache in his heart could not possibly deepen, but as he crossed the hall and stood peering into Johanna's shadowed room, a stab of fresh pain took his breath away.

She sat in the darkness, her small, thin figure illuminated only by the weak glow of moonlight from outside. Her head hung down, her arms dangled loosely at her sides. She looked for all the world like a small, discarded rag doll.

He hesitated only a moment before crossing the room to stand in front of her. For a long time, she gave no sign of recognition. Finally, she lifted her face, tear-stained and smudged with dirt. Daniel swallowed hard against his swollen throat as he met the torment in her gaze.

At last he held out his arms to her. Her eyes traveled from his face to his hands, but still she hesitated. Then, her face crumpling to an expression of raw grief he knew he would never forget, she began to jab one finger into her chest, over and over again, as hard as she could. As she poked at herself, she sobbed, a terrible silent, choking sound that Daniel thought the saddest cry he had ever heard. The jabbing went on, until finally he could bear it no longer and moved to stay her hand with his own.

"*No!*" he fairly shouted, wincing at the sound of his own voice in the quiet of the room. He gripped her hand tightly. "No," he said again, "it wasn't your fault! It wasn't, Johanna!" Only then did he realize she wasn't looking at him and so had no idea at all what he was saying.

Suddenly, she exploded from her crouch on the window seat like a wild animal sprung from a trap. Leaping to her feet, she yanked her hand away. As if to isolate herself from him, she hugged both arms to her chest, clawing at her shoulders as she rasped her grief-stricken, voiceless cry.

Something warned Daniel not to touch her again, that she might fly apart entirely. All he could do was stand there, helplessly watching her flail herself while he tried to persuade her that she had no fault in Little Tom's death.

Daniel was one of the few persons Johanna had allowed into her silent world. He had made an effort to learn the abbreviated hand language Morgan had devised for the family. With this and the natural understanding that seemed to flow between them, he had managed to make himself her friend.

But now he could almost hear the door to her heart slamming shut in his face, could almost see her backing off, retreating to that strange, silent place inside herself where no one else could go.

And he could do nothing, nothing except to stand, tears tracking his own face, as he bit down on a vicious, bitter anger, an anger he had not felt for a long, long time. Not since Johanna's sister, Katie, had died.

God help them all, Johanna's entire family was gone! Katie. Their mother, Catherine. Thomas, their father. And now…now, Little Tom. Only Johanna was left. Johanna, who could neither hear nor speak, whose wee brother had been the delight of her silent life.

Suddenly, Daniel identified the object of his anger, and it only heated his rage. *"Oh, God!"* he choked out, cringing as his words echoed in the darkness of the room. "Did you have to take Little Tom, too? Couldn't you have left her *something*? Can't you ever leave us *anything* at all?"

The hellish scene in front of the theater defied belief. It looked for all the world like a battlefield. Horses snorting, bullets whistling, thousands of blood-crazed men running back and forth, hurling stones at the soldiers, even trying to wrest their weapons away from them.

The streets were hot and bitter with the smell of gunpowder. "The soldiers—they're only firing blanks!" someone in the crowd shouted with bravado. Then, before the echo of the words had faded, one of their own, a green youth, was shot in both feet, crumpling over into the street.

One filthy-looking thug with a large stone braced between his knees suddenly ripped open his jacket, exposing a red flannel shirt. "Fire into this!" he cried. "Take the life of a free-born American for a bloody British actor! Do it, aye, you daren't!"

But the soldiers did dare, firing at him where he stood.

Michael watched in horror as a tall, fine-looking gentleman made himself an open target by standing in the middle of Astor Place. "You, man!" Michael shouted. "Get away before you get yourself killed!" The man ignored him. A second later, a bullet drilled his skull, and his head exploded.

Sick to his stomach, Michael took up with a band of his men who had come to the aid of the beleaguered militia. By now the mob was out of control entirely. Boys no more than sixteen seemed to make up most of the front ranks—at least three or four hundred of them. They were still hurling their stones at the building as well as at the militia.

The look on most of the soldiers' faces was pitifully revealing. These same men who only moments before had been begging for permission to fire into the crowd now clearly recoiled at the idea of shooting their own countrymen. Yet shoot they did, as much as possible aiming low, hoping to frighten or, at the least, wound the worst of the rioters instead of killing them.

"Chief Matsell's been hit!" a policeman called out. "In the chest—by a huge stone!" Michael whipped around and started back toward Eighth Street, thinking they would take the chief inside. But before he ever reached the door, Denny Price intercepted him, waving a piece of paper.

"Mike! Mike—here! From your wife!"

Distracted and disoriented by all the noise and word of the chief's injury, Michael stopped, staring at Price blankly. "My wife?"

Price handed him the note. Michael frowned at the scrawled words, so uncharacteristic of Sara's usual neat hand: "Little Tom drowned in an accident at the park this afternoon. I've gone to Brooklyn. Come when you can."

Denial, then dismay slammed through Michael. The poor wee tyke! *Drowned?*

He looked up from the note. For a moment he could do nothing but stare into the nightmare of killing and insane rage going on about him. Murder and madness. Slaughter in the name of patriotism. People shooting their neighbors in the street and killing the very men sworn to protect them.

On the fringes of his consciousness lurked a thought he knew to be irrational, yet sometimes it came to him in the midst of some horror he encountered in his role as a policeman. When he viewed some evil inflicted by one human being, or an entire group, upon another, he couldn't help wondering if perhaps in this life it was the *nightmare* that was the reality and peace only an elusive pretender. Was it madness to aspire to peace when human nature seemed so bent on turning on itself— destroying itself?

Again he glanced down at the note in his hand. Slowly, he shook his head. One thing was certain: There would be no peace this night. Not here, in the streets of the city, and not in the little frame house in Brooklyn.

God help them all, would there ever be peace again?

4

The Gypsy and the Rebel

I know not whether Laws be right,
Or whether Laws be wrong;
All that we know who lie in gaol
Is that the wall is strong;
And that each day is like a year,
A year whose days are long.

OSCAR WILDE (1854–1900)

Dublin, Ireland
Mid-June

Tierney Burke passed his seventeenth birthday in the cold, dark cell of a Dublin jail.

Had he been at home for the event, no doubt his da would have treated him to a corned beef dinner at the Wells Cafe and perhaps a boxing match afterward. As it was, he celebrated with bitter water and stale bread. The bread was always stale in this place, as was the air, thick with mildew and the smell of unwashed bodies.

It had been quiet for the most part tonight. The only sound was an occasional shout from one of the guards or a muffled moan from a prisoner. Once in a while a cell door clanked open, followed by scuffling noises that signaled a new arrival.

He had been here two weeks now. Two weeks and *three days*, he reminded himself, marking off another day on the wall with a small stone. He made the mark with an awkward jab of his left hand. His right arm had been broken and was suspended in a dirty sling.

Sinking down onto the hard slab that served as a bed, Tierney leaned his head back against the wall and shut his eyes. He thought it might be nine o'clock or thereabouts, although he couldn't be sure. His watch was gone, as were all his other personal effects—confiscated for "purposes of security" by the prison officials.

Any question about the time, or anything else for that matter, brought only taunts from the guards. Especially the one called "Boiler Bill"—so named by the prisoners for the angry-looking boils in evidence on the back and sides of his thick neck.

"What's time to a prison rat?" he would say, his furry broken teeth bared in an ugly laugh. "Hah, I know! I bet you're impatient for your next fine meal, is that it?" Invariably, he and the other guards would goad the prisoners about the food, which was so foul even the rats turned up their noses at it.

The guards defied all belief. They were like caricatures created by some drunken madman in his dreams. They seemed happiest when hammering a prisoner against the wall or putting out their smokes on the poor man's hands. A few of them stopped short of being altogether vicious, taking only a mild satisfaction in degrading the prisoners in the cells. But most of them, like Boiler Bill, struck Tierney as altogether deranged.

He had a broken arm and a few cracked ribs to prove him right.

The scene of domestic tranquility in the great room at Nelson Hall should have brought contentment to Morgan Fitzgerald. His wife, Finola, and his newly adopted daughter, Annie, sat sewing for the coming babe, while Sister Louisa hovered near, inspecting their progress with a watchful eye.

No doubt he would have reveled in such a setting under different circumstances. But there seemed to be no serenity for his soul this night, no peace for his aching heart.

It had been three days since Evan Whittaker's letter had arrived with the dire tidings of Little Tom's death. Even now, the waves of shock and grief roared through Morgan with such force he could scarcely bear the pain. He had read the letter over and over again, as if he'd somehow missed a part of the story, some saving grace hidden amid the lines which, when deciphered, would reveal that it was all a mistake.

But it was no mistake. Little Tom was dead, and Morgan felt bruised and raw with the anguish of it. It almost seemed that each time he believed he had finally come to grips with the loss of his family—that he had at last been able to store the memories away where they would no longer wound him so—another tragedy would strike. Once again, the cumulative pain of the past would wash up, overwhelming him with regret and sorrow.

His gaze returned to the scene across the room for another moment, lingering on Finola's golden head and Annie's dark one, bent low over their sewing. The quiet pleasure he usually found in moments like these now eluded him. Tonight he craved only solitude. He needed to be alone with his memories.

With one last reluctant glance at Finola, he turned and wheeled himself out of the room.

Tierney opened his eyes as keys jangled outside in the corridor. Heavy, shuffling footsteps signaled the approach of Boiler Bill.

Tierney tensed, waiting. After a moment, the cell door opened, and the barrel-chested guard sent a new prisoner scrambling into the cell.

The new arrival let go a stream of invective that sounded like a foreign tongue. With one heavy-booted foot, the guard kicked the prisoner in the back and sent him sprawling against the wall.

"Got some company for you, Yankee-Boy!" the guard announced to Tierney. "You've had the royal suite to yourself long enough."

Tierney glared at him, pulling in a long breath. The pain in his ribs reminded him that he was in no shape for a pounding from Boiler Bill, so he remained silent.

"The both of you should make a sterling pair," sneered the guard. "A Gypsy horse thief and a Yankee dock rat."

Deliberately, Tierney studied the disgusting boil that bulged just below the guard's left ear, then transferred his attention to what appeared to be a large gravy stain on the front of his shirt. Out of the corner of his eye, he saw the new prisoner slowly uncoil himself from the wall and stand, hands clenched, glaring at the slovenly guard.

Tierney straightened a little to get a better look at his new cellmate. *A Gypsy horse thief*, the guard had called him. He looked the part, right enough.

There had been some Gypsies in New York, mostly in and about Shanty-town. In their strange-looking clothes and brightly painted wagons, they attracted attention and suspicious stares wherever they went.

This one was young, probably not much older than Tierney him-self, and looked to be about the same height. Long-legged and lean, he wore stovepipe trousers with several rows of stitching around the bot-tom, a bright yellow shirt, and a blue-and-white printed scarf knotted loosely about his throat. Dark brown boots, apparently of fine quality, showed beneath his trousers. A small gold earring glinted in one ear. His hair was the color of pitch, as was his roguish mustache. He was dark-skinned, though not as dark as most of the Shantytown Gypsies Tierney remembered.

The door clanged shut, and Boiler Bill shuffled on down the corridor, taking the lamp with him. Only a faint trace of moonlight slipped in from the small barred window high on the outside wall.

The two prisoners stood appraising each other in the shadows for a moment. The Gypsy was the first to break the silence. "Did that happen in here?" he asked, motioning to Tierney's arm.

Tierney nodded but offered no explanation.

The Gypsy's black eyes took on a knowing look. "One of the guards?"

"No," muttered Tierney. "*Two* of them."

The other winced as if he, too, had felt the pain. "How long have you been here?"

Tierney's arm inside the grimy bandages itched, and he tried to work it back and forth in the sling to gain relief. "Close on three weeks," he said, making no attempt to mask his frustration. "It seems like three years."

The Gypsy nodded, studying him. "The guard called you 'Yankee-Boy.' You are not Irish, then?"

"American. *Irish* American. My parents emigrated."

"You have come from America recently?"

Tierney gave a bitter laugh. "So recently that I managed to get myself thrown into jail less than an hour after getting off the ship." The disap-pointment of having his plans so rudely thwarted washed over him again, renewing the pain, reviving his anger.

The other's dark eyes glinted with interest. "I have never met an Amer-ican." He paused. "Have you come to visit family? I thought these days most ships sailed *away* from Ireland."

Tierney remained silent. He was in no mood to relate his life history. Certainly not to a Gypsy.

"Forgive me. It is not my place to ask." His new cellmate turned his eyes away, looking down at the floor. After another moment, he said quietly, "I am Jan Martova. And I am sorry for your pain."

Tierney looked up, surprised. He was caught off guard by his cellmate's good manners. In New York, the Gypsies were viewed as little more than filthy, thieving savages. Ignorant beggars to be shunned.

Still, he'd had no one to talk with for weeks now, except for the brutish guards—and they seldom made a sound beyond a grunt or an oath. Though he admitted it grudgingly, even to himself, he was lonely. Lonely and homesick—for his da, for his pals and his old neighborhood.

"My name is Burke," he finally offered. "Tierney Burke." He paused, then asked, "So—why are you here? What did you do?"

The Gypsy sighed and shrugged. "I am accused of stealing a horse." He looked at Tierney with a faint smile. "All Gypsies are horse thieves, no?"

As a matter of fact, that was pretty much what Tierney had always heard. Even Da, a man not given to bigotry, had had little use for the Gypsies and what he called their "thieving ways."

Still smiling, Jan Martova crossed his arms over his chest. "What happened was that I came upon a British soldier caning his horse. A fine animal—the horse, that is—but far too spirited for the soldier's liking. And smarter, too, no doubt."

Abruptly, his expression sobered. "I undertook to relieve the soldier of his cane and free the horse. As it happened, there were other soldiers on the street at the time." Again he shrugged. "And so now I am in jail, for horse stealing." He met Tierney's gaze straight on. "Not such an uncommon circumstance for a *Rom*."

"*Rom?*"

"Romany. My people are Romany Gypsies."

They fell silent for another moment. Tierney was intrigued by his cellmate, somewhat taken aback by his almost refined speech and courteous demeanor.

"I hope your offense is not grave," the Gypsy finally said.

Tierney uttered a grunt of scorn. "My *offense*," he bit out, "was to try and set two drunken sailors off a wee, scrawny lad before they killed him! They claimed he picked their pockets." Twisting his mouth into a semblance of a smile, he added, "And he probably did. But I could see he was half-starved. I wasn't about to let them murder him for being hungry! Unfortunately, one of their pals called the police on me. They socked me in jail and took the boy off somewhere else."

The Gypsy nodded, as if Tierney's tale were a familiar one. "Not exactly the best of welcomes. Do you have anyone in the city who will be anxious for you? Anyone who could help?"

"I was on my way to find my father's old friend. I'm supposed to be staying with him, at his estate just outside Dublin."

He twisted sideways, and a sharp, searing pain shot along his tender ribs, making him catch his breath. At the same time, a different kind of pain gripped him, a pain made of resentment and frustration at the mess he'd gotten himself into. After all these years, he had finally achieved his dream of seeing Ireland, only to have it ripped away before he was scarcely off the docks!

"Your father's friend has an estate? He must be a wealthy man."

Immediately Tierney's guard went up. The Gypsies were notorious for swindling and robbing the rich. "It might not be an estate exactly," he hedged. "I think the place belonged to his grandfather."

Jan Martova regarded Tierney with a studying look. "And does your father's friend know what has happened to you? That you are here?"

Tierney shook his head, still smarting from the reminder of his foiled plans. "I've had no way to get word to him."

The Gypsy nodded, saying nothing. Turning, he crossed the cell, the heels of his boots clicking loudly on the stone floor. For a moment he stood staring at the mean excuse for a bed. With a look of distaste, he remained standing.

Scraping at the floor with the toe of his boot, he seemed to consider his words carefully. "I might be able to help you," he said. "Perhaps we could arrange for you to get a message to your father's friend. If he's wealthy, he must have influence. Perhaps enough influence to get you out of here."

Tierney heard the undertone of a bargain in the making, but he was unable to bank the fires of interest that rose at the Gypsy's suggestion. "And just how could you manage that?" he asked warily. "It seems to me that you're locked up as tight as I am."

The Gypsy's answering smile was cryptic. "But my people are not. One of my cousins is out there somewhere, right now, keeping watch," he said, gesturing toward the high, narrow window. "He will be acting as lookout for my older brother, in order that no undue harm might come to me. It would be a small matter to pass a message outside and have it delivered."

He stopped, rubbing his fingertips along his chin. "But it would have to be a *written* message. Your wealthy benefactor is not likely to believe the word of a Gypsy."

Tierney didn't miss the barbed edge in the other's tone. Nor did he give any further thought about bringing trouble on Morgan Fitzgerald. If there were any chance, even the slightest, of getting out of this hellhole, he'd be a fool not to take it!

"What is his name, your father's friend?" asked the Gypsy.

Tierney hesitated only an instant. "Fitzgerald. Morgan Fitzgerald."

Jan Martova looked at him. "The one they call the *Seanchai*? The great poet in the wheelchair?"

"You know him?"

The Gypsy shook his head. "Only the stories I have heard. Morgan Fitzgerald is a man of much controversy—and great respect."

Tierney would not be distracted from his purpose. "What would you expect," he asked bluntly, "in return for helping me?"

Jan Martova gave a small gesture with one hand, then smiled. "Perhaps I might hope the great *Seanchai* would help me as well. I've been here before, you see, and I don't like the place any better than you do."

Tierney would have promised him Ireland itself if it meant a way out of this foul-smelling hole! "You said a written message. Where am I to find pen and paper in *here*?"

Still stroking his chin, the Gypsy said nothing. Suddenly, he caught the sleeve of his shirt at the elbow and began tugging at it until a piece of the material ripped free. Dangling it from his fingers, he motioned toward Tierney's broken arm and said, "This will serve as your paper. But I hope that is not your writing hand."

Tierney glanced over the makeshift splint. "It is," he muttered. "You'll have to do the writing."

Jan Martova gave him a long, steady look. "I'm afraid I cannot. You must manage with your other hand."

It took Tierney a minute, but he finally realized his mistake. He remembered his father telling him that most Gypsies could neither read nor write, that they refused to send their children to school, and so each generation continued to grow up illiterate.

Embarrassed, Tierney nodded curtly. "I'll manage." Pushing himself up from the bed, he stood watching in bewilderment as the Gypsy went to the cot on the other side of the cell and, dropping down on his knees, began to search underneath and at the sides. At last he stopped, his face breaking into a wide smile. He got to his feet, holding up a nail for Tierney's inspection. "And this," he said, still smiling, "will be your pen."

Tierney stared at him.

"We will need ink, of course," said Jan Martova, clearly undaunted.

It struck Tierney that, not only had he gotten himself mixed up with a Gypsy, but a *daft* Gypsy at that. "And where," he asked impatiently, "do you propose to find *ink*?"

The dark eyes took on a glint. "Blood," replied the Gypsy, withdrawing a small knife from inside the heel of his boot. "Blood will do the job very nicely, I think."

"*Blood?*" Tierney echoed incredulously, braced to defend himself in case this crazy Gypsy made a move toward him.

Jan Martova grinned. "Blood," he said again. "Don't worry, Yankee-Boy," he added. "We will use *Gypsy* blood. I have plenty."

5

You Will Always Have Your Memories

Those we love truly never die....
The blessed sweetness of a loving breath
Will reach our cheek all fresh through weary years.

JOHN BOYLE O'REILLY (1844–1890)

In the library, Morgan poked the logs in the great stone fireplace back to life, scowling at the unseasonable cold that seemed to permeate the house.

Wheeling himself back to his desk, he idly shuffled through some papers for a moment, then slumped back in the wheelchair.

He was heartsore and bone-weary, but it was not late enough to retire. He had enough trouble sleeping as it was, spending most of the early nighttime hours with his nose in a book, until his eyes and his mind grew numb with fatigue. Since the news about Little Tom had come, even those precious few hours when he normally slept were often interrupted with painful memories and unsettling dreams.

He was greatly concerned for his niece, Johanna—the last remaining member of his brother's family. Poor lass, she had more than her share of misfortune as it was, what with not being able to hear or speak. Her baby brother had been like a gift from heaven to her. From the beginning, she had doted on him like a little mother, caring for him, playing with him, hovering over him. What might the loss of wee Tom do to her?

He sighed, wiping the dampness in his eyes with his sleeve as he sank even farther back in the wheelchair.

To take his mind off Little Tom, Morgan deliberately turned his thoughts toward Tierney Burke. The lad should have showed up long before now.

Michael's letter about his son's troubles and his passage to Ireland had come more than a week past. Ever since, Sandemon had been going to the docks daily in anticipation of the boy's arrival. Then, just this past Friday he had learned that the ship had actually put in more than two weeks ago. Yet Tierney Burke was nowhere to be found.

Upon receiving Michael's letter with the news that his son would be coming to Ireland, Morgan had felt a mixture of eagerness and uncertainty. While he looked forward to meeting the son of his oldest friend, he could not help but wonder what sort of problems Tierney Burke might bring to Nelson Hall.

Michael had been characteristically candid in his letters about the conflict between him and his son, occasioned—at least according to Michael—by the boy's rebellious, hotheaded temperament. Throughout the years of their correspondence, Morgan had been unable to ignore the apparent similarities between Tierney Burke and *himself*. As a youth, he, too, had been frowned upon as being factious and rebellious. When they were boys back in Killala, Michael had often—and only partly in jest— accused him of chasing trouble as a hound did a hare.

Morgan smiled faintly at the thought. What a bitter irony for the practical, sensible, reliable Michael to have a son who was apparently a mix of quicksilver and fire—much like the friend he had always found so exasperating.

Imagining Michael's frustration and pain, Morgan realized that *there* lay the difference between him and young Tierney Burke. His own father had been little troubled by Morgan's rebellious ways. Aidan Fitzgerald's fatherhood had been almost entirely characterized, if not by actual indifference, at the least by a kind of lethargy—even when sober, which was not often the case. Except in the area of education, Morgan and his older brother, Thomas, had virtually reared themselves. Their father's lack of interest had allowed them an excessive amount of freedom while growing up, a freedom keenly envied by other youths in the village.

Perhaps it was his own careless upbringing—as well as Michael's faithfulness as a friend—that now made Morgan so determined to do his best by Tierney Burke, to provide the boy a home and whatever guidance he might allow. In time, he hoped they might even become friends.

Unhappily, he seemed to have failed in his good intentions before ever laying eyes on the lad!

He dragged his hands down both sides of his beard, closing his eyes for a moment against the dull ache that had set in along his temples.

"Morgan?"

He looked up to see Finola standing just inside the doorway. As always, his heart warmed at the sight of her. Straightening in the chair, he motioned for her to enter. "Did you grow tired of the sewing?"

She shook her head, giving a shy smile as she came the rest of the way into the room. "Actually, I came...to see about you," she answered, her voice soft. "Are you thinking of your nephew tonight, Morgan?"

He nodded. It was almost unnerving, the way she always seemed so in tune with his thoughts. "Aye, I am. I cannot seem to think of much else. Except for the whereabouts of Michael's son, that is. I'm growing more than a little concerned for the boy."

He wheeled himself out from behind the desk, stopping to draw the heavy, rose-colored drapes against the darkness. "Come, sit with me," he said, gesturing toward the fireplace, "although I know I'm poor company."

He watched her settle herself carefully into the large fireside chair. He loved the way Finola moved. In spite of the fact that she was growing heavy with child, her every movement, every gesture, was as graceful as a waterfall.

Her flaxen hair fell in a heavy braid over her shoulder. In her honey-colored gown, her fair skin glowing in the firelight, she appeared golden and fragile and exquisitely lovely.

"There has been no word, then, about Tierney Burke?"

"None," Morgan said, dragging his eyes away from her and looking into the fire. "Perhaps I should have expected the ship sooner. One of the importer's clerks told Sandemon it was a new vessel, one of the Farmington packets—and a great deal faster than most of its predecessors."

"Sure, nothing would have happened to the boy? You did say he was close on seventeen."

Morgan lifted his hands in a gesture of puzzlement. "How can we know? And there's the rub. Where do we even begin to look? The lad could be *anywhere* by now!" He stopped, giving a heavy sigh. "I do not seem to be having much success as a guardian."

"Whatever do you mean? Why, you're *wonderful* with Annie!"

He looked at her, then turned back to the fire. "I cannot seem to stop thinking of the last time I saw Little Tom and the rest of my family...the night I set them aboard the ship for America."

Squeezing his eyes shut against the wrenching image, he said nothing for a moment. These past few days had brought back so many painful memories he had tried to put safely away: seeing Thomas, his brother, shot down before his eyes, slain in his attempt to save Morgan's life...the terrified eyes of the children as they were hurried, half-carried aboard ship...Nora's anguish...the loss of her eldest son before the ship ever left the harbor....

"I can still remember the boy's arms about my neck when he said goodbye... so thin, *those little arms...he didn't want to let go...."*

When he realized he had spoken aloud, he started, glancing quickly at Finola, who was studying him with undisguised sympathy.

"Your little nephew?" she asked softly.

Morgan nodded, hugging his arms to his chest. "He was scarcely more than a babe then...not even three years yet. He and the little girls were so frightened, with all the uproar on the docks—I've told you most of it...."

She leaned forward, touching his hand but saying nothing.

"I thought—I was convinced—that I was sending them off to a better life, a land of hope...."

He shook his head, tormented by the still-vivid memory of wee Tom's enormous green eyes—the "Fitzgerald eyes," Thomas had always called them. He remembered the fear and bewilderment in that startled gaze when the tyke had first understood that his daddy was dead and would not be going with them to America.

First Katie, now Little Tom, God have mercy on them. Even in America, they had found no hope....

Finola's soft voice broke into his troubled thoughts. "You did what you thought best, all you could do. You gave them all you could give, Morgan. You must cling to the assurance that, at least for a time, they were surely happier than they would have been if they had stayed in Ireland." She paused, still touching his hand. "And your memories, Morgan...you will always have your memories. How you must cherish them now—"

At the sound of much throat-clearing outside in the hall, she broke off, and they both turned toward the door.

Artegal appeared in the doorway. The pallid, cadaverous footman stood unmoving, his usual disapproving expression fixed firmly in place.

"Begging your pardon, sir, but there is—" He swallowed with obvious effort, as if a wad of grapeshot had lodged in his throat. "There is a *Gypsy* boy at the back door. He insists on seeing you."

Morgan stared at him. "A *Gypsy* boy? *Here?*"

"I'm afraid so, sir. Shall I send him on his way?"

"What reason does he give for wanting to see me?"

The footman rolled his pale eyes in contempt. "He *says* he has a message for you."

Morgan considered this announcement for another moment. "Very well. Bring him in. And send Sandemon to me, please."

Artegal's eyes widened. He made no reply, nor did he make any attempt whatsoever to mask his disapproval. "Very good, sir."

As soon as the footman was out the door, Morgan turned to Finola. Unbidden, every old tale he'd ever heard about the Gypsies' penchant for stealing children and settling curses on the unborn came flooding upon him. Impatience with himself for entertaining such nonsense battled with a fierce sense of protectiveness for his young wife.

"Perhaps...it might be best if you go back to Annie and Sister Louisa." She looked at him blankly.

He expelled a deep breath, still irked with himself. "One never knows what to expect from the Gypsies, you see. They are a very...peculiar sort of people."

Her expression was still puzzled as she got up, smoothed her skirts, and left the room.

As it turned out, it was Sandemon, not Artegal, who ushered in the mysterious messenger. The black man towered over a small boy, somewhat ragged and none too clean.

Upon entering, Sandemon's dark eyes glinted with an uncharacteristic guardedness. His usually serene features were drawn taut.

Studying the boy, Morgan would have reckoned him to be no more than ten, perhaps younger. His black eyes were hooded, his narrow face smudged, and about his neck he wore a faded print kerchief. That he was Gypsy was evident. No doubt he came from one of the Romany tribes that often camped in vacant lots about the slum districts, such as the Liberties.

Morgan wheeled himself back behind his desk. "What's this about?" he asked, glancing at Sandemon.

The West Indies black man raised one dark, dubious eyebrow. "This boy claims to have an urgent message for you, *Seanchai*. I asked for proof, but he refuses to show it to me."

Morgan frowned, turning his gaze on the Gypsy boy. "So, then—what is this urgent message?"

The shaggy-haired youth thrust his chin up in a defiant air. His black eyes snapped with what looked, incredibly, like indignation.

"The message is here," he said, tapping the front of a very dirty white shirt. With an arrogance Morgan found slightly amusing, the Gypsy boy continued to study Morgan and the wheelchair. "I am to give it to nobody else but the *Gorgio* called Morgan Fitzgerald," he finally said.

"*'Gorgio'?*" questioned Sandemon.

"That's what the Romany call anyone who's not a Gypsy," Morgan answered, not taking his eyes off the boy. He had known a few Gypsies over the years, none well. He doubted that any *Gorgio* ever knew a Gypsy *well.* They were a secretive, primitive, insulated people, the Romany—a race of strangers who lived behind a seemingly impenetrable fort of their own exclusiveness. It was a rare outsider indeed who ever managed to breach the wall.

"I am Morgan Fitzgerald," he said to the boy. "And, now, if you please, I will have this message you claim to bear."

The black eyes raked over him. Morgan thought this was likely the first time he had ever known the contempt of a green *gorsoon*—and a Gypsy at that. Had the lad not been so young, he might have been annoyed. "The message?" he prompted firmly.

He watched as the Gypsy boy dug inside his shirt and withdrew what appeared to be a piece of material. Without a word, the youth closed the distance between Morgan and himself and handed over the swatch of cloth.

"What—" Morgan unfolded the material, stretching it taut between both hands. His gaze went from the boy to the cloth. For a moment he stared at it blankly, not comprehending.

"*Seanchai?*"

The worried tone in Sandemon's voice roused him. Finally, he took in the words crudely scrawled across the material.

His throat tightened, and his heart began to drum heavily in his chest. "Where did you get this?" he snapped, looking up at the Gypsy boy.

The boy studied him for a moment, then said curtly, "From my cousin. In the prison. He passed it out through the window of his cell."

"The *prison*?" Morgan stared at him, dumbfounded.

The Gypsy youth bristled. "My cousin Jan Martova is in gaol—falsely accused!" Drawing himself up to his full height, he added, "He entrusted me with this message for his *Gorgio* cellmate."

Cellmate...

Morgan groped for understanding. Then, his eyes still on the Gypsy boy, he handed the torn piece of material to Sandemon. "The message," he said, his voice low, "is from Tierney Burke." Pausing, he swallowed against the dryness of his mouth. "Apparently, he is in gaol, here in Dublin."

Sandemon scanned the words on the material. When he looked up, his expression was startled. "This looks as if—"

Morgan nodded, feeling somewhat ill. "As if it were written in blood."

6

Meeting in a Dublin Gaol

We fell by each other—though it was senseless,
It was the encounter of two heroes.

NINTH CENTURY IRISH

he cell door flew open. Metal clanged against stone, jarring Tierney
out of his sleep.

There was no time for his head to clear or his eyes to focus before
Boiler Bill and Rankin, one of the other guards, came charging into the
cell, curses flying. Red-faced, Rankin went after Jan Martova with his
fists doubled. At the same time, Boiler Bill hurled himself toward Tierney.

"*What—*" Scrambling to his feet, Tierney ducked the guard's intended
blow. Boiler Bill pivoted, coming at him again. Tierney saw the heavy
chain wrapped around his knuckles and averted his head just in time to
avoid a savage blow. Thrown off-balance, Boiler Bill stumbled against the
wall with an explosive oath.

Tierney saw that Jan Martova was taking a pounding from Rankin,
a hulking dimwit twice the size of the Gypsy, and poison-mean. But he
knew he had no hope of helping his cellmate. He had all he could do to
ward off his own raging assailant.

"*You conniving Yankee scum!*" The guard was on him again, his beefy
hands circling Tierney's throat. Panicky, Tierney felt his breath crush out
of him, his windpipe about to collapse. His head reeled. Flecks of light
danced in front of him, and he flailed his free arm, lashing out at the guard
in blind desperation.

Teeth bared, the guard roared and flung Tierney against the stone wall of the cell. "Sneak your messages out with the dirty Gypsies, will you? You made a bad mistake, you American dog!" He spat in Tierney's face, then drove a fist into his stomach.

Tierney gagged on the pain that slammed through him. Feeling his knees buckle, he fought to retain consciousness. Boiler Bill grinned, spewing his rancid breath into Tierney's face, clearly enjoying the sight of his pain.

Rage gave Tierney one last surge of strength. Bringing a leg up, he plowed his knee into the guard's groin. Boiler Bill's eyes bugged as he staggered backward, screaming in pain.

Out of the corner of his eye, Tierney saw the Gypsy slip under one of Rankin's punches. Stooping, he withdrew from his boot the same knife that earlier he'd used to draw his own blood. He came up with a flash of steel and a look of hatred. But before he could move, Rankin fell on him, his heavy body throwing the other off-balance. The guard swung a killing blow to the Gypsy's head, and Jan Martova went down with a thud.

As he fell, the knife flew out of his hand, clattering across the floor. Springing forward, Tierney went for the knife. But just then, Boiler Bill rallied enough to lunge clumsily for Tierney, grabbing him in the midsection and holding him fast.

Gasping for breath, Tierney twisted and struggled to throw the guard off, but with his arm splinted in the sling, he was virtually helpless in the giant's clutches. He saw Rankin retrieve the knife, then turn on Jan Martova, who was still sprawled, seemingly unconscious, on the floor.

Tierney cried out a warning, but the Gypsy didn't move.

At his back, Boiler Bill growled. "So the Gypsies sneaked a message to the gentry on the hill for you, did they?" His fetid breath washed over the side of Tierney's face. "Well, precious little good it will do you!"

His beefy arms tightened around Tierney's abdomen, squeezing the breath out of him, making him feel sick and lightheaded.

Somehow, he managed to find the strength to kick back, gouging the guard in the knees with his heels. At the same time he twisted, finally wrenching himself free.

Lurching forward, he whipped around and saw Boiler Bill coming at him. The big guard's hands were clenched above his head, ready to launch a murderous blow.

Tierney stiffened, then deliberately lifted his splinted arm, gasping at the pain the movement caused him. He aimed the crude, sharp edge of the makeshift splint at the guard's neck—and shoved it directly into the center of the angry red boil. The guard screamed out in agony, clutching his neck as he fell to the floor.

In spite of the hatred and anger pulsing through him, Tierney winced at the man's agony. Turning back to Rankin and Jan Martova, he saw that the other guard had been temporarily stopped by Boiler Bill's scream of pain. Knife in hand, Rankin stood gaping at his cohort, now a whimpering heap on the floor of the cell.

Tierney hurled himself at him with a roar, his good hand outstretched to seize the knife from the guard's hand.

Raising the knife as if to throw it, Rankin exploded in a savage roar. *"Stop!"*

At the rumbling shout behind him, Tierney whirled around, Rankin momentarily forgotten.

"Drop the knife! Now!"

Just inside the open doorway of the cell sat a fiery-eyed, copper-haired giant in a wheelchair, holding a pistol on Rankin. Behind him stood a big black man in a purple shirt and a seaman's cap.

Lifting the gun, the big man in the wheelchair growled out his warning once more. *"I said...drop the knife!"*

This time Rankin obeyed.

The piercing green eyes of the man in the wheelchair drilled the guard another instant before turning their full force on Tierney.

An involuntary shiver skated down the boy's spine. He swallowed hard, then again. For a moment, he felt his eyes riveted to the blanket-draped, lifeless legs of the man who sat glaring at him. Finally, he dragged his gaze upward, to the gun, then to the bronze-bearded face, flushed with obvious anger.

The man sat, his back rigidly straight, one large hand holding the gun perfectly level, the other gripping the arm of the wheelchair. Feeling himself seared by the look of incredulous fury in the big man's gaze, Tierney had to force himself to stare back.

He knew who the giant was, of course. Although his appearance was unexpected, their surroundings unlikely, he recognized Morgan Fitzgerald at once.

Before him was the hero of his boyhood imagination, the subject of countless stories his father had related over the years about the old friend of his childhood: stories of boyhood pranks and young men's daredevil antics and, later, wondrous tales of the roving rebel-poet who had assumed almost legendary proportions in Tierney's mind.

The man's presence, even confined to a wheelchair, was compelling. He had the bearing of a monarch, an ancient chieftain, a warrior prince. The strength that emanated from him seemed to fill the small, mean cell with a humming energy.

For as long as Tierney could remember, he had idolized this man, had yearned for the day he would finally meet him face-to-face, this giant who seemed to embody so many of his own grand hopes and ideals. But even though he had been aware of the injury that had paralyzed the man, seeing the grim evidence in front of his own eyes struck him like a blow.

It occurred to him that the dread wheelchair was but another kind of cell, a prison from which there could be no release. For a moment, an inex-plicable wave of bitter disappointment washed over Tierney: disappoint-ment and outrage that a man like Morgan Fitzgerald should be forced to suffer such an atrocity.

The dark images passed, leaving him shaken and somewhat stunned at the realization that he was actually standing in a Dublin prison cell, in the presence of Fitzgerald himself. Humiliation was an exceedingly rare, almost alien feeling to Tierney. But at this instant, he felt himself to be humiliated. That his first encounter with the man who had inspired him since his childhood should be a crude scrambling in the middle of a dank, filthy cell made him feel small and insignificant and altogether foolish.

The hard green gaze went over him, raking him thoroughly in one sweep. "If you are quite finished with maiming your warders, perhaps you would be good enough to confirm what I already suspect: that you are Tierney Burke, son of Michael."

The voice was a surprise. Deep and rich, its distinctly Irish cadence held a touch of quiet refinement. Yet, Tierney sensed an underlying power that, if unleashed, could shake the very walls of the prison. Growing more miserable by the moment, he forced himself to meet the big man's eyes with far more confidence than he felt. "I am, sir. I am Tierney Burke."

The great copper head gave one brusque nod. For a second or two, Tierney could have sworn he saw a glint of amusement in that steady green gaze, and the thought made him bristle with anger.

But when Morgan Fitzgerald spoke, his tone was dry, his words clipped. "Aye, somehow I thought as much."

For a moment, Morgan was seized with the unnerving sensation that he had been catapulted back in time twenty years. The slender, lean-faced youth standing, legs spread, in the middle of the cell, looked so much like his father that Morgan almost voiced his old friend's name...

Michael...

The same proud, unyielding jaw, evident despite a growth of black beard. The thick dark hair. The familiar glint of confidence in the eye. The well-set wide shoulders. The roguish good looks, marred only by an angry white scar that slashed over his left eye. Morgan thought he could have picked the lad out of a crowd of thousands.

Suddenly caught up in a fierce yearning for the friend of his youth, it was all he could do not to throw open his arms and embrace the boy. Instead, he darted a cursory glance at the slavering guard, collapsed in a heap on the floor, then the other, upon whom he still held a gun. At last his eyes went to the unconscious boy near the wall.

"That would be the Gypsy—the cousin of the lad who brought your message?" he asked, now turning his attention back to Tierney

"Yes—he...it was his idea to write the note...he said one of his people would deliver it, but in truth I didn't really hope..."

The boy let his words drift off, unfinished. Morgan noted his obvious discomfort and decided it was more than likely a rare feeling for the young rascal.

Sandemon had gone to the Gypsy boy on the floor and was down on his knees, examining him. "He is unconscious," he said, looking up, "but not badly hurt, I think."

Morgan nodded. "What exactly is all this about? The cell door standing open, you fighting with your gaolers—"

"They charged in here and began to beat on us!" The boy's mouth thinned to a hard, indignant line. "They were furious because we got a message to the outside!"

"You're fortunate it didn't go worse for you! I doubt that you've any idea the kind of thugs you're dealing with in a place like this."

"Oh, I think I do," the boy grated, pointedly glancing at the arm encased in a grimy sling. "This came about, for example, because I demanded some clean drinking water."

Morgan grimaced. "Aye," he said quietly. "I am not unacquainted with the penal system myself." He studied the boy for a moment. "You have been released into my custody. I trust you will give me no cause for regret."

The boy flushed, and—ah, yes…there it was again, that arrogant toss of the head, the defiant flare of the nostrils. Like a young and spirited thoroughbred.

So like his father…like Michael…

"I can explain all this, sir."

"No doubt," Morgan said. "And I am sure I will be altogether fascinated by your explanation. But that will have to wait, I fear. The first order of business is to get you out of here."

He turned to Sandemon, who had come to stand near the door again. The black man's expression was impassive, but Morgan knew him well enough to recognize the disapproval and guarded curiosity in his eyes.

"Find the chief warder. Tell him we need a physician at once." He stopped. "Make sure he knows he has guards who need attention, not only a prisoner. Then I shall speak with the governor again before we leave for home."

"Sir?"

Morgan turned back to Tierney Burke, who motioned toward the Gypsy youth, still lying on the floor.

"Can't we take him with us? Please. I owe him, you see."

Morgan stared at him. "Impossible! The boy is a total stranger to you. A prisoner." He paused. "And a Gypsy."

The blue eyes flashed. "He's a friend! He opened a vein for me! I won't leave him here like this. They'll murder him."

Morgan considered him, feeling an odd sort of approval for his heated outburst. So, then, it would seem there was even more of his father in him than mere good looks. Loyalty and a keen sense of fairness had always been strong in Michael.

Sandemon had stopped just outside the doorway and stood watching them. Morgan met his gaze and saw the troubled look, the doubt there.

Turning back to Tierney, he said, "One can't simply take a Gypsy off as he pleases. We might very well bring the wrath of the whole tribe on Nelson Hall. His people would not take kindly to our interference."

"Our interference would surely be preferable to leaving him here to be slaughtered! You *know* what they will do to him. He pulled a knife on the guards!"

He was right, of course. The boy was as good as dead if they left him. Gypsies were mere animals to bullies like these—of no consequence whatever. Indeed, most of the population despised the Romany, bitterly resented their numbers in the city.

But even if he were willing to take the boy to Nelson Hall, he couldn't just whisk him out of gaol! "I have no legal right to take him away," he said, frowning.

"How did you get *me* released?" Tierney Burke countered.

Morgan gave a grim smile. "You might say that I combined my deceased grandfather's influence with a generous donation to the penal system," he answered dryly.

The boy needn't know that it had been an out-and-out bribe, coupled with a veiled threat. "I did promise your father that I would assume responsibility for you, you see."

"I don't *need* anyone to assume responsibility for me," Tierney Burke said evenly. "I am seventeen years old."

"And I am much older," Morgan said just as evenly, "and, we will hope, a good deal wiser. Now, then, what do you know about this Gypsy?" He motioned toward the boy, still unconscious on the floor.

"Only that he freed a horse from two soldiers who were caning it," the boy replied. "And that he was willing to write a message in his own blood to help a stranger."

Those disconcerting blue eyes fastened on Morgan's face in a look of undisguised challenge.

Relenting, Morgan sighed. "I will see what I can do," he said wearily. "But if we all end up murdered in our beds by a band of Gypsies, let it be on your head, and not mine."

7

The Open Door

King of stars,
Dark or bright my house may be,
But I close my door on none
Lest Christ close his door on me.

EARLY IRISH

Peering through a crack in the kitchen door, Annie Fitzgerald and Fergus the wolfhound were having a close-up look at not *one* new boy, as had been expected, but *two*—one of whom was a *Gypsy*! A *real* Gypsy, not just an ordinary tinker or one of the traveling people who affected to call themselves Gypsies—but a real-life *Romany* Gypsy!

It was almost too much to take in, such excitement in one night! Her first encounter with a real Gypsy—and an *American* as well! Well, not an *encounter*, actually: not yet, that is. For now, she could only peep through the partly open door into the kitchen, where the *Seanchai* and Sandemon were watching the surgeon patch up these two strangers to Nelson Hall. But she *would* have an encounter, and very soon, sure. She intended to make quite certain of it.

"This is an EVENT, Fergus," she whispered under her breath to the wolfhound, who was also craning his neck to view the curious scene in the kitchen. "Of course, *you* may have seen many a Gypsy and even some Americans before you came to live with us, but as for me, I can assure you that this is indeed a great EVENT."

Annie expected that she would have been keen enough to identify the

Gypsy for what he was, a Romany, even if old Artegal, the footman, hadn't been in such a state, muttering to himself and carrying on for anyone to hear. Sure, who else but a Gypsy would dress so?

And wasn't he a sight! He was a *real* Gypsy, no doubt about it. With that dark, wicked-looking mustache, the bright-colored kerchief about his neck, and a gold ring in one ear, he looked bizarre and mysterious and perhaps even a bit dangerous!

She shivered slightly at the idea, then turned her attention to the other newcomer. As intriguing as the Gypsy might be, it was the *other* stranger who fascinated Annie most—the American, Tierney Burke.

Whereas the Gypsy would be returning to his own people, Tierney Burke would be living right here, at Nelson Hall. Indeed, as the son of the *Seanchai*'s oldest friend, wouldn't he be almost like *family*?

And wasn't he a grand-looking boy? Annie kept the thought to herself, not even sharing her impression of Tierney Burke with her best friend, Fergus.

Sure, Sister Louisa would go a bit wild-eyed were she to get wind of the fact that Annie had paid heed to a boy's looks. Especially an *American* boy who was a virtual stranger to them all. Nuns, Annie had observed, were not very tolerant of boys in general.

Squinting, she watched as the surgeon moved the Gypsy boy to the bench against the wall. He slumped back, holding in his lap two items the *Seanchai* had passed to him earlier: a scarred violin and a leather pouch on a rope. He looked altogether weary, but still a sight better than he had before Dr. Dunne had worked on him.

Next, the surgeon moved Tierney Burke into the chair at the table and began to help him remove his shirt. Annie knew it was past time for her to leave, but a combination of curiosity and fascination with the astonishing events of the night made her loath to miss even a moment of what might come next.

For the sake of decency, she tried not to gawk at Tierney Burke's broad chest. But she couldn't help but conclude that her earlier expectations of the American had been wrong entirely. Perhaps because the *Seanchai* routinely referred to him as a *boy*, she had been expecting just that: a squat, red-faced toad of a boy like one of the awful O'Higgins twins, or perhaps a scarecrow of a *gorsoon*, with muddy freckles and big ears.

Tierney Burke was neither. Even sprawled in the chair as he was, Annie

could tell that he was tall, with wide-set shoulders and a fine, strong chin—
what she could see of it beneath the ragged dark beard. And while he
was in truth as lean as a high-spirited yearling, he had the hard-muscled,
somewhat threatening look of a man grown. And he had a *scar*—a rakish,
piratelike scar that ran down from his forehead, puckering one dark eyebrow, and ending with a pinch at the outer corner of his left eye.

Any fear of retribution for her outrageous behavior vanished as she saw
the mass of angry bruises over the American boy's midsection. Why, didn't
he look for all the world as if someone had attempted to murder him?

Annie put a fist to her mouth, bracing her other hand on Fergus's
strong back. She was struck by an unexpected wrench of pain at the
thought of some of the more vicious beatings she had suffered at the
hands of her drunken stepfather. But how, she wondered, had anyone
managed to trap a fierce-looking boy like Tierney Burke long enough to
wreak such abuse on him?

She saw his face go pale when the surgeon removed the disreputable
sling and then the splint. Involuntarily, Annie winced for the American
boy's pain. Dr. Dunne muttered something about "breaking the bone all
over again," and Annie felt the blood drain from her head.

She decided she had played the peep long enough. Besides, she wasn't
at all sure she wanted to watch what came next. . . .

"Aine Fitzgerald! Explain yourself at once!"

Annie stiffened, expelling a sharp breath of annoyance at being caught.
For a moment, she deliberately remained fixed in place, unwilling to face
Sister Louisa's wrath. The nun's blistering tone was bad enough. Sure, the
fire in her eyes would be a terror.

"I *said*. . . explain yourself."

In the second before Annie turned around, Fergus gave a convincingly
pitiful whimper, which Annie hoped might help to soften the nun. But
Sister ignored the wolfhound entirely, fixing Annie with a terrible gaze,
sharp enough to part her hair.

"Why, Sister, wasn't I just coming down for some warm milk to help
me sleep, when I heard all the commotion and looked in to see what was
happening? And didn't I find strangers and Gypsies all about the house? Of
course, I intended to come and fetch you. . . but before disturbing your rest,
I thought I should investigate and find out what all the ruckus was about—"

"I'll have none of your blather, Miss! I'm far too cross."

Annie could see that, all right. Her mind groped for a reasonable explanation that might help to placate the nun. "Well, you see, Sister—"

"You should have been asleep hours ago!" Sister Louisa railed on, ignoring Annie's attempt to explain. "Instead, I find you sneaking about the hallway, spying on things that I am certain are none of your affair, none at all. Whatever has possessed you, child? And what, exactly, might be so engrossing that you would demean yourself in such a fashion?"

Now she was in for it! Annie braced herself for the worst, screwing up one side of her mouth in grim anticipation as Sister elbowed her out of the way to have herself a look into the kitchen.

"May the saints preserve us!" Sister whipped about, her skin as stark as the white linen framing her face. The raisin-dark eyes looked about to roll up into her brain. Annie's mind went spinning in one last desperate attempt to redeem herself before the nun lost all control. Another conciliatory whimper came from Fergus.

"*This* is what you are spying on? Heathen Gypsies and half-naked strangers?"

Annie twisted her face as if bracing for a blow. She waited for the enormity of her sin to settle over her, for the full measure of her disgrace to sink in and make her properly repentant.

"Didn't I only want to see what was happening?" she offered feebly, hoping Sister would hear for herself the genuine remorse in her voice.

Suddenly, a brilliant idea seized her. "And wasn't I about to go to sleep, Sister? Truly, I was! I had been studying my lessons, don't you see, but what with all the disturbance I simply couldn't concentrate. I feared something disastrous must have happened!"

"And it may, if you're not at the top of the stairs by the time I count to ten, Miss! And under the covers by the count of fifteen!"

Immensely grateful for this unexpected mercy, Annie began to move. "Come, Fergus—"

"*Wait*—"

Annie stopped in mid-flight, turning back. She might have known Sister would retract such uncharacteristic leniency.

The nun, not a great deal taller than Annie, who was slight herself, closed the distance between them. "You will stay away from those two," she warned, her eyes snapping. "There is no telling *what* to expect from a tinker—or an American!"

"Why, Sister, isn't Tierney Burke the son of the *Seanchai*'s oldest and dearest friend? As for the Gypsy—"

"As for the Gypsy, you will ignore him entirely!" the nun rejoined, wagging a finger and shaking her head. "Is that *quite* clear, Miss?"

"Oh, it *is*, Sister!" Annie's eyes went to a small stray curl of dark hair that had slipped defiantly from beneath the nun's wimple. "Well, then... I'll just be off to bed, Sister, if you will commence to count, please."

Sister's eyes narrowed suspiciously, but she merely gave a brief nod of dismissal. Fergus dared one last look over his shoulder, as if to be certain the nun was not in pursuit, then raced Annie up the stairs, easily pulling ahead before they reached the landing.

It would seem, Annie concluded, *that even a wolfhound knew enough to stay clear of a nun on the rampage.*

Louisa watched them go, the girl's white nightdress slapping her thin legs as she took the stairs two at a time. Easily outdistancing her, the wolfhound stood at the top of the landing, waiting.

Suppressing a smile, Louisa stood reflecting on whether she should retire to her own room or see if she were needed. She had been roused from her devotions at a time when most of the household would ordinarily have been abed. Half-expecting to be summoned downstairs, she'd hurriedly changed back into her habit and come down to find the child at her mischief.

She turned back toward the kitchen, then changed her mind. Certainly, an entire roomful of men could attend to things on their own.

Starting up the stairs, she wondered again at the wisdom of the *Seanchai*'s willingness to take on this American boy, who, by his father's own admission, was a rebellious son. If it had occurred to Morgan Fitzgerald that he might be inviting trouble, however, he was keeping it to himself.

At the landing, Louisa looked down the hallway and saw that Annie's bedroom door was securely closed. No doubt the child and the wolfhound were waiting at the keyhole to hear her footsteps go by.

Faith—*that* one was more than enough challenge for the *Seanchai*, indeed for the most stalwart of guardians! She hoped he would not eventually rue taking in yet another willful youth.

Going on down the hall, she wondered if the *Seanchai* had given enough thought to what he was doing. Certainly, he already had a formidable responsibility on his shoulders, with a newly adopted daughter and a troubled young wife. Not to mention the new babe on the way!

The man had either the heart of a saint or that of a fool—Louisa was never quite sure which. Bringing yet another difficult youth into a household that was already turbulent, to say the least, could prove a grave mistake. And what was he thinking, God help them all, to bring a *Gypsy* under the roof?

Louisa had served often enough in the Liberties and other slums throughout the city to acquire a fair measure of distrust for the Gypsies. Their heathen ways, their disregard for the property of others, their resistance to integrating themselves into society—even to the point of refusing their children an education—made them highly suspect to the church.

Yet, if she were to be entirely honest, she had also known those few who might have been said to possess some unexpectedly *decent* traits and, even more difficult to figure, a peculiar kind of nobility. Nevertheless, there was much that gave credence to the dark tales told about them, and they were not, as a whole, a people to be trusted—at least not by those outside their own.

That being the case, it seemed to her that the sooner the Gypsy was sent on his way, the better for them all.

8

Strangers at Nelson Hall

They call us aliens, we are told,
Because our wayward visions stray
From that dim banner they unfold,
The dreams of worn-out yesterday.

AE (GEORGE RUSSELL) (1867–1935)

Morgan felt the stab of pain in his own arm as he watched the surgeon reset Tierney Burke's broken bone.

The boy had grit, he would give him that. White-faced, his jaw set, Tierney uttered not a sound, but simply clenched his fists and bore his pain with rigid self-control.

"He should go to bed and stay there for a time," said the surgeon as he applied fresh bandages. "He has a bit of a fever and will be needing rest." He glanced up at Morgan. "Rest and proper food. And that one," he said, nodding at the Gypsy who looked to be half-dozing across the room, "should at least stay the night. I believe he will be fine, but he appears to have taken a nasty blow. He shouldn't be traipsing about until I have another look at him tomorrow, to make certain—"

"I am fine," interrupted the Gypsy, who apparently had not been sleeping after all. "I need no further attention."

Morgan studied him, feeling torn between reluctance to have a Gypsy in the house and uncertainty as to whether the lad was truly fit to leave. The Gypsy—*Jan Martova*, he called himself—held the battered violin that had been among his personal effects from the prison, cradling it as if it were a rare and precious instrument.

He looked exceedingly weary, and Morgan decided he was no boy, though he had a youthful appearance, a kind of innocence that was no doubt deceptive. He would be older than Tierney, he figured—perhaps twenty or more.

"There is a room for you here tonight," he offered impulsively.

He saw Sandemon glance at him with surprise. The Gypsy looked even more startled. His head came up sharply, the dark eyes locking on Morgan's face.

"You did a kindness for my friend's son," Morgan went on. "I would not repay you by putting you at risk. You may stay the night."

The Gypsy's dark gaze was direct but unreadable. "I expect no repayment. You have already done me a great service in rescuing me from the prison. I would not impose further on your generosity."

Taken aback by the youth's fine manners, Morgan gave a wave of his hand. "It will be no imposition to give you a bed. Tomorrow will be soon enough for you to leave."

"You are very kind, but I cannot stay." The Gypsy was polite, but the finality of his tone brooked no argument. "It is forbidden."

"Forbidden?"

"You are *Gorgio*. I am *Rom*." The Gypsy's gaze never wavered, but there was a slight hesitation in his voice that Morgan somehow took to be regret. "I cannot stay under your roof, but I am most grateful for your invitation."

Had he not been curiously insulted, Morgan might have found the youth's remarks amusing. So strong was the popular aversion to the Romany that he could not help but wonder how most of his contemporaries would react to the idea that a Gypsy considered Nelson Hall "forbidden."

"The stables then," he countered. "I'll see that you have bedding." Inexplicably, he found himself determined that the Gypsy would stay.

"If *he* sleeps in the stables, then so do I!" Tierney blurted out.

Suddenly impatient with the both of them, Morgan snapped, "Don't be foolish! He sleeps in the stables by his own choice. *You* will sleep in a bed, where you belong—and the sooner we get you there, the better! The rest of the household could do with some sleep, too. I, for one, am exhausted entirely!"

Tierney looked at him, clearly unconvinced. His mouth was set in a hard, thin line, but he said nothing more as he allowed the surgeon to help him shrug into his shirt.

Not for the first time that night, Morgan found himself questioning the wisdom of taking on this most recent responsibility. He glanced again at Jan Martova, who still sat balancing his violin, then at Tierney Burke, who met his gaze with an expression that stopped just short of being sullen.

In the instant of that silent encounter, it suddenly occurred to Morgan that, of the two, the Gypsy might well be the less troublesome to have under his roof.

The small camp was on the edge of the Liberties, in a long-abandoned, dusty lot. When Nanosh slipped in among the wagons, it was late, but the campfires were still high, the voices lively. Most of the men sat, smoking and drinking, around the fires. A number of the women were already asleep, most of them in their wagons because of the unseasonably cold night.

The dogs heralded Nanosh's approach, and some of the children playing about the wagons called out to him. But he ignored their greetings, stopping only long enough to scan the cluster of men near the fires. Spying his cousin Greco, he started toward him.

As soon as Greco saw him, he leaped to his feet. "What are you doing here? You were told to stand watch over your cousin at the prison!"

Greco's mouth was tight with anger, his black eyes accusing. Two other men in the circle also stood.

Nanosh stopped short. "Wait, Cousin, you don't know—I must tell you—" he gasped, out of breath from his run. "Jan passed me a message from the prison, told me to take it to the Big House on the hill, on behalf of his cellmate. I went back, just as soon as I delivered the message, but the guards discovered me, and I had to run away!"

Greco's stormy expression darkened. "What message? What foolishness is this?"

Nanosh had no wish to feel his older cousin's wrath. Quickly he rushed to explain about the message written on a piece of cloth, his audience with the big man in the wheelchair at the place called Nelson Hall, and, finally, about his close escape from the prison guards.

"They found me in the brush, soon after the men from the Big House arrived at the prison. They threatened to lock me in a cell, too! One even threatened to disembowel me!"

Anger leaped in Greco's eyes, but this time, Nanosh knew the anger was directed at the guards, not at *him*.

"They were large and clumsy…I slipped out of their hands and ran like the wind! I ran all the way here to tell you what happened!"

His cousin's black gaze raked over him, one long finger tracing the line of his mustache. Finally, he gave a curt nod of approval. "You did well. Go, now, and stay with your mother. I will go to the prison to find out what has happened to Jan."

"Take me, Cousin! I should go with you!" Nanosh protested.

Greco looked at him. "You cannot go, Nanosh," he said firmly but not unkindly. "The guards might try to hold you again. You must stay here. But your cousin will be told of your courage this night. Go along now. I will see to Jan."

Although greatly disappointed, Nanosh knew better than to argue with Greco, and so he reluctantly trudged off to his own campfire.

By two hours past midnight, most of the household had retired. Morgan listened at Finola's door for a moment, hoping all the confusion had not awakened her. Hearing nothing, he gave a nod to indicate that Sandemon should help him into bed.

"*Seanchai,*" Sandemon said as he laid out Morgan's nightclothes, "I have been thinking—"

Morgan slanted a look at him. "You usually are," he quipped.

Sandemon shrugged off the jibe and continued. "I have been *thinking*," he repeated, "of a way we might give you a bit more freedom—an arrangement to allow you to get yourself in and out of your bed."

Morgan cocked an eyebrow at the bed, which had been lowered to the height of his wheelchair. "You have already cut the legs off my grandfather's two-hundred-year-old bed," he said. "What else do you have in mind?"

Sandemon smiled, his dark eyes sparkling. He pointed toward the ceiling.

Morgan looked up at the gloom-shrouded rafters. "So?"

"A meat hook," Sandemon said. "We fix a meat hook in that rafter directly overhead, attach a chain, and—"

Morgan rolled his eyes. "First you truss me up like a turkey for my own wedding, and now you want to hang me from the rafters like a side of beef!" He let out an exaggerated sigh. "What else—"

A sudden, savage pounding downstairs startled them both. Still in the wheelchair, Morgan instinctively yanked open the draw of the night table by the bed and withdrew his pistol. But Sandemon stopped him with a firm hand on his shoulder. "Let me see to it first," he said, already starting for the door.

The pounding continued uninterrupted until finally Morgan heard the front doors open. Loud voices ensued, and Morgan wheeled himself out into the hall, the gun in hand.

He stopped at the banister and looked downstairs. To his astonishment, he saw a tall, thick-chested man with black hair and a drooping mustache push roughly by Sandemon and come to stand in the middle of the entryway.

The intruder snarled something unintelligible, and Sandemon, his expression as cold as Morgan had ever seen it, replied in strident tones. "You will have to return tomorrow, at a civilized hour! I cannot disturb the *Seanchai* at this time of night!"

But Morgan had already wheeled the chair onto the lift. All the way down the stairs, he purposely trained the pistol at the stranger. "Identify yourself."

The man below stood his ground, his hands splayed on his hips, staring at Morgan with hostile eyes.

"I am Greco Martova, and I will have my brother!"

Martova. Of course! He should have realized the man was a Gypsy at first glance. Rugged and dark, the Romany was an imposing sight. His hair and mustache were thick and raven-black. He wore leather riding boots, numerous gold rings on his fingers, and one thin gold earring. Across his wide chest dangled a chain, on which hung several gold coins. A bright blue silk kerchief was knotted loosely about his neck.

"Jan Martova is your brother?" Morgan finally asked.

"My brother, yes. And I was told by the prison guards that he is here. Is that true?"

Morgan gave a short nod. "He is asleep in the stables."

"In the stables?" the Gypsy repeated, his tone incredulous. "My brother sleeps in your *stables*?"

"Only because he would not accept a bed under my roof!" Morgan snapped, exasperated by the man's rudeness.

The Gypsy gave a short grunt in reply.

"Your brother took a blow on the head from one of the warders," Morgan went on, determined to ignore the man's bluster. "A surgeon examined him and suggested that he spend the night here, for his own protection."

The Gypsy frowned, his concern evident. "He is injured?"

"No," Morgan quickly assured him. "Not seriously. He will be perfectly fine. The surgeon simply thought it in his best interests to stay the night."

The Gypsy crossed his arms over his chest. "If he is not injured, then I will take him home. At once."

Morgan drew a long breath, containing his temper at great effort. "That would not be wise, I think. Not when the surgeon has advised against it."

"The advice of a *Gorgio* medicine man is of no account to me! I will take my brother home, where he will receive proper care."

By now Morgan was at the end of his patience. "That is altogether up to you," he said caustically. "But if he suffers any ill consequences from your foolishness, that will also be your doing."

He paused. "You might want to have a look at him, in the stables—to satisfy yourself that he is quite all right and is comfortable. Perhaps then you could let *him* decide whether he feels strong enough to leave in the middle of the night."

The Gypsy seemed to consider Morgan's suggestion for a moment, then shook his head. "He will do as I say. He is my brother. I will take him back to the camp with me tonight."

Galled by the man's stubborn resistance to reason, Morgan snapped, "As you wish, then! Sandemon—show him to the stables."

Back upstairs in his bedroom, Morgan sat seething. He had had quite enough for one day of gaols and Gypsies and hotheaded boys!

Just then, the clock in the downstairs entryway chimed three. Morgan groaned. In less than five hours, he would be expected in the classroom to hear sleepy recitations and stumbling theorems. Any man with half his wits knew that such a task could not be borne with so little sleep.

He was beginning to question the wisdom of agreeing to take in an old friend's son. There was a great deal to be said, after all, for leading a quiet, uncomplicated life— especially if this night were any example of things to come.

9

Of Friends and Family

Our friends go with us as we go
Down the long path where Beauty wends.
OLIVER ST. JOHN GOGARTY (1878–1957)

In the morning, the Gypsy boy was gone. Sandemon reported to Morgan at breakfast that there was no sign of Jan Martova in the stables, indeed no sign that he had ever been at Nelson Hall.

His thoughts elsewhere, Morgan nodded distractedly. "I expected as much. That brother of his no doubt hauled him out in short order."

Alone at the long dining room table, he glanced up from his coffee. "Finola did not come down this morning. I wish you would go up and inquire, make certain she is all right. And *where* is Annie? This is the second time this week she's been late to breakfast."

"I am here, *Seanchai!*"

As always, the girl did not so much enter the room as *explode* into it. Out of breath, she gave Sandemon a sheepish grin as she squeezed by him through the door.

With weary eyes, Morgan took in his adopted daughter's uncommonly neat appearance. The heavy dark hair, which ordinarily began its escape from confinement well before breakfast, seemed to have been restrained by extreme force into two thick, heavy braids. The elfin face had been scrubbed to a polish, and the always alert black eyes fairly snapped with restless energy.

He offered his cheek for her quick kiss. "I was beginning to think I was the only one astir this morning."

"But I would have thought you'd have all sorts of company." Annie blurted out, her gaze sweeping the room. "Where are the others?"

"The others?"

"Aye, Tierney Burke from America—and the Gypsy."

She stopped suddenly, biting at her lower lip.

Morgan lifted one eyebrow, exasperated but not surprised that she had evidently been doing a bit of snooping in the night. The imp missed very little. "And how is it that you know about Tierney Burke and the Gypsy?"

Chin up, she thrust her hands behind her back and locked eyes with him. "And wasn't there enough commotion to rouse the dead? A body could scarcely sleep with such a fuss."

"Your curiosity will cost you yet," Morgan said, lacing his words with a perfunctory note of sternness. "I'll expect you to be alert during recitation today, despite your late-hour eavesdropping."

"Aren't they coming down?" she asked bluntly, pulling her chair up to the table. "Tierney Burke and the Gypsy?"

"The Gypsy," Morgan replied, "has already gone. And Tierney Burke will be abed for a day or so, at Dr. Dunne's advice. As for you, lassie, you had best be having your pottage."

She wrinkled her nose. "Pottage *again*? I'm bored with pottage!"

"You will eat it and be thankful!" Morgan snapped, the previous long night and scant sleep making him unduly short. "There are thousands all across the land who would bless God for even a spoonful!"

Her startled look made him instantly contrite, but he would not have the girl given to whining, and her having so much.

No words were exchanged as she ate. Finally, in a milder tone of voice, Morgan broke the silence between them. "No doubt you will meet Tierney Burke later today, perhaps this evening. But he will be weak, mind you, from his ordeal, so you must not weary him with your chatter."

She delayed a spoonful of pottage in midair. "Oh, I *shan't*! I'm hoping he will tell us all about America, though, when he's strong enough." She paused. "And where did the Gypsy go, then, *Seanchai*? Back to his tribe, I imagine."

Morgan nodded. "His brother came for him," he said sourly, recalling the elder Martova's demands.

Annie suffered one last spoon of pottage, then bounced up from her chair. "More's the pity," she said, swiping her mouth with the table napkin.

"I had hoped to meet him as well. I've never had conversation with a real Gypsy before."

Morgan looked at her. "Your education will not suffer from the lack, I'll warrant."

As he watched her tear out of the room, he could not restrain a fleeting smile. It was a bittersweet feeling this, watching her bloom so quickly from child to young woman. She would be thirteen soon. A little girl no longer.

At times he felt an almost overwhelming urge to stop the clock so that he might have more time to savor her childhood. Admittedly, he entertained a great curiosity about the sort of woman Annie would become, but he cherished these years of her youth, when he could still be a father to the child in her.

She had come to him so late…and had quickly become so dear. It never failed to shake him, the realization that he was, at last, a father. Father to a fey, star-chasing child with a quicksilver mind, a child who viewed life as one vast wonder after another and had not allowed even the agony of abuse to dim the light of her soaring spirit.

He reminded himself that soon…frighteningly soon…he would also be father to *another* child. A wee babe.

Finola's child. As her time drew near, Morgan grew both eager and anxious. Eager for the waiting to be done, for the child to arrive, but anxious, too, for Finola, for her well-being.

He found himself increasingly fearful that the birthing itself—an act he found nothing short of terrifying—might somehow cause her harm, might even take away from the progress she had made since the attack, the attack which had left her both physically and emotionally shattered.

At times he even worried that the *babe* might prove harmful to Finola, simply by being an inescapable reminder of the violent assault that had brought her such anguish. And yet she seemed, if not entirely content with her condition, at least accepting of it. She sewed with Sister Louisa and Annie, took part in the planning of the nursery, appeared conscientious of her health. If she seemed reluctant to speak of the impending birth, whether out of respect for convention or her natural shyness, he thought it only to be expected—although in truth he would have welcomed more candor from her.

The candor of a wife who shared her deepest secrets with her husband.…

He forced the thought aside. He already had far more than he could have hoped for. For the first time in his life, he had a home and family: a daughter he cherished, a babe to anticipate, and Finola as his wife.

True, she was his wife in name only, but at least she was *here*, under his roof. She was close by, ate at his table, shared his hearthfire. And they had become friends—no small blessing in itself.

Aye, he had far more than any man in his condition could dare to hope for, especially in these troubled times. It would behoove him to simply maintain a thankful heart and live one day at a time.

For now, he decided, wheeling the chair out from behind the table, he would go upstairs and make certain that she was all right. He still had time to treat himself to her smile before starting the day in the classroom.

"Sandemon was just here to inquire about you," Lucy told Finola. "The *Seanchai* was concerned."

Finola glanced up from her rocking chair by the window. Small One, her black and white cat, stirred impatiently in her lap and then turned once, settling back into the crook of Finola's arm. "I hope you told him I was well?"

"I did." Lucy closed the door to the bedchamber as she entered. "I explained that you simply did not feel up to breakfast yet this morning. But I'm thinking you might expect a knock on the door any moment now. The *Seanchai* will not rest until he sees for himself that all is well with you."

Finola frowned. "Perhaps I should go down. But he frets so when I don't eat…"

"Because he wants what is best for you and the child."

"I know." Finola scratched the cat's ear thoughtfully. "It's just that I feel so…dull this morning. So huge. Everything seems such an effort, I can't think I would be able to swallow a bite. It would stick in my throat, sure."

Lucy stood looking at her, shaking her head. "It's anything but huge you are, child! You are still too thin, in spite of the babe's weight. Far too thin, I'm thinking. You need every bite you can take in."

Finola managed a smile. What a turn Lucy's feelings had taken since she'd found the Savior! Whereas she had once dared to suggest that the child be aborted, now she hovered like a mother herself, intent that both Finola and the babe should thrive.

And they *did* thrive. Until a few days ago, she had almost begun to feel strong again. Recently, however, the burden of extra weight had begun to tell on her in terms of discomfort and sheer ungainliness.

It embarrassed her these days to be seen at all, especially by Morgan, although he was kindness itself and pretended not to notice her awkward girth. He remained ever the gentleman, unfailingly attentive and concerned.

At the thought of him, a swell of love rose in her, almost dizzying in its intensity. Her arms tightened around Small One until the cat squawked indignantly and jumped to the floor. Finola looked up, surprised, when Small One landed with a loud *thump*. She had been very far away...far away with Morgan. At times she thought she could not bear the sweet ache of gladness the very thought of him evoked.

Her feelings for this man who was her husband—and her dearest friend—both frightened and bewildered her, for she did not understand the painful yearning in her heart to simply be near him. Even less did she understand the agonizing emptiness when they were apart.

She fervently hoped he did not sense her confusion, her unaccountable foolishness. How humiliating it would be if he were ever to discover that, even in the throes of her disgrace and ungainly condition, she harbored such an affection for him—the one who knew more than most about her shame.

She could not bear to do anything that might mar the wonder of their friendship. No matter what, she would not risk this precious gift.

Morgan hesitated just inside the threshold, waiting until Lucy left the room. For a moment, he sat transfixed, taking in the sight of her, the golden aura of her loveliness.

Her flaxen hair, almost to her waist, was unbound and fell loosely over the soft cream-colored dressing gown. The morning light seemed a gentle halo encircling her there, in the chair by the window. Never in his wildest imaginings would he have thought that a woman so great with child could wrench his heart with the sheer radiance of her beauty!

Not that he had had all that much experience with women great with child, of course. But who would believe that an old rake like himself would end up playing the consummate fool over a glory of a girl half his age—a girl who undoubtedly had little on her mind but the imminent birth of her babe?

Wheeling himself the rest of the way into the room, he said uncertainly, "I was concerned for you."

She smiled at him, and the room seemed to brighten still more. "I'm sorry. I didn't mean to worry you. I'm afraid I'm feeling somewhat idle this morning. Perhaps I should have come downstairs anyway—"

"No, of course you shouldn't, not if you don't feel up to it," he said quickly. Taking her hand, he brushed it lightly with his lips, then released it. "I simply needed to reassure myself that you're all right."

I had to see you...drink in the sight of you before another hour went by, or I would not be able to bear the loneliness....

"You must not worry so, Morgan. I am quite well. Truly."

"Still, as your time draws near, I'm afraid I will only fuss more," he said without thinking. He felt his face heat, for like any Irish male, he was sorely ill at ease in the presence of an expectant mother, more uncomfortable yet at the mention of her condition.

As if embarrassed for him, she looked away. "I will be fine. Please don't worry yourself on my account. You have done enough...more than enough."

"Impossible!" he blurted out. "I could never do enough for you."

Immediately awkward at the words that had spilled from him unbidden, Morgan gripped the arms of the wheelchair. What *was* there about the girl that invariably enfeebled his mind and entangled his tongue?

Her startled look only heightened his discomfort. "It's quite a beautiful morning," he said, attempting to change the subject. "I thought perhaps you might like to enjoy the sunshine with me."

Up until recently, they had made a practice of spending at least a part of the late morning outside, often doing nothing more than sitting by the small stream that bordered the west side of the estate, where they would watch the swans and talk quietly. Sometimes they visited the stables or merely roamed about the grounds. Of late, however, Morgan was hesitant to suggest an outing, having noticed her shortness of breath and an apparent tendency to tire easily.

For a moment she looked tempted, but just as quickly she shook her head. "I don't think I feel—"

She stopped at the sudden rapping on the bedroom door, followed by a soft query from Sandemon.

An inexplicable coldness touched Morgan's spine the moment the black man entered the room. Something in the midnight eyes put him instantly alert.

"*Seanchai*—" Sandemon stopped for a moment, and again Morgan sensed something amiss, as if his usually eloquent West Indies companion could not find the words to say what needed to be said.

Morgan nodded. "What is it?"

"I fear I have bad news for you, *Seanchai*." The black man paused, his gaze wandering to Finola, then back to Morgan. "It is about Father Joseph. Word has come just this morning. I am sorry to have to tell you this, *Seanchai*...but Father Joseph has passed on to be with the Lord."

Sandemon's words hit Morgan like a physical blow. The touch of cold dread he had felt only a moment before now slipped over him like a shroud.

As if from a great distance, he heard Finola's soft gasp, felt her hand clutch his arm. He was aware of Sandemon's additional murmurs of sympathy, the black man's own features shadowed with sorrow.

"*Joseph?*" he choked out. "Joseph Mahon? Surely not..."

Grief swept over him, and suddenly his hands and arms began to shake erratically.

Morgan clenched his jaw, desperately willing the shaking to stop. *Finola must not see; she must not know....*

Furious at this betrayal of his body, he slammed at the wheels of the chair with his quaking forearms, and whipped himself to the door. He *had* to escape—now, before he was utterly humiliated. "I'm sorry," he muttered, and scrambled blindly from the room.

Somehow he managed to reach his bedchamber and wheel himself inside, where he sat, mortified and sorrowing. Sandemon knocked just once, but Morgan told him in an unsteady voice that he needed to be alone, instructing him to ask Sister Louisa to take his morning classes. After a moment, he heard the black man's quiet footsteps retreat down the hallway.

Morgan sighed and rested his head against the back of the chair. *This wasn't the first time....*

For several weeks now, the seizures had been coming upon him—gradually, at first, like a muscle tic, then with increasing intensity. There could be no doubt—something was wrong, and getting worse. So far he had managed to hide it from Finola—God knows she had enough to think about with the babe nearly ready to be born. But this time she had seen—he was certain she had seen.

Morgan shook his head. It was bad enough to be a useless lump of a man confined to this cursed chair…but to be plagued with seizures as well?

He shot a fierce glance into the dark rafters over his head.

"God," he said in a throaty whisper, "my legs are gone. Must I lose my dignity as well?" He took a deep breath, and the full realization of his losses washed over him. "And *Joseph,*" he breathed. "Ah, Lord…did it have to be Joseph Mahon?"

Weakened by shock and the nervous seizure, Morgan sat sprawled in the chair, trying to absorb the news of this latest loss—a loss as critical to the entire County of Mayo itself as to him personally. Memory after memory slammed through him. At last, unable to still the tides of sorrow cresting in his heart, he wept.

He could scarcely recall the time he had not known Joseph Mahon. The gentle priest had been a vital part of his life, indeed a vital part of the village of Killala, where Morgan had grown to manhood. And although he had not seen his old friend for well over a year, Joseph's thin, ascetic face, lined with years of hardship, came as clearly to his mind now as if he had been with him only yesterday.

The aging priest had been a comforting, familiar presence at most village events, but more to the point for Morgan, he had been an instrumental presence of change in his life. Joseph had prayed for him unceasingly over the years, Morgan knew. And, God be thanked, the good man's prayers had not been entirely in vain!

But the kindly priest, while concerned for Morgan's soul, had been every bit as concerned for his neck. Hadn't he effected the pardon that saved him from the noose at almost the last hour?

It had been Joseph who brought about the reconciliation with Morgan's English grandfather, Richard Nelson. And it had been Joseph who had knelt with the weary prodigal in the dust to lead him back into the arms of a forgiving God.

Of late, Morgan had been working in a fever to edit the failing priest's writings. Joseph's journals of the famine in Mayo would, once published, disclose the truth about Britain's monstrous betrayal of the Irish—and at the same time reveal an inspiring, incredibly courageous account of the Irish people's indomitable spirit. The brutally frank writings of the elderly priest had given Morgan an agonizing glimpse into the heart of his friend—a good, simple man who had remained faithful to his God during an entire lifetime.

Through his tears, Morgan stared out the window onto the gentle, rolling hills, now lush and vibrant with the emerald and rainbow hues of springtime. It seemed to him that there was no calculating the loss of such a man as Joseph Mahon, no counting the souls he had led to the Savior, no measuring the influence of the life he had poured out for others.

And yet there should be something…some acknowledgment…some tribute to such a man.

Oh, Joseph…Joseph…I will do what I can to ensure that your work will be known…and your words will be heard…by our people…perhaps by the people of other nations as well. This much I can do for you, old friend…this much I will do for you…

Finola could bear it no longer. The memory of his pain-filled eyes, his stricken face, when he fled the room would give her no peace until she went to him.

Going to the door that connected their bedchambers, she knocked quietly, then again.

"Come…"

His voice was so low as to be little more than a whisper, but Finola did not hesitate. Stopping just inside the threshold, she stood, studying him with an aching heart.

His back was to her, his massive shoulders slumped, as he sat, looking out the window. The awful trembling seemed to have subsided.

"Morgan," she said softly, uncertainly. "Morgan, I…I will leave you alone if you want. But I…wanted to tell you how sorry I am. I know Father Joseph meant a great deal to you."

For a long time he said nothing. Finally he turned, and Finola's breath caught in her throat when she saw his tear-tracked face, ravaged with grief.

"Oh…Morgan…I am sorry!"

His attempted smile failed. He lifted a hand, then dropped it. Finola thought her heart would shatter for the sorrow in his eyes.

Impulsively, she went to him. Awkward with her weight, she nevertheless knelt in front of the wheelchair and clasped both his hands in hers. "Is there anything I can do? Anything at all?"

He shook his head, squeezing her hands. "I'm sorry for my behavior," he said in a strangled voice.

"Don't be foolish!" Aching for the pain she encountered in his eyes, she gripped his hands. "May I stay with you, Morgan? Please?"

A look very much like gratitude went over his face, and he nodded. "Forgive me if I frightened you."

Finola frowned. "What are you talking about?"

"The tremors," he said, his voice so low she could barely make out his words. "I know you saw them." He paused. "It doesn't happen often," he added, "but I expect it's a bit—unsettling to others."

His face was set in a look of misery. As understanding dawned, Finola could have wept. She had noticed the trembling once before, but they had been outside at the time, and, sensitive to his embarrassment, she had deliberately pretended not to see.

It humiliated him....

"It bothers me only because I know it troubles you," Finola said, holding his gaze. "But what does it mean?"

As soon as the question left her lips, she wondered if she should have asked it. But he merely shrugged. "Dr. Dunne isn't certain. It began some weeks back," he explained, still holding her hands. "He's pressing me to consult with a new physician. But for now, I can't quite face another surgeon prodding at me."

"Perhaps you should at least consider it," she ventured.

"Perhaps," he murmured, glancing away.

There was so much Finola longed to say to him. She ached to tell him that she felt his pain, wanted to ease it somehow. She wished, too, she could communicate how brave she thought he was, how much she admired him for all he had managed under such impossible circumstances.

But it would sound too much like pity, and she suspected that if there was anything Morgan could not bear from her, it was pity. So she simply squeezed his hands once more and, with some difficulty, hauled herself to her feet. She even managed a smile at her own clumsiness.

"I think I would like to go outside after all," she said, forcing a note of brightness into her voice. "I'll go and change. You will go with me?"

He hesitated, then nodded. "Aye. Sister Louisa has taken my recitations." He paused, studying her. "Thank you, lass."

At Finola's puzzled look, he added, "For caring. Thank you for caring."

Finola had to fight back her own tears. "I do…care, Morgan. I care very much."

Turning then, she hurried from the room before she foolishly said more than she intended.

10

The Arrival
of Quinn O'Shea

Some come with rattle of drum...
Joyous epiphanies.
Others gain a place through secret pain
And silent agonies.

ANONYMOUS

New York City
Late June

Perched on the edge of her bunk, Quinn O'Shea held her breath against the foul stench that seemed to ooze from the hull of the *Norville*. It was early morning, and although she could not see outside, she sensed that the day was fine.

They had put in at New York Harbor five days ago, but instead of being allowed on deck they had been held "between ships," as the sailors referred to steerage class, the entire time since their arrival. Steerage passengers like Quinn had been set to scrubbing and scraping with sea water and lye, trying to rid their part of the ship of its accumulated filth and vicious odors.

As if any amount of scrubbing could hope to rid this rotting old heap of its stink, Quinn thought with a scowl. She was quite certain that the disgusting smells of decay, unwashed bodies, and an entire host of treacherous diseases were imbedded in the damp wood of the hull forever.

Ignoring the blather of the women nearby, most of whom were either arguing the merits of America or exchanging fearful imaginings about

what lay ahead, Quinn turned back to her letter writing. She already had
at least a dozen or more letters ready to post to Molly, but she went on
with today's, for she had promised her younger sister not to spare even the
smallest detail about the voyage.

She had not kept that promise, however; not entirely. There were *some*
things about this ocean journey she would keep to herself, for fear of
frightening the girl. When the time came, she didn't want Molly to balk
at making the trip.

But for the most part, Quinn had written honestly of the ship's
crowded conditions, the spoiled rations and food shortages, the miserable damp cold, and the seasickness—the relentless, enervating seasickness that had stricken so many, but which somehow Quinn had managed
to escape. She was determined that Molly must not be allowed to harbor
unreasonable expectations about the crossing, for wouldn't that only make
the truth more bitter still?

At least for now, however, Quinn would keep some things to herself:
the worms and vermin in the food stores, the stench of vomit, the dysen-
tery that had become epidemic by the third week of the voyage, the countless dead bodies tossed out to sea like so much worthless rubbish, the
ever-present terror of almost everyone in steerage throughout the journey.

...It is rumored that today we will all be inspected for
disease. Everyone has been busy praying that no serious
illness will be found among us, for otherwise we could be
kept at hospital for weeks.

The sooner we can get off this coffin ship the better, to my
way of thinking! I am eager to manage a bit of privacy
and begin looking for a position. The sooner I find work,
the sooner I'll be able to send you your passage money.

Remember now, Molly, you must be patient and have faith,
for it will take me some time to locate a position....

Her little sister would have to have faith for them both, Quinn thought
grimly, for she had precious little left, once the law and Millen Jupe had
finished with her.

She ended the letter, addressing the envelope to Molly alone. For an
instant she held the pen suspended above her sister's name, then went on

in firm strokes. There was no use in adding her mother's name, after all. To Mum, she was as good as dead, and there was no changing the way things were.

It was midafternoon when word came down that the ship would more than likely be held in quarantine.

All sick passengers would be taken to the hospital on Staten Island for detention, while "further medical inspections" were continued aboard the *Norville.*

Quinn had already suffered one shipboard medical examination, and, even though she knew nothing at all about such procedures, she was sure it had been little more than a hoax. With at least eight hundred or more passengers aboard the *Norville,* it would have required an entire team of medical inspectors to do a thorough job. Instead, one health officer and two assistants had made a brief walk-through of the ship, nodding or jabbing a finger at those passengers who were either blind, deaf and dumb, or simply too ill to stand. Quinn had passed the preliminary inspection as slick as goose grease.

But now they were coming through again, and this time they seemed to be taking a closer look at some of the steerage passengers. Quinn knew for a fact that the ship's officers had hidden several passengers before the inspections even began, especially those who appeared to be suffering from communicable diseases, such as smallpox and typhus. Evidently, the ship's master was willing to resort to any deception at all if it would avoid a long delay in quarantine.

Obviously, they hadn't considered her cough a serious threat. Nor did she. Who would *not* have a bit of a cold after spending more than a month in the frigid, wet belly of a rotting old ship like the *Norville?*

But the incessant hack made her vulnerable. When the fish-eyed medical inspector jerked a finger in her face and pronounced her "fevered, probably consumptive," her heated protests met only a stony stare. The inspector moved on, and Quinn was herded to one side with the others who had been culled from the steerage list. Moments later, they were ordered to board the skiffs below for transportation to the hospital.

Like a condemned prisoner, Quinn could now only stand and watch with growing horror as others were singled out for the same fate. Families were torn apart during the selection process: wailing mothers dragged away from their children, husbands separated from their anguished wives, screaming orphans snatched from one another's arms.

It was like being trapped in a nightmare, where the ill and afflicted were punished for their infirmities by being sent off on a journey to hell. And their loved ones could do nothing but stand and watch, looking on as their families marched off to their doom.

It was almost dark when the crowded launch swung around in the shallow water just off Staten Island. The patients for the hospital were ordered out of the boat, and Quinn immediately found herself plunged knee-deep in water. Nearly losing her footing, she hoisted her small poke holding her letters to Molly and her one change of clothes as high as she could manage while she scrambled for the shore.

Suddenly, she heard a child cry out behind her. Whipping about, she saw a small girl with panicked eyes submerged almost to her neck in the water.

"Mum! Mum! Help me, Mum!" Flailing her hands, the child bobbed erratically as she screamed.

Quinn lunged forward in the water, thinking of nothing but the child. Without warning, she slipped, losing her balance. In sick horror, she saw her parcel sail out of her arms and into the river.

Quinn staggered, grasping for the small poke that held her few meager belongings and the letters over which she had labored for weeks. But it was already sinking from view.

For a moment she could only stare in disbelief. Then the child's shrill cry roused her, and she again started toward the little girl. By now, however, others had reached the panicked child, and a woman, whom Quinn took to be the mother, had her firmly under the arms and was pulling her to shore.

Quinn turned and headed back, finally collapsing on the beach, out of breath and badly shaken from the loss of her things. All her letters were lost to her—and to Molly! Moreover, she now hadn't a clean change of clothing to her name! How could she apply for a position looking like a tinker?

But she had no time to mourn her misfortune. An official-looking man wearing an armband marched up and immediately began to herd everyone up the beach toward the hospital.

In the gloom of early dark, Tompkinsville, as it was called, appeared a dismal, squat structure, much like a prison. Even before they reached the building, Quinn's senses were almost overwhelmed by some deadly, vile stench that must, she was certain, pervade this entire island.

The smell of death. A great tide of death, all about her, waiting to suck her into its ugly mouth.

Quinn's stomach rebelled. Her mind scrambled for a way of escape, for as sure as she was standing on the shores of America, this was a death-island!

Just when she would have bolted and run, big Bobby Dempsey came up beside her. "Don't be a-scared, lassie," he said in his deep, lumbering voice. "We don't need to be staying in this place too very long."

Surprised, Quinn looked up at him. "Why, whatever are *you* doing here, Bobby Dempsey? Sure, and there's nothing sickly about you!"

The burly man shifted his weight, staring down at the rock-strewn beach. "They said I looked to be an eejit, said I'd maybe have to go back to Ireland."

Quinn stared at him in astonishment. Bobby Dempsey was a big, clumsy rock of a man, with eyes as sad as an orphaned pup set deep in a face that looked to have been battered in one too many faction fights. He was a bit dull and slow-thinking, no great bargain as brains went, but he was no idiot either and didn't deserve to be humiliated in such a way.

For some reason, the ungainly giant had appointed himself Quinn's protector aboard ship. Whether it was due to her small size and tender years, or the fact that she had treated him kindly, poor Bobby had become her constant shadow.

Suddenly, her own loss of personal belongings seemed less important. Feeling a surge of pity for the man, Quinn put a hand to his thickly corded arm. "You just pay them no heed, Bobby. Their kind can't be telling a fool from a fig, and that's the truth."

As they approached the entrance doors, she lowered her voice. "What did you mean, Bobby, about not staying in this place too very long?"

His reply was delayed by the arrival of the tall, thin official who had preceded them up from the beach and who now began to herd them through the doors. Inside, the place seemed but an extension of the misery

Quinn had seen aboard ship. Every bit of available space had been plugged with beds and cots, all of which were occupied by moaning, shrieking immigrants. The very walls reeked with the smell of disease and death, and echoed with more keening than Quinn had ever heard in any one place, even on the *Norville*.

At the far end of the narrow room, Quinn saw a line of women and children. Most were crying—some aloud, others weeping softly. Sensing that she and Bobby would soon be separated, Quinn turned to him. "I asked you, what did you mean about getting away from here, Bobby? I'll be going with you!"

Bobby glanced about them with a furtive look. "Aye, 'tis no fitting place for a wee lass like yourself. This be a bad place—a very bad place— I'm thinking."

Suddenly impatient with him, Quinn pressed. "But how will you manage to get away, Bobby? You didn't say *how*!"

Glancing toward two other rough-looking men in the next line, Bobby lowered his voice to a whisper. "Jack Roche and Owney Boyle—and their women—we plan to take one of the skiffs what brought us over and get us away to the city. To New York."

When Quinn would have probed for more information, the big man hushed her, saying, "Just do what I say, lass, when I tell you. Can you be faking a swoon, then?"

Quinn bristled. "Well, I'd *have* to be faking it, I expect!" she shot back. "Sure, I'm no silly hen myself, to be swooning and taking on so."

Bobby blinked, then grinned at her. "Aye...well, then, when I snaps me fingers, you swoon big. Make a grand show of it, mind. I'll be catching you, so never fear, you'll not hit the floor."

"But—"

Behind her, a gruff voice interrupted Quinn's protest. "Women to this line, men over there!"

Quinn whipped around, about to make an acid retort.

Something in the narrow-faced official's eyes stopped her. "You must be inspected for lice," he said, his nostrils flaring as if he could actually see them crawling along Quinn's face.

"*Lice?* I don't have bugs! I have but a bit of a cough, not *bugs*!" Nervously, Quinn glanced again toward the end of the line, at the door through which the women and children continued to disappear.

Other worried voices now raised in protest. In truth, Quinn knew a number of them were indeed infested with bugs. It had become almost an obsession with her aboard ship, to avoid the filthy vermin that rode so many heads but hers.

"If they find bugs on us," moaned a woman just down the line, "they will cut off all our hair!"

Quinn's blood chilled. Not *her* hair, they wouldn't! Nobody would be cutting off Quinn O'Shea's hair! Indeed, not! And sure, not for bugs she did not have!

"I do not have lice!" Quinn renewed her defense, raising her voice still more.

"Don't be too sure, lassie," said Bobby Dempsey, still standing behind her.

Quinn whirled around, her eyes blazing. But Bobby only gave her a clumsy wink. "Don't I just see one, right there?" He pointed to the brush part of Quinn's long braid and winked again, an exaggerated grimace.

Quinn stared at him, then caught on. She gave a fierce, loud wail, then buckled to a swoon that would have done the Queen herself proud. Bobby caught her in his powerful arms just before she hit the floor.

11

A Long Night in Brooklyn

Come down, O Christ, and help me! reach my hand,
For I am drowning in a stormier sea
Than Simon on thy lake of Galilee.

OSCAR WILDE (1856–1900)

M r. Whittaker?"

Evan Whittaker glanced up from his accounts receivable ledger. Harry J., one of the office boys, stood in front of his desk. The youth was bright-eyed and fidgety, obviously excited about something.

"They say you're wanted at home, Mr. Whittaker! Right away! Your stepson sent word by one of the neighbor boys!"

For a moment, Evan could only stare blankly at Harry J., whose large dark eyes looked even wider than usual with the importance of his message. At last the words penetrated his consciousness. Springing to his feet, he grabbed his jacket from the corner coat tree. "What exactly d-did he say?"

Harry J. came round to help Evan with his jacket. "Why, that's all, sir. He just came at a run, saying you're needed at home. Would you like me to take you in the buggy, Mr. Whittaker?"

Evan was already on the way out the door. His heart pounding, he nodded. "I'll just tell Mr. Farmington and then m-meet you outside."

"But Mr. Farmington went across to the attorney's with Mr. Donaldson," Harry J. called after him. He followed Evan out into the corridor. "Said he wouldn't be back till late afternoon."

Evan tried to think. "Very well. When you return with the carriage, b-be sure to tell him where I am."

The carriage ride took only moments, but it seemed like hours. The last time Evan had been summoned home with such urgency was the afternoon of Little Tom's death. Since that woeful day, now more than a month past, every hour he spent away from home he lived in tension, half-expecting another panicky call, this one from Nora.

It was still some weeks before her time, but she had been so distraught since Tom's tragic accident—distraught and unwell—that Dr. Grafton had cautioned Evan to be prepared for any emergency. Since the quiet-spoken physician did not seem given to alarm, Evan had heeded his admonition with an anxious heart.

He had seen for himself Nora's failing, of course. It would have been impossible *not* to notice. She slept fitfully when she slept at all, moaning, often weeping softly, at other times crying out as if from a nightmare. Her appetite, never robust, had waned to nothing. She ate only at Evan's or Aunt Winnie's coaxing—and then, Evan was certain, only for the sake of the child she was carrying.

She was listless, uncharacteristically nervous, and distracted. So intense was Evan's anxiety for her that his own appetite and sleeping habits suffered. He was never quite at peace, and it was taking its toll.

With a sigh, he stared out the carriage window at the river, which glistened in the fading afternoon sun. Ordinarily, he loved this view and never tired of it. The river itself seemed alive, with hundreds of tall-masted ships, their sails furled and flags flying. Ferries scurried back and forth, carrying people and cargo from Brooklyn to Manhattan's shore, lined with countless warehouses and wharfs.

But today the bustling scene he usually found so stirring was all but obscured by a thickening fog of fear. He found particularly terrifying the thought that the baby might be born prematurely. Dr. Grafton had stressed the fact that Nora should be hospitalized for the birth, that he felt the risks of having the baby at home far too great for her frail condition.

What if the baby came early and there was no time to move her to the hospital?

Choking down another wave of apprehension, Evan tried to pray. He prayed that this baby, which Nora wanted so desperately, would be born healthy and strong, and would somehow restore Nora's joy, her sense of purpose and enthusiasm for life.

With gnawing guilt, he again contemplated the fact that from the beginning, it had been *Nora* who wanted this baby, Nora who had fashioned all the dreams and hopes for the child, not he. The truth was that at times he almost dreaded the new life that was growing inside her, perhaps even resented it, for fear it would somehow bring harm to Nora or... *please, God, no...* even take her from him.

Suddenly, he found himself praying even more fervently, from the depths of a guilt-ridden heart, that God would help him love this child. It was *his* baby, too, after all, not Nora's alone. It would devastate her if she were ever to suspect that he loved their child any less than she did.

Evan shuddered at the significance of his own silent prayer. *What kind of a man was he that he found it necessary to pray for the capacity to love his own child?*

"Forgive me, Lord," he whispered. "It's just that I fear I love her more... I can't imagine loving anything or anyone as much as I love Nora..."

Daniel stood at the front door, looking anxiously out on the gathering dusk, in hopes of some glimpse of the doctor or Evan.

Although he had gained considerable experience as Dr. Grafton's assistant, he had never witnessed firsthand an actual birth. Expectant mothers were sorely embarrassed even to have a male physician in attendance during delivery, much less a boy with no training.

In spite of his lack of experience, however, he had read enough in the medical books to know his mother's situation could be grave.

Turning away from the door, he began to pace the parlor. His mother had said the baby was coming. If she was right, that meant the baby was coming *early*—weeks before her time. The prospect frightened him more than he cared to consider.

She seemed so fragile these days, so visibly weak and unwell, that he could not bring himself to think what a premature birth might mean for her. Or for the baby.

Had it not been for the constant, plaguing fear, he thought he would have found the idea of a new brother or sister pleasing. He also thought it might be a good thing for Johanna, who was obviously still sorrowing over the loss of Little Tom.

Certainly, he understood that this baby was important to his mother.

He knew she was determined to give Evan a child of his own. But he suspected that she was far more concerned for the baby's condition than she wanted anyone to know. He found himself praying daily that God would give her the strength she needed when the time came.

And now it seemed the time *had* come.

Still engulfed by uneasiness, Daniel turned from the door and started down the hallway to the bedroom. When he entered, he found both his mother and Johanna just as they had been when he left. Johanna, her eyes huge with undisguised fear, stood beside the bed, hovering close to Daniel's mother, who was awake but obviously in the throes of great pain.

Crossing the room, he stopped on the opposite side of the bed from Johanna. "Sure, Evan and Dr. Grafton will be here any moment now, Mother," he said, taking her hand. "Is there anything I can be getting for you while we wait? Anything I can do?"

Her skin was ashen, her eyes smudged with dark shadows. Pain sharpened her features as she gripped his hand. But she merely shook her head, tugging at him to urge him closer. When she spoke, her voice was so low he could scarcely make out her words. "I want you to go now, Daniel John. Leave Johanna with me until the doctor comes. You should not—"

Abruptly, she stopped. Her eyes went wide, and, as if seized by an unbearable spasm of pain, she clamped Daniel's hand with a strength he would not have thought her capable of. Her entire body seemed to stiffen. She lunged upward, arching her back, crying out and squeezing his hand until he thought his bones would surely snap.

Expelling yet another hard gasp, she sank back onto the pillow. Trying not to show his own anxiety, Daniel met Johanna's anxious stare across the bed. He motioned that she should bring a cool cloth, then bent over to touch his lips to his mother's forehead, flinching at the heat of her skin.

Staring into her pain-darkened eyes, he had all he could do to mask his fear. Somehow he managed a smile and said again, "Dr. Grafton will be here soon, Mother, he and Evan. Everything is going to be perfectly fine. Truly, it is."

Even as he spoke, Daniel realized his reassurance was as much for himself as for her.

❧

Lewis Farmington had left the shipyards as soon as he learned about Evan's abrupt departure.

Upon reaching the cottage and seeing his assistant's haggard face, Lewis was glad he had come, more grateful still that he'd had the forethought to send for Winnie. The small house would not hold too many, but he knew Evan would want his aunt with him. And, admittedly, Lewis wanted Winnie with *him.*

Nicholas Grafton had preceded Lewis's arrival by only minutes and had already ordered everyone out of the bedroom—everyone except Johanna. Nora had insisted that she stay, and the child seemed pleased— if a bit anxious—about being chosen.

Lewis smiled to himself. After the terrible tragedy of Little Tom's death, the girl *needed* to be needed again, needed to feel special. It was just like Nora to think of it, even in her own pain.

An obviously nervous Daniel John sat perched on the very edge of the settee beside a white-faced Evan, who looked positively stricken.

Lewis turned back to the front window and resumed staring out into the night. Only a few streetlamps and faint light from behind curtained windows relieved the darkness. He sighed. They were in for a long night. A *very* long night, he feared.

He hoped Winnie would arrive soon. Her presence would lighten things up a bit for them all. She did that, Winnie did. The woman had a way of brightening a room by just walking through it. Certainly tonight, Evan could use a generous measure of his aunt's lively cheer.

Lewis smiled ruefully as he considered how taken he was with Winnie, wondering if he were as obvious to anyone else as he was to *her.* She seemed to tolerate his attentions well enough, but he could only hope she wasn't merely being kind because he happened to be her nephew's employer.

There's no fool like an old fool....

Grimacing at the direction his thoughts had taken, he forced himself to think about Evan instead of Evan's *aunt.*

Over the past two years he had come to care a great deal for the mild-mannered young Englishman. Evan was—well, the truth was, Evan had become almost like a son to him. He trusted the man completely, enjoyed his company greatly, and depended on him more every day.

Should he feel guilty, he wondered, that he respected Evan more than he did his own son? Oh, he loved Gordon, of course, but the unfortunate truth was that his only son was simply not very *likable*.

This latest caper—taking his family off to California in pursuit of yet another moneymaking scheme—had hurt Lewis far more than he cared to admit. Gordon had it in his head to open a bank for the gold miners flooding the western part of the country. So, just before Christmas past, with scarcely any warning at all, he'd simply up and moved his rather foolish, excessively spoiled wife and two equally spoiled children to California.

It saddened Lewis that his son, already a wealthy man, seemed obsessed with acquiring still more riches. From the time they were small, Lewis had done his best to teach both Gordon and Sara that, although the Farmingtons might have more than their share of money, the accumulation of a fortune should not motivate their lives. At the same time, he had tried to instill in each of them the sense of responsibility he believed should accompany great wealth.

Sara, God bless the girl, was generous to a fault and held her material possessions lightly. But Gordon—Lewis felt that he had failed his son in some way, and that failure continued to weigh upon him.

Still, he had to admit that even before Gordon's defection, he had grown extraordinarily fond of Evan and Nora Whittaker. The immigrant couple were almost as much family to him by now as his own offspring, and he intended to do whatever he could to make life a bit easier for the two of them.

The exasperating thing was that there seemed very little he *could* do in a situation such as this. Nora was to have been hospitalized for the delivery, but now that was impossible. Nicholas said it would be far too dangerous to try to move her.

Gripped by frustration, it occurred to Lewis that here was yet another circumstance which *ten* fortunes could not redeem. Again he saw the truth with piercing clarity: those things which counted most in life were beyond the control of mere human beings and all the means at their disposal.

There would always be times, and this was one of them, when enormous wealth could do absolutely nothing to make a difference. Tonight, in this modest small home, there was only the skill of a good physician—and the power of the *Great Physician*—to rely on.

Lewis comforted himself with the reminder that, on numerous occasions of which he was aware, that particular combination had been more than enough.

12

The Mystery, the Miracle

For He is our childhood's pattern,
Day by day like us He grew,
He was little, weak and helpless,
Tears and smiles like us He knew
And He feeleth for our sadness,
And He shareth in our gladness.

CECIL FRANCES ALEXANDER (1820–1895)

Unable to carry on any sort of conversation with the others who had gathered in the parlor, Evan had gone off in a desperate search for solitude.

Now, alone in Daniel John's bedroom, he closed the door, hoping to shut out the agonizing sound of Nora's pain. Every cry, every moan, was like a knife slashing at his heart. Yet the last report from Dr. Grafton had indicated that it might be hours yet before the baby was born.

Aching with weariness and worry, he sank down on the side of the bed. For a long time, he sat, numb and unmoving, rubbing his hand over his eyes.

From the other side of the door, he could still hear Nora's cries echoing down the hall. He had dreaded this night, had lived in terror of it. Yet the worst of his apprehension hadn't come close to the reality. She was suffering even more than he had feared, and there was nothing—dear God, *nothing*—he could do to help her!

Being shut out from her, banished from the bedroom by convention and his wife's pleas, only made things more difficult. If he could have stayed with her, held her hand, sponged her forehead—anything—at least he might have somehow shared a part of her pain.

He remembered how helpless he had felt when she'd been ill with the scarlet fever, months before their marriage—how he had stayed in the hospital room, watching over her. Throughout that long siege, his own skin had burned with the heat of Nora's fever. His heart had pounded with the hammering of her pulse. His body had ached from the viselike grip of the treacherous disease. He had been with her throughout the entire nightmare—and somehow, that had almost made it bearable.

But tonight—tonight, Nora seemed so…*separate* from him, so *distant*. Enshrouded in the mystery and the miracle of birth, she was more like a stranger than his wife.

Just down the hall, only heartbeats away, she struggled and gasped and labored through the most wondrous, miraculous event imaginable… while he sat here, utterly helpless, feeling an entire world removed from her. He thought he could not *bear* the thought of her pain, could endure even less the reality that she must go through it alone.

Newly consumed by fear and frustration, he hauled himself up from the bed and sank slowly to his knees. He found himself seized by a fit of trembling, and for a time he could do nothing but weep, quietly, desperately, like a frightened boy. The prayer he had thought to voice seemed lodged in his throat, buried beneath a tidal wave of terror.

"Oh, God! How much longer m-must this go on? She has already had so much pain tonight…and b-before tonight! So much p-pain, Lord—and to face it alone—oh, Lord, won't You p-please just…stop the pain? Deliver her from the hurting, let it end. She's so alone…."

She is not alone. I am with her in the pain…

Evan drew a deep breath, faltering. "But she—she has such agony…."

I had Gethsemane….

"Lord, she suffers…."

I suffered Calvary….

"If I c-could only be with her, Lord…."

I am with her, Evan. I am as close to her in her pain, as she struggles to bring forth your son, as I was to my own mother the day she watched her son die on a cross….

Evan's weeping subsided, at least a little. The bleeding of his heart seemed to slow. "You...are there with her—truly, Lord? You are there, in that r-room, with Nora? At this very moment, in her p-pain...You are there?'"

Evan...Evan...do you not yet realize that I am closer to my children in their pain than at any other time? I hold you in my arms when you hurt. I rock you like a child when you suffer. Quiet your soul, Evan. I am holding Nora now...at this moment. She is not alone, son...never alone. Nora is in her Father's arms.

Evan opened his eyes, then quickly squeezed them shut again as he basked in the light and warmth that seemed to fill the tiny bedroom. "Lord..." he ventured. "Lord? Did I hear...d-did You say... *son?*"

Theodore Charles Lewis Whittaker was born at three o'clock in the morning.

The longest night of Evan's life finally ended with a timid cry from his newborn son, a wan, fleeting smile from his exhausted wife, and weary, relieved hugs from those who had stayed the night, keeping vigil: Daniel John and Johanna, of course, and Aunt Winnie and Lewis Farmington. Later Sara Farmington Burke had arrived and proved a great source of comfort. Also present was Jess Dalton. The big, curly-headed pastor had stopped by early in the evening and, after one look at Evan, had remained for the duration.

Even now, after repeated reassurances from Dr. Grafton that both Nora and the child seemed to be doing nicely, Evan could do nothing but sit and stare in numb amazement at them both.

In the bedroom, her new son nursing contentedly at her breast, Nora watched Evan with eyes that refused to stay open for more than seconds at a time.

Surely she had never been so depleted in her life. The births of her other children had all been long and never easy. Yet none had wreaked such havoc on her body as this wee boy-child in her arms. But, oh, wasn't it worth it all, to hold a new, fresh-faced babe at her breast and see the dazed look of happiness in Evan's eyes!

"You are quite sure he is healthy?" she asked again, as if she had not already heard the answer more than once.

Clutching her hand, Evan nodded. "You've c-counted his t-toes and fingers yourself, dear...how m-many times now?"

"There's more to it than fingers and toes," Nora said, surprised at the effort it took simply to speak. "I never told you, Evan, but from the beginning, when I first learned I was with child—I was frightened. Frightened that perhaps the Hunger or the scarlet fever might cause something to go wrong with the babe."

She saw a change in his expression, just for an instant. "Well...I, ah, I admit that I wasn't without m-my own fears at times," he said, his voice low. "But you c-can see for yourself," he added, his eyes clearing, "that he is quite p-perfect."

Nora nodded, straining not to fall asleep. She didn't want to miss a moment of this special time with her husband and their new son. "And don't I thank the Lord for that?" She sighed deeply. "I'm so glad it's a boy, Evan. For you. And for Johanna."

Evan frowned. "Johanna?"

"She misses wee Tom so. She still grieves for him, as do I." Nora's joy faded, and for a moment she said nothing. Even now, as she held her new son next to her heart, the thought of Little Tom's drowning brought a shudder of sadness.

Instinctively, she touched her hand to her son's small, downy head in a reassuring caress. "Perhaps now," she finally went on, "Johanna will begin to let go of Tom, at least a little." She looked at Evan. "You don't think I was wrong, to let her stay through the birth? She was with Catherine, you see, when Little Tom was born."

Evan squeezed her hand. "I think you d-did just the right thing," he said firmly. "And it helped me to know Johanna was with you. I...I wanted to stay, you know. I didn't w-want to leave you alone."

Surprised, Nora searched his face. "Why, I wasn't alone, Evan."

Lifting his head, he looked at her closely.

Nora smiled and nodded. "I wasn't alone at all. Oh, Evan—it was really quite wonderful! Truly."

He leaned forward still more, his hand tightening on hers. "But...you were in such pain."

Again Nora turned her gaze to the delicately formed little head snuggled against her breast. *He was so perfect!* He was the most beautiful of babies, this new son! "Well, now, there's no having a baby without the pain, and that's the truth. But isn't it worth whatever it takes?"

"Of course," Evan conceded. "But...*wonderful?* I d-don't understand."

Nora thought for a moment, struggling to find just the right words to explain something she suspected might be beyond explanation. *A mystery.*

"You are the one who's good with words, Evan, not I," she said, smiling faintly. "It's just that...something happens...not always, but sometimes...amid the pain..."

Again she paused, studying him. His face was drawn, even haggard, reflecting the long, arduous night. But Nora sensed that this was important to him, and so, in spite of her own exhaustion, she weighed her reply with great care.

"'Tis a difficult thing to explain, you see. When the other children were born, and when I had the scarlet fever—and then again tonight—it's as if I'm in the very center of the pain, and yet, in a way, I'm not a part of it at all. It almost seems as if—"

She stopped, turning to look toward the window. The baby sighed, warming her breast with his sweet breath, and Nora suddenly felt such a peace, a contentment. For a moment, the room didn't exist for her. Her thoughts wandered.

She was remembering, remembering the excruciating pain...but more than that, she remembered the Other: the sense of something else...no, *Someone* else, Someone whose presence made the pain seem small, even insignificant. She remembered the warmth, enfolding her, holding her... protecting her....

She turned toward Evan. His expression was intent, his eyes locked on her face. "This is what it's like, Evan, as near as I can give words to the feelings. It's as if the Lord Himself comes to me and scoops me up in His arms and somehow carries me through the pain. And when it happens, when I realize who is holding me, it does seem for all the world that everything—even the pain—is nothing at all but a glory."

She stopped. "This much I do know and believe, Evan: that I am closer to our Lord during those times than at any other moment of my life."

She felt his hand tremble in hers. For a long time, neither of them spoke, and Nora felt herself drifting off to sleep. With an effort, she forced her eyes open to find him studying her with a tearful gaze.

"Evan...Evan, you *are* pleased? About the baby?"

Leaning forward, he brought her hand to his lips. "What a qu-question for you to ask!" His voice sounded gruff with emotion. "Of course, I'm pleased! I am...I'm *overwhelmed*!"

Nora smiled at him. Her head was spinning with weakness, but she could not take her eyes off her husband and her tiny newborn boy, now sound asleep. "I have given you a son at last, Evan. A beautiful, healthy son, thanks be to God."

"Yes...thanks b-be to God," he echoed quietly, and Nora wondered at the trembling in his voice.

"What shall we be calling him, Evan?"

"Why, I thought we had already d-decided on his name, dear!"

"Yes," Nora said, marveling anew at the baby's fine dusting of sand-colored hair, the tiny ears so amazingly perfect. "But what shall we *call* him? Sure, such a big name is too much for the wee wane to carry until he's older."

Evan seemed to consider her words a moment. "Teddy," he finally said, nodding slowly. "Why don't we call him Teddy?"

"Teddy," Nora repeated thickly, feeling herself fast losing the battle to stay awake. "Aye, then...we shall call our son Teddy. Teddy is a fine name...."

13

Enemy Territory

Men of the same soil placed in hostile array,
Prepared to encounter in deadly affray.

ROBERT YOUNG (1800–c. 1870)

Simon Dabney's Fourth of July parties had been a society event for the past five years. State senators, congressmen, city aldermen, and other notables were among the illustrious guests who never failed to make an appearance—in addition to select members of the police force.

Tonight's affair promised to be the largest and most lavish to date. The ballroom of the Dabney mansion was ablaze with light. Throughout the spacious hall, crystal chandeliers glittered like diamonds dancing in fire, while hundreds of candles fluttered in the soft summer breeze drifting through the open windows.

Sara's dress was a triumph of emerald satin and silk, triple-skirted with deep flounces. Only on rare occasions did she wear her mother's jewelry, but she had deemed tonight a special enough event for a diamond pendant. Such finery, topped off with a sprig of summer flowers tucked into her hair, made her feel positively elegant.

But it was the open approval in her husband's eyes that accounted for the giddiness that swept over her every few moments. Tonight, sitting across from her father and Winifred, with Michael at her side, Sara thought she must be the most fortunate woman in the room—indeed, in New York City! She had a wonderful family, a good, good life—and a handsome husband who still looked at her with undisguised admiration, still paid her court with his gallantry and attentions.

"Did you wear that gown just for me, Sara *a gra?*" Michael's voice was low, his words meant only for her, but when Sara glanced over at her father and Winnie, she saw that it really didn't matter. The two of them were altogether engrossed in each other, too absorbed to take note of anyone's conversation but their own.

Sara smiled. "Then you approve?"

"You know it's my favorite." He squeezed her hand, his dark eyes going over her face with a warmth that made her heart leap. "You are," he said, his voice still low, "quite the loveliest woman in the room. I am one lucky Irishman, I'm thinking."

After six months of marriage, he could still make her blush with one of his lingering looks or murmured endearments. "This setting would be flattering to any woman," Sara pointed out to mask her quick flush of pleasure. "It's like being in the middle of an entire sea of candlelight."

Michael glanced around, his expression dryly amused. "Quite a bash just to throw some politicians together, wouldn't you say?"

Sara's father dragged his gaze away from Winifred long enough to make an observation of his own. "You'll find that Simon never does anything halfway. Least of all a party. It's planned to impress—and I expect it does."

Still studying the dance floor and the crowded tables around the ballroom, Michael shook his head. "I'll warrant half the police force is here."

Sara's father nodded. "Mostly the captains, I should think. Simon's interest in law enforcement extends only to the boys with the clout."

"Clout or corruption?" Michael returned, his smile not reaching his eyes. "Most of the brass have their hands so deep in the till they can't find their elbows."

"Still, they're the pillars of the local party."

Michael scowled. "More like puppets, I'm thinking, than pillars." He paused. "I'm not sure I understand why *we* were invited. Except for your friendship with Dabney, of course."

Sara's father shook his head. "You're here because Simon intends to add you to his political camp. Surely you know that by now. He's hardly subtle."

Michael's scowl only deepened as he answered. "He means to *buy* me, you mean."

Sara had heard most of this conversation before tonight. Apparently, there was no disputing the fact that a number of the local police, many of them captains, were snug in the pockets of the Tammany bosses, but she couldn't believe they were *all* corrupt. Michael had managed to avoid being seduced by the politicians and the crime bosses, after all; certainly, there must be others like him.

"No, I don't think Simon has too many illusions about you, Michael," her father replied. "Jaded as he is, I believe he can distinguish between a man with integrity and those with none. No," he repeated, toying with his watch fob, "it seems to me that Simon is genuinely trying to attract you to the political arena by making it seem…respectable—and far more attractive than it really is."

Sara was taken by surprise at the surge of relief that washed over her when she heard Michael's reply. "I've no real interest in politics. At least not at the present."

Her father nodded, darting a look at Sara. "Nevertheless, New York politics has taken an interest in *you*, son. And you'll find Simon Dabney a tenacious sort, once he sets his cap for something."

Michael shrugged, his features unreadable. "He'll find I can be just as—"

He stopped, his entire expression darkening as he stared at the entrance doors across the room. Turning to follow the direction of his gaze, Sara caught her breath at the sight of Patrick Walsh entering the ballroom. His wife, Alice, was at his side.

Michael half-rose from his chair. Laying a restraining hand on his arm, Sara felt her own temper flare. She didn't know what she found more outrageous: the idea that Simon Dabney would invite a man like Patrick Walsh into his home—or the fact that Walsh actually had the gall to show up.

Michael shot her a look, and Sara saw the fire in his eyes. "Michael, you mustn't," she said, tightening her pressure on his arm.

By now he was on his feet. This time Sara's father intervened. "Sara's right, son. This is Simon Dabney's home. He can invite whomever he chooses. Besides, the man's wife is with him. You wouldn't want to humiliate her."

Sara held her breath. For a moment, Michael stood poised like a panther ready to spring. With relief, she finally felt the muscles in his arm relax slightly, saw his white-knuckled fists unclench as he slowly lowered himself into his chair.

"Why?" His question was directed to Sara's father. "Why would Dabney have any truck at all with a snake like Walsh? He has to know what he is!"

Folding his hands on top of the table, her father studied Michael. "Simon Dabney," he said after a long sigh, "is the consummate political power-broker, Michael. He's far bigger than the hoodlums at Tammany Hall, bigger even than the state party establishment. He has a string attached to every political boss in New York, every ward leader, every party henchman in the city—and quite a few in the state. Simon courts power like some men woo women—he never misses an opportunity to make a conquest."

He paused, drumming his fingers lightly on the table. "What you must understand, Michael, is that, like it or not, Patrick Walsh happens to wield a great deal of power in Manhattan. No one has been able to prove he's anything but a shrewd, highly successful, if somewhat questionable, businessman. He pours a considerable amount of money into the party coffers, and he has more ears at Tammany Hall than any other crime boss in the city, except perhaps for Isaiah Rynders."

"It's a wonder *he's* not here tonight as well," Michael muttered, his words laced with contempt.

Sara's father spread his hands. "Rynders is a different breed than Walsh in one respect." At Michael's skeptical look, he went on to explain. "Oh, he's just as corrupt, mind you, but the difference is that Rynders doesn't pretend to be anything other than what he is—a gambler, a saloon owner, and a gang leader. His political weight was more or less donated to him. He didn't scramble for it, but, of course, he took what was offered. He's a crook, and doesn't seem to care who knows it. Walsh, on the other hand, would have us believe that he's entirely respectable. Just another hardworking, influential businessman."

"He's nothing but a *pirate!*" Michael grated, leaning forward. "The sharks at Tammany know it, and so does the entire police force!"

As Michael's voice rose, Sara again squeezed his arm to subdue him. He looked at her, then leaned back, raking a hand through his hair in a gesture of frustration. "We would have had him in jail months ago if those ledgers hadn't been burned up in the warehouse fire—and if his thugs hadn't had their throats slit before they could talk."

Sara's heart wrenched with sympathy for her husband. He seemed to meet with nothing but frustration in his attempts to bring Patrick Walsh to justice. In spite of a number of eyewitness accounts of Walsh's involvement in a child-slavery ring, the man was still free, going on about his obscene business as if nothing had happened. Two of his henchmen had been arrested after the fire, but they had been murdered in their cells before they talked.

Even the firsthand evidence from Michael's son had accomplished nothing but to place Tierney's life in danger. As a result, the boy had fled the country for Ireland, while Patrick Walsh went right on expanding his corrupt empire. Small wonder that Michael could scarcely stand the sight of the man!

"I'll have him yet," he said, his face taut, his tone chillingly hard. "No matter what it takes, I will see that devil behind bars where he belongs."

Sara glanced at her husband's long-time adversary across the room. Walsh stood, casually elegant in his well-tailored evening apparel, chatting and laughing with his host, Simon Dabney.

She could scarcely look at the man without shuddering. Her first meeting with Walsh had given her a sense of a deceitful, possibly deadly, evil presence. Tonight, that same presence seemed to pervade and darken the entire ballroom, as if a sudden summer storm had blown up unawares and now hovered in their midst, waiting to strike.

Turning back to Michael, Sara was momentarily seized by a cold feeling of dread. Lately, she had begun to wonder if his determination to expose Patrick Walsh might not be turning into something more than a natural desire to see justice done—something much darker, perhaps even dangerous.

She almost thought it bordered on obsession, this hostility he harbored toward the notorious crime boss. Yet, in his defense, Michael had reason enough to despise the man. Patrick Walsh represented every evil that Michael had spent his life fighting against.

What troubled her most was the fear that he might have begun to blame Walsh for the chasm between himself and Tierney. And there, Sara admitted uneasily, she could not agree with her husband, at least not entirely. Oh, it was a terrible thing Tierney had done—a foolish and dangerous thing—getting involved with Walsh in the first place. Even if the boy had been innocently duped in the beginning, by his own admission he had known the extent of Walsh's corruption at the end.

While it was true that there had seemed no choice for Tierney but to leave New York, Michael had confided long ago that the gulf between him and his son had been widening for years. Yet, more and more, Sara was afraid her husband had somehow managed to convince himself that Patrick Walsh was at least in part responsible for the loss of his son.

Up to now, she would not have believed Michael capable of an irrational thought. He was by nature a fair, reasonable, and thoroughly practical man. But in this one instance, she could not help but wonder if his fixation about Patrick Walsh hadn't blinded him to the truth.

Studying her husband's profile as he sat glaring at his adversary across the room, Sara felt chilled, almost as if she were seeing the hard, unyielding set of his features for the first time. The sultry July night seemed to have turned suddenly cold, and even the solid weight of Michael's arm against hers failed to warm her.

Alice Walsh had come to dread events like tonight's gala. Not that they were invited to all that many social affairs. With Patrick being Irish and in *business*, they received precious few bids to society functions. Despite his enormous success and influence in certain areas of the city, the Walshes were still not "acceptable" in a number of society circles.

Alice wasn't sure she really minded, at least not terribly. She had always been shy, had never been comfortable in large crowds; certainly, she would never feel at ease among New York society.

What bothered her, when she thought about it at all, was the insinuation in some quarters that they were less than desirable—not so much because of Patrick's Irishness, but because of his varied business activities.

She could have understood, had they been living in England or one of the other European countries where merchants were still regarded with a certain snobbery. But this was America. In America, making one's fortune was supposed to be not only acceptable, but admirable. *Wasn't it?*

The country, after all, had been built by self-made men who attained success through their own hard work and ingenuity. Why, then, were she and Patrick continually kept at arms' length by everyone except the *nouveau riche* and the politicians?

Up until now, she hadn't thought much about the reasons for their exclusion. It had been enough to have a few acquaintances from among their local congregation and Patrick's political and business associates.

Lately, however, Alice found herself questioning a number of things she had once ignored. Patrick seemed to have changed over the past few months. Before, things had been blessedly serene at home. Their marriage, if somewhat uneventful and…predictable…had at least been *peaceful.*

Uncomfortably, Alice realized that the reason for that tranquility might lie in the fact that she spent so much time seeing to Patrick's comfort. She disciplined the children herself, because "Papa mustn't be bothered when he comes home late and feels so weary." She made most of the decisions regarding the servants so Patrick needn't be distracted from his work. Even in questions of household decor and furniture selections, Alice usually made the choices—paid for, of course, out of the more than generous household allowance Patrick provided.

Lately she had begun to realize that her entire life seemed to revolve around Patrick: keeping him happy, at ease, and undisturbed had seemingly become her reason for existence. To a point, even the children took second place to their father's comfort.

For most of their married life, Alice had not examined their relationship too closely. The truth was, she had avoided analyzing whether Patrick was entirely happy with her and the children. She adored him and devoted her days to being an ideal wife and mother. Why *wouldn't* he be happy with her?

He had never given her reason to doubt his affection. If he had complaints, he voiced them, and Alice took care of the matter at once. She more or less took it for granted that if Patrick became dissatisfied about anything in particular, she would know it without delay. Her husband wasn't a man to keep his opinions to himself.

These days, however, he didn't seem the same at all. Alice found it more and more difficult to anticipate him. Was something amiss in their relationship, or was he merely distracted by his business affairs—or perhaps some worry he was keeping to himself?

Whatever the reason, she couldn't avoid the fact that Patrick's behavior was peculiar. He was edgy, easily irritated—short with her and the children.

Of course, he had *always* tended to be somewhat impatient with them. But recently he became downright testy over the smallest things, things that really didn't matter one way or the other.

Unaccountably, he even seemed to resent the time she spent helping out in the Five Points mission work. At first, he had said little. Lately,
though, he seemed to take as a personal affront her involvement with the
boys' choir, or the few hours a week she spent helping Sara Burke with
inspections of the children's homes. He snapped at her when she tried to
discuss either subject, grew almost petulant when she mentioned some
small achievement with one of the children.

He was, she had noticed, particularly irascible where Sara Farmington Burke was concerned. Even the mention of the woman's name would
most often bring a sneer or a sharp retort.

Alice found this the most confusing issue of all. Sara Burke was
respected, even loved, by just about everyone who knew her; she was
especially revered by those who worked with her in the mission projects.
It was common knowledge that there was no task beneath the Farmington heiress. No need brought to her attention was left unexplored. She
seemed to have the endurance of a strong man when it came to work, the
patience of a mystic when it came to spiritual matters.

Alice could not fathom anyone—least of all Patrick, who scarcely
knew Sara—*disliking* her. She felt nothing but respect and a growing fondness for the young woman—fondness and gratitude. For Sara Burke had
given her, for the first time in her life, something worthwhile to do for others besides her own family.

Seeing her now, across the ballroom, Alice started to lift a hand to
wave, then stopped at the sight of Sara's husband. Captain Burke was staring at Patrick with a look of such open animosity that Alice involuntarily
shuddered.

She had seen this hostility between her husband and the police captain
before, yet she had no inkling as to what was responsible for their antago-
nism toward each other. She would have thought that Patrick's treatment
of the Burke boy when he was so badly injured the past year—taking
him into their home and seeing that he had the best of care—would have
formed a bond between them. Yet, the bad feeling between the two men
was so obvious as to be almost a tangible presence.

It hurt, this mysterious enmity between her husband and the husband
of a woman for whom she held only the highest of respect and admiration. With all her heart, Alice wished it could have been different. She had

even daydreamed about becoming good friends, close friends, with Sara
Burke—not just social acquaintances.

Again her gaze went to the granite-faced Captain Burke. With a sharp
pang of regret, she now realized how terribly hopeless her daydreams had
been.

14

Dancing Dreams

I bring you with reverent hands
The books of my numberless dreams.

W.B. YEATS (1865–1939)

Michael had excused himself just long enough to say hello to Chief Matsell and his wife. On his way back to the table, Simon Dabney stopped him.

"So glad you and your lovely wife could make it tonight, Captain. I hope you're enjoying yourselves."

"It's a grand evening, Mr. Dabney. You were kind to invite us."

Simon Dabney was a big, pleasant-faced man with an impressive mane of silver hair. Sara had commented that "Simon looks like everybody's favorite uncle—not the sly fox he really is."

Michael thought "sly" a good word for the smooth-voiced lawyer. Dabney struck him as a bit too much the good fellow—too quick with the slap on the back and the ready smile that did not quite meet his eyes, too eager to strike a note of camaraderie, even with those he scarcely knew. In fact, he would be surprised if Simon Dabney were not, at heart, somewhat callous and calculating. A true "sly fox."

"I confess that I've been hoping for an opportunity to talk with you at more length, Captain, about what we discussed a few weeks ago."

"The position of alderman, you mean," Michael said directly.

Dabney smiled. "Exactly. I hope you've had time to think about it."

"Enough to know I'm not your man."

Dabney's smile never flickered. "You underestimate yourself, Captain. If the party thinks you're qualified—"

Michael shook his head, interrupting Dabney before he could finish. "I wasn't referring to my qualifications. The fact is, I'm simply not interested in leaving the force. Not at this time."

The lawyer studied him with what was probably meant to be good-natured understanding. But Michael thought he caught a glimpse of something else behind that avuncular expression. "May I be frank, Captain Burke?"

Michael waited, but said nothing.

The big attorney laid one hand on Michael's shoulder. Despite himself, Michael stiffened. "The party is looking for a certain kind of man, Captain. A man of intelligence and integrity—a man who can't be compromised. Because certain leaders in the party know your reputation and think you're just the kind of fellow we're looking for, the decision was made to bypass some of the usual routes and put you directly in place for alderman."

Dabney stopped, leveling a meaningful look on Michael as he added, "I don't think I'd be presumptuous in suggesting that Congress might be next."

Michael found himself irritated by the man's assumption that he would be so eager to jump into the political arena, even more by the hand on his shoulder. "I appreciate the interest, Mr. Dabney, but as I said, this isn't the time for me."

As if he sensed Michael's annoyance, the lawyer dropped his hand away. "May I ask why, Captain?"

Out of the corner of his eye, Michael could see Patrick Walsh, standing off to one side as if he were surveying the ballroom. His stomach knotted as he turned his attention back to Simon Dabney, but he kept his tone carefully noncommittal. "Let us just say that I have some things I want to accomplish before I leave the force."

The lawyer studied him for another moment, then inclined his head and shrugged, smiling. "Very well, Captain. But I have to say that I hope you're not making a grave mistake, passing up this opportunity. It would be only the beginning of what I foresee as an extraordinary career for you."

Michael heard the edge in his own voice when he replied. "Sometimes a man has to finish what he started before he can think about new beginnings."

Simon Dabney broke into one of his most charming smiles. "I understand, Captain," he said agreeably. "And I must say, you're to be admired for your dedication to the police department. But we'll talk again, you can be sure of it."

As Michael threaded his way through the couples on the dance floor, he hoped he wasn't being as rash as Dabney had hinted. It was true that he was passing up a fine opportunity; it wasn't every day that a police captain was solicited to run for alderman. It was also true that he'd had vague political ambitions for a number of years.

But he was convinced that only in the police department would he find the power to topple Patrick Walsh from his evil empire. That being the case, he was prepared to stay right where he was for however long it might take.

With a familiar sense of longing, Sara watched the grandly dressed couples whirl around the ballroom floor. It seemed that everyone was dancing except her and Michael. Winifred had even managed to talk Father into a waltz.

She caught herself tapping her foot to the beat of the music, stopped, then almost at once began tapping her fingers on the table. The orchestra was particularly fine tonight, she thought, strong and lively and inviting. The ballroom was awash with flowing colors, the women radiant in their ball gowns of summer hues as their partners swept them over the dance floor at a dizzying pace. It was obvious that Simon Dabney's guests were enjoying themselves immensely.

Sara had never danced. Never. She had come out as a debutante, as was expected of Lewis Farmington's only daughter, had attended endless balls when she was younger, both as a guest and as her father's hostess—again, because it was expected of her. But because of her lameness, she had never danced.

Occasionally, a young fortune hunter brash enough to call attention to her handicap had offered to slow his steps to match hers, as if doing her a great favor. Sara most often responded by leveling a withering look and an acid remark on the witless suitor, making it clear that she would not be in the least flattered by the favors of a fool.

What she had never admitted to anyone—not even to her father—was that she had more than once daydreamed about what it might be like to have at least one dance, despite her hateful limp.

Especially appealing to her was the waltz. Apparently tonight's orchestra shared her enthusiasm for the popular dance form, which was literally sweeping Europe and the United States, for they seemed to be playing more waltzes than anything else.

Some were scandalized, of course, by this new ballroom craze, appalled at the idea of partners touching as they glided across the floor. Sara thought such censorship a bit absurd, considering the voluminous gowns and chaste distance between the dancers.

Besides, before now she wouldn't have been much interested in dancing with anyone other than her brother or father—neither of whom ever suggested it, out of respect, she was sure, for her handicap. Most of the fellows who trailed the debutantes about the city were far too clumsy on the dance floor to make it look very appealing.

But she would so love to dance with Michael....

She had imagined countless times what it would be like to glide over a ballroom floor in his arms to the tune of a stirring waltz. She wondered if it might not be a little like flying.

Of course, she would never know. Years ago, alone in her room, she had attempted to whirl around the floor, to the beat of music that sounded only in her head, pretending. Pretending that she was feather-light, with movements as fluid and graceful as those of a French ballerina. But then she would catch sight of herself in the mirror and, feeling hopelessly awkward and ugly, she would fall across the bed and close her eyes against her own foolishness.

For a moment...only a moment...she would give in to a wave of self-pity. Then, feeling altogether miserable that she had compounded the sin of her wasteful daydreams with the wickedness of regret for the way God had made her, she would jump up from the bed and go storming through the house in search of a more useful—and wholesome—pastime.

Naturally, those occasions had all been before her marriage to Michael. It would be folly indeed for a woman as fortunate as she to continue indulging in idle daydreams. She was married to one of the finest, noblest, handsomest men in New York—*surely he was*—a man who made no secret of the fact that he adored her.

Why should she care about something as frivolous as *dancing,* for goodness' sake?

"Dance with me, Sara."

Sara whipped around to find Michael rising from his chair, his hand on her arm.

She stared at him as if he'd gone mad. "*Dance* with you? Good heavens, Michael, you know I can't dance!"

He studied her for a moment, then straightened, pulling her up with him. "You've never danced, Sara?" he asked quietly.

Sara felt herself flush. "Certainly not," she said tightly, avoiding his gaze.

"Sara?" Her name was little more than a whisper on his lips, but his hands on her forearms were unyielding. "You will dance with *me*, then."

In spite of the way her heart leaped at his words, Sara was still unable to meet his eyes. "I *can't,* Michael! I can't manage—"

"You needn't," he interrupted, his voice infinitely gentle. "I will manage for the both of us. Come along, now. A man wants to dance with his wife, after all." With that, he began to lead her around the table.

"I'll embarrass you," Sara mumbled, looking wildly around for an escape route somewhere among the sea of dancers.

Michael stopped, turning toward her. For an instant something flared in his eyes. Then, very deliberately, he gathered her into his arms, placing one of her hands on his shoulder as he clasped the other in his. "Never, Sara *a gra*," he said, trapping her in the force of his dark-eyed gaze. "You could never embarrass me. You may mystify me every now and then, even astonish me. Certainly, you *delight* me. But you could never, ever, embarrass me! And now, sweetheart—you will dance with me. Don't mind the others. Just follow my lead. It will be as if I'm carrying you, you'll see. I'll not go any faster than you can follow."

Suddenly, Sara felt herself swung out into the midst of the other dancers, felt Michael half-lift her from her feet, buoying her along with his strength. For one fleeting instant, her lame leg locked. But, feeling her hesitate, Michael increased the pressure of his hand at her waist and whirled her out still farther onto the floor.

Sara knew an instant of panic, but pushed it aside as the orchestra swung into yet another lilting waltz. The room swayed, her head spun, and now she realized that Michael was sweeping her toward the glass doors opening onto the garden patio.

Outside, the night was nothing but moonlight and the scent of summer flowers, heady and sweet on the warm July breeze. Michael pulled her along with him, and the star-sprinkled sky began to spin as they whirled across the patio.

"I'm doing it! I *am*, Michael!"

He held her tighter. "Of course, you are. Didn't I tell you all you had to do was follow my lead?"

"Well...the truth is, you're very nearly carrying me...."

He searched her eyes for a moment. "And do you mind, sweetheart?"

"No," Sara said softly. "I don't mind at all, Michael."

Sara's feet scarcely touched the smooth flagstone. She was aware of nothing but dancing stars overhead, the strength of Michael's embrace, the white flash of his smile as he carried her smoothly beyond remembrance of her lame leg and her fear of clumsiness.

Tonight, for the first time, Sara danced. She danced with her husband, bathed in the magic of moonlight and the fragrance of flowers. Unable to contain herself as she floated in Michael's arms, she laughed aloud for the sheer joy of it all. He laughed with her, laughed at her delight and, Sara thought, with a delight all his own, to be dancing in a summer garden in the moonlight with his wife.

Seeing Sara and Michael disappear through the patio doors, Lewis Farmington guided Winnie in the same direction. He stopped just inside the ballroom, riveted by the sight of his daughter dancing.

He had never seen Sara quite like this, certainly had never seen her look so lovely or so happy. And, of course, he had never seen her dance, although he had sensed her longing, seen the yearning in her eyes more than once as she stood on the sidelines, watching others.

Michael was virtually carrying the girl over the patio, and her face was brighter than the halo of moonlight and stardust that framed the two of them. They looked so incredibly young, so infinitely happy—and so thoroughly in love—that Lewis had to wipe his eyes at the sight of them.

Beside him, Winnie put a hand to his arm. "Aren't they splendid, Lewis? Aren't they just *splendut*!"

He nodded, unable to take his eyes off the couple on the patio. "They are, indeed," he choked out.

"It must make you feel very happy, Lewis, seeing them like this."

Lewis turned to study his own dancing partner. Winnie was a vision tonight, she truly was! All pink lace and diamond fire, with that magnificent silver-blond hair piled high—why, she looked like something right out of a fairy tale!

Suddenly, before he could stop himself, he blurted out what had been on his mind for most of the evening—and for most of the week preceding the evening.

"Only one thing could make me happier, and that's a fact."

Winnie looked at him with an ingenuous smile. "Whatever would that be, Lewis?"

Fumbling to reach his inside coat pocket, he withdrew the small velvet box he had tucked there earlier. "Seeing this on your finger!" he said bluntly, flipping the ring box open so abruptly it almost went flying out of his hand.

For a moment, Winnie continued to stare at him with that odd little wondering smile of hers. Finally, her eyes went to the diamond and sapphire ring glittering on the velvet cushion.

When she finally looked back to Lewis, still smiling, her eyes were twinkling like diamonds themselves.

"Well, then," she said, extending her dainty left hand, "do put it on for me, darling. Please, do."

Feeling twenty-five again—well, thirty at the most—Lewis put the ring on Winnie's finger and spun her back onto the dance floor for the next waltz.

15

On the Golden Streets of New York

My heart's oppress'd, I can find no rest,
I will try the land of liberty.
ANONYMOUS (IRISH STREET BALLAD C. 1847)

Quinn O'Shea stood staring out across the river to the island known as *Brooklyn*. It had been another miserably hot day. The river had a stench that made her think of garbage and death. The sun was going down, but its heat remained cloying and oppressive.

Workers had begun to spill out from the warehouses onto the docks, wiping their faces with large kerchiefs as they grumbled about the ongoing heat wave. Heavy iron gates and shutters clanged shut behind them, and soon the wharves grew quiet with the anticipation of approaching nightfall.

Quinn shuddered at the thought of another night on the docks, without shelter. She had been living on the riverfront for days. *Like a harbor rat,* she thought to herself, *though not near so adept at sniffing out food.*

After bolting from the quarantine hospital, she had spent the first two days wandering aimlessly about the city with Bobby Dempsey and the others. At first, she had been too dumbfounded by the sights and sounds of New York to fret much about her empty belly. Before long, though, she had been forced to face the reality of their situation: they had no food, no jobs—not even a place to sleep, other than in the alleys, among others as impoverished as themselves.

Finally, at the coaxing of some other Irishmen on the docks, Roche and Boyle decided to take their women off to a place called Five Points. According to the weaselly characters that talked them into the idea, there were decent boardinghouses and the prospects of jobs to be had in this Five Points place.

Quinn already knew she didn't want to attach herself to the others. They were a rough, dirty bunch, as coarse as they came. When Bobby made known his intention of staying on the docks to find work, she decided, at least for the time being, to stay with him.

So far, though, he hadn't found even the hopes of a job, and Quinn was beginning to think she should get away, on her own—as much for Bobby's sake as for her own. He was too concerned for her by far. He spent more time looking after *her* than he did looking for work.

What she could not seem to make the slow-thinking Bobby understand was that she did not *need* looking after. Indeed, his continual hovering was beginning to annoy her. This afternoon, for example, Quinn had practically had to get cross with him just to get him out of her shadow for a spell.

Bobby could not know, of course, that Quinn had resolved before ever leaving Ireland to never again be beholden to a man—not even to a kindly intentioned man like Bobby Dempsey. Once had been enough. She would not be paying the piper twice for the same tune.

She was seventeen, a woman grown, and from now on, she was on her own keeping entirely. She had decided that tomorrow, while Bobby was off searching for work, she would simply disappear.

At the moment, however, she was feeling a bit uneasy about the man. He should have been here long before now. Added to her concern was a growing weakness and light-headedness. Her legs would scarcely hold her up, so wobbly were they from the lack of food.

She was beginning to think she had merely exchanged the Hunger at home in Ireland for yet another hunger here in the United States.

The land of golden streets...

Quinn uttered a brief sound of disgust. Perhaps somewhere out there in the city, those golden streets did, indeed, exist. Somewhere far and away from *this* place, where the starving and the ill huddled like rats just to stay alive, where men fought like animals for a bite of food from the rubbish barrels...perhaps there truly *were* streets paved with gold and opportunity.

But so far, the only thing Quinn O'Shea had seen on the streets of New York were drunken sailors, Irish immigrants, and wild pigs.

And only the pigs, Quinn had noticed, appeared to be well-fed.

Sergeant Denny Price was deep into the Bowery, a ways off his beat.

He had come down to meet a nervous informant who refused to budge from the bar of the Blue India saloon. Although this particular pigeon had proved valuable in the past, Denny was feeling just irritable enough from the heat that he begrudged the time and the effort he was expending for what might turn out to be nothing.

He curled his lip as he neared the bar, disgusted by the ripe smell of garbage rising off the streets. The steady high temperatures of the past few days had only made the stench worse. Nights brought no relief, either from the foul odors or the oppressive heat. Nights like these made Denny remember with a great fondness the sweet, clean air of Donegal.

It was just past ten when he rounded the corner of Chatham and started toward the saloon. He stopped dead at an outcry just ahead. Seeing nothing, he waited. Again came a shriek, a cry that sounded like that of a young girl.

Pulling his pistol, Denny moved, quickly but cautiously. There was no lack of people in the streets. The Bowery was a blaze of light, pouring out from the gin palaces and the free-and-easys. Street vendors, men and boys on their way in and out of the saloons, prostitutes, youths out on the town—this was the East Side's center of night life.

But the crowded streets didn't necessarily mean safety, Denny knew. As with anywhere else in the city, the Bowery was no place in which a policeman dare let down his guard.

Nevertheless, when the next scream shrilled through the streets, he threw caution aside and took off at a run.

Quinn had intended to keep her distance from the gambling den. She had gone in search of Bobby, but after futile hours of looking, wandering farther and farther from the riverfront, she'd given up.

She told herself that Bobby was all right. With his hulking size and his heavy fists, why wouldn't he be? Deciding that this was as good a time as any to go off on her own, she had set about making her way deeper into the city.

She hoped to find a respectable area, a place with nice homes and families who would be looking for healthy girls to do housework and the like. When she'd first heard the loud music and seen the men going in and out of the public houses, she hadn't meant to come this close. But the tempting food odors had gathered her in like a net.

Unable to stop herself, she had eventually drifted in closer to the taverns, reasoning that perhaps she could find a job that would allow her to eat until she found something more permanent. She was beginning to fear she might swoon and end up facedown in a pile of rubbish if she did not soon manage a meal.

She had almost mustered her courage to go inside the public house when the two dandies came staggering out. Young, they were—astonishingly young, Quinn thought, to be flaunting brocade vests, gold watch fobs, and glittering rings. Still, they looked like gentlemen, and so when one stopped her and asked in a slightly slurred tone if she had need of assistance, she wasn't afraid. Not until the other began to laugh like a drunken lout and asked if he, too, could be of assistance.

Alarmed by the way he reached for her, Quinn backed off and tried to run. They caught her easily and began to drag her along between them.

Quinn's initial reaction was rage. The old fury that Millen Jupe had bred in her flamed to a blaze, and she began to twist and try to claw her way free of the two soaks. But weak as she was from the hunger and exhaustion, she had no strength left for such a struggle. When she realized their intent to haul her off down a dark alley, she managed only one feeble cry for help.

"Stop fighting, you little slut! We're not going to hurt you. If you weren't after some fun yourself, you wouldn't be down here in the first place!" The taller of the two—the one who had first approached Quinn—held her arm behind her back in a relentless viselike grip. Every time she attempted to wrench away, he would yank, hard, taking Quinn's breath away with the pain.

The other one, the one with the foolish little spectacles perched on his nose, held her by her other arm as he helped his cohort drag her into the darkness.

When Quinn first heard the shouts at the entrance of the alley, she panicked, thinking it was another of their kind, coming to join the others in their sport. But after another moment, a gunshot exploded and feet pounded down the alley toward them.

"Police! Hold up there, or this time I won't miss! Let that girl go! Let her go right now, i say!"

Quinn had never swooned in her life, but she came very near now to passing out in the street. She had the Irish combination of grudging respect and fear for the law, but at this moment, the glint of a copper star on a sturdy chest and a pistol in a large hand brought an enormous wave of relief roaring through her.

As soon as they saw the policeman, both swells dropped Quinn as if she were a leper. But when they would have turned and run toward the other end of the alley, the officer stopped them in their tracks with another pistol shot.

"Move a hair and the both of you will leave the bowery in a meat wagon!"

Quinn couldn't see the policeman's face very well in the darkness, but when he turned to her his voice was kind.

"You all right, Miss? Have these two hurt you at all?"

Quinn shook her head, her teeth chattering from fear and a fresh seizure of weakness.

"All right, then, get on with you two!" the policeman ordered. "We'll be getting out of this alley and into some light."

The officer formed a small caravan of his three charges, first gripping Quinn with a protective arm, then prodding the two surly drunks with his pistol all the way to the alley entrance.

When they reached the street, he gave two shrill blasts of his whistle, then turned to make a thorough inspection of Quinn. "What are you doing down here, lass? The Bowery's not a safe place for little girls or decent women."

"I'm not a little girl!" Quinn bit back. "But I take your meaning right enough about this place!"

The policeman had a pleasant, good-looking face and a jaunty smile. "Ah, you've just come across! I might have known. And looking for a position, I'll warrant." He went on without giving Quinn so much as an instant to reply. "Well, you'll not find any decent sort of work down here, lass. If it's service you're hoping for, you'd do well to go uptown."

Quinn was about to ask for more information about this "uptown" when another policeman came rushing up to help with the two soaks, who now stood muttering in thick tongues to each other, all the while glaring at Quinn.

The second officer—a younger version of the one who had rescued Quinn—appraised her molesters with a humorless grin. "Why, sure, I've seen these two fine gentlemen only recently, Sergeant Price! Just this past week, if I'm not mistaken. On *that* occasion they were even heavier on their feet than they are tonight. Giving one of the dance-hall girls over to Karringtons a bit of a problem, they were!"

"Get the wagon and give them a ride," said the one called Sergeant Price. "Perhaps a night's stay in the stinkhole will sober them up a bit."

The taller of the two dandies flushed crimson. "A night's stay?" he sputtered. "We're not staying anywhere tonight but at home, you ignorant paddy!"

Quinn's hand flew to her mouth at this unheard-of defiance of the law. Sergeant Price leveled his gun, while the other policeman stroked a wicked-looking wooden stick.

"Have it your own way, son," said the sergeant in a low rumble of a voice. "If you'd rather be dealing with us, sure, we're up for it."

The swell went pale. Wide-eyed, Quinn stared with weary relief as the young officer herded the two, staggering, down the street.

Sergeant Price turned back to Quinn, frowning. "So, then—do you have a place to stay, lass? Or anyone who can give you a bit of help? Family, perhaps?"

Quinn hesitated—apparently too long, for he gave a knowing nod. "On your own, is it? Well, then, I expect we'd best be taking you to one of the department's lodging houses for women, at least for—"

"Can we be of some help, Sergeant?"

Surprised by the female voice that had come up behind them, Quinn whipped around to find two well-dressed ladies appraising her and the policeman. She found herself looking into sharp, probing eyes in a face that was angular and austere. In spite of the overwhelming heat, the tall lady with the unnerving gaze was dressed in a severe black suit. Her companion, not quite so tall or forbidding in appearance, studied Quinn with a faint, uncertain smile.

Inclining his head to each, the sergeant gave a smile. "Miss Crane," he said politely, then, "Mrs. Deshler." His eyes went from the women to Quinn. "Perhaps you can at that. The young miss here will be needing temporary lodgings while she looks for a position. I was about to take her to one of the department's lodging houses for the night."

The tall lady with the disturbing eyes raked Quinn up and down. "Are you healthy, girl?"

Quinn hesitated, then gave a grudging nod. Had it not been for the sergeant, she might have told the cross-looking woman it was none of her affair at all whether Quinn O'Shea was healthy or diseased. When a cough unexpectedly shook her, she half-hoped the other would turn and run.

Instead, the black-clad lady merely continued to inspect her. "You're a Roman, I suppose?"

Irked by the woman's gall, Quinn remained steely-eyed silent.

"If it's a bother, Miss Crane," the sergeant put in, "I'll just be taking the girl with me."

"Not at all, Sergeant. Mrs. Deshler and I will take her to the Shelter, if you will be so kind as to accompany us."

"Aye, I will," said the policeman—ever so eager, Quinn thought, to oblige. No doubt he could not wait to be shut of her.

Well, *she* would have a say as to where she spent the night, she would!

"That will not be necessary," Quinn said with deliberate emphasis. "I have friends in the city."

The policeman looked at her as if she were daft. Abruptly, he took her arm, saying, "I'll have a word with the girl, ladies, if you will excuse us."

Not waiting for their reply, he moved Quinn a few steps away from the two women. Still holding her arm with a firm grip, he turned to face her. "Now see here, lassie, you'll be going with Miss Crane to the Shelter. It's a far sight better than one of the police lodging houses. They'll give you something to eat there, at least, and a bed to sleep in."

Quinn glared at him. "Have I broken the law?"

He reared back a bit. "What's that?"

"Have I broken any law at all, Sergeant, that gives you the right to say where I'll sleep?"

His mouth twisted. "My badge gives me the right, lassie, and you'd do well to be remembering it."

Quinn flared. "If I haven't done anything wrong, then I can't think it's any of your business where I happen to be lodging."

He was riled, but was obviously making an attempt to hold his temper
with her. With a long, exaggerated sigh, he softened his tone somewhat.
"Here, now, lass—what's your name anyhow?"

"Quinn O'Shea."

"Well, see here, Quinn O'Shea," he went on in a long-suffering sort
of tone he might have used with a disobedient child, "the Women's Shelter is a decent place. You'll be safe there. And you'll be fed until you find a
position. In fact, if you like, Miss Crane might even allow you to work to
earn your keep until you locate something more permanent. She's a fine
Christian lady—"

"A bit of a sour one, it seems to me."

"A fine Christian lady," the policeman repeated, raising his voice slightly,
"who has dedicated her life to helping get young girls and women off the
streets. And Mrs. Deshler, the lady with her? Why, isn't she a prosperous
widow from uptown—who just might be able to help you locate a position? She contributes her time as well as her generous financial support
to the Shelter."

The sergeant paused, then added, "I'm telling you, girl, you'd be doing
the wise thing to go along with them and make no more trouble."

It was the remark about the wealthy widow that decided Quinn. If she
were truly a rich lady from "uptown," as the sergeant said, then indeed she
might assist Quinn in getting a job.

"I'll take no charity," she said stubbornly.

"Well, that's fine, lass. An honorable attitude," the sergeant replied,
already guiding Quinn back to the two women, who stood waiting. "Let's
be telling the ladies here what a fine, respectable girl you are. You're just
the sort they like to help, don't you see?"

Without delay, Quinn found herself securely tucked between the sergeant and the black-suited Miss Crane. "You ladies must be more careful
about being out so late at night," he said conversationally.

"The Lord protects His own," said Miss Crane, her eyes straight ahead.
"The kingdom's work must be done when it can."

"Ah, that's so," murmured the sergeant.

Feeling very much out of place in their company, Quinn walked along
for a time in silence. Suddenly, a thought struck her.

"I couldn't find Bobby," she said, tugging at the sergeant's arm.

"Bobby?"

"My friend, Bobby Dempsey. I was supposed to meet him on the docks, but he never showed. If you see him, would you tell him where I've gone? Please, Sergeant?"

The policeman stopped, studying Quinn with a disapproving look. The two women also stopped to wait, Miss Crane with an exasperated look on her gaunt face.

"You're too young a lass to be having anything to do with the likes of the dock workers!" scolded the sergeant. "They're a rough bunch of fellows, don't you know?"

"He's not a dock worker!" Quinn shot back. "At least, not yet. Why, if it hadn't been for Bobby Dempsey, I'd hate to think where I might be now!"

Gentling her tone a bit—the man was a policeman, after all—Quinn pleaded, "Please, Sergeant, say you'll try to find him. Just to make sure he's all right, and to let him know where he can find me."

The sergeant studied her for a moment, then nodded. "Aye, then, if I run into your Bobby Dempsey, I'll be sure to tell him where you are."

"The women at the Shelter are not allowed visitors."

Quinn turned to stare at the one called *Miss Crane*. Something in her voice seemed to hold a threat with every comment.

Quinn decided then and there she did not like the woman at all. Not at all. "I will not be there but a short time," she said, addressing her words to Mrs. Deshler, who gave her a vague smile. "Only for as long as it takes me to find a good position for myself."

Silently, Quinn hoped this…Shelter…turned out to be a sight more cheerful than Miss Crane, the "fine Christian lady" who seemed to be in charge of the place.

16

Shooting Star

When I remember all
The friends, so link'd together,
I've seen around me fall
Like leaves in wintry weather;
I feel like one
Who treads alone
Some banquet hall deserted,
Whose lights are fled,
Whose garlands dead,
And all but he departed!

THOMAS MOORE (1779–1852)

Dublin
Late July

Morgan enjoyed these early morning sparring sessions with Tierney, although he found that he often neglected his breakfast in favor of their lively conversation.

He had not been surprised to find the lad sharp-witted, even mercurial. In his letters, Michael had often referred to his son as a "shooting star," and Morgan thought it an apt description.

The boy had a keen intelligence, though probably not a bent for scholarship. Tierney, Morgan suspected, was the sort who learned more by doing, preferring action over academics. He had already discovered vast holes in the lad's education, but he wondered just how eager the young scamp would be to fill in the gaps if given the opportunity.

This morning, most of the brisk exchange across the table was taking place between Tierney and Annie. Morgan found himself too distracted to participate, other than in a vague, preoccupied fashion. There was a great deal on his mind, most of it unpleasant.

Today he would go to Richmond Prison to bid William Smith O'Brien farewell. Exiled to Van Diemen's Land by the Crown, the former Young Ireland leader had lost his protest against being transported. Although the law was clear that one convicted of high treason be either executed or granted a full pardon, British officials had, with customary efficiency, simply hurried into passage a *new* law. As a result, in a matter of days Smith O'Brien would be leaving his country—the country to which he had devoted his entire adult life.

O'Brien's demand for execution instead of exile had been denied, God be thanked, although Morgan thought he understood his friend's preference for death over banishment. Still, as long as William was alive, there was hope, no matter how slight, for a pardon.

It was believed among the former members of Young Ireland that O'Brien was hoping to resume his leadership role one day. Morgan disagreed. William certainly knew that his exile would mean political oblivion. O'Brien would have stood more of a chance to become Ireland's hero if he *had* been executed. The nation had a long list of Irish martyrs who had died for their country. But it would be far more difficult, if not impossible, to assume the role of hero after leading a failed revolution and being sent into exile for life. Especially for a leader whose reputation had been blackened by the ugly stain of ridicule.

It was with a keen sense of loss that Morgan considered O'Brien's leaving. With Joseph Mahon passed on and William exiled, he would virtually be without close friends, other than Sandemon. There was Michael, of course, his oldest friend—but he was an entire ocean away.

Morgan found such encroaching isolation more unsettling than he would have expected. There was something about friendship, he had come to realize, that gave one a sense of permanence. In some inexplicable way friends helped to affirm the importance of one's life—a gift not to be taken lightly when everything else seemed uncertain....

"What do we think about the Queen coming to Dublin, *Seanchai*?"

Morgan glanced up, momentarily at a loss to comprehend Annie's question. "The Queen?"

"Aye. How do we feel about her visit to Ireland next week?"

"Ah, yes…the Queen's visit." Recovering, Morgan restrained a smile at the girl's ingenuousness. "Why, I can only speak for myself, of course, but it seems to me that if 'our darling little Queen'—to quote the O'Connell—feels compelled to accept the tributes of her Irish subjects, then why not?"

Annie gave him a blank look, obviously not satisfied. "But what is our *opinion* on Queen Victoria's visit, *Seanchai*?" she pressed.

Morgan leaned back, still smiling at his precocious daughter. "You must think for yourself, *alannah*. Suppose you tell *me*…'our opinion,' eh?"

Obviously warming to the opportunity, Annie plunged in with her usual energy. "I expect we might be wondering why the Little Queen is coming just *now*. It wouldn't seem the most…propitious moment for a royal visit."

Not for the first time, Morgan found himself struck by Annie's insight. "Aye," he answered thoughtfully, "your question is well-taken." Indeed, he thought grimly, why *was* the Queen coming to Dublin at this particular time? The country was altogether devastated, had come through yet another year that was nothing but one long night of sorrow. Almost all of Britain's relief effort—if *effort* was the word—had ceased. The people were fleeing the land by the thousands, and the masses were forsaking Dublin to escape the cholera epidemic.

Even as he spoke, Morgan felt the old indignation and bitterness rise up in his chest. "An incisive question, indeed, *alannah*," he grated out. "The Irish people might well ask why the Queen is coming to Dublin in the midst of a cholera epidemic."

Not quite meeting his gaze, Annie frowned. "Are you fearful of the cholera, *Seanchai*?"

"That man is a fool who does not fear a cholera epidemic, child. That's why I have asked the entire household to avoid the city as much as possible, until it passes. We cannot afford to take risks."

Annie nodded. "Especially with Finola's babe about to be born."

Another fear. Morgan swallowed, managing only an agreeing murmur. "So, then," he returned, "you could say that my opinion…*our* opinion, if you will…about the Queen's visit is somewhat skeptical, at the least."

"Perhaps," Annie ventured slowly, "she only means to help the Irish people."

"A noble sentiment on her part, though somewhat belated, I fear,"

Morgan said, struggling to keep the full force of his resentment under control. "Unless, of course, she intends to decorate the common graves about the land."

"I think it's obscene!" Tierney's outburst didn't surprise Morgan in the least. During the few weeks in which the boy had been a guest at Nelson Hall, he had proved himself to be nothing if not assertive.

"She has the gall!" he went on, snapping his knuckles as he rose to his tirade. "Coming here with her decadent pomp, while the country is starving! All this fuss about 'illuminations' throughout the city and the need to redecorate the Vice-Regal Lodge for her stay. I think it's a disgrace!"

Morgan let him go on for a moment. Tierney seemed to feel compelled to establish his loyalties to Ireland at every opportunity.

Finally, when the boy stopped for a breath, Morgan offered an observation. "The Queen isn't altogether responsible for the foolishness of her officials. They seem to be the ones calling for all the expense."

He ventured no comment on the fact that Victoria and her prince were bringing their four children and a host of servants—a party of some thirty-six people altogether, according to the papers. An entire army of workmen had appeared in the city weeks ago to begin preparations for the royal visit. Triumphal arches, platforms, and the like were being hastily erected, St. Patrick's Hall redecorated, and Dublin Castle thoroughly cleaned and repainted.

He was surprised at Annie's next remark. "Well, I expect my opinion is the same as the *Evening Mail*'s," she said solemnly. "'If we have funds to spare, let them be spent not on illuminations, but on Her Majesty's starving subjects.'"

Morgan smiled at her. "Aye, lass, I concur. For once—although it's rare—I, too, agree with the *Evening Mail*."

Folding his breakfast napkin, he turned his attention to Tierney. "I am going to Richmond Prison today, to bid William Smith O'Brien farewell before he sails. You may accompany me if you'd like to meet him."

The boy was eagerness itself. "I would, sir, thank you! What time shall we leave?"

Annie interrupted before Morgan could answer. "And shall I be going too, *Seanchai*?" she asked eagerly.

Morgan looked at her. "Why...no, lass. Not today. The prison is no fit place for you."

Immediately, her features darkened. "I don't see why I can't go. Mr. William Smith O'Brien is a hero. I would like to say goodbye to him, too." That said, she favored Tierney with a fierce glare.

Ignoring her petulance, Morgan shook his head firmly. "I'll not take you to the prison, and that's that. Aside from the fact that it's a mean place for a man, much less a lass, I want you here with Finola."

One eye narrowed, just slightly, and the pouting mouth pursed still more. But finally she yielded. "I suppose that's best, then."

"Thank you, lass." Morgan reached to squeeze her hand. "You *will* keep a close eye on Finola?"

"You know I will," she said, leaping up from her chair. "Is Sandemon going with you to the prison?"

"Of course. And before you go upstairs, would you remind him that I'd like to leave within the hour?"

"He needn't go," said Tierney. "I can help you manage just as well."

Morgan looked at him. Even before today he had sensed something vaguely disturbing about the lad's attitude toward Sandemon—a certain coolness, a subtle undercurrent of resentment that almost seemed to border on jealousy. On occasion he had the distinct feeling that Tierney only condescended to Sandemon out of deference to Morgan's obvious affection for the man.

Morgan found the boy's bearing toward Sandemon unsettling. At times, he thought he sensed a disturbing streak of cruelty—or at the least, a certain pettiness—in Tierney. Most often, it would manifest itself as arrogance or even rudeness. Whatever it was, Morgan found it troubling, for it seemed in stark contrast to the boy's other, finer character traits.

Often, he could almost feel the conflict going on in that restless young spirit. He was quickly learning that Michael's son was every bit as complicated—and as difficult—as he had been heralded to be. Tierney could be generous to a fault, yet displayed an occasional spark of malice toward the younger scholars. He was charming, capricious, and engaging—yet quite capable of withdrawing and turning cold as a snake.

Even with Sister Louisa, the boy could be impudent—no easy feat, to Morgan's thinking. Toward Sandemon, he showed no hint of emotion or respect. Yet, with Annie, he seemed to be fitting into the mold of the proverbial elder brother and comrade. And, though he teased her unmercifully, the lass did seem to dote on him—most of the time.

Besides Morgan himself, the one person in the household toward
whom Tierney showed a genuine respect was Finola. Though seldom in
her company, for Finola rarely came downstairs these days, Tierney was
every bit the gentleman when they chanced to meet.

But, then, Morgan reasoned with a faint smile, didn't Finola hold virtually the entire household in the palm of her slender hand?

The very thought of his delicate young wife and the imminent birth
of the babe made Morgan's hands tremble slightly on the table. To avoid
Tierney's probing gaze, he straightened and said firmly, "Sandemon will
go with us."

He did not miss the flicker of impatience that passed across the boy's
face.

"I would like the two of you to become friends," he went on, as if he
hadn't noticed. "Sandemon has much to offer a young man like you. You
would do well to seek his company."

Tierney made no reply, but his insolent stare spoke enough to make
Morgan uncomfortable.

Deciding to confront him now, before things went any further, Morgan braced both hands on the edge of the table. He studied the boy for
a moment, then said, "What, exactly, is this problem you seem to have
with Sandemon?"

Tierney looked down at his plate. "I don't know what you mean."

"I think you do," Morgan returned, more sharply than he had intended.

The boy lifted his head. Those unnerving blue eyes met Morgan
straight on. "He's arrogant. For a Negro."

With some difficulty, Morgan kept his voice even. "Sandemon is anything but arrogant. You misunderstand him entirely."

"It's different in America," the boy countered. "Perhaps that's why I
don't understand. Negroes aren't treated the same there."

Inwardly, Morgan seethed at his insolence. "I know very well how
black men are treated in America...by *some*." He paused, then added, "I
would have thought you above such ignorant behavior."

The boy flushed. "I won't insult your friend, sir," he said harshly. "But
you needn't think I'll be his chum, either."

Morgan leaned forward, struggling to keep his temper. "Understand
this: You will treat Sandemon with nothing but the utmost respect at all
times. He deserves it—and I insist on it. Do you understand?"

The boy's face was a mask. "Of course, sir. It's your home, after all."

Morgan eyed him for another moment, then sighed. "It is also your home, lad," he said wearily. "For as long as you want. I simply thought it best that you understand how things are with Sandemon."

Tierney's gaze held steady. "I do understand." Abruptly, he rose. "If you'll excuse me, sir," he said shortly, then turned to leave the room.

At the door, he met Sandemon, who was just entering. As Morgan watched, the boy hesitated for an instant, then gave a brief nod to acknowledge the black man's greeting.

Sandemon turned slightly to watch Tierney's exit. Morgan tried to read his expression as he came the rest of the way into the dining hall, but could detect nothing in those noble features other than what might have been a trace of puzzlement, or perhaps even disappointment.

17

Among Men

Three coins tossed by a fool:
Pride of face, pride of name, and pride of manhood.

MORGAN FITZGERALD (1849)

Most of the way back in the carriage, Tierney reflected on the surprise William Smith O'Brien had turned out to be.

He couldn't have said what, exactly, he had expected of the imprisoned Irish leader, but the stiff, ascetic-looking man at Richmond Prison certainly belied his expectations.

Instead of the anticipated glint of fire in the eyes, there had been only a hint of restrained anger. Far more apparent had been O'Brien's weariness and sense of defeat. The polite, even elegant bearing seemed to announce the consummate aristocrat, not the zealot Tierney might have imagined him to be. Indeed, Tierney thought with some disdain, Smith O'Brien more closely resembled an English landowner than an Irish rebel.

If O'Brien had proved surprising, his circumstances had been downright astonishing. Rather than being submerged in the bowels of a cold, filthy dungeon, O'Brien had been given rooms in the home of the governor—the warden—of the prison. Not only did he have access to two large gardens, he was allowed his regular servant on hand to provide for his needs! There seemed no actual restrictions on him, save that he could not leave the grounds.

Unable to keep his silence any longer, Tierney finally blurted out: "What sort of imprisonment *is* that, anyway? It's more like he's a guest in a swank hotel!"

"Richmond Prison is under the control of the Dublin Corporation," Morgan explained with a grim smile. "Public opinion in the city is such that the authorities dare not treat O'Brien with anything less than deference. They're smart enough to know they don't need another Irish martyr to stir up the people."

Tierney shook his head. "Well, sure, he's not that, now is he? He doesn't seem to have much to complain about, I'd say."

"Once he's transported, his situation will be vastly different, I can assure you."

Tierney thought Morgan's reply sounded rather testy.

"O'Brien will be a felon, and no doubt will be treated as such. He will be without country, without family, and without any real hope of ever changing his condition, although a number of us will continue to work for pardon."

Unable to shake his disappointment, Tierney blurted out, "He doesn't even seem Irish! He's nothing at all like what I thought he would be!"

Morgan crossed his arms over his chest, studying Tierney. "What were you expecting, lad? A wild-eyed warrior with long hair and a spear in his hand?"

He stopped, glancing out the window of the carriage before going on. "Don't make the same mistake that many others do about the Irish, Tierney. Don't try to force them into your own preconceived notion of what they are, instead of discovering the truth for yourself. The English have been doing it for centuries, and consequently they still don't understand what we're all about. Smith O'Brien, like many others in leadership roles, is a highly educated, cultured man who could have done most anything he wanted to with his life. The fact that he chose to spend it on what some see as a hopeless cause makes him no less the man. Perhaps it only gives him that much more nobility."

Feeling himself chastised—and grudgingly admitting that there was some truth in Morgan's rebuke—Tierney merely nodded and said nothing.

The black man had been silent throughout their return journey. But now Sandemon spoke, his tone distracted, as if he were thinking aloud. "I suspect," he said slowly, "that most of the ancient prophets were also greatly misunderstood. More than likely, their contemporaries viewed them as madmen—or as fools."

Morgan nodded. "It does seem that we have a way of relegating anyone whose motives we don't understand to one category or the other."

He turned back to Tierney. "Your father often wrote of your interest in Ireland—and its people. I would hope that you will take the time and make the effort to discover the truth about both. That may mean having a number of your illusions shattered, but if you truly want to explore your own Irishness, you need to begin from the point of reality."

Tierney thought about what Morgan said. The truth was, the young man had already had a number of his illusions shattered, and he was beginning to think Morgan Fitzgerald might be one of them.

The man sitting across from him was not the heroic figure of his childhood fantasies. Oh, in some ways he was everything that Tierney had imagined him to be. In size and strength, despite his crippled legs, he was very much the giant who had trod through Tierney's boyish daydreams, polished his ideals. Morgan's intellect was staggering, almost beyond comprehension; he could not be outdone in conversation or in chess— although he insisted that he disliked the game.

But where was the fire, the relentless zeal? Where was the blazing love of country, the passion for Irish freedom, that had fired the youthful renegade of Da's memories?

This man spent his hours teaching in a classroom or buried deep in the pages of some dead priest's journal. When he wasn't thus involved, he could be found either mooning over his wife—understandable, Tierney admitted—or else coaching his daughter in her lessons. He seemed to spend the rest of his time either writing or playing the harp.

Whatever he was, he was definitely not the phoenix Tierney had envisioned. Indeed, the Irish hero of his childhood would seem to be something of a disappointment.

Why, the man was even a teetotaler! Who had ever heard of an Irish rebel who wouldn't take a drink?

Tierney had looked forward to sitting around the great stone fireplace of an evening, lifting a glass with Morgan Fitzgerald while listening to tales of his heroic exploits. Obviously, even that was not to be.

Disgruntled, Tierney thought it might be high time to look up his Gypsy friend, Jan Martova. The Gypsies were known to like the drink, weren't they?

Not that that was the only reason for searching out Jan Martova, he quickly rationalized. He had liked the Gypsy well enough, thought they would get along just fine. He wanted to see him again, that was the thing.

On impulse, he leaned forward. "Where would I find the Gypsy, Jan Martova, sir? He said he was from the city."

Morgan looked at him, then nodded. "No doubt they're camped in the Liberties."

"The Liberties?"

"It's a section in the western part of the city. A slum, actually. And a good place to avoid."

"A dangerous place, surely," put in Sandemon.

Tierney gave him an impatient glance. "Still, I'd like the chance to see him again. To thank him."

"Then it would be best to invite him to Nelson Hall," Morgan said firmly.

"I doubt that he'd come. He was uncomfortable there."

Morgan considered him with a look that made Tierney vaguely uneasy.

"Couldn't you just drop me, sir? I can make my way home on my own later."

Morgan shook his head adamantly. "Must I remind you of the cholera epidemic in the city? It will be even worse in a place like the Liberties! No, it would be more than foolish! You would be putting yourself and the entire household at risk. Absolutely not!"

Tierney glared at him. It was on the end of his tongue to remind him that he had no right to tell him what he could or could not do. He was seventeen years old, a man grown—and certainly not answerable to Morgan Fitzgerald. But he reconsidered, acknowledging, if grudgingly, that he would do himself no good at all by deliberately provoking the man. He was living under his roof, after all.

He would have to be patient, wait for the right time to slip away into the city. As for managing a drink before then, his instincts told him that the watery-eyed old butler had himself a stash somewhere on the grounds.

Tierney had a hunch that for the right price, Artegal might be convinced to share his secret store.

18

A Momentous Occasion at Nelson Hall

And I that would be singing
Or whistling at all times went silently then....
PATRICK MACDONOGH (1902–1961)

Morgan knew there was something wrong as soon as the carriage turned and started up the lane to Nelson Hall.

Annie was standing just outside the wide front doors, squinting as if she were awaiting their arrival. As always, the watchful-eyed wolfhound stood beside her.

The moment she saw the carriage approaching, she bolted away from the door and ran to meet them. Fergus raced ahead of her, leading the way.

"Seanchai! Seanchai!"

Morgan leaned out the door as Sandemon hurried around to help him with the chair. "What is it, lass? What's wrong?"

"'Tis Finola! The babe is coming, *Seanchai*! Sister Louisa says the babe is coming!"

Seized by a mighty wave of fear, Morgan stared at her. "The babe—you are sure?"

The girl shifted from one foot to the other, her head bobbing wildly up and down. "Aye, Sister says!"

"The surgeon—have you sent for Dr. Dunne?" stammered Morgan as Sandemon tugged him from the carriage into the wheelchair.

"Aye, *Seanchai*! He should be here any moment," Annie assured him. "Sister sent Colm O'Grady for him nearly an hour ago!"

Finally settled in the wheelchair, Morgan allowed Sandemon to wheel him hurriedly up the ramp into the house. All the while Annie chattered beside him, answering his questions with more of her own.

Sister Louisa met them in the entryway. "Ah, thank the Lord, you are back! But where *is* that doctor?"

Beside Morgan, Annie asked, "How long do you think it will take, *Seanchai*?"

Feeling lightheaded, Morgan looked at her. "How long?"

"For the babe to be born!"

"How should I know such a thing?"

He looked to the nun for help, but she merely lifted her eyebrows. "Only our Lord and the babe could be knowing."

Morgan's hands trembled on the arms of the wheelchair. "How…how is she? How is Finola?"

"She is—anxious, of course," answered Sister Louisa carefully. "She will feel easier when the doctor arrives, I expect."

"Where *is* he, anyway?" Morgan muttered. "He could have been here and back by now!"

Upstairs, a cry came from Finola's bedroom. Morgan reared in the chair, his entire body breaking into a tremble to match the shaking of his hands. "She is in pain!"

Sister shot him an impatient glance. "No child is born without pain, sir." Her look clearly said that men were ever the great fools about such matters.

Morgan started the chair toward the lift. Sister Louisa stepped in front of him. "It would be best for you to wait here for the surgeon, don't you think, *Seanchai*?"

Morgan stared at her, then looked up at the hallway, toward Finola's bedroom door. "Is Lucy—"

"Lucy will not leave her. Nor will I."

He knew he should not—perhaps *could* not—go into that room. Yet, every part of his being cried out to be with her, to go to her side.

It was unheard of, of course. An Irishman in the birthing room? Unthinkable!

Convention aside, he did not *want* to be in the birthing room, or anywhere near it, for that matter! But the thought struck him that she might be frightened, might want him there, even need him with her. They had grown close, after all, she had come to depend on him, at least in small ways....

"*Seanchai*, I must go back upstairs." Sister Louisa's voice jarred him from his frantic thoughts. "Send the surgeon up the moment he arrives." She gave him a sharp look, then turned to Annie. "It would not be a good idea to detain him with questions."

Morgan's mouth seemed numb. "Do you think I should go up…"

Sister turned an almost pitying glance upon him. "Surely not," she said evenly. "It's quite late. Why don't you have Mrs. Ryan serve tea?"

Tea—the nun's answer to any and every crisis.

"I do not *want* tea!"

What he wanted, God forgive him, was a drink! And wasn't the nun glaring at him as if she knew it?

Well, then, but what of it? At such a time as this, could not the strongest man be forgiven a momentary weakness?

Another cry came from Finola's room. This time Morgan nearly catapulted from the wheelchair. "I will go to her—"

Again Sister Louisa blocked his passage, a small but formidable sentry. She opened her mouth to speak, then stopped when Lucy Hoy came hurrying down the stairs.

Morgan cast accusing eyes on Sister Louisa. "Didn't you say the woman would not leave Finola's side?"

"Oh, sweet pity—" The nun broke off, rolling her eyes toward heaven as Lucy came to a halt at the landing.

"What is it?" Morgan demanded. "What has happened?"

Lucy stopped, looking from him to Sister Louisa.

"Happened? Oh, nothing, sir! Nothing at all! It's just that Finola asked me to fetch—"

Morgan braced himself, fought down still another attack of panic. "I will go up," he managed bravely.

Again Lucy looked at him peculiarly. "I—I don't think that would be best, sir. But she did ask—"

"What?" Morgan interrupted, ignoring the relief that washed over him. "What did she ask? She must have anything she wants, anything at all!"

"Aye, sir, thank you, sir. She was wondering if your daughter would come up, sir. She would like Miss Annie to be with her, if she pleases."

Morgan stared at her. "My daughter? Annie?"

At his side, he heard Annie's sharp intake of breath. He glanced at the girl, now poised like a spring. Her eyes were huge, her mouth agape. "Finola—wants *me* with her?"

"Aye, Miss, she does that. If you're willing, she says."

"Truly?"

Now *Annie* began to tremble. But though her hands were indeed shaking, her back was straight, her chin high and firm as she turned to Morgan. "It will be well, *Seanchai*. It will almost be the same as if *you* were with Finola, my being your daughter and all."

She stopped, searching his eyes as if looking for affirmation. "I will be…standing in for you, as it were. In a way, you will be right beside her, isn't that so?"

Morgan's eyes locked with hers. He felt a sudden surge of pride for her: pride and gratitude for all that she had come to mean to him, for the strength she was now offering him, and for the depth of love that gazed out at him from behind those dark, seeking eyes.

After a moment, he reached for her hand. "You are quite certain about this, *alannah*? It will not be—too difficult for you?"

The pert chin lifted a fraction more. "I am quite certain, *Seanchai*," she said quietly. "It is what I should do."

Morgan pressed her hand, studying her. Finally, he nodded. "Aye…I believe you are right. As my daughter, it seems fitting that you should be with Finola at this most important time. You will tell her for me…" he faltered, glancing about at the others, then lowering his voice. "Tell Finola that I am with her." He put a hand to his heart. "Here, in my heart…I am with her."

Annie beamed, squeezed his fingers once, then sprinted toward the stairs, taking them two at a time.

When the wolfhound whimpered and would have followed, Morgan put a restraining hand on his great head. "Not this time, old boy," he soothed. "For now, I fear you have been relegated to the estate of all Irish males. It would seem that it's our lot to feel utterly worthless and quite helpless upon momentous occasions such as this."

As he spoke, he looked directly at Sister Louisa, who merely gave a brief nod, as if satisfied that at last he understood the way of things.

19

A Child Is Born

Thread from silver moon at night,
Dust from evening star's soft light,
Kiss of sun from summer morn—
Angels smile...a child is born.

ANONYMOUS

In his bedchamber, Morgan willed the minutes, then the hours, to pass. He had chosen to wait here, where he might be as close as possible to Finola. He could hear her moans and cries through the thick walls and heavy connecting door, yet this very closeness to her as she labored seemed to make the waiting more bearable.

He felt a small comfort, almost as if he were linked with Finola, what with Annie at her side and himself just on the other side of the door. If he could not share firsthand the actual birthing, perhaps this was the next best thing.

Sandemon had offered to wait with him, but Morgan had declined, asking him instead to go to the chapel. "Do what you do best, my friend. Pray for Finola...and for the child. Pray until all is accomplished, if you will."

And so now he sat alone, waiting in the silence. He had thought before tonight that Nelson Hall was not an especially quiet place after the sun went down. There were always muffled noises in the night, the reassuring sounds of a large estate being well kept by a competent, if slightly aged, staff. A small retinue of kitchen servants baked and prepared for the day ahead. The classrooms were cleaned and straightened. Minor repairs that might inconvenience the household through the day were carried out quietly in the late night hours. Routine but necessary tasks were performed inconspicuously, with a certain vague hum that indicated an ongoing life in the rambling old dwelling.

This night, however, seemed vastly different. Tonight, it sounded as if all activity in the house had been suspended—indeed, as if the very heartbeat of the house had paused, hushed, to await the birth of the new babe. Finola's child.

And mine, Morgan reminded himself. *I promised her that, Lord. I promised the child more than my name, now didn't I, more than my protection? I promised my love...my fatherhood.*

A shudder seized him, almost overwhelming him with the magnitude of the commitment he had made.

What if the child were not normal? A shattering rush of dread flooded him, unbidden thoughts of all the pain and torture Finola must have endured during the brutal attack that had left her with child. What if the beating, the savage punishment to her body and her mind—*dear God, the unspeakable evil of her attacker*—what if it had damaged the babe in some hideous way?

What if he could not love the child, after all?

He moaned aloud, furious with his own weakness. Determined to banish from his mind the paralyzing fear, the ominous imaginings, he wheeled the chair over to the corner and retrieved his harp. Going to the window, then, he sat staring into the night, plucking the strings in a quiet, underlying harmony to the desperate prayer of his heart.

In the labor room, each attendant had her own responsibility. Lucy had quite naturally assumed the role of the surgeon's nurse, working side by side with him as he administered what little assistance he could offer Finola. Sister Louisa took charge of supplies and keeping the laboring young mother as comfortable as possible under the circumstances.

Annie, with an occasional assist from Sister, provided Finola a strong hand to grip and an ongoing flow of encouragement.

It had been nearly three hours now since Dr. Dunne had arrived, the three longest hours of Annie's life, she was certain. For a panicky few moments at the beginning, she had been tempted to bolt from the room and leave it all up to Sister and Lucy.

The initial sight of Finola lying there, her ashen face, her writhing body, her glorious hair now limp with perspiration, had knocked the breath from Annie. It had taken every bit of courage she could muster to approach the bed and clasp Finola's hand.

But then Finola had smiled…a poor, weak smile it was, in truth, but a smile meant just for Annie, all the same…and she had somehow managed to put aside her panic.

"Will you stay with me, Aine?" Finola had asked in a voice that was little more than a whisper. "You are the babe's sister…and mine, in my heart of hearts. Will you stay with me? I need your strength…."

Annie had felt about to burst with pride and love. *Finola had called her "sister"!*

"Sure, and I will stay, Finola!" she promised, squeezing the slender, damp hand clinging to hers. "I will not leave you for a moment. I will be your strength, Finola…all that you need. I will stay for the duration."

And she *had* stayed. Now, long hours later, she felt nearly as wrung out and limp as Finola herself. Every pain that brought a cry from Finola put a knife to Annie's heart. Every moan, every gasp, seemed her own pain finding voice. But she would not leave. She had promised Finola and the *Seanchai* to stay, and so long as God enabled her to stand, she would keep that promise, she would.

Pain again. And such pain. Wave after wave of it, roaring through her, bearing down on her, then passing, only to leave her thoroughly depleted, almost without the strength to take a breath.

Finola was all too familiar with pain, remembered its torment, its savagery. But this time it was different. No less vicious, no less enfeebling— but different.

Before, the pain had been dark. Dark and obscene and deadly cold. Not so tonight. This pain somehow seemed borne of light and warmth and meaning. Its force was violent but cleansing, demanding but with a purpose. There was a kind of…purity about the very force of each fresh new wave that pounded her body.

Somewhere outside the room she heard Morgan's harp…a soft tune, sweetly gentle. Somehow it gave her strength, knowing he was near, that he was waiting. The music seemed to undergird the pain, lift it from her….

At last the final raging tide of pain slammed through her, making her arch her spine up from the bed and grip Annie's hand on one side and Sister Louisa's on the other. She cried out in one last piercing shriek that seemed to shatter the ball of agony inside her and send it exploding into the room—not a cry of desperation, but a white-hot shout of exultation.

Finola's scream all but annihilated Morgan's last thin shred of control.

Moments after the sound pierced the door between them, it still seemed to echo in the dimly lit corners of his bedchamber. The paralysis that had claimed his legs now seemed to seize his entire body. He sat, his hands locked in a trembling vise upon each arm of the wheelchair as he stared in raw panic at the heavy oak door between their rooms.

He tried to swallow, but his throat seemed frozen. He felt his blood slow, then churn through him like a river current. His pulse thundered a dangerous rhythm in his head as the hateful shaking began again in earnest.

How long he sat there, a palsied coward listening to the silence on the other side of the door, he could not say. It seemed hours before he caught the low murmur of women's voices, followed by a lusty wail, then the incredible sound of Dr. Dunne's soft chuckle.

As the trembling of his body subsided, the voices in Finola's bedchamber seemed to brighten. Morgan stared hard at the door, holding his breath, willing it to open. When it was suddenly flung wide, he reared back so sharply he almost set the chair on end.

Sister Louisa stood in the doorway, her peppery features creased in a weary but reassuring smile. Morgan looked from the nun's twinkling eyes to the bed, caught a glimpse of Annie, face stark white but dark eyes ablaze, standing beside Finola.

Finola. She lay, propped demurely against a mountain of pillows, surrounded altogether by snowy-white linens, a small bundle in the crook of her arm—

"*Seanchai—*" Sister Louisa's voice cracked for an instant with the announcement. "You may now come in."

Had Finola's bedchamber always been so far distant from his own? Had the wheelchair always rolled so slowly?

Finally reaching the bed, Morgan stopped. His gaze went from Finola's exhausted smile to the wee bundle she was balancing so carefully against her shoulder. He looked back at Finola, saw for the first time the uncertainty in her searching eyes.

"So, then...it is over at last? Are you...all right, Finola *aroon*?"

Still the uncertain smile, the searching gaze. She beckoned him closer, closer still, until he was but a hand length away.

He stared. First at her...a vision, even weary and depleted as she must be. Then his gaze went to the tiny bundle she hugged close to her. *So small...*

Startled, he saw her lift the bundle to him, saw her falter with the effort. Instinctively, Morgan reached out to take the burden from her, balancing it clumsily in his big paws, scarcely knowing which way to turn it, then forming a cradle of his arms.

Such warmth! How could something so small be so warm?

Trembling, he looked at Finola. She was loveliness itself...even in her weakness and fatigue, she seemed to glow.

"Morgan? Please...would you choose the name? Would you name him, please?"

Him. *A boy-child, then...*

Finally, Morgan dragged his eyes away from her. Wheeling himself and the babe over to the window near the bed, he pulled aside one corner of the drape to reveal the first faint glow of dawn.

Heart pounding, he gathered the child up, cradling him in one arm, and with awkward, unsteady fingers edged the blanket away from the tiny face.

A rush of light-filled wonder swept over him. *Golden hair, just like his mother's. Skin so delicate...so fair...*

The eyes squinted, opened, met his and held. *Round blue eyes...like his mother's, as blue as an Irish sky on an afternoon in spring.*

No evil there. No stain of darkness. Nothing but light. Warm and golden. He held light itself in his arms.

One trembling finger touched the soft, round cheek, then a fair wisp of hair. Golden hair.

A golden child, sent from God.

Once again, the Lord had turned ugliness to beauty—pain to glory—in the gift of this boy-child.

A son. *My* son.

Gabriel...

The name leaped up from somewhere deep in his spirit.

"Gabriel," he murmured, then said it again, louder this time, testing the sound of it on his lips. "He shall be called *Gabriel.* 'Man of God.'"

Braver now, he lifted the babe in his arms for a closer look. After a moment he turned back to Finola. "You have given me a fine son, Finola *aroon*," he said quietly, his gaze holding hers. "I choose to name him *Gabriel.* Do you approve?"

She nodded, making no effort to brush away the tears that spilled over. Despite her weariness, despite the tears, she smiled, smiled at him in a way that made Morgan feel like a giant in the land.

His eyes clung to hers for another moment. "He will be a fine man, this Gabriel," he said. "He will be noble and strong and—"

Morgan broke off abruptly and looked down at the child. The tiny golden-haired babe had reached out a flailing fist and caught Morgan's little finger in a fierce grip, hanging on as if to prove by sheer infant strength the proof of the prophecy.

Caught up in a rush of bittersweet delight, Morgan started to laugh. But an unexpected sob came instead, and he had to fight to swallow down the lump in his throat. As he gazed down at the child in wonder, great unshed tears clouded his vision.

At last he looked up and saw Sandemon framed in the doorway, his dark face shining with relief and elation.

Morgan's eyes swept the room. Sister Louisa stood at the foot of the bed, so very weary, yet so obviously pleased. Beside her, the doctor smiled at his handiwork with understandable pride and satisfaction. Behind them, Lucy Hoy...faithful Lucy, looking worn and tired and slightly stunned.

Ah, and there was Annie...his dark-eyed Aine, full of the joy and awe of this miracle of birth. Morgan reached out to her, and she came around from the other side of the bed to stand next to him.

Unable to stop the fountain of joy welling up in him, Morgan lifted the child in his arms, threw his head back, and laughed aloud.

"Our son!" he proclaimed in a voice that was almost a shout. Raising the child higher still, he presented him to the family. *"This is Gabriel! Gabriel... Thomas...Fitzgerald! Finola's son—and mine!"*

Part Two

LIGHT OF TRUTH

Gathering Darkness

He reveals deep and hidden things; he knows what
lies in darkness, and light dwells with him.

Daniel 2:22

20

A Candle in the Dark

Like a candle lifted in the night,
God's love is a light in the darkness.

ANONYMOUS

Late September

Billy Hogan huddled alone in a dark corner, his arms clasped about his propped-up legs, his head resting on his knees.

It would soon be dark. He could tell by the narrow, fast-fading ribbon of light leaking in from the crack on the outside wall.

Nobody in the building knew about the small storage press off the coal cellar except Billy and his uncle. And so far as Billy knew, nobody but Uncle Sorley had a key. Even his mum didn't know about the cramped space, nor about the hours Billy spent inside it.

At first, Billy had almost welcomed the occasional banishments to the cellar. Until recently, they had seldom lasted more than an hour or so, and the isolation provided at least a temporary reprieve from his uncle's rage and the threat of another beating.

Of late, however, Billy had begun to dread the musty, dark hole, even fear it. Uncle Sorley was locking him up more and more often, and for longer periods of time. Yesterday, he hadn't come to let him out until well after the supper hour. Not daring to ask for food past the mealtime, Billy had gone to bed with an empty belly.

The thrashings came more often now, too, sometimes for purely imaginary offenses. These days, it seemed that Billy could do nothing right.

159

The slightest fault would set his uncle off. If he couldn't find Billy guilty of any particular offense, he would simply accuse him of "impertinence," and either give him a pounding or jostle him down the stairs to the cellar. Sometimes both.

Uncle Sorley was at the drink all the time lately, which meant he was in a constant state of bad temper as well. Billy's mother no longer begged him to quit, as she once had, even though there was seldom enough money left over from the drink to buy food. Nagging at him accomplished nothing but to bring on yet another fit of rage—which invariably ended in a renewed bout of drinking.

Billy raised his head, trying not to think about his uncle. He knew he should try to concentrate on brighter things, to make the time go more quickly.

Had it been any other day, he might have turned his thoughts to Mr. Whittaker and the boys in the singing group. But not today. Today, he was missing the weekly rehearsal. For a moment, he tried to pretend he was in the upstairs practice room with the others. He even opened his mouth to sing, but all that came out was a sob.

Singing with Mr. Whittaker's group was the one pleasant hour of the entire week for Billy. It was the one time he felt safe and even worthwhile. But now Uncle Sorley had taken *that* away, too.

A faint rustling sound came from the opposite corner. Billy stiffened. He peered into the darkness, holding his breath, listening. For a moment all he could hear was the roar of his own pulse in his ears. Then the sound came again.

Rats!

Billy's heart pounded, accelerating as he heard the scrabbling, scratching noises coming nearer. He wished he had a stick, a rock—*anything* that would serve as a weapon. He wished, at least, that he could *see*.

How many were there? he wondered. *One or two? What if there were more?*

Billy hated rats beyond imagining. And New York seemed to be teeming with them! They were down here, they were upstairs—they were *everywhere*! Often they found their way into the flat. Indeed, his mum lived in terror of them.

Many a night he would lie awake on his straw-filled cot, his stomach churning with dread, his eyes wide open to make sure the filthy creatures didn't come near his younger brothers.

Swallowing hard, Billy again strained to see more clearly, but the darkness was closing in. Any moment, he realized with a sick sense of dread, Uncle Sorley would be leaving for work, leaving him locked in the cellar room for most of the night.

His uncle worked as a houseman—a bouncer—at Tiny's Place, one of the gambling dens in the Bowery. He seldom came home before one or two in the morning. Some nights he didn't come home at all.

Another rustling sound from the shadows made Billy pray that this would not be one of those nights.

"I say, Mrs. Walsh, would you m-mind playing through this for me? Just a b-brief run-through, so I can check the harmony."

Alice Walsh gave a cursory glance to the score Evan handed her, then began playing. As he stood looking over her shoulder, listening, Evan admired, not for the first time, the woman's command of the keyboard. Her sight-reading was impeccable, her rhythm flawless. She made it look so easy, coaxing those wonderful sounds from the keys. A person could easily forget how much time and effort must have gone into attaining such competence.

When she finished the piece, she looked up at Evan. "Why, Mr. Whittaker, this is very nice! It's one of your own, isn't it?"

"Ah...yes, as a m-matter of fact, it is," Evan said, embarrassed by her praise. "It's become m-more and more difficult to find music for the boys, you see, and so I find m-myself either rearranging what we have, or simply writing something new. It's difficult, though, since I c-can't really play all the p-parts to check my work."

"Your work is excellent. In fact, I think you should consider showing some of your arrangements to a publisher."

Evan laughed at her enthusiasm. "I'm afraid I'm n-no Stephen Foster, Mrs. Walsh! My compositions are strictly amateurish attempts."

"Oh, I don't agree with that at all, Mr. Whittaker. Would you like me to take this home and make an accompanist's copy, as I have your other pieces?"

"It would be most helpful, of course, but I really d-don't want you going to any more trouble—"

She smiled warmly at him. "It's no trouble. Actually, I enjoy it. Now that the children are older, I find myself with a great deal of time on my hands."

Evan nodded absently and began to collect his music. "No d-doubt you've noticed that we have a problem developing," he said. "I'm beginning to think I m-made a mistake in not setting an age limit for our membership."

Unwilling to exclude those who expressed an interest in singing, Evan had made a practice of welcoming any boy into the group who didn't appear to be a troublemaker. As a result, he now had quite a mix in ages among the boys, with some as young as eight or nine, and others, like Daniel John, approaching their late teenage years.

The problem was that the older boys' voices had either changed altogether, or were in varying stages of deepening. Consequently, it was becoming more and more difficult to develop practical arrangements for the group as a whole.

"Perhaps some separate numbers for the older boys would help," suggested Alice Walsh.

"Perhaps. But I fear they're losing interest, and I'm not sure we can d-do much about it. Have you n-noticed their impatience with the younger boys lately?"

She nodded. "I suppose it's to be expected. Other than one or two, like Billy Hogan, the younger boys require much simpler music. The older ones get bored waiting for them to learn their parts."

At the mention of Billy Hogan, Evan looked up. "Did you n-notice that Billy was absent again today? It's happening m-more and more frequently, don't you think?"

"Have you talked with him about it?"

Evan nodded. "It's always the same. He apologizes but n-never really offers much by way of explanation."

Looking up from his music case, he hesitated, then blurted out what had been on his mind for several weeks. "I tell you, Mrs. Walsh, I think there's something very wrong with B-Billy. I'm actually quite worried about him."

She rose, stacking her own music neatly on top of the piano. "I'm afraid I agree," she finally replied. "The poor little boy just wrings my heart. He tries so hard. Obviously, he enjoys every minute of rehearsal. And that incredible voice! But there's such a sadness about him—" She stopped, letting her words drift off, unfinished.

As if deliberately trying to change the subject, she turned toward Evan, smiling. "And how is *your* little boy, Mr. Whittaker?"

Evan brightened. "Oh, he's quite well, thank you! He's such a joy to us, you kn-know. I f-fear we'll spoil him terribly. He's quite a good baby, though—so quiet and good-natured. Why, he scarcely cries at all!"

"I'm so happy for you. And how is Mrs. Whittaker?"

Evan continued to smile, but even as he murmured his usual reply, that Mrs. Whittaker was "well and quite busy these days, with the baby and all," he felt the familiar stab of doubt as to how well Nora really was.

He couldn't help but think she should be stronger by now. Teddy was nearly three months old, but even so, Nora seemed to have regained little strength or vigor. Evan found it difficult not to fret about her; she was pale all the time, and even the smallest task seemed to exhaust her. Yet she insisted that she felt stronger every day.

He had confided his worry to Dr. Grafton, of course, but the other had offered little reassurance. Evan had grown accustomed to the mild-mannered physician's reserve—he was, indeed, a man of few words. Nevertheless, something about the doctor's vague nods and understanding smiles only served to sharpen his concern.

Still, there could be no doubt that Nora was enjoying their infant son. The radiance about her when she held Teddy in her arms never failed to make Evan's heart swell with love.

Teddy was a delight to them both—and a continual wonder to Evan, who up until now had had virtually no exposure to babies at all. He held him as often and for as long as Nora would allow, endlessly fascinated by the delicate perfection of tiny fingers and tiny toes. And when the little fellow gazed up into his eyes and made that funny little chortling sound—as if he found his father highly amusing—Evan would laugh aloud with pleasure.

"About the boys, Mr. Whittaker—I might have a suggestion."

Alice Walsh gave an uncertain smile, waiting for Evan's nod of encouragement before continuing. "It's just a thought, of course, but you might consider starting a band—for the older boys, that is."

Evan looked at her. "A band?"

"It might be just the thing. Some of them already read music and play instruments—like Daniel John and Casey Dalton."

Evan didn't want to risk offending the woman, but he scarcely considered a harp and a flute the makings of a band.

As if warming to the idea, she went on, her words hurried and eager now. "Some of the boys are quite musical. I'm sure they could learn instruments quickly," she said. "And a band of their own might restore their interest in staying together."

Even as she spoke, Evan could anticipate all manner of obstacles. "But we have n-no instruments—"

She waved a hand as if the problem were negligible. "I'm sure I could locate some used instruments among the merchants and other members of my congregation."

"I'm afraid I know n-nothing at all about *b-bands*," Evan again attempted to protest.

"Oh, but you know a great deal about music! And the boys are so dedicated to you, I'm sure you'd have no problem capturing their interest."

In spite of his skepticism, Evan actually found himself considering the possibilities. "Still," he pointed out, "I couldn't m-manage both the singing group *and* a band. It would involve n-new music arrangements and additional rehearsals—"

Alice Walsh seemed to have an answer for every argument he raised. Indeed, Evan was beginning to wonder just how long she had actually been considering her suggestion.

"I believe I know someone who would help," she offered. "One of the members of our congregation, Mr. Harold Elliott, is an employee of Firth, Pond—the music publisher. I could speak with him about donating some easy arrangements. I'm sure he'd be happy to help. As for the extra rehearsals…" She hesitated, but only for an instant. "Perhaps—perhaps I could manage the younger boys while you work with the older ones. Just for practices. You'd still be their director, of course."

Evan stared at the woman, somewhat bemused. He had never seen Mrs. Walsh like this. She was usually so…*quiet*. "Well…I suppose it's worth considering," he said slowly. "If you really think we could m-manage, that is."

"Oh, I'm sure we could," replied Alice Walsh in an uncharacteristically firm tone of voice. "The boys are intent on pleasing you. They're quite devoted to you, you know."

Inordinately pleased by her words, Evan busied himself with erasing the chalkboard that Lewis Farmington had recently donated. "Yes, well, they're good b-boys. I enjoy them no end."

Again he thought of Billy Hogan. "I believe I shall m-make a call on the Hogan family. I've been thinking that I should at least introduce myself to the boy's parents. Perhaps this would b-be a good time to begin."

"But you don't plan on going this evening, do you?"

Evan turned, realizing at once what she meant. "Oh...n-no. No, I suppose not. One d-doesn't linger in the Five Points after dark. Certainly n-not alone. I'll have to go another time."

Directly on the heels of his words came an unsettling thought: if he, a grown man, could not face the Five Points after dark, what must it be like for a small boy to spend his *life* there?

The cellar closet was now completely dark. Billy knew his uncle Sorley would not be coming to let him out. At least not soon. For the first time, he would have to spend the night alone in the inky blackness of the cellar.

Billy bit his lip to the point of pain, squeezed his eyes tightly shut to stop the tears. A boy his age shouldn't be crying, shouldn't be afraid of the dark. He was nine years old, after all. He shouldn't be afraid of *anything*.

"I'm not afraid," he said to the darkness. He heard the trembling in his voice, and said it again, this time louder. "I'm not afraid of *anything*."

As the minutes passed and he heard nothing more, Billy wondered if he could have imagined the sounds. He wished he had a lantern. Or even a candle. Anything that would enable him to see what was in the corner.

In truth, he wasn't at all sure he *wanted* to see. Still, if he had a light, perhaps they wouldn't bother him and...

Something tugged at his thoughts. Unexpectedly, the memory of one of his recent reading lessons came squeezing through his fear. Because he was reading ahead of the other boys, Mr. Whittaker had assigned him an additional lesson to study: some Bible verses from the book of Psalms.

Once Billy had mastered the verses, Mr. Whittaker had given him a big smile and said the word that all the boys worked hard to hear: "*Splendid!*" he said. "*Splendid* job, Mr. Hogan!"

With his eyes still closed, Billy groped to remember the words, trying to see them just as they had appeared on the printed page:

"For thou wilt light my candle: the Lord my God will enlighten my dark-
ness...even the darkness will not hide from thee...the night shines as the day...
the darkness and the light are both alike to thee...."

Slowly Billy opened his eyes. The pounding of his heart eased a bit,
and he sat up straight. At last—his voice clear, and stronger this time—he
spoke again to the darkness. "I'm not afraid," he said. "I'm not."

Mr. Whittaker often reminded them that God was everywhere, that
those who belonged to the Lord could never be out of His sight. "Even
in the blackest night," he once explained during the practice of a hymn
tune, "He sees you. He is with you. His love is your shelter in the daylight
or in the dark."

That being the case, God was right here, in the cellar closet. And the dark
wouldn't be a bit of a bother to God, none at all. He could see everything that
was going on, even in the hidden corners.

So Billy kept his eyes closed and asked God to stand watch over him
in the darkness. And after a time, he truly was no longer afraid, for he realized he was no longer alone.

21

The Chatham Charity Women's Shelter

Father in Heaven, give us bread;
(God, make us want to live, instead.)
May we be clothed by charity;
(Oh, give us back our faith in Thee.)
For our sick bodies, give us care;
(God, save our souls from this despair.)
Shelter us from the wind and rain;
(Oh, help us learn to smile again.)
Grant that our babies may be fed;
(But what of hopes forever dead?)
Father in Heaven, give us bread—
(Oh, give us back our dreams instead!)

AUTHOR UNKNOWN
(YOUNG WOMAN REFERRED TO NEW YORK'S CHURCH MISSION OF HELP)

And what sort of a day will you be having, sweetheart?" asked Michael. He frowned at his reflection in the vanity mirror as he struggled with the top button of his shirt.

Still in her dressing gown, Sara crossed the room to help. "A busy one, more than likely. I'm visiting Nora this morning, then coming back to tour one of the women's shelters in the Bowery. Helen asked me to help out during Emily Deshler's illness."

He turned, locking his arms around her waist as she conquered the stubborn button. "Which shelter would that be?"

"I believe it's on Chatham Street."

He lifted an eyebrow. "The one run by Ethelda Crane?"

"Yes, I think so. Have you been there?" she asked, smoothing the front of his shirt.

"No, but I've met Miss Crane. The subcommission interviewed her when we first began to set up our committees."

"She serves on one of the committees?"

He shook his head. "No. The general consensus was that Miss Crane might be a bit...difficult to work with." He grinned, pulling her closer. "You'd be wise to approach that one with caution, sure," he said, grinning at her.

"The shelter or Miss Crane?"

"I believe Miss Crane *is* the shelter. It was my observation that she takes her work very, ah...seriously. I got the feeling she might also take a dim view of anything that could be interpreted as interference."

Sara looked at him. "Is she really all that formidable?"

"Terrifying," he said, still smiling. Lifting her hand, he brought her fingers to his lips for a moment. "But no match for my Sara, of course. Still, you'd best have a care. You're not going over to Brooklyn alone, I hope?"

"No, Robert's going to drive me to the ferry, then go across with me."

He made a face. "Robert is practically doddering, Sara. Not much of a protector, I'd say."

"We'll be fine, Michael. Don't hover."

He gave her a look, but said nothing.

"Will you be home for dinner?"

"Not tonight. I've a meeting at seven."

"The subcommission?"

"Aye, we're finally getting down to the reason I agreed to serve in the first place."

He turned back to the mirror, and Sara watched him. "The crime bosses, you mean?"

"And the pirates who work for them, that's right."

"You'll be investigating Patrick Walsh?"

He met her gaze in the mirror. "Among others."

"Michael...you know what a dangerous man he is. You'll be careful?"

He ran a brush through his hair, then turned to her. "I can be a dangerous man, too, sweetheart, if need be. You're not to worry."

"He terrifies me! I wish—"

He took her by the shoulders. "What, Sara?"

Sara searched his eyes. She knew the hard glint reflected there wasn't for her. "I wish...you'd let someone else see to Patrick Walsh."

His jaw tightened as he turned away to shrug into his jacket. "Walsh is mine," he said flatly, his tone clearly leaving no room for argument. "Come along, now," he said, taking her arm, "or I'll not have time for breakfast. And you'd best be looking to your own welfare instead of fretting about mine. You'll need all your defenses in place to brave the formidable Miss Crane."

"Good heavens, Michael, you make the woman sound positively intimidating."

He opened the bedroom door, stopping just long enough to plant a quick kiss on her cheek. "Well, now, and wouldn't I know a terrible, fierce woman when I see one, being married to you?"

Sara had hoped to find Nora improved from their last visit, but there seemed little change, if any.

Although the baby appeared to be thriving, Nora was another matter altogether. She was too thin by far, almost as gaunt as when she had first arrived in America, ill and devastated by the famine. Even her hair seemed to be graying more quickly than was reasonable. Indeed, to Sara's eyes, Nora simply did not look *well.*

When questioned, though, Nora continued to insist that she felt "perfectly fine."

"Oh, I'm a bit tired, perhaps," she admitted. "A baby does take work, though Teddy is so good I scarcely know he's about."

Sara studied her across the kitchen table. "I think you could do with some help, Nora," she suggested. "At least for a while, until you're stronger. Especially now that Johanna has gone back to her lessons with Miss Summer."

"Oh, I'm managing fine, Sara—truly!" Nora insisted. "Johanna is here in the evenings, and Aunt Winnie still comes often to help."

"But you've told me yourself that Johanna seems reluctant to handle the baby," Sara reminded her. "And Aunt Winnie will soon have her hands full, looking after her own home again. If Father has his way—and he almost always does—they'll be married before year's end."

Nora nodded and smiled. "Aunt Winnie is positively glowing, isn't she? I think it's quite wonderful about her and your father."

"I couldn't be more pleased," Sara agreed, her enthusiasm genuine. "Father's been alone long enough, and Winifred is an absolute delight. I think they'll be wonderfully happy. But don't go changing the subject. Promise me you'll give some thought to this," she urged, leaning forward to clasp Nora's hand across the table. "If there's a problem with finances, you know Father or I would be more than happy to help. For that matter, we could send one of the day girls over for a few weeks."

Nora had a certain strength, a quiet dignity about her that often went unnoticed because of her retiring nature. But there was no mistaking it now. "You and your father have done far too much for us as it is, Sara," she said firmly. "Please don't think me ungrateful—I can't think what would have become of us without you and Mr. Farmington. But Evan and I want to make our own way from now on, don't you see? Besides, one day, when Evan can send for his money in England, things will be easier for us."

"What money in England?" Sara stopped, embarrassed by her own bluntness. "I'm sorry—that's none of my business, of course."

Nora waved off her apology. "When Evan was employed in London, he managed to accumulate some savings. But after going against his employer's instructions and helping us get away—well, he fears some sort of retaliation if his whereabouts were to be discovered. That's why he's made no attempt to contact the bank before now."

"But couldn't Evan's father get the money and send it to you?"

Nora's expression clouded. "Evan thought of that as well. In fact, he wrote to his father about it some months past. But Mr. Whittaker has been too poorly to manage the trip to London."

Not wanting to press, Sara said nothing further. But she had already decided to take the subject up with her father at the first opportunity. He was fond of declaring that he couldn't get along without his British assistant, that the man was invaluable to him. Sara thought this might be a good time to remind him of Evan's usefulness—and suggest a raise in salary. A *generous* raise. Perhaps then Nora would be more open to taking on help.

In the meantime, she would ask Nicholas Grafton to make a call. He could drop by on the pretense of checking baby Teddy, but surely when he got a look at Nora, he'd insist on examing *her*, too.

If there was one thing Quinn O'Shea despised with a vengeance, it was sewing. For as long as she could remember, she had been all thumbs with a needle.

Although she had never voiced her suspicions, she expected the reason for her clumsiness with the sewing had to do with her eyesight. Close work had ever been a bother to her, for such things as tiny stitches and fine patterns seemed to blur and run together.

In spite of her protests to Miss Crane, however, Quinn had spent almost the entire time since her arrival at the Shelter—close on three months now—hunched over a stack of shirts, stitching buttonholes and shirt cuffs. Her fingers were pricked raw from her clumsiness with the needle, and her eyes watered and burned incessantly.

Today she was finding the sewing particularly difficult, what with the room being dim and gray from yet another rainy afternoon. Her stomach knotted with bitterness as she jabbed the needle through the shirt front she'd been working on.

She had hoped to catch a glimpse of the ladies touring the Shelter today, on the chance that the society widow, Mrs. Deshler, might be among them. Quinn was almost certain she had sensed a hint of kindness in the woman's eyes that night back in July, in the Bowery—a kindness she could appeal to, if given the chance.

Somehow, she must make known the truth about this place they called a *Shelter*. But stuck up here in the crowded, cheerless sewing room, there was no likelihood of that ever happening, she reminded herself despairingly. Ladies from the various missionary societies never visited the third floor.

No doubt, there would be some questions to answer if they *did*. Crowded with eight women—two of whom were in advanced stages of their pregnancies—the narrow sewing room would have been cramped with four. It was dimly lighted by only two flickering candles at each end, and cold and damp in the late September chill.

When she first arrived at the Shelter, Miss Crane had set her to work in the kitchen, which suited Quinn just fine. She had always been fairly handy with food, and if Mrs. Cunnington, the cook, had not turned out to be such an old shrew, the work might even have proved enjoyable.

On Quinn's third day in the kitchen, however, the hatchet-faced Miss Crane had relieved her of her duties, assigning her instead to the sewing room upstairs. Quinn's objections were met with the terse statement that "Miss Cunnington is disturbed by your cough. She feels it might be unhealthy for a consumptive to be handling the food."

"*Consumptive?*" Quinn had shouted. "I'm not *consumptive*! I have a cold, 'tis all!"

The administrator had fixed her with a look of such distaste that for an instant Quinn felt as if she were, indeed, diseased. Recovering, she informed Miss Crane that since she had planned to leave by the end of the week all along, she might just as well be on her way immediately.

To her amazement, Ethelda Crane proceeded to inform her that it would be "quite impossible" for Quinn to go just yet, that she would be required to stay on until she had "paid her debts."

"*Debts?* What debts?" Quinn demanded, stunned by the woman's remark. "I have no debts!"

The other's thin lips curved slightly in the mockery of a smile. "To the contrary, Miss. You owe us for two days' room and board, not to mention the expenses incurred for your medical treatment."

Quinn seethed anew at the memory of that confrontation. The *medical treatment* to which Miss Crane had referred had been some weak tea with a drop of camphor! She had seen no surgeon, received no medication whatsoever. Medical treatment, indeed!

In spite of the ridiculous allegations, Quinn had stayed. Miss Crane's final thrust had been too frightening to ignore. "Penniless immigrants who cannot pay their debts find themselves in jail in *this* country, Miss. Either you stay for a full month hence, or I shall turn you over to the authorities."

So Quinn had stayed on, forcing herself to hold her tongue about the blatant injustices and unfair treatment that went on at the Shelter. Determined to "serve her time" and be done with the place, she followed the rules and worked hard, without complaining.

But when the month finally drew to an end, she was told that she had incurred "new debts" which must be paid. The threat of jail was once again hung out to her.

This time Quinn exploded in rage, making a few threats of her own. In the midst of her outburst, however, Ethelda Crane quietly produced what appeared to be a detailed list of Quinn's current obligations. To an unsuspecting eye, the list would seem to prove that Quinn's meager "wages" in no way covered her considerable expenses.

Quinn was not one to give up easily, but the threat of being locked up was the one thing that could intimidate her. More than anything else, she feared imprisonment.

She had left Ireland to avoid a cell. It made no difference at all that Millen Jupe would have beat her to a bloody pulp if she hadn't knifed him. He had meant to kill her, and that was the truth. She had acted only to save herself. But the authorities would not have listened to a word of defense on her behalf. In their eyes she was naught but a strumpet—a *murdering* strumpet. It would have been the hanging tree for certain, had they caught her.

She could not bear the thought that she might have escaped one prison cell only to land in another!

And so, months after her arrival, she was still caught—as were the other residents of the Shelter—in a seemingly hopeless, inescapable trap.

Meanwhile, she had grown to detest Ethelda Crane as she had never disliked another human being in her life, except for Millen Jupe. Her bitter feelings toward the woman had begun to fester that first night at the Shelter. Even then Quinn had sensed that the seemingly virtuous Miss Crane might turn out to be more foe than friend to someone like herself.

Time, she now acknowledged wearily, had proved her instincts sound.

How she wished she had heeded those instincts from the beginning! Had she known then the ugly truth about the Chatham Charity Women's Shelter, she would never have allowed that smooth-talking policeman to send her here.

Although the place was altogether miserable and grim, apparently it had once been the fine home of a wealthy Dutch family. But that had been many years ago, and there was little left to suggest its past elegance. The wall coverings had long since faded, and the few remaining pieces of furniture looked tired and outdated. To Quinn, it seemed a bleak, inhospitable place with not a single cheering attribute to mark it as anyone's home. Indeed, sometimes it seemed little better than the prison she was so determined to avoid.

The first thing required of any roomer was to give up her own clothing—right down to her petticoat, if she had one—in exchange for an ugly, shapeless brown dress. "We adopt a practical, modest attire here," Miss Crane was fond of saying when a new resident attempted to hold on to her own apparel. "We do not conform to the world."

The place was supposed to house women down on their luck, but in reality most of the residents were young girls, some mere children of nine or ten. Others arrived "in disgrace," as Miss Crane referred to their situation: unmarried mothers-to-be who had no recourse but to seek charity.

The few mature women who did board at the Shelter worked outside, at the factories, while the younger girls cleaned and cooked, or else took in piecework from the shirt mills to earn their keep. No one was allowed to keep even a small part of her pay, but instead was required to turn each week's wages over to Miss Crane, to pay for their "board," or, in the case of the expectant mothers, to accumulate for "forthcoming medical expenses."

Even the pregnant girls worked until they were ready to drop. Nobody rested until bedtime, and they were hauled out well before dawn the next morning.

On the rare occasion when one of the newer residents ventured to protest, she was threatened—as Quinn had been—with immediate expulsion to a police workhouse or a jail cell for "unlawful indigents."

Ethelda Crane frequently reminded her charges that "idle hands are the devil's workshop," and that "she who does not work, does not eat."

It seemed to Quinn that the long-nosed administrator did little enough work herself, other than when she whipped through the building with a flock of society ladies in tow. These were usually from one of the big city churches uptown, interested in seeing the fruits of their financial support. All residents were warned ahead of time that there was to be no conversation during these excursions, and no reply to questions other than a simple yes or no.

There were few questions, of course. On those rare times when she had been downstairs during a tour, Quinn had not missed the fact that most of the finely dressed women flouncing through the halls, while duly impressed by the Shelter's "cleanliness and order," displayed little if any interest in the residents themselves.

And why would the place *not* be clean and tidy? Ethelda Crane seemed obsessed with "cleanliness and order." Let the woman spot so much as a fleck of dust or a ball of lint, and didn't she act as though a mortal sin had been committed?

Oh, she was a strange one, was Ethelda Crane! According to Ivy Meeks, the one truly close friend Quinn had made at the Shelter, Miss Crane was a devout Christian lady, a spinster woman who had been administrator for nearly four years. Apparently, she was a loyal member of a small congregation who met in each other's homes. Their leader was a man they called "Brother Will."

The entire group had come to hold services at the Shelter once since Quinn had been there. They seemed a fiercely religious bunch, just as sour as Miss Crane, every last one of them, except for Brother Will. A big man, with a full head of curly gray hair and a great wide mouth of white teeth, he often flashed a smile that Quinn noticed was not reflected in his eyes.

He appeared pious enough, leading the services in the parlor with loud prayers, even weeping as he pleaded for souls of the "lost." At first Quinn couldn't figure what there was about the man that gave her the shivers, until she realized that he had a look about his eyes that was familiar.

She had seen that glint before, in the eyes of Millen Jupe. It was the look of a falcon set on his prey.

Ivy shared Quinn's doubts about Brother Will. In truth, she and Ivy shared many of the same feelings. Had it not been for her new friend, Quinn would have been unbearably lonely, for most of the women seemed either silent and embittered, or too timid to develop close friendships.

Ivy was just a year younger than Quinn—sixteen—and had come up to the city with her folks from Pennsylvania. They were farm people, Ivy explained, who had lost their homestead when the illness of her younger brother drained the family's resources. Despite their efforts, the little boy had died, and Ivy's father decided to pull up roots and move to the city to find work.

A month later he was dead of the influenza, leaving Ivy and her mother, who was expecting another child, on their own in the city. The two of them came to the Shelter at the recommendation of a street mission worker. When her mother died giving birth to a stillborn child, Ivy could think of nothing else to do but stay on.

Ivy was a pretty, lively girl with fair hair and a quick smile. She worked days at a shirt factory; evenings, after performing her chores about the Shelter, she stole off by herself to study her reading. Her daddy had taught her the little he knew, she told Quinn. "But I'm going to learn more, as much as I can, so I'll make a good impression when I apply for service."

As a rule, Quinn divulged little about herself. But seeing the younger girl struggle night after night, she finally offered to help.

"I can read a streak," she told Ivy somewhat gruffly. "It'll be no trouble to teach you."

Millen Jupe had taught her to read, early in her employment at the Big House, before he turned mean. She told Ivy nothing of this, of course, nor did she let on how it strained her eyes to make out the words. Ivy's gratitude for her help was so childlike, so eager, that Quinn would not have spoiled her pleasure for anything. Didn't the girl have little enough to smile over?

Didn't they all?

Quinn wished Ivy were here with her now. Perhaps they could have given each other the courage to sneak downstairs.

She felt a growing urgency to try *something*. What if the Widow Deshler were here in the building, right at this very moment?

Disregarding the possible consequences of her behavior, Quinn suddenly flung the shirt from her lap onto the rickety table near the window. As she started toward the door, Marjorie Gleeson looked up. "Where are you going?"

"I am going to be sick," Quinn said, not stopping.

It was the first thing she had thought of to say, but as she hurried out the door and down the dim hallway, she wondered if she might not live up to the lie. Now that she had set her head to making a move, the full import of her decision washed over her.

Her stomach heaved, but she went on. Below her, from the hallway, came the muffled voices of women. Quinn gripped the banister, took a deep, steadying breath, and started down the stairs.

22

The Space Between

The innocent and the beautiful
Have no enemy but time....
W.B. YEATS (1865–1939)

Late in the afternoon, long after Sara had gone, Nora awoke with a start. She was dismayed to realize she had actually fallen into a sound sleep while nursing the baby. Sweet angel that he was, Teddy dozed contentedly at her breast, but the idea that she could drift off so easily with him in her arms—and while sitting upright in a chair—disturbed her.

Carefully, so as not to wake the baby, she fastened her bodice and got to her feet. The room tilted, and she had to wait an instant for her head to clear before taking the baby down the hall to his crib.

Teddy barely stirred as she tucked him in. For a moment, Nora bent over the crib, gazing down at him. The delicate perfection of her infant son never ceased to fascinate her. She delighted in his round little face, rosy-cheeked and smooth, the tiny hands that reached for her so quickly, the light down of hair that framed his features.

Straightening, she glanced across the room. The high double bed suddenly looked all too inviting, and she longed to lie down, just for a bit. But there were the dishes to do, and didies to fold, supper to start—

Time. There was never enough of it these days. It seemed that even the smallest task required great effort, wearing her down long before she could finish all that needed doing.

Without warning, the weariness that often came over her of late now enfolded her like a shroud. Lightheaded, she felt her heart give a sickening lurch, then begin to hammer against her chest.

Forgetting the work that awaited her, she crossed the room and sank down onto the bed. She had time, she told herself. She would have a short nap before Evan came home. That was all she needed…just a short nap.

She lay back, feeling as if she were sinking to the bottom of the mattress, her ears roaring as if the very sea raced through her head. Only in the vaguest sense was she aware of a familiar, dull pain spreading across her rib cage. Soon she drifted off into the peaceful darkness of sleep.

Sara stood, pretending to listen to the exchange between Ethelda Crane and some of the other women in the group. In actuality, she was trying to sort out her feelings about the Shelter's administrator.

Because she rarely took an instant dislike to anyone, she tried to convince herself that *dislike* might be too strong a word. All the same, she had to acknowledge that her response to Miss Crane was extremely negative—and puzzling.

The woman seemed to be everything she had been touted to be: virtuous, courteous, pious—above reproach. As for the Shelter itself, Sara thought it might serve as a model of efficiency for other similar endeavors throughout the city. Impeccably clean and almost severe in its order, the building and entire operation—at least what she had seen of it so far—would appear to be under the supervision of a highly competent manager. The few residents they had encountered—young women, mostly—had looked healthy and decently groomed, although Sara found their uniform brown dress demeaning. The aromas from the kitchen were inviting, and the tables in the dining hall were set with good quality, if institutional, dinnerware.

In spite of the overall appearance of a well-oiled operation, however, Sara could not shake the feeling that something wasn't quite right. It was a bit like passing one's fingers over an expertly crafted painting while sensing all the while that just beneath the surface lay an entirely different picture.

More unsettling still was the fact that Ethelda Crane gave her exactly the same feeling.

As she watched the tall, sharp-featured administrator field questions from the women's group, it occurred to Sara that their guided tour had seemed rather too brisk thus far, perhaps too tightly structured. Some rooms—indeed, entire areas of the building—had been ignored without any explanation. It was clear from the exterior that there were three levels, yet Miss Crane had made no mention of the third floor. Instead, she had brought their excursion to a halt after showing them the second-story dormitories, leading them back downstairs to entertain their questions.

Sara waited until Miss Crane replied to Helen Preston's query about food and medical supplies before venturing a question of her own. "What about the third floor?" she asked, stepping forward a little. "Is that dormitory space as well?"

Ethelda Crane turned to her. Sara noticed that, although the woman did not meet her eyes when she answered, the deferential manner she had adopted throughout the tour never slipped. "No, the third floor is reserved as a work area for some of the residents, and for extra storage as we may happen to need it."

"Oh, what sort of work is that? I thought most of the residents were employed outside the Shelter."

Sara was genuinely curious; she hadn't meant to press. But the look of annoyance that passed over Ethelda Crane's features plainly said that she found the question inappropriate.

"Those who aren't able to work outside the Shelter do sewing and other piecework upstairs." Her tone clearly communicated dismissal. The subject was closed.

But Sara wasn't to be dismissed so easily. "I'm not sure I understand. What prevents them from working elsewhere?"

Miss Crane seemed to be maintaining her patience at great effort. Sara merely waited, holding the woman's gaze.

"A number of the...unfortunates are in the family way, and we do not encourage them to flaunt their condition in public." Tight-lipped, the administrator went on. "Then, too, a great many of them are Irish, and therefore are considered undesirable in the workplace. They encounter great difficulty in finding outside employment."

"Yes, so I've been told," Sara said evenly.

Helen Preston, standing nearby, cleared her throat. Two of the other women in the group darted uncomfortable looks in Sara's direction.

"I'm sure you've seen the signs posted throughout the city," continued

Ethelda Crane. "None of the respectable businesses will hire the Irish, so we have to resort to whatever means we can to help them earn their keep."

"Indeed," Sara managed. "It must be very difficult for you."

Warming to her subject, Ethelda Crane continued. "Oh, well, one can hardly blame the merchants, can one? Not only are the Irish altogether ignorant, they're often diseased. And, of course, they can't be trusted. They've no morals at all." She sighed. "I can't think why we allowed them entrance to the country in the first place, with their filth and disease and pagan ways. The city is infested with them already, and they're still coming."

Out of the corner of her eye, Sara saw Helen Preston, always slightly flushed, turn positively crimson, her upper lip dotted with nervous perspiration.

Sara drew in a deep breath, one hand knotted at her waist, the other clenched at her side. "But how extraordinarily charitable of you," she managed to grate out, "to take them in, feeling as you do."

At that moment she saw Ethelda Crane's eyes cut upward, then flash with anger. Sara turned to follow the direction of the woman's gaze.

A young girl stood about halfway down the stairs. Her large, dark eyes were riveted on the Shelter's administrator in a look that seemed to reflect both apprehension and defiance.

Sara glanced from one to the other, and her instincts snapped to attention at the expression on Ethelda Crane's face. She was sure she saw a crack in the armor. At that moment there was no mistaking the blistering fury that contorted the woman's features.

Miss Crane's words cracked like a pistol shot. "What is it, Miss?"

Sara heard a world of contempt in her use of *Miss*. For an instant, the girl appeared uncertain, and Sara thought she might simply turn and run. But then her chin lifted, and she came the rest of the way down the stairs, stopping at the landing.

"I was feeling sick to my stomach, ma'am, and thought to go to the infirmary."

The brogue was thick, the voice surprisingly firm. Sara studied the girl who had aroused such an unexpectedly strong reaction from Ethelda Crane. She decided she didn't look at all ill. The face was unusual: delicately molded, yet sharply defined, with a firm jaw that stopped just short of being square, and a light, tawny-shaded complexion, flawless except for a few freckles that danced over the nose. It wasn't quite a pretty face in the conventional sense, but held a singular attractiveness that was compelling in one so young,

And she *was* young, Sara was certain. In spite of the air of strength and the keen look of intelligence that burned out of those wonderful eyes, she doubted the girl could be more than sixteen or seventeen at the most.

Puzzled, Sara watched the girl scan the group of visitors as if she half-expected to find a familiar face.

"You are excused to the infirmary," Ethelda Crane said. "But return to your work once you're feeling better."

The girl gave a distracted nod, her gaze now darting from one face in the group to the other, as if she were still intent on finding someone she knew.

"I *said*, you are excused, Miss." The administrator's tone would have frozen a hot coal.

Sara wondered at the look of disappointment that crossed the girl's features. For an instant their eyes met. Sara found herself smiling, feeling an inexplicable desire to make contact.

Something flickered in the other's eyes, and Sara acted on impulse. "Miss Crane? If this young lady wouldn't mind, I think we'd all be interested in hearing a firsthand account about the Shelter from one of its residents."

The administrator turned toward her, slowly, and Sara felt the resentment in those depthless eyes like a blow. She actually took a step backward.

Recovering, Sara repeated her request, this time with more emphasis, adding, "Perhaps she has suggestions as to ways our women's group might be of more help to the Shelter's residents."

Some of the other women murmured their agreement, and Sara turned her attention to the girl, who was now regarding her with obvious astonishment.

"Another time, perhaps," said Miss Crane. The look she turned on Sara was smug. "As you heard, Miss O'Shea is feeling ill."

"Just one or two questions," Sara countered, turning to the girl. "If you're up to it, that is?"

The full mouth curved faintly in a somewhat wry expression, as if to concede that Sara had found her out, that she wasn't really ill at all.

"Aye, ma'am. Ask what you will."

Sara moved a little closer. "What's your name, dear?"

"Quinn O'Shea, ma'am. Anna Quinn O'Shea, but I'm called Quinn."

"What a lovely name. You're Irish, aren't you?"

The strong, firm jaw tightened even more. "I am."

"So is my husband," Sara said mildly, glancing only for a fraction of a second in Ethelda Crane's direction. She had the satisfaction of seeing the woman gape at her in amazement.

Quinn O'Shea eyed Sara with disbelief. "Your husband—is *Irish*, ma'am?"

Sara nodded, smiling. "My name is Mrs. Burke. How did you happen to come to the Shelter, Quinn?"

The girl regarded Sara as if to measure her sincerity, then darted a quick glance at Ethelda Crane. "Well, ma'am, what brought me here was that I had nowhere else to go. I was just off the boat, don't you see, and was looking for a position when these two no-account—"

"A police officer rescued Miss O'Shea from an attack in the Bowery," interrupted Ethelda Crane. "He placed her in our care and asked us to look after her."

Sensing the tension in the girl, Sara resumed her questioning even more gently. "How long have you been here, Quinn?"

"Nearly three months, ma'am."

"So long?" Sara hesitated. "Are you employed somewhere nearby?"

The girl looked surprised. "Why...no, ma'am. I work right here, at the sewing."

"She was ill when she arrived," Ethelda Crane put in abruptly. "We feared she might be consumptive and thought it best to give her only light tasks on the premises for a time."

Quinn O'Shea flushed but remained silent.

Sara watched her. "And...are you happy here at the Shelter, Quinn?"

Something sparked in the magnificent eyes. The intensity of the girl's stare belied her mumbled reply. "*Happy*, ma'am?" Her expression hinted that Sara must be slightly mad to ask such a thing.

There was a long silence. Uncomfortable beneath that defiant stare, Sara could not quite think what to say.

Ethelda Crane broke in. "If you're still feeling ill, Miss O'Shea," she said, her tone clearly indicating she didn't believe the girl, "I would suggest that you go on to the infirmary."

The girl's eyes clung to Sara for another instant before she finally turned away and walked slowly down the hall toward the back of the building.

As she watched her go, the slender back rigidly straight in the shapeless brown dress, Sara felt a sudden wave of compassion—and a kind of respect—sweep over her. She found herself unduly curious about Quinn O'Shea. Why had she stayed here so long? What was her story?

Inexplicably, she shivered. No doubt every woman and child in this bleak place had a story. Sara could not help but wonder how many of those stories had been woven from the fabric of broken dreams or tragedy.

Something told her that Quinn O'Shea's story had been formed of both.

23

Closed Doors

I close the book;
But the past slides out of its leaves to haunt me
And it seems wherever I look,
Phantoms of irreclaimable happiness taunt me.

C. DAY-LEWIS (1904–1972)

Quinn raged at herself all the way down the hall. *Why,* when she had finally found a chance to speak out—why had she held her silence? *Because she had lost her nerve, that's why....*

If only there had not been so many of them. Perhaps if the lady with the kind eyes and gentle voice had been alone...and if Miss Crane had not hovered so...

She wanted to strike out at herself. She wanted to weep. Her one opportunity, and she had spoiled it! And who could say when, if ever, she might have another chance.

It was just that she had been overwhelmed by them all, with their fine hats and fancy suits—and herself standing there on exhibition, in the hideous brown dress, looking like an inmate from a madhouse. *And there had been the unmistakable warning in Ethelda Crane's stare....*

Seeing the closed door of the infirmary straight ahead, Quinn hesitated, then went on. She would have to put in an appearance after her ridiculous tale about being ill. Miss Crane had not believed her for a moment, of course—the woman was the devil to fool. Still, it was best to go on with the act, though she knew that things would only go harder for her now.

She stopped just before she reached the door. Tears of self disgust and anger scalded her eyes, and she brushed them away with an angry swipe.

Quinn wished she had never come to this wretched place. She wished that she had never separated from Bobby Dempsey, and—

Suddenly she stopped. *Bobby!* She had been so caught up in her own misery that she had nearly forgotten about Bobby. Dear, gentle Bobby. He would be concerned about her, sure, would no doubt be looking for her. By now he would have a job on the docks and a bit of money. Any day now, he might find her again and help her out of this *prison of Christian charity.*

For a moment, she found herself on the verge of praying—for Bobby, for herself, for escape. A stab of unspeakable pain knifed through her as she realized how much she missed the comfort and the peace her childhood prayers had once provided.

The pain sharpened even more as she reminded herself that any prayer she might dare to voice these days would be no more than an empty echo, bouncing off the walls of her heart. The door to heaven had been closed to her for a long time now.

Evan turned and started up the walk toward home, surprised to see no sign of light from inside. Instead of the warm, cozy glow he had come to expect at day's end, he found the house dark. Instead of Nora standing in the doorway with a welcoming smile, he was greeted only by a closed door.

Inside the house, a vague uneasiness began to spread over him, especially when he called her name and received no reply. He glanced into the parlor first, then started toward the kitchen.

It was too early for Daniel to be home, of course. He seldom left the doctor's office before seven. But where was everyone else?

Definitely apprehensive by now, he hurried down the dark hallway. There was no one in the kitchen.

"Nora?" He stopped just inside the door of their bedroom, surprised to see her lying on the bed, apparently sound asleep. In a chair between the bed and the crib sat Johanna, as if keeping watch. The only light in the room came from the window, where the last faint glow of evening was giving way to encroaching darkness.

Evan glanced toward the crib, where the baby lay, wide awake, making small sounds of contentment.

Johanna's eyes filled with relief at the sight of him. Immediately, she put a finger to her lips, as if to caution him that Nora was sleeping.

Frowning, he went and sat down on the edge of the bed, taking Nora's hand. She stirred a little, then turned onto her back.

Her eyes opened, and for a moment she seemed confused. "Evan?" Her hand went to her throat. "Why are you—" She broke off, glancing over at the baby and Johanna. "What time is it?"

Evan withdrew his hand from hers, fished in his vest pocket, and snapped open his watch. "N-nearly six." He bent to kiss her, and when he drew back he thought her eyes looked slightly swollen. "Nora? Are you all right?"

"*Six?*" Tossing the quilt off her legs, she scrambled up from the bed.

Evan saw her sway on her feet and rose to steady her. "Nora! What is it? Are you ill?"

"I'm not," she insisted, shaking her head. "I just got up too quickly, is all. I can't think what came over me, to sleep so long, and in the middle of the day!"

"You were up with Teddy late in the n-night," Evan reminded her. "I'm glad you m-managed a rest." Still holding on to her arm, he continued to study her. "Are you quite certain you're all right?"

She nodded, kissing him lightly on the cheek. "You didn't know you married such a slugabed, I'm sure." Starting for the crib, she paused long enough to touch Johanna's hair. "And weren't you good, to watch over Teddy while I slept, *alannah*."

Taking up the baby, she shot Evan a look of dismay. "I haven't even started the supper yet! Oh, Evan, I'm so sorry, and you home from working all day—"

"Nora, *will* you stop fussing!" Going to take the baby from her, he was struck by how exhausted she appeared, even though she had just awakened. Not for the first time, he wished they could afford some extra domestic help for her, at least until Teddy was older. She was simply not regaining her strength as she should.

"I'm sure we'll be n-none the worse for a late meal now and then," he said firmly, adding, "You go along and get things started. I'll entertain Teddy."

Still she hesitated. "He needs changing…"

"Yes, I can see that," Evan said dryly, still smiling. "Johanna can help m-me."

He recognized the brief look of uncertainty that passed over Nora's features as she left the room. Johanna's continued resistance to handling the baby was a concern and a disappointment to them both. Although the girl was as eager as ever to help Nora with anything else about the house, she stopped short at direct contact with little Teddy. She would watch over him in his crib, would stand nearby and assist with changing or dressing, but she simply refused to pick him up or handle him in any way.

It was obvious that she was determined not to form any sort of real attachment to the newest member of the household. Yet, Evan had seen the longing in her face when she thought no one was looking—an unmistakable desire to hold the baby.

He thought he understood, and it grieved him no end. Johanna was still blaming herself for Little Tom's death. The entire family had done their utmost to convince the girl she was not at fault, that she must not hold herself responsible for what had been, in fact, a tragic accident.

But Johanna had borne the responsibility of looking after her little brother for so long that Evan suspected she would have held herself accountable, whatever the circumstances of Tom's death had been. Months had passed, but the girl was obviously still grieving for her baby brother, still condemning herself for his death.

Her attitude toward Teddy as much as confirmed it. Evan wondered if this…this *distancing* of herself from the baby might not be her way, at least for now, of dealing with her feelings of loss and guilt.

It struck him that she might also be *afraid* to take care of Teddy. Perhaps she feared another accident, in which, at least to her way of reasoning, she would again be to blame. The girl had lost her entire family, after all. Wasn't it understandable that she might temporarily withdraw from a close relationship with another child, perhaps as a way of protecting herself from still even loss?

Even Daniel, to whom Johanna had always been able to turn when confused or troubled, no longer seemed able to comfort her. It was as if she had closed the door on herself and refused to open it to anyone.

He was keenly aware of Johanna's quiet presence beside him as he clumsily attempted to change the baby with his one hand. She moved to help, but carefully avoided Teddy's wide-eyed scrutiny.

For a moment, a wave of pity for the girl almost overwhelmed Evan. She was little more than a child herself, twelve years old, living in a silent world where grief and guilt could grow unchecked. He could not imagine the crushing pain in her troubled heart, could not help but wonder how long it might be before that young heart broke beneath the enormous burden she was trying to carry alone.

Johanna tried not to look directly at Teddy as she helped Uncle Evan with the changing. Even though the baby seemed intent on staring up at her and smiling, she pretended not to notice. And when her hands ached to reach for him and bring him close against her heart, she simply clenched them that much tighter.

She didn't understand the rush of warmth that coursed through her every time the baby waved his tiny fists in her direction, and she did her utmost to ignore it. But sometimes...like now...when he lay staring up at her in seeming fascination, the desire to pick him up was almost more than she could bear.

She knew she was disappointing Aunt Nora and Uncle Evan by refusing to hold their new baby. She had seen the looks that passed between them when they thought she didn't notice.

It was just that they didn't understand. How could they? They had not been there that day when Little Tom was carried from the pond, his wee body limp and lifeless. How could they possibly understand what she had felt at that moment...what she had been feeling ever since?

It had been her fault, her fault entirely. Had she not grown so impatient with him, lost track of time, forgotten him—oh, dear Jesus, forgive her—she had *forgotten* him, her own little brother!

Didn't they realize why she could not care for Teddy? Didn't they know that something awful might happen *again*? And just see how they loved him! They had forgiven her for Little Tom's death—he had not been their own, after all—but, sure, they would *never* forgive her if anything should happen to their Teddy! Just as she could never forgive *herself* for not having saved Little Tom.

This, then, would be her penance for neglecting her own brother—and a means of making sure she could never hurt the new baby boy. She would not allow herself to become fond of him or attached to him, not at all.

It was a terrible fierce hurt, when she wanted so much to be his big sister. It would be a fine thing to have a little brother to play with and look after again.

Perhaps if she accepted her penance and tried her utmost to be entirely responsible from now on, the Lord Jesus would forgive her. Perhaps she would even come to forgive herself, and eventually, to trust herself with little Teddy.

Of course, by then Teddy might no longer need—or want—a big sister.

Late that evening, Sergeant Denny Price was standing at the station desk, scanning a number of police reports for the preceding week when he came across the name *Dempsey, B.* It sounded vaguely familiar, but he couldn't think why. He went on reading, then stopped. His eyes went back up the page to rest on the name and the statistics that followed:

> *Dempsey, B., longshoreman. Accidental death from head injury while loading freight.*

Denny frowned over the entry, suddenly remembering the Irish girl he had come upon in the Bowery some months back, the feisty one who had been looking for her friend. Hadn't the friend's name been *Dempsey?*

Sure, that was it. *Bobby Dempsey.* The girl had fairly begged Denny to try to find this Dempsey fellow, to let him know where she would be staying. And he had asked after the man during the next day or two. When he learned nothing, however, it had slipped his mind shortly thereafter.

More than likely, this was the fellow. Too bad. The lass had looked as if she could use a friend.

What had she called herself? He rubbed his chin, searching his memory. *O'Shea,* he thought. Aye, that was it: *Quinn O'Shea.*

Poor lass. Whoever this Dempsey character had been, the girl had called him her *friend.* Denny hoped by now Quinn O'Shea had found herself another friend, for wasn't it hard enough as it was, being Irish and strange to America, without having to go it alone? And herself such a wee thing, at that.

Perhaps he ought to look her up, just so she'd know. But she wouldn't likely be at the Shelter after all this time, and those places seldom kept account of anyone's whereabouts once they'd gone. Still, next time he was in the Bowery, perhaps he would just stop by and inquire.

24

To Face the Dragon

Consumption has no pity
For blue eyes and golden hair.

RICHARD D'ALTON WILLIAMS (1822–1862)

Daniel Kavanagh swallowed hard, looking on in misery at the exchange taking place between Dr. Grafton and Elizabeth Ward, a widow and young mother who was slowly dying of consumption.

At one time, Mrs. Ward had obviously been quite beautiful, before the killing disease had so mercilessly ravaged that beauty. She had delicate, perfectly balanced features, large blue eyes, and a full cascade of dark blond hair. There was a way about the woman that spoke of a genteel, sensitive nature. But her body was now wasted, her skin dry and flushed with fever, and her refined voice often thin and strained.

Mrs. Ward no longer came to the mission clinic on a regular basis. These days her visits were sporadic. Usually she brought her baby daughter with her, but today she had left the child with a neighbor. "I have a responsibility to little Amanda that depends upon your answer to my question," she had told Dr. Grafton. "I would not tax your kindness to the extreme, Doctor, for you have been most generous already with your concern and your time. But I simply must have an idea from you as to how long I may expect to live so that I can make arrangements for my little girl in advance of the end."

Even Dr. Grafton, who, according to his own admission, had seen "about all there is to see of sorrow in this city of broken hearts," was obviously shaken by the woman's directness.

Daniel had been at the clinic the day Elizabeth Ward calmly related her background to Dr. Grafton. The daughter of a wealthy English barrister and his wife, she had left her home and family to wed an Irish stable hand employed on the estate. Her mother was deceased by then, and her father, still living, had disowned her entirely. Daniel still remembered the look in her eyes that day when she told Dr. Grafton, "I am as good as dead to my father."

Apparently the husband had succumbed to typhus only weeks after their arrival in America, and not long after that, their child—now thirteen months old—had been born. The young widow had been forced to take in piecework at their flat, earning not nearly enough to pay the rent and buy food as well. Charity from one of the Mulberry Street missions helped them survive, but barely.

By then the young mother was consumptive and had been failing steadily ever since. To Daniel, she seemed a very brave woman who appeared to be reconciled to her coming death, although greatly concerned for her child's future.

"Surely if you write to your father," Dr. Grafton was saying to her now, "he will relent. From your own account, little Amanda is his only grandchild."

Looking dangerously fragile and extremely ill, Mrs. Ward sat without moving on a straight wooden chair. "Yes," she said, nodding sadly, "that's true. And I have written to my father, Doctor—many times, in fact—but he has never once answered my letters. My father isn't a heartless man, Dr. Grafton, not really. But he is a very stubborn man, and I disappointed his hopes for me."

The thought seemed to distress her, and the doctor moved to put a gentle hand to her shoulder. "Is there any way I can help you, Mrs. Ward? Anything I can do?"

As Daniel watched, the young widow drew a deep breath, as if to calm herself. "You can tell me the truth, Doctor. Please. I must know how long."

Dr. Grafton studied her for a moment, then nodded and straightened. "You understand, of course, that all I can do is tell you what I think. There's no way in the world to be exact."

By now, Daniel had come to know his employer for a tenderhearted, compassionate man, and he had no doubt that this was extremely difficult for him.

When Dr. Grafton finally spoke again, his tone was low and almost apologetic. "In my estimation…you can expect a few weeks. Perhaps as long as two months." He paused, and Daniel sensed the conflict taking place inside the man. "I'm so sorry, Mrs. Ward. I truly am."

The young widow appeared remarkably serene in the face of such an appalling pronouncement. She raised her head and even managed a faint smile. "Thank you, Doctor. I had to know. And now, I must ask you for one more kindness, in addition to those you've already extended to me."

Dr. Grafton inclined his head. "You've only to ask, my dear."

"As I told you, I've had no reply—not a single one—to my letters. I do believe, however, that if my father were to receive a message in a strange hand, with a respectable address from a professional like yourself, he might not be so quick to disregard it. I was wondering if you'd mind terribly… if you would write to him…just a brief note to explain my circumstances and tell him about Amanda. Ask him if—" She broke off, covering her face with her hands. For the first time, she seemed overwhelmed by the hopelessness of her situation.

Daniel thought she would break down entirely. But after a moment, she looked up and, with visible force of will, went on with her request. "Ask him if he would consider taking Amanda in and raising her. Not because of me, I wouldn't expect that. He will never forgive me for the way I hurt him. But she *is* his only grandchild—my brother is unmarried— and I know he would grow to love Amanda in no time at all if he would only make the effort. Would you do that for me, please, Dr. Grafton?"

"Of course I will," the doctor replied quietly. "I'll make a note of the address before you leave and write to him this very night."

After Mrs. Ward had gone, Daniel and Dr. Grafton stood looking at each other, neither speaking for a long time. Finally, the doctor let out a weary sigh. "She is quite a courageous young woman, isn't she? These things defy all understanding. I must confess that a patient like Elizabeth Ward tests my faith to the extreme."

Daniel looked at him in surprise. The physician rarely ventured comments of a personal nature.

For a while they worked in silence, collecting instruments and supplies, then packing them in the doctor's medical case.

"It strikes me," Dr. Grafton finally said, "that it must take a supreme act of grace on God's part to keep a doctor from becoming either mortally cynical or altogether mad. The peculiar thing is that my faith in Infinite goodness seems to have grown in direct proportion to the tragic cases I've encountered over the years."

Daniel found himself intensely interested in the doctor's words. He struggled almost daily with anger and unanswered questions about Little Tom's accident. For some reason, he had found this latest sorrow even more difficult to accept than the tragic deaths in his own family.

He wondered if it wasn't partly because of Johanna. Little Tom's death had devastated her, and she seemed as sad and as lost today as when it happened. Everything was so much harder for Johanna, living in her silent world, so out of touch with others. Her ongoing grief was a torturous thing to watch, and somehow seemed to fuel Daniel's own frustration.

He looked up to find Dr. Grafton watching him. "I'm not sure I understand what you mean, sir."

The doctor closed his medical case, then looked up. "I suppose it has to do with the idea that a man's faith grows only as it's stretched. Some would say that faith untried is no faith at all." He paused, regarding Daniel with a thoughtful look. "It's been a while since we've talked about *your* plans for medicine, son. Are you still committed to becoming a doctor?"

Daniel frowned. "I thought I was. In truth, I never hoped to do anything else. But...I confess I'm no longer certain. I can't make plans anyway, not for a time. Not with things as they are at home. They need me there for now."

Dr. Grafton nodded. "The thing is, Daniel, you really need to be thinking of going on to university soon. I've taught you just about everything I know."

Daniel didn't meet his eyes. "It will have to wait. Besides...I...I'm just not sure that I really want to spend my life dealing with tragedy."

Again the doctor gave a nod. "Certainly I'd be the last to pretend it's an easy life. Yet, for some of us, it's the *only* life. And you know, Daniel, for all the tragedy and disappointments, it's also a fulfilling life." He stopped, and for a moment his thoughts seemed to drift elsewhere.

Daniel hesitated, then blurted out, "Would you do it again, sir? If you were to start all over, would you become a doctor again?"

Dr. Grafton looked at him with surprise. "Why, yes, Daniel, I would. I definitely would." He paused, then went on. "Although there was a time, early in my practice, when I very nearly gave it all up."

At Daniel's look of astonishment, the doctor nodded, his expression turning pensive. "I lost half a dozen patients in the first year, three of them children under twelve, to deadly diseases and one horrifying accident. I thought I simply could not go on, pretending to be some sort of a 'healer' when in fact I felt more like a charlatan every day! All the schooling, all the training—what was it worth when it came right down to it? I couldn't even save a little girl from scarlet fever—three years old, and she died of complications. I believe I *would* have given up had it not been for a certain young woman—about the age of Elizabeth Ward."

Going to the window, now veiled with darkness, the doctor stood staring out as he continued his story. He spoke quietly, with a kind of fond remembrance, almost as if Daniel were no longer in the room. "Her name was Felicia. She was one of those golden young women who seem to bring light into any room they enter. She was lovely and bright and sunny-natured—a small woman, but one of monumental faith. Everyone who knew her adored her, with good reason.

"She had just given birth to her second little girl when we discovered the cancer."

Daniel's throat tightened. He already knew he didn't want to hear the rest of Dr. Grafton's story, yet he could not help but listen.

"It took her nearly a year to die, and it was one of the most agonizing, heartrending deaths I have ever witnessed. Everyone grieved. Even the most resolute Christian believers suddenly found themselves questioning a God who could allow a woman like Felicia to suffer such agony. Just to be in the room with her toward the end was enough to devastate the strongest man. There were times when I actually felt myself caught up and trapped inside her pain—it was that vicious. It was unbearable... simply unbearable."

He stopped, and Daniel saw the doctor's shoulders lift as he drew in a long, steadying breath. "Yet I never, in all that time, heard her utter an angry or accusing word against her God."

He turned around, and he suddenly looked much older. A veil of sorrow seemed to have slipped over his features. "I'm afraid I can't say as much for myself. I raged at God—I believe I may have even threatened Him a time or two. I expect I'm living proof of His mercy, for He could just as easily have struck me dead for my blasphemy. Perhaps He took pity on me, for I believe by then I might have been a little mad."

For a moment the doctor said nothing more, but simply stood, his hands clasped behind him, looking across the room at the chair Elizabeth Ward had recently vacated.

Slowly, then, he lifted his eyes back to Daniel. "Felicia was my wife," he said quietly.

At Daniel's sharp intake of breath, the doctor raised a hand to indicate he had not finished his story. "A few weeks after she died, I found her diary, which she had kept up until the time she was no longer able to write. It was a revelation. For all her suffering, her agony, she had written beautiful things. Her words were almost like songs of exultation. I found page after page of surprises, amazing insights and feelings that had come from her heart…her soul…things that changed forever my ideas about pain— and where *God* is in the midst of pain.

"She wrote about the Lord holding her hand, about how He carried her over the mountains and above the valleys of pain and showed her wondrous things—promised glories. There was this incomprehensible…*joy* in everything she wrote. Even when she wrote directly of the pain, she seemed to be rejoicing somewhere deep inside her, closed to the rest of us.

"One entry was written directly to me…" He faltered, wiped a hand over his eyes, then went on. "She told me how God had come to her in what she called her 'valley of pain,' how He had come close, closer than He had ever been before and lifted her up into His arms. She said He had carried her through it all, had held her so close…so very close…that she almost thought she could hear His very heartbeat."

Shaken, Daniel clung to his every word. His mother had spoken of an experience something very like what the doctor was relating after she gave birth to Teddy. She, too, had talked of the Lord "carrying" her through her pain.

Dr. Grafton looked weary and gray, but his eyes were filled with a faint glimmer of wonder as he went on. "Felicia apparently found a kind of… *glory*…in her suffering. To this day, I can't begin to comprehend what she must have experienced. But her words gave me a hope that I believe has made me a better doctor than I might have been otherwise."

He looked at Daniel. "It's my observation that you will make a fine, fine doctor, son, and I truly hope you'll pursue your dream. If I may, though, let me give you this caution, in hopes it might ease your way a bit. This is the best time—now, while you're young and life hasn't worn you down—to face the reality of pain and suffering. As a doctor, you're going to encounter horrible things, wretched, heartbreaking things. This is the time to confront that reality, not when you're caught up in the middle of an emotional storm. Face the dragon now and decide just how you intend to deal with it. It is for you to choose whether you're going to blame God for the ugliness life is sure to bring—or whether you're going to trust Him with it all and keep on going.

"For I tell you, Daniel, I am convinced that what you believe, really believe, about the Great Physician and His workings in our poor human lives will make a very real difference in the kind of physician—and the kind of man—you ultimately become."

Daniel stood staring at this man he had come to admire and trust, in whose footsteps he hoped to follow. He couldn't speak. His feelings were too overpowering, his thoughts racing in too many directions.

But he was moved almost to tears with gratitude. For somehow he knew that today, thanks to Nicholas Grafton's willingness to bare his heart, he had already faced the dragon and made his choice.

25

Portrait of a Woman

The certainty that I shall see that lady
Leaning or standing or walking
In the first loveliness of womanhood,
And with the fervour of my youthful eyes,
Has set me muttering like a fool.

W.B. YEATS (1865–1939)

Dublin
Late October

This child spends far more time in his mother's bedroom than in his nursery," Lucy observed good-naturedly as she watched Finola cuddle baby Gabriel on her lap. "He will not recognize one from the other, I'm thinking."

In the rocking chair by the window, Finola ruffled the golden head snuggled next to her heart, smiling down at her son. "He is far too small for that big drafty room, I think. Although it *is* quite grand, as nurseries go," she added. "Besides, he will be hungry soon, so I shall keep him here for now."

Lucy watched them for another moment. "Then I will take the diapers downstairs to the laundry. Do you want anything from the kitchen when I come back?"

Finola shook her head. "I am growing far too round as it is."

"Would you *listen* to the girl!" Lucy burst out, propping her hands on her hips. "For the first time in memory, she has a bit of meat on her bones, and doesn't she fret?"

Finola laughed at her. "All the same, I will have nothing from the kitchen."

After Lucy left the room, Finola nursed baby Gabriel contentedly. She treasured these times of quiet closeness with her son. And how she did adore him!

Her golden child had charmed the entire household. Except for Artegal, that is. The sour-tempered footman obviously found even a sweet baby boy only a bother.

But everyone else did dote on the new heir of Nelson Hall. His big sister, Aine, could not pass him by without a squeeze and a kiss. She picked him up so often that Lucy had taken to scolding: "The babe hasn't a chance! He will be spoiled entirely!"

Sister Louisa, however, declared that there was little likelihood of spoiling such a sweet-tempered child. "He will know himself to be cherished, so where's the harm? Just see how well he takes it all in his stride. The child is an angel."

"You see, my precious? You have captured an entire treasure of hearts for your very own!" Finola continued to affirm her son with soft reminders of how important he was to her and his family at Nelson Hall. She often carried on long conversations with the babe when they were together. She would speak to him of the day's events, discuss decisions that needed to be made, and he would rub his tiny hand along the column of her throat as if to reply.

But at times like these, it seemed that words were not enough! Her heart threatened to burst with the joy of being a mother—*Gabriel's* mother. Without warning, a song welled up inside her, a frivolous, but delightful, little children's air.

These days, she frequently found herself singing, although silently. In her heart she sang lullabies for Gabriel, joyful hymns to her merciful Lord, and even timid, secret songs of affection for Morgan.

Only now did she realize that she was singing the happy little children's song *aloud*! Surprised at herself, she went on singing, elated at how easy it seemed.

The words seemed to fairly dance over her tongue! Irish words, bright and carefree. They came easily, spilling out like sparkling clear water from a fountain. How perfectly they seemed to fit her emotions this night.

Obviously, baby Gabriel appreciated her song. He nursed eagerly, his tiny hand locking hold of her thumb as she went on singing.

Morgan stopped the wheelchair outside Finola's partially opened door, caught off guard by the sound of singing. He recognized the lighthearted children's song, and after a moment realized with amazement that *Finola* was singing it!

What kind of voice was this from one so young, so timid and fragile?

He had always admired her speaking voice, for it was crystalline and gently rhythmic, like a pure, sweet waterfall. But this...this was a voice that could scale the Mountains of Mayo, a voice that could put wings to the heart and sweep it over the sun! This was a voice one would never forget.

It was also a highly *trained* voice, Morgan suddenly realized. Aside from the glorious quality and tone, there was an obvious discipline and control, as well as a technical perfection that even a simple children's song could not obscure. This was no young girl's fancy of a voice, but a well-polished instrument, fine and rich and wondrous.

Understanding came rushing in on him like the tide. Of course! Why had he not realized it before now? Her love of music, the way her throat had seemed to caress the words of a song in those days before she regained her voice, and, later, after she had at last begun to speak, the smooth, flowing rhythm of her words—he should have seen long before now!

Sometime...somewhere, in the dark, unknown chamber of her past, Finola's voice had been trained. Someone had coached her, taught her how to use that splendid instrument to perfection.

The door to the bedroom was partly ajar, and he turned the wheelchair just enough so that he could see inside. She was there, sitting by the window in the dim glow of candlelight, her back to him, her head bent low over the child. She was singing to Gabriel, her voice low and tender and caressing. A mother singing a lullaby to her babe.

Morgan could tell by her pose that she was nursing the baby, and for a moment he felt embarrassed, almost like a voyeur. But as quickly as it came, the awkwardness passed, and he allowed himself the luxury of watching that golden head bent over her child as she sang her tender songs of love to her son.

As he sat there, drinking in the sight of her, his heart melting, his head swimming, an awareness of something different about her slowly dawned inside him. For the first time he saw Finola as more than the lovely, enigmatic girl with wounded eyes, whom he had grown to cherish with a fiercely protective kind of love. He saw her as an infinitely lovely, mature young woman. A woman, a mother...and his wife. In his house, under his eyes...Finola had gently passed from girl to woman. A mystery!

They made such a beautiful picture, the two of them, that he wished he could have a painting of the scene.

The thought of a portrait nagged at him, teased his mind, as if there were something he was not seeing, something important....

It hit him so suddenly he almost gasped aloud. If he had a portrait to send to Frank Cassidy, surely it would aid him in his search! Cassidy had been frustrated at every turn in his quest to uncover Finola's background. Every attempt to locate her family had been futile.

But a likeness of Finola—it might make all the difference! And even if he couldn't locate a trace of her family, there must be others—others who would recognize that unforgettable face! If he were right about her having been trained in the singing, then somewhere there must be a vocal coach, an instructor.

A portrait was what was needed, right enough!

But there *was* no portrait, nothing at all except for the large family portrait Sister Louisa had painted as a wedding gift.

Sister Louisa! Whipping the wheelchair around, Morgan sped down the hall toward the nun's room, almost ramming the chair against the door when he reached it.

"A portrait of Finola?" Sister Louisa stared at the *Seanchai*, his face eager and expectant in the open doorway. "Why, yes...I expect I could. But—"

"I would need it as soon as possible, that's the thing."

Sister Louisa had been altogether startled by the fierce pounding on her door, more startled yet when she opened it to find the *Seanchai*, looking somewhat wild-eyed and impatient.

Her first thought had been of Finola and the child, or young Annie. Panic had gripped her, but the *Seanchai* quickly assured her that nothing was wrong. "But I would ask a favor of you, Sister, if I might impose."

His request made, he still seemed quite agitated. The urgency behind his words made Sister Louisa more than a little curious. But clearly, he was not going to explain.

"I shouldn't imagine it would take long." She paused, still hoping for an explanation. "Is it to be a surprise?" she asked. "Should I not mention it to Finola?"

"That's right. I'd rather you say nothing about it. It can be small, Sister, as long as it's a fair likeness. And...quickly rendered."

Sister Louisa nodded, still bemused by his behavior as she watched him wheel himself off down the hall toward his bedroom.

The *Seanchai* could really be quite strange at times, in a rather endearing manner.

Closing the door, she crossed the room and set a clean sheet of drawing paper on the small easel that Sandemon had made for her as a gift. Within moments, she had the beginnings of what she considered an attractive—and highly realistic—portrait of Finola Fitzgerald.

26

The Midnight Thief

Oh! thou, who comest, like a midnight thief,
Uncounted, seeking whom thou may'st destroy;
Rupturing anew the half-closed wounds of grief,
And sealing up each new-born spring of joy....

JOHN KEEGAN (1809–1849)
(VICTIM OF THE DUBLIN CHOLERA EPIDEMIC OF 1849)

It was one of those clear, piquant autumn nights that seemed made for music and merrymaking. In the Gypsy camp there was always plenty of both.

The *Romany* caravan might have been in the middle of a country meadow instead of on the fringes of a Dublin slum, for all the attention the traveling people paid to those around them. About a dozen painted wagons were spread out to form a wide half circle, which gave a measure of privacy to the Gypsies. In the camp, children whooped and played outside until all hours, subdued only when their parents grew tired of the din. The men drank and laughed and made music late into the night, until they either fell asleep by the dying campfires or the weather turned bitter enough to drive them inside the wagons.

If other denizens of the Liberties objected to the noise, they grumbled mostly to themselves. To approach the camp of the *Rom* with a complaint, no matter how legitimate, would be foolhardy. And for an inhabitant of such a notorious, crime-ridden slum to carry a grievance to the law would be more foolhardy still.

Everyone knew that the Gypsies were quick to exact their revenge. The wisest course was to tolerate them from a distance.

Indifferent to the chill in the air and the noise in the camp, Tierney Burke lay propped up on one elbow beside the fire. He felt sluggish and idle, but supremely content. The cheap wine he'd been drinking for well over an hour had thickened his blood, and the festive mood of the Romany camp had infected him with a kind of drowsy euphoria.

Across from him, Jan Martova perched on a rock, cleaning a piece of harness. Each family shared their own campfire, although a great deal of intermingling went on. At the moment, Tierney and Jan were alone at the fire, the elder Martova brother and other relatives having gone to care for the horses.

Someone across the camp was softly playing a squeeze-box. On the outer fringes of the wagons, the Gypsy dogs—fierce, wild things that seemed to growl with every breath—took up an eerie howling as if to echo the music. Children raced in and out between the wagons, shouting and laughing as they played their games.

Tierney was no longer a stranger to the tribe. Tonight marked the third time he had managed to slip away from Nelson Hall to visit the Gypsies. Although the cholera epidemic had long since ebbed, Morgan had as yet refused to lift his ban on entering Dublin. He made no exceptions, not even when Annie had begged to go and see the Queen ride through the city.

What Annie did not know was that Tierney *had* sneaked off for a look at the royal procession. Just as he would have expected, the "Little Queen" was not much to see, nor was the rest of the royal family. He had thought the entire show in abominable taste and obscenely extravagant. Worse yet were the Dublin fools who stood in the streets and cheered the English queen, as if she were not responsible for shoveling dirt on countless Irish graves.

The Gypsy camp was one of the first places Tierney sought out when he began slipping off at night. In the beginning, he had been welcomed with only a sullen courtesy by the *Rom,* especially in the case of Jan's older brother, Greco. As a *Gorgio*—an outsider—Tierney was automatically suspect by the Gypsies, even though they acknowledged that he had helped to save the life of one of their own.

By his second visit, however, the story of the experience at the jail and the subsequent hospitality extended to Jan at Nelson Hall had circulated the caravan, gaining Tierney a warmer reception. Even Greco, though still somewhat gruff in his demeanor, no longer behaved as if the young American might be carrying the plague.

Having been exposed to all the prejudices against Gypsies in America, Tierney had acquired no small contempt for them. Yet he found himself drawn to the Martova camp more and more often. Here there was always food and drink, stories of faraway places, tales of ancient mysteries—and beautiful, exotic girls who seemed to find him dangerously intriguing.

One of those girls was Jan's sister, Zia. Only fourteen, she looked more like eighteen, with black, almond-shaped eyes, flashing white teeth, and skin the color of honey. An immense mass of dark hair flew about her face, and her slightest movement seemed imbued with the lithe grace of a young wildcat. She was a stunner, the kind of girl Da would call *trouble*.

Never one to shun trouble, Tierney would have liked nothing more than to get to know Zia a great deal better. But he was no fool. Early in their friendship, Jan had explained the way of things with Gypsy women, warning Tierney that any man foolish enough not to heed the law of the *Rom* in this regard might very well end up with a knife in his back.

Tierney had been surprised to learn that the Gypsies lived by a rigid code of laws, a code which apparently combined ancient decrees with strict morals and a confusing mix of customs—some religious, some distinctly pagan. For the women, the code required chastity and modesty. For the men, it occasioned a surprising lack of emphasis on sexual prowess and a serious, almost businesslike approach to marriage. Most marriages were arranged by the couple's families. Infidelity brought a variety of harsh punishments, especially for women, for whom banishment from the tribe was not uncommon.

While not exactly warning him to stay away from his sister in particular, Jan Martova had conveyed to Tierney the importance of keeping his distance from Gypsy girls in general.

Still, he could not resist an occasional question about the alluring Zia. Glancing at Jan across the low burning campfire, he stretched to hand him the nearly empty wine bottle. "The last is yours," he said magnanimously, feeling the effects of the wine and the heat from the fire.

Jan smiled and shook his head. "Thank you, but I have had enough."

Tierney shrugged and casually drained the rest of the bottle. "What were you talking about, last time I was here, when you said a match would soon be made for your sister?"

Jan didn't reply right away, but went on carefully cleaning the harness. "Zia is promised to Tenca, the leader of another *kumpania*," he finally said.

"*Kumpania?*"

"A tribe of families, like my own," Jan explained.

"But you said your sister is only fourteen years old! She's just a kid."

Jan looked up with an expression of mild rebuke. "Gypsy girls are pledged at a very young age, sometimes when they're no more than eight or nine years old. They don't always marry until much later, but the match is arranged in their early years."

Tierney found himself strangely repulsed by the idea. "How old is this man they're making her marry?"

Again the look of faint censure. "Gypsies do not measure years as the *Gorgio* do. Tenca is well past his thirtieth year, like my brother, Greco. But understand that Zia will not be forced to marry him. The arrangement can still be canceled, if Greco agrees. My brother is a reasonable man. He will not bully our sister. Our women are not slaves."

From what Tierney had seen, Greco was anything but reasonable. And while the women might not be slaves, they seemed to be treated with a certain heavy-handedness that left little doubt as to their standing in the camp.

"You are attracted to my sister?" The question was asked easily enough, but Tierney heard the slight edge in Jan's tone.

He shrugged off an answer. "Like I said, she's only a kid."

The other boy's hands stilled as he met Tierney's eyes over the fire. "Zia is not considered a child among the *Rom*, but a young woman, to be cherished and closely protected."

He paused, again taking up the harness in his hands. "You and I are friends, Tierney Burke," he said quietly as he went on working. "Your household extended aid and kindness to me when I was injured. Indeed, had it not been for you and the *Seanchai*, I might have died. But please understand that our friendship would be of no account whatsoever should you ever disregard our laws. The *Rom* is loyal to his friends—but only when his friends are loyal to the *Rom*."

The pleasant buzz going on in his head made it difficult to take anything seriously, but Tierney gave a solemn nod, as if to indicate his understanding and acceptance.

On his knees in the pantry, Sandemon heard the sound of stamping feet behind him and knew the child was on the march.

He sighed, hauled himself upright, and turned around.

"Whatever are you doing in the pantry, Sand-Man?"

Her petulant tone and thunderous frown told him immediately that young Annie did not care in the least what he was doing, that her real mission most likely had nothing to do with him.

Nevertheless, he would humor her. "Mrs. Ryan insists we have a mouse. I am setting a trap to appease her."

"Sure, you would *not* kill a wee mouse!" Annie stood rigid, her hands on her hips, one eyebrow arched, a foot thrust forward. The wolfhound, who had been standing in the middle of the kitchen eyeing a loaf of bread on the counter, now came to join the exchange.

Sandemon recognized the girl's battle posture, and quickly moved to defend himself. Crossing his arms over his chest, he leveled a stern look on her. "Have you ever known me to kill a living thing, even a mouse? Shame on you, child, for even thinking it! I have set a catching trap, not a killing trap. If the mouse is foolish enough to enter, he will merely find himself confined until I can rescue him."

"Oh." She appeared satisfied—and not at all interested. "Where is Tierney Burke, by the way? Have you seen him tonight?"

Amused at the way she managed to turn the boy's full name into one— *Tierney-Burke*—Sandemon replied, "I'm sure I do not know. Is there an emergency?"

She gave a saucy toss of her braids and fixed him with a thoroughly guileless look. Of late, the child had been practicing the fine art of being a woman. "Of course not," she said airily. "If there *were* an emergency, why would I be looking for Tierney Burke?"

"He seems a competent young man."

She narrowed her eyes. "I suppose he's sneaked out again."

Sandemon sensed he was being tested. "Is that a question or an observation?"

"You must know what he's up to," she countered. "I saw him once, with my own eyes."

Sandemon *did* know. But he had not realized that anyone else suspected. Young Tierney was most enterprising, and evidently well-experienced at slipping in and out at all times of night.

"Artegal helps him, you know," Annie announced rather peevishly. "He leaves the kitchen door unbolted so Tierney Burke can come and go as he likes. It strikes me that they are *both* deceitful."

Sandemon frowned at her. "It strikes *me* that you know entirely too much, that apparently there has been a considerable amount of prying on your part. And it strikes me as well that it is long past time for you to retire."

Instantly her face screwed up, a mirror of the child she used to be. Just as quickly, she regained her dignity. "I don't require as much sleep, now that I'm older." She paused, but when Sandemon said nothing in reply, she turned to the wolfhound. "Come, Fergus, we might as well go upstairs. Sand-Man is cross tonight."

Sandemon smiled as he watched them go, the girl flouncing out the door with deliberate impudence. The wolfhound was right at her heels, glancing back only once with a longing eye at the bread.

Alone again, his mood turned solemn. The child's comment about Artegal's complicity in Burke's late-night antics reminded him of a situation that was worrisome, to say the least.

He was aware of the irascible footman's duplicity, of course. Moreover, he suspected him of slipping spirits to the boy. He had passed by young Tierney's quarters when the door was partly ajar, and the stale, sour odor from within was unpleasantly reminiscent of the days when the *Seanchai* had been given to the drink.

For months, he had suspected Artegal of being a secret tippler, but as the man's vice didn't seem to affect his job, Sandemon had made the decision to hold his tongue, at least for the time being. This collusion with Tierney Burke, however, was a different matter entirely. If Artegal was indeed giving the boy alcohol, in addition to encouraging his deceit, was it right to allow them the protection of silence?

He didn't think the *Seanchai* had a hint as to what was going on between the footman and the American boy. These days, when the young master was not busily involved with his family or the school, he was working intently on the final editing of Father Joseph's famine journal, readying it for publication. He seemed unaware of anything amiss in the household.

But Morgan Fitzgerald was far too shrewd and discerning to be duped indefinitely. He would eventually discover the truth, and when he did, he would no doubt give young Tierney reason to regret his actions.

In the meantime, Sandemon was still troubled by his responsibility in the situation, still concerned that his silence might only make matters worse. His first loyalty was to the *Seanchai*, after all. Wherever the incorrigible Tierney Burke was sneaking off to—and he had his suspicions about the boy's nocturnal exploits—there was always the risk that his surreptitious behavior would bring trouble on Nelson Hall.

There had already been more than enough grief in this house. Sandemon sensed that the time was approaching when he would have to take steps to prevent more.

He decided he would start by confronting Tierney Burke. He would face the boy with what he knew and give him the opportunity to tell the *Seanchai* himself.

With a deep sigh, he drew a chair up to the table to wait. Tonight when the errant young rogue came sneaking into the kitchen through the back door, he would not find an empty room.

As soon as Greco and the other men came back to the fire, somebody called for music. Across the camp children came running, and at the same time the women began to gather in. One of the older men started to sing, and soon others joined in, Jan and his brother among them.

The Gypsies sang with full, strong voices and deep emotion. Sung in a language that Tierney could not understand, the lyrics sounded ancient and sad. Some of the older men had tears in their eyes as they lent their voices to the music.

The song ended, and Greco stepped into the circle of men who had crowded about the campfire. He began to hum what sounded like a dance tune, the rhythm brisk, the melody happy. The other men and boys took up the humming, then burst into song, clapping and beating out the rhythm with their feet.

Someone among the young men called for Jan to get his violin, and with a faint smile he left the fire to fetch it. By the time he returned, leaping into the open space near the fire, the other men had moved back to give the Martova brothers more room.

Fascinated, Tierney got to his feet, clapping with the rest of the Gyp-sies as the usually thunder-faced Greco began to circle the campfire, his strong white teeth flashing to the obvious mirth of the music as his boots pounded out a hailstorm of staccato beats.

But it was Jan who captured his interest and held it. Tierney knew next to nothing about music, had never played an instrument in his life, and in fact had never understood the passion of those who did. But as he stood there watching and listening to his new Gypsy friend, his instincts told him that Jan Martova was an exceptional violinist, a master of the string and bow. He could almost feel the power and the artistry in those long, slender hands as they coaxed one enchanting tune after another from the violin.

The music grew in intensity, and a second dancer joined Greco, then another, until an entire throng of men and boys had entered the dance. Tierney was disappointed when Zia attempted to lead some of the women into the circle, only to be stopped by Greco's restraining hand. One curt shake of his head, and she backed away from the others.

Tierney couldn't help but wonder if Zia would have been allowed to dance had an outsider like himself—a *Gorgio*—not been present.

At last Jan ended the set of dances with a flourish and a grin, and there was much hand clapping and bursts of whistling. This time when the young violinist touched his bow to the strings it was to evoke a slow, tender melody, so achingly beautiful and sad that a shiver ran down Tierney's spine.

It was almost as if Jan Martova were playing the strings of his heart. He felt his own emotions accompanying the violin as bittersweet memories and old dreams came rushing up, swelling his mind, stealing his breath.

Something about this music called up feelings from deep inside him, from a place he hadn't even known existed. If Jan Martova's music could accomplish such a thing with someone as unmusical and heretofore unin-terested as himself, what kind of magic would it work on those more sen-sitive to such things?

Right then and there he decided that Jan Martova must play at Nel-son Hall, for Morgan. Perhaps it would help to gain a measure of accep-tance for his Romany friend.

Another hour passed, an hour of music and dancing and merriment, before Jan finally stopped playing and came back to the fire. "Come," he said to Tierney, "I want you to see my *vardo*—my wagon."

He led him to a small square wagon that had been pulled away from the others, but was still parked not too far from the camp. It was obviously new, its deep-toned natural oak walls freshly varnished, with shutters painted bright blue. A variety of symbols—flowers, moon, and stars—had been stenciled here and there as decoration. Fitted at the rear of the frame, in between the wheels, was a large box, presumably used for storage.

Jan opened the double doors at the back, bowed formally to Tierney, and said, "Welcome to my home, Tierney Burke."

Following him inside, Tierney let out a low whistle. "Some digs," he said, turning to look at the Gypsy. "This is yours?"

Jan nodded. "I built it." Again, the faint note of pride without arrogance.

Impressed, Tierney's gaze swept the room. "You *built* this?"

Jan grinned. "With a little help from Greco and my cousins," he said. "It took us many months. I don't really need my own wagon, of course, since I have no wife as yet. But Greco's *vardo* is quite crowded, with Elena and the younger children, and I was beginning to feel in the way."

There were curtains on the windows, pots and pans hanging on nails, but no furniture—only a few cushions tossed randomly about the floor, and some plump, colorful quilts spread out in one corner,

"This is grand," Tierney said in earnest. "I envy you, having your own place."

"It's only a wagon," Jan said with a small shrug, but Tierney could tell he was pleased.

They plopped down on the cushions, sitting in companionable silence for a time as Tierney considered his new friend's impressive, and varied, talent. Jan seemed slightly distant, as if he were still lost somewhere in the music.

"How did you learn to play like that?" Tierney finally asked. "You said you never went to school, that you can't read or write. How do you know so much about music?"

Jan smiled a little. "It is true that I did not go to school and I cannot read or write. As for the music—" He shrugged, looking up at the window on the opposite wall. "I believe I was born with it in my soul. My tribe is a part of the *Rom* known as The Musicians," he explained with a faint trace of pride.

Tierney stared at him. "You mean it just comes natural? You never took lessons or anything?"

Jan laughed. "Gypsies do not take violin lessons, Tierney Burke." His smile faded, and Tierney was surprised to hear him say, "Although I confess there have been times when I've wished to do so."

"Why? You should be *giving* lessons, not *taking* them."

Still staring into the fire, Jan shook his head. "There are many sounds inside me I cannot give voice to because I don't know how to go about it. Besides, I have often thought I would like to go to school. It is not our way, but I would be glad for an education."

Abruptly, he turned and grinned at Tierney. "But what foolishness is this? A Gypsy who cannot read or write, talking of violin lessons and going to school, eh? As you Irish would say, 'A daft notion entirely!' What about you? What will you do here in Ireland? Will you take a job?"

Tierney shrugged. "Morgan wants me to get more schooling, but I'd rather work. First, though, he's talking about a tour across Ireland. Soon, I hope. Nobody knows more about Ireland than Morgan does. But he says we'll have to wait until the baby gets a little older. He won't go without his family."

Morgan's insistence on waiting irked Tierney. He didn't know why the two of them couldn't just go off on their own. Of course, Morgan would insist on taking Sandemon along; he was admittedly dependent on the black. But even that wouldn't be as much fuss as traveling with a wife and baby.

Jan broke into his thoughts. "I could offer you more wine if you like."

Tierney grinned at him and leaned back against the wall.

Then a strange thing happened.

His legs began to twitch, at first only sporadically, then with more force. Abruptly, it stopped, and then a sharp, knifing pain struck his knees and his calves. It fled as quickly as it came, but had he been standing, his legs would have buckled under him.

He gaped at his limbs in astonishment, clutching his knees as a fresh blast of pain hit first one, then the other. *"What—"*

Seeing his distress, Jan jumped to his feet and came to stand in front of him. "What is it? Are you ill?"

Ill? Yes…oh, he was ill! Nausea rose in him like a wave. His stomach blazed with fire, and his heart seemed to stop beating….

"What is wrong, my friend? What can I do?" Jan's voice seemed miles away, muffled, as if he were shouting from the depths of a well. "I will get help!"

A fierce heat swept Tierney's loins, raged down his legs. Jaws of pain clamped down on him, shaking him.

His head spun, and the floor of the wagon seemed to pitch. He looked up. The door to the *vardo* flew open, and the fierce form of Jan's brother, Greco, swirled above him.

There was a terrible rumbling in his stomach. Tierney ducked his head to retch, but nothing came.

He was hot, so very hot....

"It is the cholera!" Greco's voice came, rough and angry. *"The* Gorgio *has cholera!"* He spewed out something in *Romani,* then, *"Get out of the camp! You must leave at once!"*

Tierney groaned, twisted, tried to push himself onto his knees.

"He's not *able* to leave the camp! Have pity, Greco! We must help him! He is my friend!" Jan pleaded with his brother, at the same time trying to help Tierney to his feet.

Incredibly, Tierney managed to stand, one arm flung around Jan's shoulder for support.

"You would kill us all for this Gorgio?*"* Greco went on roaring a stream of invective, as Jan slowly began to tug Tierney toward the quilts in the corner. *"I told you! Didn't I tell you? You see now what comes from letting the* Gorgio *into our midst? Get him out of here or I will drive him out with the whip!"*

"Come, my friend," Jan urged Tierney, dragging him to the bedding on the floor, then helping him lie down. "He will not leave my *vardo*, brother," he said, glancing back over his shoulder. "I will drive the wagon outside the camp, where there is no danger to you and the others."

"No!" Dimly, Tierney saw Greco lift a burly arm as if to strike his brother. "Are you mad? You would risk your life for him?"

Jan Martova paused, then covered Tierney with a quilt. "You have forgotten that I *owe* my life to him," he said quietly. "He is my friend."

"He will be your *doom* if you do not heed what I say, little brother!"

Tierney squinted, saw Jan get to his feet and face his brother. "I am more than twenty years," he said quietly. "I am no longer your little brother, Greco. I am a man. You will not order me about like a child. Tierney Burke is my friend," he said, "and I owe him my loyalty. Now get out of my way. This is my *vardo*, and I will take it—along with Keja, my mare—wherever I choose."

Greco pierced Jan with an intense glare, his eyes narrowed. "If you leave the *kumpania* this night, little brother," he said through clenched teeth, "you will never be welcome here again."

Then he turned on his heel and strode off into the night.

After hitching Keja to the *vardo*, Jan Martova stood, thinking. Thinking and worrying. He had no special ability with sickness, especially one so deadly as cholera. The women in the camp saw to all the healing measures, not the men.

Finally he went seeking Nanosh, his young cousin. "There are two things I need you to do," he told the eager-faced boy. "And they are both very important. Can I trust you not to fail me?"

Nanosh straightened his slim shoulders and puffed out his chest. "You can trust me, Cousin."

"Good. First, you must ask your mother to send me any medicines at all that are good for cholera. Tell her I will need enough for—I don't know how long. Then I want you to run all the way to Nelson Hall on the hill and tell the big black man who works for the *Seanchai* what has happened."

Jan paused for breath. "Explain that Tierney Burke has been taken ill with the cholera, and that I am bringing him in my wagon to the land that runs across the stream from the big house. Tell him I will come that far only, no farther, so as not to endanger the *Seanchai* or his family."

His young cousin nodded and started to turn. Jan put a hand to his shoulder. "You must hurry, Nanosh. And you must do exactly as I say. Your word?"

"My word, Cousin."

Jan watched him turn and run, his heart sinking within him. He had made his choice. He hoped that neither Nanosh—nor any others among the family—would be stricken with the cholera. And he hoped with equal fervency that once all this was past, his family might find a way to forgive him for putting an outsider before them. Given Greco's parting words, however, he already knew his hope was futile.

27

Bad Tidings

This heart, fill'd with fondness,
Is wounded and weary....

FROM WALSH's IRISH POPULAR SONGS (1847)

Sandemon was dozing at the table, his head resting on his arms, when the pounding came at the back door.

He looked up, disoriented for a minute as he waited for his head to clear. The chair scraped the floor when he lurched to his feet, and he banged his leg against the corner of the table.

Was the boy drunk, to make such a racket at an unlocked door?

The sharp reprimand on his tongue died when he flung open the door to find, not the errant Tierney Burke, as he had expected, but a small Gypsy boy. It took a moment for him to realize that this was the same shaggy-haired child who had appeared at Nelson Hall some months past, the one who had carried the message to Nelson Hall from the Dublin gaol.

The boy appeared to be wearing the same soiled white shirt he had worn that night, and his face looked only slightly cleaner. His dark eyes brimmed with obvious excitement.

"I've a message for the *Seanchai* from Tierney Burke!" he burst out with no preamble.

So his suspicions had been right: the American boy HAD been consorting with the Gypsies on his late-night expeditions.

"The *Seanchai* is abed, as you might expect at such an hour," Sandemon responded sharply. "What is the message?"

The boy studied him as if to assess his reliability. Remembering the little Gypsy's impudence the night he had hauled him into the library to face the *Seanchai*, Sandemon crossed his arms over his chest and fixed the child with a stern glare. "The message?" he demanded again.

"You are to tell the *Seanchai* that Tierney Burke is ill," announced the boy, preening with the importance of his errand. "He has the cholera and has been banished from our camp."

Stunned, Sandemon instinctively stepped back. *"Cholera?"* An entire flood of memories assailed him. He had encountered the killer disease in Barbados and again in Ireland, where he and the priests had fought helplessly to stem its spread as hundreds died. It was an ugly, vicious plague. The word itself struck fear into the bravest of hearts.

Suddenly, the boy seemed to throw off his arrogance and give in to the drama of his mission. His next words poured out of him like grapeshot. "The American boy is very ill, I think! My cousin Jan Martova is bringing him in his *vardo*—his wagon—to the land across from the stream!"

A storm of emotions roared through Sandemon as he stood staring in horror at the child in the doorway. If only he had heeded his instincts and confronted the treacherous youth before now! He should never have put off telling the *Seanchai*, should not have withheld what he knew. This, then, was the deadly result of his delay.

"Why do they think it is cholera?" he challenged. "The epidemic is long past."

The boy bristled. "My cousin Jan Martova knows all about the cholera! He is a man and has seen such things."

"And he is certain?" Sandemon pressed.

The Gypsy boy studied him. His indignation with the persistent questioning seemed to wane, almost as if he had sensed, and understood, Sandemon's fear. His tone was less challenging when he answered. "Jan is certain. It is the cholera." After a slight hesitation, he asked, "Will the American die?"

Sandemon looked at him, still struggling to absorb the boy's bitter tidings. The unexpected question jolted him, and he made no attempt to reply. "They are coming *here*? You are sure of this?"

The boy nodded. "Jan sent me ahead to warn the *Seanchai* of their arrival. They should be here soon, but will not approach the house. My cousin will park the *vardo* in the field on the other side of the stream."

"And then what?" Sandemon asked the question of himself, not the child. *They would need a physician...medicine...nursing care....*

A momentary shudder of despair seized him, but he shook it off. By sheer force of will, he suppressed the panic threatening to engulf him. Finally, his mind slowed and reason returned. No matter what, the household must not be exposed, must not be put at the slightest risk. The *Seanchai* must be protected at all costs, as well as the family.

A thought struck him, and he leaned over, searching the Gypsy boy's eyes. "Have you been exposed? I must know the truth."

The boy shook his head.

"You are absolutely certain?"

The sharp little chin lifted defiantly. "I am certain. I was nowhere near the American—only Jan."

Straightening, Sandemon said, "Very well, then. You go out to the stream and watch for the wagon. When they arrive, go close enough to make yourself heard, but no closer—stay on this side of the stream. Do you understand? You must not cross the water."

The boy frowned but nodded.

"Tell your cousin to park the wagon on the other side of the stream, and to stay there. We will send for a physician. Under no circumstances is he to cross the stream. Be sure he understands. By now he may be carrying the disease himself. He *must* stay away from the house!"

"I will tell him," the boy said solemnly. For the first time, his large dark eyes showed a hint of fear.

Sandemon regarded him, softening somewhat toward the child, who had, after all, taken on a burdensome responsibility for one so young. "We may need someone to carry messages between the house and your cousin's wagon. Are you willing to stay for a time, if you are needed?"

"I will stay," the boy said matter-of-factly. "Jan Martova is my cousin. And he calls the American his friend. I will help however I can."

Sandemon watched him for another minute, then gave a small nod and shut the door.

With heavy steps, he left the kitchen and started upstairs. Every beat of his heart, as he climbed the stairs, seemed to echo with dread. He would give anything to avoid being the bearer of this message—and at such a time, when the *Seanchai* was at last finding joy and contentment with his new family.

How could he bear to face him with the shattering news that yet another woe was about to descend on Nelson Hall? More anguishing still was the possibility that this latest tragedy might have been prevented, had he himself not waited so late to speak the truth.

For two days after the arrival of the Gypsy wagon, Morgan swung between fear and raw fury. It occurred to him more than once that it was doubtless a good thing Tierney had been isolated in the Gypsy wagon; there was no telling what he might have done to the boy if he could have gotten his hands on him.

He had considered every possible form of discipline for Tierney's irresponsible behavior and its dire consequences. He disregarded entirely the fact that he had no actual authority to punish the boy. As long as the foolish *gorsoon* was living under his roof, he *would* abide by his rules! There would be a hard price to pay, once he was fully recovered.

If he recovered…

Not for the first time, Morgan questioned his judgment in having opened his doors to Tierney Burke. The boy had proved nothing but trouble from the very start. A harrowing rescue from a gaol cell. Sneaking alcohol on the very premises from a deceitful footman. Midnight carousings with diseased Gypsies. And now—now, the fruits of his illicit behavior brought to rest on Nelson Hall.

At times he wished he had simply refused Michael's request to give refuge to his son. In his eagerness to help a friend, he had not weighed the consequences. Why hadn't he at least stopped to consider the deadly smoke that could rise from the fire of such a rebellious spirit? Wasn't his own past proof enough of sin's far-reaching effects?

There was a dark side to Tierney's nature, a darkness that too often overshadowed the finer things in him. Caprice too easily turned to waywardness, mischief to malice. The lad had intelligence, boldness, and idealism. But his intelligence often took the form of cunning; his boldness, rebellion; and his idealism was easily misplaced. More than once, Morgan had sensed the struggle of that duality in Tierney, and understood it all too well. For he, too, was a man whose spirit had often provided a battleground for light and darkness—and many was the time darkness had prevailed.

Yet, God must have thought him worth some effort, for He continued to enable him and sustain him.

That being the case, wasn't it more than likely the Almighty also believed Tierney Burke worth the effort?

Sandemon would say the boy was worth fighting for, worth a struggle, simply because he was a child of God. And although Morgan believed that, he often found it more difficult than his West Indies companion to act in accordance with his beliefs.

There had been no word from the wagon since early afternoon, indicative, he supposed, of no change in the lad's condition. The little Gypsy boy—*Nanosh*, he called himself—had stayed on at Nelson Hall, sleeping in the smokehouse when he wasn't serving as messenger.

Morgan hoped it wasn't a mistake to let him stay. There was no denying the need for a safe intermediary, and the child had sworn he'd been nowhere near Tierney the night he fell ill. Then, too, having him nearby might help to restrain the wrath of Jan Martova's elder brother, the Gypsy leader.

Morgan had not forgotten the dark insolence and volcanic fury of Greco Martova. Who could say what the man might do, should others in the Gypsy camp fall victim to the cholera? In all likelihood, the belligerent *Rom* would blame Tierney, when it was just as probable that Tierney had himself been infected by one of the Gypsies. Still, it would not hurt to have the boy on the premises, in the event of trouble from the camp.

Besides, the child had been a great help in acting as courier: shouting messages across the stream and leaving food and other supplies where Jan Martova could retrieve them.

Although the frequent reports from the quarantined wagon indicated that Tierney's condition was critical, no physician had yet been found to attend him. A number of surgeons had themselves been stricken with the cholera during the height of the epidemic, leaving those who survived excessively cautious.

Morgan suspected that Tierney's connection with the Gypsies only made it more difficult to find a willing physician. Dr. Dunne, the one surgeon who might have come, was in London and not expected to return for another week. Until then, at least, Tierney's fate seemed to rest in the hands of his Gypsy comrade, Jan Martova.

Morgan could not imagine that a Romany would know anything of the healing arts, except perhaps for a few worthless charms and spells. He had voiced this concern to Sandemon, who surprised him by disagreeing. The Gypsies, he told Morgan, were in fact highly skilled in the use of herb medicines and other healing agents. Although he admitted to not being comfortable with many of their other customs, he seemed to think that Tierney could do worse than to have a Romany looking after him.

Even so, Sandemon, by nature a tolerant man, had never denied his mistrust of the Gypsies. At any mention of the Romany, the dark eyes, usually so steady and gentle, suddenly turned shuttered and remote. More than once Morgan thought he had detected a hint of fear. He suspected that Sandemon's tragic experience with the occult in the islands might be responsible for his wariness—understandable, surely.

But even more evident than his aversion to the Gypsies was the air of dejection that seemed to hang over the West Indies black man of late. Sensing the heaviness of the other's heart, Morgan wondered if it might not be due to a self-imposed burden of guilt.

More than once Sandemon had asked Morgan's forgiveness for his failure to reveal Tierney's deception, as well as Artegal's part in it. Morgan had tried to reassure him, even admitting that in similar circumstances he might have done the same.

Apparently, he had been less than convincing. Not surprising, given the fact that, to some extent, he *did* resent his companion's silence. In a way, he *did* feel betrayed.

Tierney's underhandedness had been a great disappointment, but the realist in Morgan admitted that his own youthful exploits had been far more radical. As for Artegal, while the footman's utter lack of loyalty was infuriating, it had come as no surprise. In truth, Morgan had almost been glad for a reason to discharge the man, even though his absence placed a temporary hardship on the rest of the staff.

But the fact that Sandemon had not come to him in the very beginning continued to gnaw at him like an angry worm. He expected he would get over it, and had in fact made considerable effort in the meantime to disguise his feelings—but the resentment was there, all the same, like a stubborn wound that would not heal. And Sandemon was far too perceptive not to be aware of it. No doubt that awareness accounted for his despondency and the regret Morgan sensed when their eyes chanced to meet.

At present, however, Morgan found it difficult to attend to anyone's feelings but his own. He seemed caught in a tangle of emotions: fear, as intense as any he had ever experienced; frustration—with Tierney and with himself—for not keeping a closer eye on the boy; disappointment with Sandemon for not exposing the situation when he'd had a chance; and a personal sense of failure for falling short in his responsibility to Michael and his son.

But it was the fear—the relentless, choking, debilitating fear—that he found most difficult to deal with. Not for the world would he have the others see that he often teetered on the edge of panic, that he was constantly apprehensive—no doubt irrationally so—that the dread cholera would somehow make its way into the house, to strike Finola...or baby Gabriel...or Annie...or his entire family.

At times the fear became so overwhelming he nearly strangled on his efforts to banish it before Finola or Annie chanced to notice. The slightest sign of weakness on his part would only alarm them all the more, and he would not have it so. It seemed they had both come to regard him in terms of strength and reliability, and, although he expected it was vanity on his part, he found himself loath to disappoint them.

He drew a long breath, put aside *The Nation*, and took one more long look out the window, to the dark field where he knew the Gypsy wagon to be parked.

Finally, deciding he should try to rest, he wheeled himself over to the bed. He braced the wheelchair with the brake Sandemon had improvised and rested one arm on the bedside railing. Reaching up, he caught hold of a triangular-shaped handle attached to a chain suspended from the ceiling—also Sandemon's contrivance. He hoisted himself upright until he could pitch forward, across the bed. Then, still using the chain as support, he managed to twist himself onto his back, finally hooking the chain over the bedpost.

For a moment he lay, staring up at the ceiling, his heart pounding from the exertion. This bedtime routine had taken a great deal of practice, but once mastered, he continued to relish the small independence it afforded him. To be able to get in and out of bed unassisted would no doubt seem a small thing to those with legs that worked; to Morgan, it was a significant achievement—and one for which, once more, he had the ever-ingenious Sandemon to thank.

The truth was, he owed his loyal companion more than could ever be expressed. From the day when the big, good-humored black man had first walked into Nelson Hall, he had devoted himself to improving Morgan's quality of life—with notable success.

Guilt clamped down on Morgan's heart as he acknowledged that his friend deserved better—much, much better—than he was receiving from him these days. Perhaps Sandemon *had* made an error in judgment—what of it? The good Lord knew that Morgan Fitzgerald had made more than his share of mistakes in the past.

His throat tightened. It was a singular act of churlishness for him to question Sandemon's loyalty. The man was faithful beyond measure, yet Morgan had rewarded his fidelity with cold reserve and unfounded disappointment.

Morgan's eyes stung, and he felt weary beyond belief. Removing his spectacles, he laid them aside, promising himself that he would not allow this barrier to stand between him and Sandemon any longer. Tomorrow they would talk, and he would set things right between them.

For now, though, his body craved sleep. But as he reached to extinguish the oil lamp beside the bed, a sharp rap on the door made him halt with his hand in midair.

At his "Come," Sandemon appeared in the doorway. He entered, quietly closing the door before turning to Morgan. His expression was drawn, his eyes troubled, and Morgan knew at once he had brought bad news. Dragging in a long breath, he held it, waiting.

Rarely did the big black man remove his well-worn seaman's cap, but now he stood, holding it against his heart as he absently fingered its brim. "The little Gypsy boy was just at the kitchen door," he said, his tone heavy. "He came to tell us that his cousin—Jan Martova—has been stricken with the cholera. It seems that he, too, is now seriously ill."

When Morgan made no reply, he went on. "Nanosh—the Gypsy boy—said his cousin was so weak, he was barely able to make himself heard when he came to the stream." He paused. "What are we to do, *Sean-chai?* We can no longer leave them to themselves. They must have help."

For a moment Morgan felt as if he himself had been stricken. A grinding dread seized him, clutching his chest, wreathing his head. He felt something ominous hanging over the room. He twisted, pushing himself over onto his side. Looking into Sandemon's dark, worried eyes, he saw his own apprehension reflected there.

"Seanchai?"

Sandemon's soft prompting reminded him of the need to think, to reason, in the face of this latest dilemma. Their eyes met and held, until at last Morgan shook his head in despair. "I cannot think what to do," he admitted heavily, slumping back against the pillows. "I simply do not know."

28

A Reluctant Parting

I it is who shall depart,
Though I leave with heavy heart.
GEORGE SIGERSON (1836–1925)

Morgan raked a hand down one side of his face, trying to think. In truth, he felt little sympathy for Jan Martova. For all he knew, the Gypsy might have been the one who infected Tierney in the first place! But there was nothing to be gained by wasting time on accusations. For Tierney's sake—indeed, for everyone's sake—they must figure a way to help them both. The question was how.

"*Seanchai?*"

Morgan turned, watching Sandemon as he approached the bed.

"I think I should go and help them. I think that is the only thing to do," the black man said calmly, adding, "If you can manage without me for a time."

"Well, I *cannot!*" Morgan burst out, twisting onto his side and pushing himself up on one arm. "It's out of the question! I need you here, and that is that."

More to the point, he would not put him in such danger. Even if he could get along on his own...which he could not, of course...he was not willing to put Sandemon at risk.

"No," he said again. "We will find another way. I cannot manage without you."

Sandemon's expression was unreadable, and after a moment he looked away. In spite of his silence, Morgan imagined he could feel the other's disapproval.

"Sister Louisa has had much nursing experience," Morgan said carelessly. "She would be willing."

Sandemon raised his face, looking directly into Morgan's eyes. "Please, no, *Seanchai*. Do not put the Sister at risk. She is greatly needed here. Mistress Finola and young Annie—and the scholars—depend on her. Surely you would not endanger her so."

"She is needed no more than *you* are," Morgan said sourly. But Sandemon's words left him torn and confused. Naturally, he didn't *want* to assign Sister Louisa to such a dreadful task, though he knew without asking she would accept. But what were the alternatives?

"Someone in the city, then," he said uncertainly. "We will find a nurse—"

"No one from the city will come, *Seanchai*." Sandemon's voice was quiet, but firm, his words clipped and precise. "You must allow me to go. There is no one else. I will prepare Lucy Hoy to help you. I will make certain she knows everything that must be done in my absence."

"Indeed, no!" Morgan pushed himself up, his face flaming. "I'll not have a woman attending me! Besides," he quickly pointed out, "she is Gabriel's nurse—and indispensable to Finola. No, not Lucy."

Silence hung between them as Morgan considered the possibilities, all unfeasible. Utter frustration gripped him as he realized the hopelessness of their dilemma. Who would knowingly submit to such a task, to nurse, not one, but *two* victims of the deadly cholera?

Hearing Sandemon's long sigh, Morgan cut a glance at him.

"*Seanchai*," the black man said, "I am obviously not eager to do this thing or to leave you on your own. But I submit that it would be far easier to find someone to assist *you* than someone willing to face the cholera. And we do not have the luxury of time in this matter."

"Don't you understand, man?" Morgan burst out. "I am not willing to risk your life for a heathen Gypsy and an ungrateful *gorsoon*! I should think you would thank me!" Suddenly exhausted, his skin clammy with perspiration, he again sank back against the pillows.

For a long time, neither spoke. Morgan felt the dark-eyed scrutiny but deliberately avoided it by fixing his gaze on the ceiling.

Finally, Sandemon broke the silence. Softly clearing his throat, he said,

"Thank you, *Seanchai*, for…your concern. Please know I am moved by it, and very grateful. But let me explain that I survived the cholera once—and more than likely would do so again."

Morgan shot him a skeptical look, but the black man pretended not to notice. "It is believed in the islands," he said, "that to have the cholera once is to be protected from having it a second time. All the more reason, I think, why I must be the one who—"

He broke off at the sound of a light knock on the connecting door leading to Finola's bedchamber. Both of them turned to look, and after another soft rapping, the door opened.

Clad in her dressing gown, Finola stepped inside the room. Her hair was unbound, her features soft with sleep, her eyes wide and questioning as she looked from one to the other.

"I…I'm sorry to interrupt, but I heard voices. I thought something must have happened."

Morgan quickly reached to toss the quilt over his legs, bare below the hem of his nightshirt. "Forgive us, Finola. I didn't realize we were talking so loudly."

Sandemon, too, inclined his head in a gesture of regret.

A flourish of her hands indicated they need not apologize. "What is it?" she asked, her gaze again traveling from one to the other. "Is something wrong?"

Sandemon turned, exchanging a look with Morgan.

"Nothing that need worry you," Morgan said, unwilling to alarm her. When he saw that she was waiting for an explanation, he added, reluctantly, "It seems that the Gypsy boy has also been taken with the cholera. We were just discussing what should be done."

Her hand went to her throat. "*Both* of them are ill? But…how will they manage, then? Who will care for them?"

Morgan glanced at Sandemon, then looked away. "That's the very thing we were discussing," he muttered. "We have no solution as yet."

But Sandemon was not so easily deterred. "I was hoping the *Seanchai* might allow me to go to help the young men," he said quietly. "There is no one else."

Finola went pale, staring at him with dismay. "Oh, Sandemon! You would be placing yourself in great danger—"

Seeing her distress, Morgan immediately moved to reassure her. "He knows I won't allow it," he said, glaring at Sandemon, who appeared not to notice. "I cannot have him going off to play nursemaid when I need him here."

Sandemon turned, regarding him with a searching look. He seemed uncertain as to whether or not he should speak. Clutching his cap closer to his chest, he cast another brief glance in Finola's direction.

"Forgive me, *Seanchai,*" he finally said, turning back to Morgan, "I would not offend you, but I can't help observing that you have come to manage very well on your own. Indeed, you have attained a great deal of independence. Surely those few things for which you still require assistance could be assumed by someone else, at least for a short time."

Morgan stiffened, vaguely aware that he was being deliberately stubborn, yet unwilling to give over. Before he could comment, Sandemon went on. "I do not mean to be impertinent, *Seanchai,* but the lives of those two young men out there may very well depend upon their receiving whatever care I can provide. That much, at least, I can do." He paused, then added firmly, "And while I would not lightly ignore your wishes, that much I *intend* to do."

Morgan's temper flared. "You would defy me?"

"I would prefer not to. That is why I am asking your approval."

Morgan glared at him, all the while uncomfortable in the awareness that Finola was taking in every word of their conversation, her troubled gaze darting from one to the other.

She could not know, of course, that his heavy-handed tactics were due as much to fear for Sandemon as to simple obstinacy.

Sandemon caught him off guard with his next words. "*Seanchai,*" he said gently, "I believe you are afraid for me, and I am truly touched by your concern."

Morgan shot him a look of surprise. Sandemon smiled a little as he said, "It is a fine thing for a man to have such a loyal friend, and I am thankful."

"Aye...well...I was beginning to think I would need to paint you a picture," Morgan said gruffly.

"Nevertheless," Sandemon went on, still smiling, "I would remind you once more that I have already had the cholera...and survived. It is highly unlikely it would strike me again. Taking that into account, *Seanchai,* may I please, then, have your permission to go to the Gypsy wagon?"

Still determined to stop him, Morgan scowled and replied, "And what about me, then? Shall I employ a stranger in your absence?"

"That will be quite unnecessary," Finola said, her tone uncharacteristically assured. "I will assume Sandemon's duties in your behalf until he returns."

Her quiet announcement struck the room like a thunderbolt. Morgan nearly choked on his own breath, and even Sandemon's stoic calm appeared to falter ever so slightly.

As if entirely unaware of their astonishment, Finola crossed the room and came to stand beside the bed. Clasping her hands at her waist, she gave Sandemon a shy smile before turning an unsettlingly clear blue gaze on Morgan.

"If Sandemon truly feels he must do this, then you need not concern yourself any further about managing without him. I am quite capable of assisting you in his absence, and will be more than happy to do so."

For a moment Morgan could do nothing but stare at her in disbelief. Something in her obviously well-intentioned proposal set his heart to racing like a wild thing, even though he quickly reminded himself that she was simply trying to be helpful.

"That's...very kind of you, Finola," he managed to say in a reasonably controlled tone of voice, "but entirely unnecessary. If Sandemon has set his head to this, I will call upon one of the stable grooms to attend me."

He felt painfully awkward under her searching look. "I will...manage," he added inanely.

She continued to study him for another moment, then unexpectedly turned and said, "Sandemon, would you mind if I spoke to Morgan alone, please?"

Finola waited until Sandemon had slipped quietly from the room, then turned back to Morgan.

Moving closer to the bed, she studied him for a moment. "You are distressed about what Sandemon intends to do," she said softly. "You are afraid for him."

He nodded. "I expect what distresses me most is knowing he's right—there seems to be no alternative."

"You must try not to worry about him," Finola said, touching his hand. "I somehow think Sandemon is invincible."

He glanced at her hand, then caught it in his. "Let us hope. I confess I cannot bear to think of Nelson Hall without his presence." He paused. "I am sorry we woke you. You're troubled enough without our adding to it."

There was no denying that she was troubled. The very idea of cholera terrified her, especially when she allowed herself to think about Gabriel… or Morgan…being stricken. But she sensed this was not the time to admit her own terrors.

"I try not to dwell on it," she said, forcing a note of cheerfulness into her voice. "Sometimes I feel as if I have lived my entire life in fear. I don't want to be that way any longer. I'll not spoil the peace God has given me in this place."

He squeezed her hand, a look of pleasure crossing his features. "It means a great deal to me to hear you say that you've found peace here. It's what I've wanted for you from the beginning…that, and your happiness."

Finola felt her heart swell with love for him, for his sweet and unfailing concern, his thoughtfulness, his gentleness. It was all she could do not to blurt out her feelings. Instead, she managed to smile and say lightly, "Then you will not argue with me further. You will allow me to assist you while Sandemon is away, for it will make me very unhappy if you refuse."

He avoided meeting her gaze as he spoke, but his face betrayed his pain. "Finola, I can't expect you to understand. But it's…difficult, being as I am. Even with Sandemon, it's sometimes a struggle. But with you, *mavourneen*…"

He looked at her, and Finola's throat tightened at the torment in his eyes.

"With you," he went on after a ragged breath, "I find it much more difficult. For the most part, I can toss my pride to the wind with Sandemon. But I find myself fighting for every last shred of it where you're concerned."

Determined that he would see no pity in her eyes, Finola fought down the rush of dismay his words evoked. "Morgan…"

He shook his head, bringing her hand to his lips for a moment. "It's a bitter thing entirely for me to appear weak and dependent—helpless—in your eyes," he said softly, lowering her hand but not releasing it. "I would have you see me as invincible, like Sandemon—a tall and mighty warrior."

He gave her a faint, self-mocking smile that nearly broke Finola's heart.

Oh, my love…you could never imagine how I think of you…you are my prince,
my brave, bronze prince who makes my heart soar and my senses sing with
joy…. I think of you only with love…always with love….

Somehow she forced herself to meet his eyes. "Morgan, there is something I must say to you," she said, drawing in a steadying breath. "It is
important to me, and I ask you to please hear me. Up until now, you have
done everything for me, while I…I have done nothing for you in return."

When he would have protested, Finola silenced him by hurrying on.
"No, let me say this, please. Don't you see, Morgan, for such a long time, I
have felt as you say *you* feel—weak and dependent and helpless. Yet, I have
longed to be more than that…in your eyes."

"Finola—" With a stricken look, he clasped her hand more tightly.

She shook her head and went on, her voice stronger now. "You have
grown used to thinking of me…almost as a child—a sick child who must
be sheltered and protected. And I am infinitely grateful for your protection, Morgan—why, I can't think what might have happened to me without you! I doubt that I would have survived at all. But…I'm not sure you
realize that I've changed. I am no longer ill, don't you see? I'm no longer
weak or helpless. Indeed, I am quite healthy. I would even say I'm strong.
And, Morgan—Morgan, I am a *woman*."

She stopped, but did not look away. Leaning closer to him, she forced
herself to finish what she had begun. "I am a woman…and a mother. I am
also your wife, Morgan, and it would please me no end if you would treat
me as such. I am asking that you allow me to help *you*, just as you have
helped *me*. That would please me, Morgan, truly it would."

His eyes searched hers. Slowly he nodded, a token of assent. Finola
squeezed his hand and smiled. "Good. I will go and tell Sandemon to
prepare a brief list for me, so I will know exactly what you require in his
absence. You rest now, Morgan. I won't be long."

Within the hour, they bade Sandemon farewell. Only Morgan and
Finola were there, in the privacy of Morgan's bedroom, to send him off
with their wishes and prayers.

Still somewhat dazed by Finola's assertiveness, Morgan was finding it
difficult to take in this sudden, unanticipated change and what it would

mean in his life. At the moment, he could concentrate on little else than Sandemon's departure for the Gypsy wagon.

With his usual efficiency, the black man had taken time to gather a number of supplies he thought he might need: a roll of flannel, some laudanum and camphor, a lantern, a box of candles, and other small items.

"I will send word by the Gypsy boy as to what foods we need prepared," he told Morgan. "If they are able to take nourishment, that is." He paused, looking from Morgan to Finola. "You do understand that it may be weeks before I can return to the house. We will have to make absolutely certain all danger of contagion has passed."

Morgan nodded briefly, not eager to consider such an extended absence. "Just know that you will be sorely missed." His voice sounded gruff, even to his own ears, but this was difficult, after all—so difficult!

"Thank you, *Seanchai.*" Sandemon paused, again letting his dark gaze rest on both of them for an instant. "But I am grateful that now I can go with peace in my heart, knowing you will be taken care of with competence and affection."

Morgan glanced at Finola and saw a faint blush spread over her face. But she smiled at Sandemon, saying, "I shall do my best. But no doubt he will be beside himself with relief when you return."

"Don't be so sure," Morgan said dryly. "Your face is far easier to look at than his."

He saw the corners of Sandemon's mouth twitch. Though they were all obviously trying for lightness, the mood quickly turned somber once again.

"You will take every caution with yourself," Morgan reminded him.

"I will, *Seanchai.* Of course, I will."

"And you'll send us a report by the Gypsy boy at least three times a day."

"I will, yes."

"We'll be worried for you, mind."

"Please pray for me and the young men."

"Aye. You know we will."

"We will *all* be praying, Sandemon," Finola put in. "Morgan and I— and Sister Louisa and Annie—all of us." Her voice no longer sounded quite so confident, and Morgan did not miss the way she was wringing her hands together at her waist.

"I will find great strength in knowing that, Mistress Finola."

There was an awkward silence. Morgan's chest felt excessively heavy, as if it might sink at any instant. He cleared his throat. "You're certain you have everything you need? Of course, we can always get additional supplies to you—you've only to send word by Nanosh. Anything you need," he emphasized, wincing at the tremor in his voice. "Anything."

Sandemon nodded, saying, "I will be fine. All will be well. Please try not to worry. I will take good care of the young men—and myself."

The black man's calm was impressive. Yet, at the moment there was a look about him—a certain tightness to the mouth, a missing glint in the eye—that spoke, if not of actual apprehension, at least of reluctance.

Morgan thought he might have made it through the next few moments without losing his own composure had it not been for Finola. Without warning, she stepped forward and caught both of Sandemon's hands in hers. "We will miss you so much, dear Sandemon! You must come back to us, safe and well. And very soon!"

She dropped his hands and moved back to stand beside the bed, but the look of startled pleasure on Sandemon's face lingered.

For a moment, he stood looking at the two of them. Then he crossed to the bed, his eyes locking with Morgan's. "I will miss you, *Seanchai*, do you realize that? I will miss you grievously."

Morgan thought he would strangle. A thousand memories flashed before him, and his throat ached with the unspoken words of affection crowding his heart. All he could do was open his arms and pull the big black man into a quick embrace. "Come back as soon as you possibly can, *mo chara*...my friend," he choked out, unable to go any further.

They released each other with awkward smiles and a long last look. Then, with a quick nod to Finola, Sandemon started for the door. Abruptly, he turned back. "You will tell Miss Annie goodbye for me?"

Morgan nodded. Then Sandemon was gone.

Morgan stared at the closed door in silence. He felt bereft and heavy-hearted, already missing the steady presence, the indomitable strength and solid wisdom he had come to count on.

He felt Finola slip her hand in his and gently squeeze his fingers. Looking up at her, he saw his own sense of bereavement reflected in her eyes. Somehow it helped, knowing she understood and even shared his feelings of loss.

She stayed for nearly an hour, sitting in the chair beside the bed, allowing him to hold her hand as he told her of Sandemon's first days at Nelson Hall, how he had arrived on the very day that Finola had first brought Annie safely to the front door, then disappeared. He told her of the difference the former West Indies slave had made in his life, the enormous debt of gratitude he felt he owed him. He told her many things about the man he now called *friend,* until at last he relaxed enough to doze.

Sometime late in the night he awoke to find her gone. He imagined her slender hand still clasped in his, even lifted his own palm to his lips as if to recapture her closeness. The faint, sun-touched scent of her hair lingered near, seeming to warm the bleakness of the lonely bedroom...and his heart.

29

In the Vardo

With violins wheening
Inside that island sheiling,
I hear lost secrets breathing
Beyond the cairned mound

FREDERICK ROBERT HIGGINS (1896–1941)

At the doors of the Gypsy wagon, Sandemon deposited his crate of supplies, checking their contents one last time. He scanned the exterior of the wagon, taking in the highly polished wood and colorful shutters, the stenciled symbols and detailed carpentry.

He hesitated, still reluctant to go inside, feeling torn between the urgency to do what needed to be done and his dread of the ugly disease that awaited him inside the wagon.

"Lord God," he murmured, *"surround this wagon with a wall of Your power and angels to guard us. From this unsanctified place, expel the darkness and come with Your Light...."*

With the ancient prayer of Patrick on his lips, he stood, waiting until he felt strong enough to go inside..."*Christ with me, Christ before me, Christ behind me, Christ in me, Christ beneath me, Christ above me, Christ on my right, Christ on my left...."*

Finally, drawing the sign of the cross over his chest, he pulled in a deep, steadying breath, and entered.

Inside, he found things much as he had expected: a malignant stench of human waste and gorge, wild disarray of bedding and utensils, and the anguished moaning and outcries of young, once healthy bodies trapped in the wretched torment of disease.

He gagged, fumbling in his trousers pocket for a handkerchief, which he tied over his mouth and nose. He went first to Tierney Burke. Dropping to his knees, he saw that the cholera had advanced to the extreme stage, the deadly stage from which recovery was most rare.

The boy was obviously delirious, his face swollen, eyes bruised and deeply sunken, his skin blue—even his hands had turned dark and pulpy, like an elderly washerwoman's. He lay like a babe, his legs drawn up, his arms clasped tight about his abdomen.

As he found Tierney's pulse—dangerously faint—the boy muttered and raved unintelligible words. Standing, Sandemon then crossed to the opposite wall, where Jan Martova lay. The Gypsy boy moaned at the sight of him, a fleeting look of relief crossing his features.

"Tierney?" he whispered hoarsely as Sandemon knelt on one knee beside him. "Is he...still...?"

Sandemon nodded, then lowered his head to the boy's chest to listen to his heartbeat. It was far too rapid, but not erratic.

"I did...everything I knew to do," the Gypsy mumbled. "I tried... but nothing helped..." Suddenly, he reached up and with unexpected strength clutched the front of Sandemon's shirt. "You will help him? You won't let him die—"

He broke off, his eyes rolling back as he grabbed his stomach. With a cry of pain, he twisted onto his side, gasping for breath.

A wave of sympathy for the boy's distress swept over Sandemon, coupled with remorse that he might have allowed his old prejudices to keep him from coming here tonight. From the time he had first sensed the urging of the Spirit, he had found it difficult, even distasteful, to obey. He had known too much about the heathen Gypsy ways: their pagan gods, their secret ceremonies, their black magic. The Romany lived dangerously close to the dark side, uncomfortably near the caverns of his own past. They trafficked with the same powers of darkness that had almost destroyed him, indeed, *had* destroyed his wife and daughter.

Their way of life was repugnant to him. Yet, how could he not recognize their humanity? Even with their abhorrent ways, they, too, were the product of divine creation. The saving love of the Father was as available to the Gypsies as to anyone else.

If the Lord were to pass by this night, would He ignore this Gypsy wagon, where two youths lay suffering on the floor? Would He refuse to extend His mercy, to bind their wounds, to offer healing, simply because they happened to be outside His grace?

And could a man such as I, who has known both the depths of darkness and the miracle of God's merciful light, refuse to stand in the gap and help them?

A lump tightened in Sandemon's throat. He swallowed it down, then took in a deep breath. This was the right decision—he knew it, as surely as he knew the reality of God's intervention in his own life. The Spirit had compelled him, and he would do what had to be done.

Still kneeling beside the agonizing Gypsy, he put a hand to the youth's burning forehead. "Try to rest now," he said gently. "I am here to help you and your friend."

Jan Martova twisted onto his back, moaning with the effort. His face was flushed with fever, his eyes glazed with pain and fear as he stared up at Sandemon. Yet when he spoke, his voice was surprisingly calm. "Are we going to die?"

"We will hope not tonight," Sandemon replied. In an attempt to encourage the blood flow, he gently removed the soiled kerchief from around the Gypsy's neck, then unbuttoned the youth's shirt and removed his boots.

"Someday," he went on, "every one of us is going to die. But we will hope and pray that your time has not yet come."

Sandemon worked through the night, battling not only the vicious cholera itself, but the more insidious illnesses he knew to be lurking among the human waste and noxious fumes that the disease had generated.

He was able to at least ease Jan Martova's discomfort with laudanum and a syrup he had concocted of potassa and mint. The boy remained feverish and in much pain, but within hours his pulse had grown stronger and more regular.

Tierney Burke was another matter. His breathing was already severely labored, no doubt from the excess accumulation of fluids and the distress of the heart. Having seen this stage of the cholera before, Sandemon knew the boy's body had reached that critical point where most functions had simply ceased their efforts. Every moment counted if he were to be revived.

Grateful for the mild autumn night, he built a vigorous fire outside the wagon and boiled first a large kettle of water, then a pan of rice water, which he allowed to thicken to a syrup. Next, he heated wide bolts of flannel and took them back inside the wagon, where he sprinkled a few drops of precious camphor oil on them. Finally, with great care, he removed Tierney's outer clothing and wrapped him snugly in the warm flannel, much as he might have swaddled an infant.

The night they had first learned that Tierney had been stricken with the cholera, Sandemon had prepared a compound of powdered camphor and cayenne, plus a small measure of alcohol. His foresight had paid off. Now he took the bottle containing that mixture from the small wooden chest of herbs and medicines he had brought with him.

The mixture should have had more time to steep, but he would have to hope it would do its work as it was.

After measuring a small dose of the mixture into a cup of rice water, he undertook to make Tierney drink it. The boy fought him, as Sandemon had expected. It took almost an hour, but he managed to force a few sips of the mixture down his throat.

When he was satisfied that he could do no more for Tierney for the time being, he turned his attention to Jan Martova. He would continue to dose him with laudanum every two to three hours. That and the potassa syrup would ease the violent purging effects of the disease. Aside from this and a little rice water, there was little else to do for the Gypsy over the next few hours.

Except, of course, to pray. Sandemon knew he would do much praying throughout this night.

30

Voice of the Heart

Together...together—
The word makes music in the heart.

MORGAN FITZGERALD

M organ's first blast of the reality of life without Sandemon came early the next morning.

The day had not started badly. In fact, he had managed quite well, had even felt rather pleased with himself at first. Getting up from bed on his own, he had accomplished—if somewhat clumsily—his toilette, though keenly aware of how much easier Sandemon's discreet assistance made the process.

Dressing himself was no problem. With Sandemon's help, he had orchestrated a routine that time had only perfected. These days, it took him scarcely longer to outfit himself in the morning than it had before the injury. The procedure had been refined like a well-oiled wheel, to such an extent that he moved through it almost instinctively.

Only now, as he sat in the wheelchair looking down over his bare feet, socks in hand, did he remember the missing spoke in that well-oiled wheel.

No doubt there were those who might wonder, legitimately, why a man who could not walk insisted on wearing shoes. It had nothing to do with comfort, of course. His feet did not respond to heat or cold. Nor was it mere vanity; who cared about the feet of a paralyzed man in a wheelchair?

It had to do, he admitted to himself, with the matter of *dignity*. He simply did not feel altogether dressed without his shoes. That being the case, he made it a point not to leave his bedchamber in the morning until his feet were decently shod.

Unfortunately, he had forgotten how difficult it could be to manage shoes and socks without help.

For a moment Morgan continued to study his feet, finding it exasperating that such an ordinary, mechanical operation should pose a problem. On his first attempt he had nearly pitched headfirst out of the wheelchair. The second try was no more successful.

This time, he didn't bend quite so far forward, attempting instead to lift one foot with his hands. Again he lost his balance, catching himself by splaying both hands against the side of the bed.

With a sharp sigh of annoyance, he dangled the socks over his knees as he sat scowling down at his feet.

His head snapped up at the soft tap on the door connecting his room with Finola's.

"Morgan? May I come in?"

Without waiting, she cracked the door and stuck her head inside. "Morgan?"

"Aye, come." He fumbled for the lap robe, which had fallen from the back of the chair onto the floor, but he wasn't quick enough; she was already in the room.

She was dressed in some sort of yellow morning frock, her golden hair falling free. She looked for all the world like an early spring daffodil.

"I thought I would look in to see if there's anything I can do—" Her eyes went from the socks in his hand to his bare feet. She assessed the situation at once. "Let me help you."

"No!" The word came out far more sharply than Morgan intended, but he was mortified that she would see him in such a state.

She stopped in the middle of the room, a hand going to her throat as she gave him a questioning look.

"I'm sorry, I didn't mean to be short," Morgan said, adding self-disgust to embarrassment. "I...ah...had forgotten what a challenge it can be, putting on my shoes," he said, forcing a laugh.

She glanced at his feet. "Please let me help you," she said again.

"I would really prefer you didn't," he said, careful to keep his tone light. "It's a bit humiliating, don't you see?"

She looked at him. "Would you do it for me?" she asked unexpectedly.
"I beg your pardon?"

"If I were in your place, Morgan," she said, looking directly into his eyes,
"would you help me put on my shoes?"

Something in the simple, straightforward question hit him like a blow.
He glanced down at his hands, saw that he had rolled the socks together
into a tight ball. "Aye," he finally answered, "I expect I would."

"And would you find it demeaning, to help me so? Or would you do
it gladly?"

"Gladly, of course! It's just that—"

"Well, then," she said evenly, coming to kneel in front of him. "I haven't
had a great deal of experience with men's socks, of course, but I believe I
can manage."

Feeling foolish entirely, Morgan opened his hand. She glanced up at
him, and there was the hint of a smile in her eyes as she took one of the
socks and carefully put it on his foot.

"The other one?" she said, looking up at him.

He handed her the other sock, watching as she smoothed it up over
his foot. Her hands looked surprisingly strong and sure as she proceeded
next to slip his shoe onto his right foot. For an instant he could have sworn
he felt her touch, but that was nonsense, obviously; his feet were as useless as his legs.

For a fleeting instant, Morgan's imagination called up a sensation of
what her touch might be like, if he *did* have feeling in his feet and legs.

The effect was startling. He shut his eyes for a moment against the bittersweet joy of imagining her touch, took a deep breath, and fought for control.

When he opened his eyes again, her slender fingers still rested on his
foot, smoothing the fabric around his ankle.

He found it impossible to take his eyes from her hands, could not
help but wonder that she managed to turn such a small ordinary act into
a work of grace.

Impulsively, he reached out to touch the golden crown of her head.
Her hair was like warm satin, as he had known it would be.

She seemed to hesitate for a heartbeat, then went on lacing his shoes.

"There," she said quietly when finished, sounding as if she had accomplished something of real consequence. Looking up, she smiled shyly into
his eyes.

Reluctantly, Morgan dropped his hand away from her hair. "Thank you," he choked out, wanting more than anything in the world at that moment to gather her close and hold her. But the awareness that such an overture might repulse her or even frighten her was like a knife through his heart, and more than enough to restrain him.

"I will help you again tonight," she said, "and each morning." Suddenly she colored, as if she had hinted at some intimacy. She looked past him, saying in a low voice, "You mustn't mind my helping you, Morgan. It's such a small thing..."

She made no attempt to finish her statement, and sensing her sudden awkwardness, Morgan forced a light note into his own voice when he spoke. "Well, then—after all this exertion I am eager for breakfast. Shall we go down?"

Still caught up in a torrent of emotions as they entered the dining room, Morgan felt bemused. He supposed conventional couples might think him demented, to take on over such a small thing as the moment he had just shared with Finola upstairs. Nevertheless, he did not believe for an instant that, even if he were to spend each day with her for the rest of his life, he would take a precious second of their time together for granted.

Finola knew she was being foolish entirely, to make so much of it. No doubt the common act of helping him with his shoes had meant nothing more to him than a moment of awkwardness for his own incapacity. And no doubt the touch of his hand on her hair had been nothing but an affectionate pat, much as one might stroke a well-behaved child.

But for her, it had been more. For a moment, at least, she had actually felt like his *wife,* indeed had managed to pretend that she helped him with his shoes *every* morning, and that his gentle hand on her hair had real meaning as a touch of marital affection.

Seated to his left at the table, she kept her gaze carefully trained on her plate, though each bite she lifted seemed to stick in her throat. She had been unable to meet his eyes since they sat down to breakfast, fearful that he might detect the clamor of her emotions.

How would he respond if he were to discover the depth of her feelings for him? Would he be embarrassed? Awkward? Appalled? She was convinced that most of the time, when he thought of her at all, he thought of her as he might have a younger sister, or perhaps, even worse, a daughter!

He showed her the same fondness, the same genuine affection, he offered Annie. He was ever courteous, always thoughtful, infinitely gentle. He seemed to enjoy coaxing a smile from her, or outright laughter, and, as with Annie, he obviously delighted in drawing her into a lively exchange of ideas and opinions.

Yet, there were times...rare, unguarded times...when she caught him looking at her in a different way, a way that made her mind spin and her heart skip. She would look up and find the deep green gaze settled on her with all the intensity of a caress. Or at other times, she would turn and find him studying her with such infinite tenderness she lost her breath.

At such times, he would appear flustered and would quickly look away, leaving her to wonder if she had only imagined the subtle difference in his gaze.

He confused her, disturbed her, sometimes even dismayed her, with his manner of treating her as his ward rather than as his wife—or at least as a *woman*. Yet, in a way she could not explain, she belonged to him. She had long ago given him her heart of hearts, and the fact that he had no awareness of the gift changed nothing. For the truth was that she could no more have resisted loving him than she could have stopped breathing.

"Have you seen Sister or Annie yet this morning?"

When Morgan's question snapped her out of her thoughts, she felt for an instant as if he had read her mind, and she flushed guiltily. "Sister—oh, yes! I talked with her first thing this morning, in the nursery."

"You told her about Sandemon?"

"I did, and she suggested she might speak with Annie. I expect she already has."

Morgan nodded. "It will go hard with the lass. She still tags after Sandemon like a faithful pup."

"I plan to keep her busy, helping me with Gabriel. And perhaps, you could set her to doing things for you, as well?"

"Aye, a good idea." He studied her for a moment. "You're very good with Annie, you know. She adores you."

Finola smiled at the thought of the feisty, dark-eyed Aine. "I'm quite fond of her. Indeed, if ever I had had a little sister, I would have wanted her to be—"

Finola broke off, struck by what she had just said.

"What?" Morgan leaned toward her. "What is it?"

She looked at him. "It just occurred to me," she said, her voice unsteady, "that for all I know...I *might* have a little sister...somewhere."

He took her hand. "Does it still bother you very much, Finola, not knowing the past?"

She stared down at their clasped hands, thinking about his question. "Perhaps not as much as it once did. But it's very strange, not really knowing who I am, where I came from—if I have family, if they miss me...."

She glanced up at him, saw understanding and concern brimming in his eyes. "I'm not unhappy, Morgan. But...I can't help but wonder. I suppose I shall always wonder."

He nodded, squeezing her hand. "So long as you're not unhappy." He paused, then added, "You *do* have a family, *mavourneen*. You have me, and Gabriel—and Annie—"

Finola smiled at him. "And Sister...and Sandemon. I would say I have a very large family! And I do love you all!" she added impulsively. Quickly, she looked away, feeling her face heat as she realized what she had said.

It's true...I do love you all...but especially you, Morgan...especially you....

31

Terror on the Wind

A great storm from the ocean goes shouting o'er the hill,
And there is glory in it and terror on the wind.

EVA GORE-BOOTH (1870–1926)

L ate that afternoon, Annie stood on what had come to be called the "safe" side of the stream, watching the Gypsy wagon on the other side.

Although the distance between her and the wagon wasn't actually so great, it might as well have been miles.

She had been standing there, with Fergus beside her, for nearly an hour, hoping Sandemon would come outside. She wanted to tell him she missed him, that she was praying for him.

Of course, Sandemon would insist that she pray with equal fervor for Tierney Burke and the Gypsy. Frowning, she resisted the thought. "This entire calamity is Tierney Burke's fault, after all," she said to Fergus. The wolfhound looked up, tilting his head as if to consider her remark.

"Him and his deceitful ways! Well, it seems to me he and his Gypsy cohort got just what they deserve."

She should have ratted on Tierney at the beginning, should have gone to the *Seanchai* or to Sandemon that first night when she had seen him sneak away from the house, loping down the hill without ever looking back. So sure of himself he had been!

If only she hadn't been so determined not to tattle. Just look what her silence had allowed.

If anything happened to Sandemon, she would never forgive Tierney Burke!

Or herself...

The sun had been swallowed by some heavy-hanging pewter clouds, and the air had suddenly taken on a sharp edge. Annie shivered inside her coat but made no move to go back to the house.

There was nothing to do inside, after all. It seemed that everyone was occupied, except for her. Sister was helping Mrs. Ryan pack a food basket for Sandemon and the sick boys. Finola was helping the *Seanchai* transcribe notes from Father Mahon's journal. And baby Gabriel slept most afternoons straight through.

Since it was a Saturday, she had the luxury of free time to herself. There were no recitations or extra studies, and she had completed her chores before midday.

On a normal day, she would be glad for such a delicious pocket of time to fill however she liked. She might plop on the window seat in the library with a book, or perhaps practice her sketching. Sometimes she helped Sandemon with one of his many projects. He was forever making something new—a toy for Gabriel, an additional desk for one of the classrooms, a tool of some sort.

Sister would frequently nag at her about using her time for one of the endless "domestic arts," implying that she should conduct herself more like a young lady.

"You are growing up, Miss," she would say, with one eyebrow arched. "And as the daughter of a great man, you must learn to conduct yourself accordingly."

Annie had conflicting emotions about this business of growing up. Some things about it didn't appear too disagreeable, at least not entirely. She liked wearing new clothes well enough, especially when Finola helped her choose the patterns. Occasionally she suffered Sister's attempts to "discipline" her hair, but she liked it much better when Finola dressed it for her. Sometimes it was fun, pretending to be a fine lady with dozens of handsome suitors vying for her hand, though these days she quickly tired of playing make-believe.

If she could expect that she would ever be anything but plain and spindly-legged, she might feel a bit more eager to come of age. Finola was good to assure her that she would one day be "stunning," but it took only a close look in the mirror for doubts to rise again.

Overall, she found the idea of growing up more trouble than it was worth. It seemed to mean nothing more than increasingly difficult studies, more household chores, and more *responsibilities*—another of Sister Louisa's overused words.

It also seemed to mean feeling happy one moment and low as the grave the next—or, at other times, like now, anxious and restless for no conceivable reason.

A wind was blowing up, wailing down the hills like an old woman keening the dead. The enormous trees all about the grounds groaned and rustled, as if giants were walking among them. Again, Annie shivered. Usually, she didn't mind the wind. Huddled snugly in bed, the covers up to her chin, she liked to lie and listen to the music the wind made outside her window at night, like pipers marching over the hill, droning their battle songs.

Today, though, the wind only made her feel lonelier, and oddly frightened, as if it might be bearing some unknown terror. She glanced down at Fergus. The wolfhound, too, seemed jittery and on edge, his ears pricked as if he heard something she could not.

She was about to give up on Sandemon and go back inside when the Gypsy boy—the one called *Nanosh*—came out of the smokehouse and started toward her.

As usual, he looked none too clean. Annie had talked to him once or twice. She thought him impudent, but the *Seanchai* said they must treat him decently, that he was proving helpful and dependable in acting as a messenger between the Gypsy wagon and the house.

He walked up to her now, first eyeing Fergus, who stood perfectly still, watching him in return. Turning to Annie, he asked bluntly, "Why do you stand out here in the cold?"

Annie frowned at him. "Perhaps to keep watch on things," she said shortly.

He studied her. "Are you Tierney Burke's sister?"

"No, I am *not*! I am Aine Fitzgerald—the *Seanchai*'s daughter."

For a moment, he went on appraising her with a curious expression. "I did not know the *Seanchai* had any children," he said, following his observation with a great, unconcealed yawn.

"Well, he does. He has *two* children, in fact. A son and myself. Of course, I am no longer a child," Annie quickly added. She motioned toward the wagon. "Have you seen Sandemon today?"

"The black man? Not since early morning. I saw him burning something not long after he called out his report on my cousin and Tierney Burke." Again, he yawned, putting his hands in his pockets as he continued to watch Annie. "I suppose you live in the big house."

"Aye, I do."

"I live in a wagon," he told her. "With my mother and brothers and sisters."

"All of you live in a wagon?" Annie asked, interested in spite of herself.

"Well, mostly we live outside. We only stay in the wagon when the weather is bad or when we're traveling."

As Annie watched, he dug down in the pocket of his baggy trousers and pulled out a red ball. Fergus immediately flexed his muscles and stood at the ready.

"I don't suppose you'd want to play toss?" the Gypsy suggested.

Annie considered the ball and the Gypsy boy's hopeful expression. She looked at Fergus, who appeared more hopeful still.

"I think not," she said, feeling not at all inclined to play at *anything*. The boy's face fell, and on impulse she added, "But you may play with Fergus if you like. If you pitch the ball, he'll retrieve it."

The boy didn't hesitate, but took off running. At a nod from Annie, the wolfhound followed.

Annie watched the two charge off across the field, then turned back to the wagon. Its bright-colored exterior appeared strangely out of place in the gloom rapidly settling over the field—almost like a garishly painted smile on a sad-faced doll.

A part of Annie knew that the melancholy was on her, that the mournful wind and encroaching shadows had drawn her into their web of darkness. She felt more and more isolated, yet unnerved by the chilling sensation that she was no longer alone.

She looked around—behind her, across the stream, up toward the house—but saw nothing.

The back of her neck went cold, as if an icy finger had touched her. Something inside her wrenched as the wind moaned down the hill, sharpening the chill in the air and the ache of loneliness in her heart.

She shuddered, pulling her coat more tightly about her to shut out the wind that was coming down the hill...and whatever else it might be bringing with it. Suddenly she felt cold all through and peculiarly small and alone. Seized by an urgent need *not* to be alone, she turned and began running toward the house.

That night the moderate wind that had blown up earlier strengthened, turning into an angry, howling gale that shook the trees and hammered at the wagon.

After lighting an extra lantern, Sandemon went first to check Jan Martova, who was sleeping. The Gypsy's skin felt cooler, though he still drew his legs up with pain.

Going to Tierney Burke, Sandemon dropped to his knees, lifting the lantern over him, to see his face. He was still prostrate, his skin still darkly discolored and spongy. His breath came in short, shallow gasps.

Sandemon put his fingers to the boy's throat, alarmed by the slow, feeble rhythm. For a moment he continued to kneel beside him, watching. From time to time the slender body would jerk and twitch, the head twist and loll from one side to the other. The fingers were stiff and curled inward, like claws. From the throat came the chilling sound of the death rattles.

Setting the lantern a safe distance away, Sandemon remained on his knees with a growing feeling of helplessness as he watched the boy's struggle. If he was not mistaken, this was a soul as yet unclaimed, a soul in danger of the deadly abyss.

"This boy is not ready, Lord...not yet...he needs more time and Your patience...."

Pressing a hand to each knee, he forced himself to shake off the cold wave of dread that had been taunting him all evening. Staying perfectly still, he closed his eyes and tried to quiet his spirit.

It took a long time. At first, he was consumed with a sense of darkness. Darkness and bitter cold. Shuddering, he swallowed down the taste of terror rising like spoiled food at the back of his throat. In the woeful howling of the wind, he imagined he heard a whispering...at first, a murmur, then a rush of voices, growing nearer, as if carried on the wind itself.

Squeezing his eyes shut, he began to pray silently, then aloud. He invoked the Name of Christ, the precious Blood of Christ, the saving Cross of Christ. Beside him, the boy moaned, whimpering and thrashing about, as if waging a pathetic defense against some vicious attack.

Sensing that the attack would be prolonged and particularly tenacious—for the body was young and the spirit strong and stubborn—Sandemon prayed on. At times he prayed the words of the Church, at times the words of his heart…at times the Word itself. As the wind turned savage and the darkness heavy, he began to recite entire portions of the Holy Scriptures, until at last he was speaking only of his Jesus, retelling the story of His birth, His life, His crucifixion…then His resurrection, as if to lift the risen Savior high in the trembling wagon, high above the darkness…above the whispering…above the wind.

Tierney was trapped inside the tunnel, searching for a lantern or even a candle, something to light his way.…

He was crawling on his hands and knees, the floor hard and cold and wet. When he pushed himself upright, he swayed and pitched from side to side, blown by an angry, wailing wind. He flung his hands out into the darkness to break his fall, finding nothing to cling to but the black, threatening gale. There were no walls, and yet he felt himself to be confined in a type of dungeon, the only escape at the end of the tunnel in front of him… but how to find the end of the tunnel with no light?

The floor continued to sway and shift beneath him. The wind tossed him here, then there, like a dead leaf blown idly across the ground. Yet he fought to keep going, strained to stay upright, to push ahead toward the end of the tunnel.

But what if the tunnel *had* no end? What if he were simply chasing himself in a meaningless circle?

The pain no longer consumed him, though it still clutched at his bones with needlelike talons. A surging fear of the dark and a desperate desire to escape had pushed past the pain.

He heard whispering, a low, rustling sound like the scraping of wings or the murmuring of secrets. Slowing his pace, he flailed his arms, grabbing aimlessly to steady himself. The wind seemed to slow, and now he thought himself to be standing on a kind of bridge, a rickety, swaying footbridge with no sides, nothing to hold on to, not even a rope.

On either side of him were the whispers. He began to make his way across the bridge, holding his breath, ignoring the needle pricks of pain.

He wanted to reach out, to grab onto something…anything…but feared what he might touch in the darkness. The whispering went on, and he realized for the first time that he was walking a kind of gauntlet, with shapeless, faceless beings all along the way, beings who reached out to touch him, to stop him, as he passed by.

Terrorized, he walked faster, forcing himself not to bolt into a run and lose his balance. He knew, without knowing how he knew, that if he fell, it would be forever…a forever spent in the dark abyss that waited below him.

The whispers grew louder, the touches more demanding. Clammy hands groped at him from both sides of the bridge, pressing and prob-ing him. The whispers became voices—shrieking, angry, menacing voices who demanded something he was unwilling to give.

Suddenly, the wind began again, this time a blistering hot fury roar-ing down the tunnel, slamming at his back, then his face. He tried to run, but was caught up by the scalding wind, sucked inside it, forced into a mindless, macabre dance as he struggled to retain his footing on the bridge.

He made the mistake of looking down. His eyes filled with the hor-ror of a lake of fire, blazing up, dangerously close to the bridge. He threw out one arm, grabbed a fistful of nothing but scorching wind, screamed as a burst of fire exploded in front of his face, shaking him hard enough to hurl him from the bridge.

He slipped and pitched forward, flailing both arms as he screamed, and began to fall….

The boy's scream of terror pierced Sandemon's spirit, jolting him back to his surroundings, hauling him rudely away from the peace of the Pres-ence. Bending over the shrieking youth, he saw that his eyes were open, wide and huge, as if they beheld some mind-shattering horror. Thrusting his arms straight out, the boy grabbed at Sandemon's shirt like a drown-ing man clinging to a lifeline.

Sandemon's heart hammered like a fist at his chest as he threw his arms about the youth, holding him tightly. *"Hold on, boy! Hold on!"*

"Don't let me fall! Please, God, don't let me fall!" The boy's delirium swelled to near madness, and Sandemon clasped him even closer to his chest.

"You won't fall! Hold on to Sandemon! I won't let you fall!"

He went on crooning to the terrified youth as if he were an infant to be soothed. Finally, little by little, the boy quieted, though his hands never loosened their death grip on Sandemon's shoulders.

Easing him back just a little, Sandemon searched the boy's eyes. Tierney's gaze cleared, then finally focused. "You are safe," Sandemon assured him gently. "Don't be afraid. You're safe now."

The boy stared up at him, and even as he watched, Sandemon saw the fear return, the horror remembered. He held the boy with one arm around his shoulder, putting an ear to his chest. The heat of his body had cooled measurably. The heartbeat was already increasing in strength.

He would recover.

"What happened?" the boy asked, his tongue thick. "Where have I been? What happened to me?"

Still holding him, Sandemon searched the youthful, frightened face, damp and slick with perspiration.

"I think, Tierney Burke, that you have been to the gates of hell," Sandemon replied, his own voice weak and somewhat unsteady. "God be thanked that in His mercy, He brought you back."

The boy lay so still he seemed not to breathe. Those searching blue eyes, in which Sandemon had seldom seen anything but the darkness of cynicism or the glint of pride, were now glazed with something else. For a moment, Sandemon thought the youth would mock him, and he stiffened, bracing himself for more insult.

But Tierney Burke merely lay staring up at him, limp as a broken doll. To Sandemon's amazement, the boy grasped his free hand and clung to it. "Thank you…"

Sandemon waited, holding his breath.

"I almost fell…I would have died." He stopped, gasping. "Thank you… for holding me back. For not letting go of me. I owe you…Sandemon."

"It was not I who kept you from falling, Tierney Burke, but your merciful Savior. He held you back to give you more time—time to make your choice between death and life, between heaven and hell."

Tierney gave a weak nod, his eyes closing. Sandemon's eyes filled, but he smiled a little as he gently eased the boy down on the pile of quilts that served as his pallet. Then, getting to his feet, he went to glance out the window. The wind had stilled, leaving the night hushed and peaceful once more. He gave a weary but relieved sigh, then started to tiptoe past the sleeping Jan Martova.

"Sandemon?" the Gypsy called softly.

Stooping down beside him, Sandemon asked, "How are you feeling? Better now?"

The Gypsy nodded as if to say he was doing all right. His eyes met Sandemon's and he reached to touch his arm. "I was listening to you," he said. "I heard you praying for Tierney Burke…and speaking of your God. The One you call your Savior."

Sandemon nodded, wondering what was to come.

"Will you tell me more?" asked the Gypsy.

"More?" puzzled Sandemon.

"Tell me more about your Jesus."

Slowly, a smile broke across Sandemon's face. Forgetting his fatigue, the countless hours without sleep, he sank down to sit on the floor beside the Gypsy. "Indeed, I will," he said, patting the boy's hand. "You just rest, now, and I will tell you more about my Jesus."

In her bed upstairs at Nelson Hall, Annie stirred in her sleep. Turning over, she opened her eyes, listening.

The wind had stopped. Still she listened, just to be sure. Finally, hearing nothing, she yawned and reached over to stroke Fergus's head. Then she tugged the covers securely under her chin and murmured one last drowsy prayer for Sandemon and, after a moment, another for Tierney Burke and the Gypsy.

Turning over, she gave a soft sigh and went back to sleep.

PART THREE

LIGHT OF HOPE

Glorious Grace

See to it that no one misses the grace of God.

HEBREWS 12:15

32

Suffer the Children

We never knew a childhood's mirth and gladness,
Nor the proud heart of youth, free and brave.

LADY WILDE (1824–1896)

Early November
New York City

For the first time since the choir's inception, Evan Whittaker shortened a Thursday rehearsal. He was anxious to leave the Five Points before dark, and he still had two stops to make before going home.

With November bearing down upon the city, the days seemed much shorter. Even though it was only a little past four, the gloom of early evening was already gathering, casting deep shadows over the streets—and over Evan's spirits. He now turned Lewis Farmington's buggy onto Mulberry Street, where Billy Hogan lived, and a vague sense of anxiety churned in the pit of his stomach. Despite the boy's unmistakable enthusiasm for the singing group, Billy had shown up only once in six weeks for rehearsal. That had been three weeks past, and for the entire hour the little fellow had not once looked Evan in the eye. He had been nervous and withdrawn, tucking his chin against his shoulder as if to hide the ugly bruise darkening his temple.

Evan had sensed something unsettlingly different about Billy that day. The boy had seemed distant, withdrawn—removed from the others in the group, and from Evan.

Troubled over the lad's peculiar behavior, Evan had made an attempt to talk with some of the other boys about him, but had learned nothing. Even Billy's closest friend, Tom Breen, had been no help, although Evan sensed an odd evasiveness in the older boy's replies. Each time Evan questioned him, Tom said the same thing: yes, he still saw Billy; but, no, not recently; and no, he hadn't a clue as to where Billy might be keeping himself on Thursday afternoons.

"Workin' at his papers or shovelin' coal for the Arab, most likely" was all the Breen lad ever volunteered. On one or two occasions, Evan thought the boy had been about to add something, but instead he merely shrugged and walked away.

Today, he intended to ask his questions directly of Billy himself if he found him at home. If not, he would talk with someone in the family. He had taken quite a liking to the thin little lad with the wheat-colored hair and angelic voice. He would hate to think Billy might be ill or in some sort of trouble.

Later, Evan intended to stop by the mission clinic to see Dr. Grafton. The physician's request that Evan "drop in" concerned him more than he liked to acknowledge. He had tried for weeks to coax Nora into visiting the doctor, always with no success. Invariably, she insisted that she was "perfectly fine, only a bit tired," and he was to "stop fussing over her."

As luck would have it, Dr. Grafton had dropped by the house late one afternoon to check on Teddy. Evan had been at home at the time and, against Nora's protests, insisted the doctor examine her as well. But despite his concerns he was nevertheless caught unawares when that impromptu examination led to another, this one at the doctor's office in Manhattan. Then, just today the message had come through Daniel that Evan was to stop by the mission clinic, after hours.

He could not help but worry that his fears about Nora's health might be justified after all. In spite of her insistence that there was nothing wrong, she seemed exhausted by the slightest exertion, continued to eat poorly, and appeared altogether enervated by the end of the day.

Daniel, too, had recently confided a concern for his mother's health. Like Evan, he had noticed her extreme thinness and unnatural color. All things considered, Evan thought he had reason to feel uneasy.

Sighing heavily, he brought the buggy to a halt in front of an ugly brown tenement squeezed in between two others just like it. For a moment, he sat studying the building. It was a harsh picture of decay, with rotting doorframes and windows; the filth of decades scaled its entire frontage. At first glance it appeared strangely top-heavy, as if the building itself were leaning forward. A closer inspection revealed that its peculiar listing appearance was actually the fault of a sagging porch. It ran the length of the second floor and looked as if it might break off from the rest of the structure at any moment.

The place was so stark and ugly it appeared almost malevolent. Its neighboring dwellings were equally hideous. Evan felt faintly ill at the thought of a child like Billy Hogan growing up in such abominable surroundings.

The children playing in the street were, for the most part, filthy, dressed in rags that scarcely covered them. They seemed to pay no heed to the garbage and animal offal that was everywhere. Wild-looking dogs prowled about, ignoring the children as they scavenged for food.

One never quite got used to the abandoned children, Evan thought—the homeless, and the hopeless, forgotten little ones. Even those with a roof over their head at night often had no real home, only a place to sleep. With drunken or destitute parents, there was frequently no nurturing, no family life, no love. He had been told by Sara Farmington Burke—and he believed it—that in the Five Points, a child could simply disappear one day without a single soul ever knowing or caring where he might have gone.

"God help them," he said under his breath as he stepped out of the buggy and stood, bracing himself to enter the building. "God help them all…and please, God, help Billy Hogan."

Nora sat in the rocking chair by the front window, gazing down at the warm, sleeping infant in her arms. She touched a finger to one incredible soft cheek, then to a corner of the tiny mouth, curved in the hint of a smile as he slept.

It was hard to believe that he had been with them only a few months. Why, last year at this time she hadn't even known she was carrying him!

Teddy was such a good babe. Never a moment's trouble, not even when he was restless in the night. He seldom cried, except when he was hungry. He would lie quietly in his crib for the longest time, smiling and watching the bright-colored wooden animals Daniel had hung from the ceiling to amuse him.

Glancing out at the afternoon's deepening gloom, she gathered the baby closer, shivering in spite of the room's warmth. Like the late afternoon shadows pressing in from outside, a distant specter of uneasiness infiltrated her thoughts, dimming her earlier glow of contentment.

Over the past few weeks, she had grown increasingly aware that she wasn't well. At first she hadn't been all that concerned, only impatient with her slow recovery from Teddy's birth. But she was practical enough to realize that she was no longer a young chick, and she could hardly expect to breeze through the birthing process as if she were.

Moreover, if she were to be entirely honest with herself, she would have to concede that it had been a risk from the beginning, having Teddy. She couldn't have been overly strong when she conceived; no doubt months of famine and the scarlet fever had taken their toll on her. It was only natural, she tried to remind herself, that it would take time to recover her health.

But Teddy was over four months old now, and instead of feeling stronger, she felt her strength failing. Exhaustion was an ongoing problem. Weariness seemed to plague her from the time she left her bed in the morning until she collapsed on it again at night. Yet there was no good reason for her to feel so depleted. It wasn't as if she were overworked, after all. Johanna and Daniel John helped out as much as they could. Aunt Winnie came in once or twice a week and spent the day. And although Evan was already far too busy, he always found time for her and the children.

She had said nothing at all to Evan, of course. He fretted enough on his own without her adding to it. But he was obviously suspicious of her attempts to convince him that she was actually doing quite well. In fact, both he and Sara were set on finding extra household help for her—a notion that made Nora feel altogether useless. Just two weeks past, Sara had even gone so far as to send over a girl from one of the immigrant societies, on a "trial basis." The experiment had proved an utter failure after two days' time, when Nora caught the girl being hateful with poor Johanna and sent her packing.

Secretly, she rather hoped Sara wouldn't find anyone else. She didn't like the idea of having a stranger about the house doing work she ought to be doing herself. She liked even less the notion of a stranger helping to take care of her precious baby boy. She knew Evan and Sara had only her best interests at heart, but she couldn't help but wish they would forget the whole idea.

Something else, however, had begun to worry Nora more than the fatigue. For weeks now, at the most unexpected times, a heaviness would suddenly settle over her chest, followed by a dull, squeezing pain. It seldom lasted long—a few seconds at most—but it was occurring more and more frequently.

Although she hadn't breathed a word about it to anyone, she was afraid Dr. Grafton might have noticed something when he last examined her. He had asked her endless questions about herself, listening to her chest for what seemed an excessively long time. Although his manner had been as friendly and professional as ever, Nora thought he might have been quieter than usual. That same day, he surprised her by suggesting that she consider weaning Teddy early, hinting that she should do whatever she could to conserve her strength.

Nora was trying her utmost to appear fit and strong around Evan, determined he should not suspect anything amiss. Yet she could no longer pretend to *herself* that everything was as it should be, and she wasn't altogether certain that she was doing the right thing, trying to hide her condition from Evan. The children had to be considered, after all. What if something *should* happen to her, and Evan were caught totally unprepared? How would he manage? With Teddy still an infant and Johanna not only physically handicapped but emotionally troubled as well—how *could* he manage?

Glancing up, she caught a glimpse of herself in the mirror across the room. She lifted a hand to her hair, tucking a few gray wisps under the darker strands about her temples. Impulsively, she pinched her cheeks a bit, watching as a faint pink stain crept over them.

But the color quickly fled, and the reflection that stared back at her seemed that of a stranger: a gaunt, ashen-skinned stranger, with dull, shadowed eyes which at the moment glinted with something that looked very much like fear.

After sending one of the kitchen boys from the downstairs tavern with a message for Jess Dalton, Nicholas Grafton hastily scrawled another note, this one for Evan Whittaker:

Forgive my absence, but emergency demands my immediate attention. Will talk with you later in the week. N.G.

Grabbing his medicine case, the doctor tacked the note on the outside door of the mission room, then hurried downstairs.

He had not expected this call quite so soon, yet now that it was here, he wasn't surprised. Both he and Elizabeth Ward had known for days the end was rapidly approaching. Nicholas was convinced that the only thing that had kept the stricken young woman going was her concern for her baby daughter. She had never ceased hoping and praying that a letter would arrive from her father in England, a letter that would ease her mind about her little girl's future.

Nicholas's jaw tightened as he climbed into his carriage. Every time he thought about the foolish, stubborn man in England who had turned his back on his only daughter, he wanted to drive his fist through a wall.

For weeks he had watched Elizabeth Ward's hope turn to anguish at the deafening silence from her father. And now, at the end, the poor girl must endure not only the crushing pain of her disease, but despair and fear for her child as well.

At first he had been convinced that Edward Winston, Elizabeth's father, would reply immediately to his letter on her behalf. No matter how wronged the man might consider himself, he was a father. And a father, as Nicholas knew firsthand, had a way of putting aside any wrong to himself when the well-being of his children was at stake.

But as time went on, Nicholas reluctantly accepted the fact that there would be no reply, no last-minute letter to restore the dying young mother's hope. Apparently, Edward Winston had been unmoved by every plea for his daughter, despite the fact that his heartlessness would send her to the grave unconsoled—and might well cause his granddaughter to end up in a city orphanage.

People like Edward Winston seldom considered the consequences of their pride, Nicholas thought angrily: the long-lasting and sometimes widespread effects of their selfishness. Did they ever give a thought to the lives that might be damaged, or even destroyed, by the intractable withholding of grace, the stubborn refusal to forgive?

Shaking his head, he drove on, dreading what would be, almost certainly, his final call on Elizabeth Ward. Perhaps eventually he would be able to feel pity for the man in England, whose pride of name evidently meant more to him than his own child. But for now, the only emotion he could find in his heart for Edward Winston was a seething rage for the additional, unnecessary pain he was inflicting on his dying daughter.

With a sigh, he stepped up the pace of Little Milly, his aging mare, praying all the while that Jess Dalton would have gotten his message and would be at Elizabeth Ward's apartment by the time he arrived.

33

Be Thou My Vision

Be Thou my vision, O Lord of my heart,
Naught be all else to me, save that Thou art.

<small>ANONYMOUS (IRISH, EIGHTH CENTURY)</small>

The man who flung open the door when Evan knocked at the upstairs flat was a big hulk of a fellow, obviously inebriated.

He towered over Evan. Standing in the doorway, he raked one large hand through thinning brown hair as he looked Evan up and down. His stained, dun-colored shirt gaped open over a swollen stomach. He reeked of bad whiskey and body odor.

For a moment, Evan could only stare, hoping he had the wrong address, that this was *not* the uncle Billy Hogan had spoken of.

Clearing his throat, he finally managed to find his voice. "How—how do you d-do?" he stammered. "I wonder if I have the r-right address. I'm looking for one of m-my choir m-members—Billy Hogan."

The man eyed him with a look of distaste. Evan was beginning to wonder if he was going to answer him at all.

"You're the Englishman," the man in the doorway finally snarled. "Whittaker."

His words were slurred. Somehow he managed to make Evan's name sound like an obscenity.

Evan raised his chin slightly. "I-I am Evan Whittaker, that's correct. And you are—"

"Billy ain't here."

"I see," Evan said after a slight hesitation. Irked by the man's coarseness, he nevertheless kept a civil tone. "Are you, ah, B-Billy's uncle?"

"What do you want with the boy?"

Apparently, the man was bent on being rude. Biting down on his impatience, Evan forced himself not to reply in kind. "We've b-been missing B-Billy at rehearsal lately. I was afraid he m-might be ill." He paused. "I hope that's not the case."

"He ain't ill and, and like I said, he ain't here." The red-rimmed eyes narrowed suspiciously. "We don't need no Brits sniffin' about down here. You'd best be minding your *own* business, not ours."

It took everything Evan had to maintain his composure. Reminding himself that the man was obviously drunk, he drew in a deep, steadying breath. "I simply called to inquire after your nephew's whereabouts, to m-make certain he's not ill. Perhaps I could come b-back another time—"

"Don't bother yourself." The man's face contorted into an ugly scowl. "There's no need for you to come back a'tall—the boy don't live here anymore."

Evan frowned. "He d-doesn't live here? But, then—where *does* he live?"

"In the alleys with his newsboy chums, more than likely."

Evan caught a momentary glint of drunken cunning. Something warned him that the man wasn't telling the truth.

"I d-don't suppose you'd have any idea where I m-might find Billy and his friends," he ventured.

"I would not."

Evan stared at him, disgust and anger mingling. "Yes…well, thank you for your time. I shan't b-bother you any longer."

He could feel that baleful glare drilling into his back all the way downstairs. When he exited onto the street, he actually gave himself a shake, as if to throw off a clinging viper.

For a moment he stood outside the tenement, trying to think. Spying a policeman just up the street, he started toward him. As he approached, he recognized Sergeant Price, a familiar face about the Five Points.

To Evan's vast relief, the sergeant insisted on accompanying him in his search for Billy Hogan. "Why, the newsies are all about the place, Mr. Whittaker: in the Five Points, in the Bowery—a number of them bunk uptown, to be near the newspaper offices. You can't be going off on your own. Come along—I know most places to be looking."

Giving his nightstick a twirl, the policeman took Evan by the arm and propelled him down the street.

Billy Hogan lay curled on his side in the dank cellar, his feet drawn up almost to his chin. His entire body shook from the cold, for he wasn't allowed to have a jacket in the cellar. Bearing the cold was part of his punishment, Uncle Sorley said.

He tried to remember what, exactly, he was being punished for this time. He must have done something very bad, for it seemed he'd been here a long time. Longer than any time before. Days, perhaps an entire week.

He remembered the thrashing, remembered Uncle Sorley throwing himself at him, pounding at him, his huge, bruising hands hammering at his head, his ears. He remembered being hauled and kicked down the stairs, then thrown inside the storage press. And he remembered Uncle Sorley looming over him, the red, angry gash of his mouth shouting at him over and over, the fire in his eyes, the whiskey smell—

"This time you'll stay, boy! You'll stay down here till you learn to keep that bold mouth of yours shut!"

Then hours...days...of nothing but cold and darkness and pain. The difference between daylight and dark was vague, for he could barely see. His eyes were so swollen, the cellar so dark, he could scarcely make out anything in the storage press. First came the gnawing hunger, for he wasn't allowed food, but for the most part, the hunger had passed. His belly still ached some and burned, but he no longer thought much about food.

Most of the time he slept. His head and shoulders hurt so bad that he welcomed sleep, actually sought it. Even when he dreamed about Uncle Sorley or the rats lurking in the corners, he craved sleep, for it was his only comfort.

His belly cramped, and he drew his legs up as tightly as he could. Except for the burning in his stomach, he didn't feel much of anything at all. The weakness was on him bad again. He felt numb and lifeless. Even his feet were numb, as they had been that time back home, when he trekked through a snowstorm to find his dog, Reg.

He remembered Reg, his old red dog, as if they had parted only yesterday. He had cried and begged to be allowed to bring him to America, for he knew poor old Reg would die without anyone to feed and look after him. The dog was almost blind, and he counted on Billy to bring him his food, to rub his ears, and sometimes sing him a tune.

For weeks after leaving Ireland, Billy had prayed that someone with a kind heart would take Reg in, would give him a new home so he wouldn't be lonely or hungry. Sometimes he still thought about him, wondered what had happened to him. An old dog like Reg wouldn't live long without food or someone to talk kindly to him now and then.

His mind began to drift, as it usually did when the weakness was on him. He wanted to go to sleep, but the thought of his mother and brothers roused him.

Had Mum asked about him, he wondered? Did she or the wee boys miss him at all? Were his little brothers all right without him?

What if Uncle Sorley started beating on them in his absence?

Billy didn't think he would. Uncle Sorley pretty much ignored the younger boys. And his mum. He paid her little heed at all, except to snarl at her now and then if supper wasn't to his liking.

Perhaps Patrick or Liam would coax Mum to go looking for him while Uncle Sorley was at work. Surely *someone* would miss him.

But even if they *did* try to find him, how could they? No one knew where he was.

Uncle Sorley had brought him down to the cellar while Mum was at work and the wee boys were playing out front in the street. He said Billy had to stay here until he learned not to talk back. Billy was impudent, he said.

Billy didn't even know exactly what *impudent* meant. And he didn't remember talking back, he truly didn't. That's what Uncle Sorley always accused him of, although most of the time Billy didn't remember his offense. In fact, by the time the beatings were over, he could scarcely remember anything.

This time when he got out, he would be extra careful not to talk back. Not ever again. He would guard every word and say nothing that could possibly rile Uncle Sorley.

This time when he got out, he would be the best boy he could be. The *best*.

His head felt light again, yet he wasn't all that drowsy. He stiffened suddenly at a rustling noise from the opposite wall. Squeezing his eyes shut, he waited. After a moment, he realized he was grinding his teeth together. The pain in his jaws surprised him.

There was something…something he needed to remember….

It came to him, then, what kept the rats away. He began to hum, his voice sounding distant and strange in his ears. Words came, words that Mr. Evan had taught them. Mr. Evan often said that singing God's music or speaking God's Word was like building a fort around yourself…a fort of protection, for the things of darkness couldn't bear things of the Light….

"Be Thou my vision, O Lord of my heart,
Naught be all else to me, save that Thou art.
Thou my best thought by day and by night,
Waking or sleeping, Thy presence my light…."

Unable to remember the rest of the ancient hymn, for his mind was like a ship drifting out to sea, Billy went on singing the same words, over and over, until the scratching sounds in the corner finally ceased.

Over an hour later, Evan and the sergeant had questioned a number of newsboys. Some were small, others nearly grown. Some were huddled on doorsteps, some in alleyways around open fires. Others had pitched rude tents a distance outside the Five Points.

Without exception, no one had seen Billy Hogan for the past several days. He had not picked up his papers since last week, they said. And, no, they did not know where he might be found.

By now it was completely dark, and at the policeman's insistence, they had ceased their search. "I'll look further uptown tomorrow," the sergeant told Evan as they headed back toward the buggy. "And I'll look up Billy's pal, Tom Breen, as well. We'll find him, Mr. Whittaker, that we will."

His hopes dashed, Evan felt frustrated and increasingly anxious. And the information Sergeant Price relayed as they walked only sharpened his concern.

Billy's uncle—Sorley Dolan—was a drunk and a small-time gambler who worked as a bouncer in one of the Bowery dens. To Evan's dismay, he was not even the boy's real uncle!

"He's just a bum the mother took up with," the sergeant said. "I don't

know as they ever got married, to tell you the truth. Billy is hers by her
dead husband, but the younger two lads are Dolan's. You've got to give the
boy credit, though—he looks after those two little tykes as if they're full-
blood to him. A regular little daddy to the lads, he is. That's why I'm a bit
surprised. I wouldn't have thought that he'd take off like this and leave the
wee wanes alone with that soak of a father."

"What about Billy's m-mother?" Evan choked out, sickened by what
he was hearing. "What so-sort of woman is she?"

The policeman shrugged and tucked his nightstick under his arm.
As they walked, his eyes moved constantly, darting here and there about
their surroundings. They passed hollow-eyed men bunched together
in doorways, and streams of raggedy children shouting and torment-
ing one another. Weary-looking women hurrying home from the factories avoided their eyes as they met and went on by. Defeat and despair
fogged the streets, mingling with the uncollected garbage and filth of
several days.

"Nell's not a bad sort," the sergeant replied. "She cares for her boys as
best she can. But she works days at the shirt factory and tends to drown
her troubles in the drink at night. You can't help but feel sorry for Nell.
She's had it hard."

"I d-didn't know what it was like for him," Evan said softly, more to
himself than to the sergeant. "Poor little fellow."

"Aye, I expect Billy has had his troubles," the sergeant agreed as they
came up to the buggy. "Well, then, you'd best be away, Mr. Whittaker. 'Tis
almost dark. I'll keep an eye out for the lad, you can be sure."

"Thank you, Sergeant. And you'll let m-me know right away if you
learn his whereabouts?"

The policeman tipped two fingers to his forehead as in a jaunty salute.
"I will indeed, sir. And I'm sure we'll be finding the lad soon. Try not to
worry, though it's good of you to care."

By the time Evan reached the mission clinic and found Dr. Grafton's
note, he was exhausted and nearly ready to snap from the strain of the
day. The appalling revelations about Billy Hogan's home life, added to

the worry about Nora, had brought on a sour stomach and a throbbing
headache.

Yet, on the ferry across to Brooklyn, his mind refused to let go of the
implications of what he had learned. Like bees swarming to a hive, the
unsettling images of Billy's "uncle," the ugly tenement that was home to
the child, and the countless poor boys living out their existence in doorways or back alleys, continued to torment him.

And where was Billy now? He felt a terrible burden for the sad-eyed
little boy, an almost desperate urgency to find him without delay.

But how? He did not even know where to look.

Before the ferry docked, something…a thought, a memory…began to
nag at him, insinuating itself into the fringes of his mind. What had Sergeant Price said about Billy and his brothers?

"…*a regular little daddy to them, Billy is…. I wouldn't have thought he'd
take off like this and leave the wee wanes alone with that soak of a father…."*

Troubled, Evan rubbed his chin, thinking. Thinking of the many times
he had noticed bruises and cuts on Billy, the boy's evasive answers when
asked about them, the way he often attempted to hide his face, the eyes
that seemed to hold a lifetime of heartache…

*What if Billy hadn't run away at all? What if he had been hurt…badly
hurt…or worse?*

Something deep within Evan's spirit moaned as if bereaved. He sat,
unmoving, scarcely breathing, as the full impact of what he suspected
seized him, engulfing him in dread.

He was convinced now that he had not heard the truth. Sorley Dolan
had been lying, he was sure of it. There was something wrong, dreadfully
wrong, in all this.

He *had* to find the boy! He would search until he *did* find him. As his
sense of desperation grew, Evan wished he had not left the Five Points at
all. Yet his reason told him it was no place to go wandering about at night,
even with a policeman at your side. Besides, Nora would be frantic with
worry. He had never been this late getting home after rehearsal.

Tomorrow he would go back. He would go back to that terrible place
and that horrid man. But this time he wouldn't go alone. He would take
Sergeant Price with him.

34

Hope for the Hopeless

I stood beside the couch in tears
Where pale and calm she slept,
And though I've gazed on death for years,
I blush not that I wept.

RICHARD D'ALTON WILLIAMS (1822–1862)

To Nicholas Grafton's great relief, Pastor Jess Dalton was waiting for him outside the tenement where Elizabeth Ward lived.

As the two men shook hands, Nicholas newly considered what it was about the big, curly-headed pastor that gave others such a sense of calm. Being in Dalton's presence was like taking a deep, cool drink of serenity. The man seemed to exude a steady kind of strength and warmth, a magnetism that attracted individuals from all walks of life, in particular those who hurt. The lonely, the troubled, and the suffering were drawn to Jess Dalton like starving children in search of a banquet.

Nicholas had come to count on this big, gentle bear of a man in times of crisis, and had never been disappointed. Dalton had left one of the most prosperous, influential pulpits in the city to take on a ministry among the destitute and outcasts of society. There were those among the pastor's former parishioners who were quick to label him a "lunatic abolitionist," a "madman." Others scorned his actions, sneering that with the fortune he had inherited from his father and the income he earned from his writing, he could afford to "indulge his pet causes."

Nicholas knew that none of the gossip was in the least justified. Jess

Dalton might indeed be what some would term "a fool for God," but he was no madman. As to an inheritance, that might be the case, but certainly the pastor's unpretentious lifestyle gave no credence to great wealth. He *had* authored a number of books protesting slavery and oppression, which, at least among the more temperate abolitionists, were extremely popular. Still, from the little Nicholas knew of the publishing world, it was unlikely that Jess Dalton was getting rich off his books.

After resigning his Fifth Avenue pulpit, Dalton had moved his wife and son to a modest brownstone on West Thirty-fourth Street. The seemingly tireless pastor could be found almost anywhere in the city: ministering to the poor, afflicted residents of the "freak shows" in the Bowery, preaching the gospel to the downtrodden immigrants in Five Points, or presiding over a burial service in Shantytown. To those who had long assumed themselves to be forgotten or despised by God, Jess Dalton was hope incarnate.

Nicholas prayed that, tonight, the big pastor could impart at least a ray of that hope to Elizabeth Ward.

"Since I've never met your patient," the pastor said, following Nicholas through the door, "I thought I'd best wait for you."

Nicholas nodded. "I've told you about Mrs. Ward, haven't I? About her illness, her little girl, the estrangement from her family?"

The pastor's kind blue eyes turned sad. "Yes, I remember. And your note said you believe this to be the end?"

Again Nicholas gave a nod. "One of the neighbors sent for me," he said, pausing at the landing before starting down the steps to the basement apartment. "I appreciate your coming, Jess. This is a difficult one."

"It never gets any easier, does it, Nicholas?" The pastor put a hand to his shoulder.

"No," Nicholas said, shaking his head. "And I don't expect it ever will."

Inside the small, dingy apartment, which in reality was nothing more than two cramped rooms—a kitchen of sorts and a bedroom—things were pretty much as Nicholas had expected. A neighbor had taken the baby, while another woman—an Italian matron named Mrs. Silone—sat by the patient's bed.

At the sight of the doctor and the pastor, Mrs. Silone rose and, giving a resigned shake of her head as she passed between them, left the apartment.

Elizabeth Ward, awake, attempted a smile as the two men approached the bed.

The young woman's darkly shadowed eyes seemed to brighten for an instant as Nicholas introduced Jess Dalton. "It's…good of you to come, Pastor." Her voice was so weak she could scarcely be heard. "I'm afraid… I haven't been able to attend services for a long time," she said, moistening her fever-cracked lips.

Unexpectedly, her eyes widened, and she lifted a frail hand to Nicholas. "Doctor…has there been…any word?"

His throat tightening, Nicholas took her hand. "Not yet, I'm afraid." At her stricken look, he quickly added, "Why don't I write again? Perhaps my first letter didn't reach your father."

Closing her eyes, she said simply, "There's no more time."

A wave of anguish washed over Nicholas, and for a moment he couldn't answer.

Elizabeth Ward drew a deep, ragged breath, which triggered a fit of coughing. Quickly, Nicholas moved to slip a hand behind the pillows to hold her steady. He was almost surprised at the blood that came. The poor girl was so emaciated and pale she appeared bloodless. But when the spasm ended, the small white rag in her hand that served as a handkerchief was stained with crimson, as was the bodice of her white nightgown.

Gently releasing her, Nicholas smoothed the thinning hair away from her face. *Dear girl, I would give up my entire practice if I could somehow make this night easier for you….*

Her eyes closed, Elizabeth Ward murmured a word. *"Amanda."*

"Amanda is just fine," Nicholas assured her, again taking her hand. "Mrs. Modine is looking after her."

Her eyes opened and she looked at Nicholas. "But she can't *stay* there, Doctor! The Modines have four children of their own. They can't possibly—" Her voice broke and she gasped, fighting for breath. "Please…I want to see her…I want to see my baby…."

Nicholas quickly checked her pulse, which was perilously weak. Giving her hand a gentle squeeze, he turned to Jess. "If you'll stay, I'll go across the hall and get the baby."

Little Amanda Ward, fifteen months old and the image of her mother, was a friendly, happy little girl. She was all blue eyes and dimples and bouncing blond curls.

Even now, in spite of his heavy heart, Nicholas found himself responding with a smile to the child in his arms.

He stopped just inside the bedroom door, waiting. Jess Dalton stood beside the bed, head bowed, holding both of Elizabeth Ward's hands in his as he prayed. Nicholas watched for a moment, then closed his eyes and said a prayer of his own, both for the dying mother and for her child, the baby girl in his arms.

Finally, the pastor straightened, standing aside for Nicholas to bring the baby to her mother. Elizabeth Ward no longer had the strength to open her arms to her little girl, so Nicholas gently laid Amanda against her shoulder.

For a long time, the frail young woman lay gazing at her child, while the baby contentedly studied her mother's face. But when another spasm of coughing seized her, Nicholas quickly lifted Amanda away, handing her to Jess Dalton.

Supporting Elizabeth Ward against his shoulder, he waited until the seizure passed, then eased her gently back against the pillows.

"I have a new bottle of cough syrup for you in my case," he said, straightening. "Let me get it."

But giving a weak shake of her head, she told him, "No. No…it's all right. It doesn't really…help any longer."

She was watching Jess Dalton with Amanda. "Do you have children, Pastor?"

He smiled at her. "A son," he replied. "Casey-Fitz is almost eleven."

Elizabeth Ward managed a weak smile through cracked lips. "Casey-Fitz. You're Irish, Pastor?"

"My wife is—and I suppose you might say I am, as well, since my roots were planted in Irish soil a few generations ago."

"I…would have liked a son," she murmured vaguely. "A brother…for Amanda."

Her features suddenly went taut. Squeezing her eyes shut, she moaned and clutched her chest, struggling to breathe. The death rattles in her throat came more insistently now.

Again Nicholas raised her head from the pillows. Fighting for breath, she stared up at Jess Dalton and her child. "Please…" she choked out. "You promised…you won't let her go to an orphanage…."

Without warning, she gave a harsh, labored breath, then Nicholas felt her sag in his arms.

It had been a long time since Nicholas had wept over a patient. But as he held Elizabeth Ward's fragile, lifeless body in his arms, he could not stop the tears from spilling over.

Dear God, it should be the girl's father weeping over her, not a doctor she's known for only a few months! What kind of man lets his only daughter die alone, a continent away, in the arms of a stranger? What kind of man?

He glanced up to see Jess Dalton—his eyes also misted—gazing down at the baby girl in his arms.

"If only she could have had the peace of knowing her child would be taken care of," Nicholas said, his voice heavy. Carefully, he released Elizabeth Ward's body, wiping away the blood from the corner of her mouth, then closing her eyes. "If only she could have had that much hope before she died."

"Perhaps she did," Jess Dalton said quietly.

Nicholas looked at him. The big pastor's eyes were still fixed on the child, who was studying him with grave intensity.

"I promised her I would take the child home," he explained. "I gave her my word that my wife and I would take care of Amanda."

Hiking the little girl higher against his massive chest, the pastor added, "At least until we can find a permanent home for her."

Nicholas nodded, vastly relieved—but not really surprised—to learn that Elizabeth Ward had been given, after all, a faint glimmer of hope before she died.

Nearly two hours later, Jess Dalton fumbled for his house key with his free hand, while balancing little Amanda and the basket that held her clothing on his other arm.

Before he could let himself in, the door flew open to reveal a slightly wild-eyed Kerry. Her red hair blazed like a cloud of fire about her face. She was in her dressing gown.

"Jess! Oh—thanks *be*! I've been so worried! You said you wouldn't be long! Where have—oh—"

She gaped as he stepped inside with the baby.

"Whatever—"

The child stirred against his shoulder, and Jess reached to free her face from the blanket. Two enormous blue eyes peered out at him, then at Kerry, who stood, a hand at her throat, her stunned gaze going from the baby to Jess.

"Jess?"

Knowing her well enough to predict her next move, he waited, smiling.

"Why…why, whatever do we have here?" Even as she asked, she was opening her arms to take the child. "Oh…isn't she lovely!"

Releasing the baby to his wife, Jess shrugged out of his greatcoat and tossed it over the coat-tree. "Kerry, meet Amanda."

He had already lost her. Kerry was tugging at the strings of the baby's bonnet, clucking her tongue as the blond curls fell free. "Oh! Such hair! Would you look at it? Angel hair, that's what it is! Oh, *aren't* you the darling girl, though!"

Jess watched as the baby returned Kerry's smile and put up one chubby hand to touch her face. "Amanda has lost her mother," he said softly. "She's in need of a place to stay just now. I thought perhaps we could take care of her…just for a while."

Finally, Kerry looked at him, touching her cheek to the baby's. "Oh, Jess," she said, her green eyes shining, "of course, she can stay with us! Haven't I prayed for a little girl?"

"Now, Kerry, it will only be for a short time," Jess cautioned, starting after her as she took off down the hallway toward the kitchen. "It's only temporary, you understand. Just until we can make other arrangements."

She hadn't heard him, he was sure of it. With the basket of baby clothing dangling clumsily from his hand, he followed them to the kitchen, where Kerry was already introducing a wide-eyed Amanda to Brian Boru, the cat, and a startled Molly Mackenzie, their housekeeper.

35

Between Freedom and Fear

The moaning wind! went wandering round
The weeping prison-wall:
Till like a wheel of turning steel
We felt the minutes crawl

Oscar Wilde (1854–1900)

Quinn had known since Monday she was going to leave the Women's Shelter, but not until Friday morning did she decide that this would be the day.

She had spent the intervening days carefully rehearsing her plan, memorizing Ethelda Crane's schedule—and trying, in vain, to convince her friend, Ivy, to join her.

She thought of her plan as an *escape*, for the Chatham Charity Women's Shelter was surely a prison in every way, except that the inmates' only "crime" was the disgrace of being alone, helpless—and usually Irish—in the New World.

Escape had become Quinn's obsession.

Every previous attempt to free herself from the Shelter's clutches had been foiled by Ethelda Crane. The sly supervisor employed all manner of devices to maintain her hold on the Shelter's residents.

The fact was, no resident at the Shelter ever got more than a peek at her own wages. The wages of the women and girls at the Shelter—including those who worked outside, in the factories—were collected weekly for such expenses as "board," or "medical bills," or "child support."

Child support applied to those residents who had infants or small children placed under the care of various members of the "church" to which Miss Crane—and the Shelter's board of directors—belonged. Care was provided at an institution on the lower East Side, and Shelter residents were required to pay exorbitant expenses for this "service."

In addition, the wily Miss Crane used the threat of "The Law" like a weapon to keep the girls in line. Failure to pay one's debts would result in a confrontation with The Law. Rebellious behavior or disciplinary problems would be dealt with by The Law. All sorts of alleged offenses—which Quinn had finally come to recognize as contrived, for the most part, for Ethelda Crane's personal use—were subject to investigation by The Law. Since most of the residents at the Shelter were either foreign immigrants or uneducated country girls with an innate fear and distrust of law enforcement in general, it was all too easy to hold them captive with a simple threat.

Quinn herself had fallen victim to this particular gambit because she knew she could not afford scrutiny of any sort by the police. But after months of being the victim of Ethelda Crane's chicanery, she had reached the point of desperation. She was convinced she must take her chances if she were going to survive at all. The threat of The Law seemed no more forbidding than the possibility of living out the rest of her days as an imprisoned drudge at the Chatham Charity Women's Shelter.

She had her strategy down pat, had gone over it in her mind a hundred times or more. Every Friday evening, after putting Mrs. Cunnington, the cook, in charge of things, Ethelda Crane would leave the building to "go calling." Sometimes she went alone; sometimes she was accompanied by one of the do-gooders from uptown—although never the sweet-faced Mrs. Deshler nor Mrs. Burke, the lady who had spoken so kindly to Quinn the day of the mission society tour.

Quinn had noticed that when Miss Crane went calling, she never failed to bring back at least one new resident for the Shelter. She had come to think of the Friday night expeditions as fishing trips. Apparently, the enterprising Ethelda Crane made it her business to nose about such places as the Bowery and the docks, where she might find women or young girls on their own keeping—girls in trouble, lost, down on their luck, or just plain simpleminded. By giving the impression that she was saving them from their misfortune, she found it easy to haul the unsuspecting poor souls into her net—just as she had Quinn.

Well, this *fish was getting away,* Quinn thought grimly as she turned her last collar for the day. This evening, once Miss Crane had left the Shelter, she would wait until that great lump, Mrs. Cunnington, was having her nip in the kitchen pantry. Then she would sneak down the fire escape at the rear of the building.

And that would be the last this place would be seeing of Quinn O'Shea.

The only real beetle in the broth was where she would go. She didn't feel she had much choice. The only place she could think of was the Five Points, where a number of those just off the boat seemed to head.

Quinn had an idea that Bobby Dempsey might have followed some of his cronies there after all, especially if he hadn't managed to find a job on the docks. She hoped to locate Bobby as soon as possible, mostly to make sure he was all right. Every time a thought of the man crossed her mind, she felt troubled. Of course, his not showing up to meet her as they'd planned didn't necessarily mean something had happened to him. He might have found a job on the docks and started in to work right off. Nevertheless, after all he had done to help her, the least she could do was look him up.

She had hoped the policeman—Sergeant Price—might have made the effort to find Bobby, after the way she'd practically begged him. But no doubt he'd forgotten all about her the minute he dumped her off on Ethelda Crane. And hadn't she been foolish entirely, to think a policeman might have a care for such as her?

Well, she didn't *need* the thickheaded sergeant's help, now did she? She would find Bobby herself. Without her, Bobby would have followed his other pals to the Five Points, she was certain. As soon as she got there, she would find them all, no doubt. There was no denying that a familiar face or two would be a welcome sight in this enormous strange city—even the rough, mean faces of Roche and Boyle and their bunch.

After listening to some of the women who worked in the factories, Quinn had at least a vague idea as to how to get to Five Points. Some of the stories they told about the place made her none too anxious to go there after dark—but she didn't see as how she could afford to be too choosy. At least there she might have a chance of finding Bobby or someone else she knew from the ship. And anything, she reminded herself, would be better than staying here.

Her only regret about leaving the Shelter was Ivy's refusal to come with her. Quinn hated the idea of going without her friend—her *only* friend, except for Bobby. Ivy had a childlike innocence about her that some-times made Quinn fear for the girl. She was too trusting entirely, too eas-ily duped to be anything but a danger to herself.

But it was the *reason* Ivy refused to leave that troubled Quinn most. Over recent weeks, despite her initial aversion, the girl had taken up with the church members who, in addition to Miss Crane, administered the Shelter: Brother Will and his "flock"—in Quinn's mind, a herd of mind-less sheep milling about after an equally mindless shepherd.

During one of the services they sometimes held at the Shelter—services the residents were required to attend—Ivy had asked Brother Will a question about something in the lesson. The preacher had gone to what seemed extraordinary lengths to answer Ivy's question, even suggesting some additional reading and providing her with a number of tracts that he claimed to have written.

This had been the start of Ivy's involvement with the "flock." She began to spend more and more of her free time reading their literature— "doctrines," they called it. When she wasn't reading, she was attending meetings with Ethelda Crane and some of the other residents who claimed to have been converted to the faith.

When Quinn had attempted to question her about the group's beliefs, Ivy gushed randomly, displaying no real grasp of their doctrines, but rather an excessive—and unwarranted—regard for the leader, Brother Will.

It didn't take Quinn long to realize that she wasn't going to change Ivy's mind about the church or Brother Will. Every attempt she made was met with an indulgent, somewhat vacant smile, along with a vague reference to Quinn's being a "lapsed Catholic," and therefore unable to comprehend the Truth. When Quinn refused to read the doctrines and sneered at the suggestion she attend some of the meetings with the others, Ivy would assume a wounded look and say, "I'll pray for you, Quinn."

Quinn was beginning to wish she had never helped the girl with her reading. Perhaps Ivy would have been better off if she had never been able to understand their drivel in the first place.

Once, when Ivy was gone, Quinn had stolen a look at some of the pam-phlets on her bunk and couldn't believe her eyes at what these people were peddling. "Mortification of the flesh," which apparently included fast-ing and other forms of self-denial, even something called "self-scourging," or "disciplining one's body into submission."

Did this blather account for Ethelda Crane's looking as if she'd been baptized in vinegar, then? Rubbish, the lot of it!

There also seemed to be a great deal of discussion on such themes as "thought purification" and "subduing the will," the "common good," and "devotion to duty." But the one that really set Quinn's teeth to grinding was the subject of "absolute obedience"—obedience to their divinely appointed spiritual guide, who in this case, of course, happened to be Brother Will.

Something about the man made Quinn suspect that he was about as spiritual as a piece of stale soda bread. In fact, she thought he might be a bit crackers. Daft. He had a way of rubbing his hands together when he prayed that never failed to make Quinn think of the times she had watched her granddad kill a chicken for the pot, back in the days when there were still chickens for the killing. He also, she had noticed, had an eye for the ladies—a distinctly goatish eye, and keen for the young girls, especially Ivy, who, to Quinn's exasperation, seemed altogether unaware of the man's peculiarities and contradictions.

She had pleaded and reasoned, argued and cautioned—all in vain. Ivy would not be moved. Finally, Quinn had resigned herself to the fact that she would leave the Shelter alone.

Lewis Farmington was surprised when his assistant, Evan Whittaker, requested the afternoon off.

He might have been amused had the man not been so obviously distraught. Evan had not asked for so much as an hour's liberty from his duties since his first day at the shipyards. On occasion, Lewis insisted that his highly capable assistant take some time off, especially on a slow day— but for Evan actually to *request* the privilege was unheard of.

"You know you've only to ask, Evan," Lewis assured him without hesitation. "Take the rest of the day, if you like. You've more than earned it, goodness knows." He paused, then added, "There's nothing wrong at home, I hope?"

Evan absently smoothed the lapel of his suit coat as he explained. "No, sir. Although Nora seems no b-better than when I last talked with you about my concerns. In fact, one reason I need to leave early is to

m-meet with Dr. Grafton. He asked m-me to stop b-by yesterday at the
clinic, b-but he was gone by the time I arrived. But there's something else,
another reason I need the time."

As Lewis listened to Evan's account of his concern for a little boy in
his singing group—Billy Hogan—he was struck, not for the first time, by
the man's obvious commitment to his work with the underprivileged children of Five Points.

Evan took an interest in every member of his singing group, and it
was no secret around the Five Points that "the Britisher," as many referred
to him, had done some fine things with the boys, in addition to teaching
them to sing. Half a dozen or more—including the little Hogan boy—
had learned to read because of Evan's willingness to spend hours teaching them. The boys had developed an evident dedication to their group
and to their director as well. Their eagerness, combined with Evan's tireless efforts and striving for excellence, had eventually molded them into a
performance choir of real skill and accomplishment.

Evan had turned out to be an extraordinary musician, Lewis mused,
and not only in his capacity as director. The man spent hours each week
arranging music for the boys, even writing some original works of his own.
His latest venture was the formation of a band for some of the older boys
who resisted singing, now that their voices were undergoing change. With
the help of Alice Walsh—a bit of a surprise, Mrs. Walsh, considering her
snake of a husband—Evan was in the process of putting together a sizable
new group that resembled some of the military bands.

The man's talents were considerable, Lewis thought, but his character was nothing less than noble. Evan was a gentleman, a devout Christian, a devoted husband and father, and a most efficient assistant. But he
was beginning to see signs of overwork and fatigue in him. There simply
didn't seem to be enough hours in the day for the man to accomplish what
he felt called to do.

Lately, Lewis had begun to despair of keeping Evan in his employ
much longer. For some time now, Lewis had sensed God working in new
ways in the young Englishman's life, grooming him, preparing him for...
something, although he hadn't a clue as to what that *something* might turn
out to be. In fact, he wasn't at all sure that Evan himself recognized as yet
the moving of the Divine Hand on his life. But that he would respond
when the time came, Lewis had no doubt. None at all.

In light of this, he was already attempting to resign himself to the fact that one day, perhaps soon, he would lose Evan from the business. He also predicted that when the time came, *he* would have to be the one to cut the ties, for Evan was loyal to a fault. No doubt the man would go on as long as humanly possible, and exhausting himself in the process.

Determined to avoid that very situation, Lewis had already asked the Lord to make him sensitive to the time…and unselfish enough to make the first move in Evan's behalf.

That afternoon, when Evan entered Dr. Grafton's office in Manhattan, he found the waiting room crowded with patients. There wasn't even a vacant chair.

It was nearly four before the doctor spied him and called him in.

"I apologize for the wait, Evan," Nicholas Grafton said, ushering him into his office. "And for missing you yesterday."

Evan hesitated only a moment before taking the doctor's outstretched hand. The American custom of handshaking still caught him unawares now and then, but he no longer found the convention quite as uncivilized as he once had.

As he sat across the desk from Nicholas Grafton, his apprehension grew. He had been decidedly anxious about this meeting ever since the doctor had sent word requesting it. His worry about what he might hear—combined with his concern for little Billy Hogan—had given him another sleepless night. The effects of going without rest and being unable to consume more than a few bites of his breakfast had left him feeling drained and slightly faint.

Dr. Grafton got right to the point. "I expect you know I want to talk with you about Nora," he said, leaning forward in his chair and folding his hands on top of the desk. "You've been concerned about her for some time now—and so have I."

Drawing in a deep, steadying breath, Evan nodded.

"Yes, well, I've found some things during my last two examinations that I wanted to discuss with you."

The physician's obvious reluctance to continue set off a painful hammering of Evan's heart. He clenched his hand, and, finding it clammy, wiped it on his trouser leg.

Nicholas Grafton regarded him with a studying look, his expression grave. "I'm afraid Nora is very ill, Evan. There seems to be a problem with her heart."

Panic rushed up inside Evan, taking his breath. He felt suddenly light-headed. "Wh-what sort of a...a problem?"

Dr. Grafton didn't answer right away, but sat looking at his hands. Finally he expelled a long breath. "When someone has been through as much as Nora has," he began, "it's not surprising that there would be certain...consequences." He glanced up. "She survived a famine, after all—and an ocean crossing that seems to be taking countless lives every month. And if that weren't enough, there's the scarlet fever and a difficult pregnancy—that's a great deal for any human being to go through...and survive."

Their eyes met. Evan's throat tightened at the kindness and compassion in Nicholas Grafton's gaze.

"What I'm trying to tell you, Evan, is that Nora's heart has taken a great deal of punishment and has apparently been damaged in the process."

Stricken, Evan tried to ask his questions, but found himself unable to speak as the import of the doctor's words washed over him.

He had known...at least he had feared...that there was something seriously wrong. He had suspected it for some time now, but managed not to face it, at least most of the time.

"Evan?"

Evan looked at the doctor. *Don't tell me anything more... I don't want to know the rest...I don't want to know...*

"Evan, listen to me. I'll not minimize the seriousness of Nora's condition—"

Evan held his breath, staring out the window directly behind Nicholas Grafton. The late afternoon light was weak and fading quickly, as if the sun could not wait to go down. The room had gone cold, and Evan shivered.

"—but I don't want to paint an excessively dark picture for you. Nora is ill, but not without hope."

Evan's eyes shot back to the doctor, who nodded reassuringly and went on. "There's a specialist right here in the city I want Nora to see: Dr. Mandel. Abraham Mandel. He's quite a fine physician and specializes in diseases of the heart. He'll see Nora as soon as next week if you want."

Struggling to control his fear, Evan gripped the arm of the chair. "Does...does N-Nora know about this?"

Dr. Grafton shook his head. "I haven't talked with her about it yet, no. But I think she knows she's ill. My guess is that she's trying to keep it from you." He looked at Evan and smiled faintly. "I'm sure it's no secret to you that Nora doesn't like to worry anyone, especially you."

Evan nodded. "She's awfully g-good at keeping her troubles to herself," he said. His eyes stung as he looked away. *Oh, Nora...Nora...my dearest heart, you must be frightened...so very frightened...yet you haven't said a word....*

"My thought was to talk with you first," the doctor explained. "Perhaps, if you like, I'll come by on Monday evening and we'll tell her together."

Again Evan nodded, turning his gaze back to the doctor. "You said she's very ill. *How* ill? Please—tell m-me the truth."

"My feeling is that with proper care and whatever treatment Dr. Mandel might recommend, we can keep this from getting worse," Dr. Grafton told him. "What I suspect is that Nora's heart muscle has been weakened from all the strain that's been put on it. I also think there might be a problem with at least one of the heart valves. That's why I want Abraham Mandel to examine her—he'll be able to isolate the problem more accurately than I can."

Finally, Evan was beginning to draw some deep breaths. "You m-mentioned proper care?"

Dr. Grafton nodded. "She's going to require absolute rest. Bed rest for a while, then a full-time regime of proper nutrition, no exertion, and extended rest. Now, I know how difficult that can be for a young mother with children and a house to take care of—and an infant to look after." He looked directly at Evan. "If you can manage it, get her some full-time help right away. The sooner the better. Someone to take care of the house and help with the baby. I can't emphasize that enough."

He paused, then added, "It just might save her life."

Standing in front of Nicholas Grafton's office, a solemn, unpretentious stonefront building just off Broadway, Evan looked out on the Astor House Hotel. Guests hurried in and out of the opulent building, some looking eager to get out of the gray November chill, others laughing and expectant as they climbed into hackney cabs.

He was badly shaken, his entire body in a tremble. He found it almost impossible to think what to do. His inclination was to forget everything and get home to Nora as swiftly as possible. He wanted to hold her, to hold her close and never let her go.

A wave of overwhelming anguish swept through him as his mind relentlessly continued to repeat his conversation with Nicholas Grafton. He felt as if at any moment fear and despair would overwhelm him, even paralyze him. Yet he knew he dared not give in to the fear, could not afford to dwell on what *might* happen, but must somehow force himself to consider what could be done…now, right now…to make a difference.

Evan had not known such oppression, such stark terror, since the night of Teddy's birth, and, before then, the time Nora had lain in the hospital, stricken with scarlet fever. On both occasions, he had feared he would lose her, and the possibility had very nearly destroyed him.

But he *hadn't* lost her, he reminded himself. She had survived. God be thanked, Nora had survived not only serious illness, but a number of other horrors that could have just as easily claimed her health, her sanity, or even her life.

Somehow he had to do everything possible—*everything*—to make sure she survived this latest peril as well. Nora must have whatever it would take to make her strong and whole again, and he would see to it… with the Lord's help…that she did.

But how? Specialists…medicines…household help—it would all take money, money they didn't have. How would they manage?

Again he swallowed down the panic clamoring to paralyze him. He couldn't worry about the money, not now. Nothing else mattered but Nora. He couldn't lose her…he simply could not lose her…he would think about nothing but Nora. Nothing.

He realized he was wheezing and tried to ignore it. His always weak lungs never failed to react at the first sign of a crisis. Struggling to breathe deeply, he willed his pulse to stop its thunderous race. It wouldn't do to have to go back inside and let the doctor treat *him*.

One thing at a time, he told himself firmly, ignoring his labored breathing and struggling to find a measure of calm. Next week Nora would see the specialist—Dr. Mandel. Before then, he would speak with Mr. Farmington—and Sara, too—to ask their help in locating a girl for service as soon as possible. He was sure Aunt Winnie, bless the woman, would help until he could find someone else.

Staring across the street, he was aware of the scene at the Astor House only in the vaguest way: the scramble of carriages, the elegantly attired men and women, laughing as they hurried on along. They appeared so light-hearted, so utterly carefree. For a moment, Evan couldn't help wondering what that sort of life might be like—a life spent in coming and going from one festivity to the other, a life without worries or fears or burdens.

Suddenly it struck him, with the force of a blow, what he had almost forgotten in the shock of the afternoon: *Billy Hogan!* He still had to go back to the Five Points to continue his search for the boy.

He gave a soft groan of dismay. He *couldn't*! He simply could not go back to that terrible place, to face that awful man. Not today.

Torn between the urgent need to be with Nora and his burden for the sad-eyed little boy, Evan pressed his fingers to his forehead, trying to think. Guilt stabbed at him as he realized that what he was feeling at this moment was a kind of resentment—resentment for Billy Hogan, and the boy's interference in his life at a time when Nora so desperately needed him. And yet he knew, beyond all doubt, that his burden for Billy was none of his own doing, but had been given by God. He couldn't simply turn his back on the boy.

Didn't God know he couldn't handle another responsibility right now? Surely the Lord wouldn't expect him to deal with yet another crisis or involve himself in anything that might take his time or attention away from Nora.

At the least, another day wouldn't matter. It would soon be dark, after all, and it was altogether foolish to think of going into Five Points alone after dark. He would go tomorrow or the next day at the latest.

But somehow Evan knew he could not wait. He must go today. If he didn't, it might be too late for Billy Hogan.

If it wasn't too late already.

The clack of horse's hooves as a hackney cab passed jarred him into action. He straightened, took a deep breath in defiance of his wheezing lungs, and started for the buggy.

He drove to Five Points in a near frenzy, praying all the way he wouldn't be too late for Billy Hogan.

Quinn O'Shea walked out of the Chatham Charity Women's Shelter at five o'clock, putting only half an hour between Ethelda Crane's departure and her own.

She left by way of the fire escape, just as she had planned, immediately after locking Mrs. Cunnington in the pantry with her bottle. The astonished cook started hollering as soon as Quinn turned the key in the lock—the key she had earlier snitched out of the woman's apron pocket. But with nothing to slow her progress except the clothes on her back, Quinn was down the iron steps in a shake and well on her way to freedom before anyone even thought to look outside.

After months of feeling like a prisoner, she welcomed the gray, gloomy evening with mounting exhilaration, her parched spirit drinking in the freshness of her newly gained freedom. She wished she could have had her own dress for the occasion; she hadn't seen it since the night she first arrived at the Shelter. But even the ugly brown dress and baggy sweater—the Shelter "uniform"—couldn't dim her elation.

Pulling the thin sweater more tightly about her, she lifted her face to the wind and headed for the Five Points and freedom.

36

In the Devil's Den

*There's nothing so bad
that it could not be worse.*

IRISH PROVERB

I t was almost dark, and Sergeant Denny Price was about to call it a day—a *long* day, he reflected wearily as he headed toward Paradise Square. More knifings than he could count, two prostitutes beaten and left for dead, a gang attack on a little newsboy—some of Rynders' worthless thugs, more than likely—and a demented drunk who had gone after Denny with a broken bottle.

Two things Denny disliked even more than the pigs running wild along the filth of Five Points: drunks and opium eaters. Get enough of their poison into either of them, and wouldn't they break your head open or slit your throat at the slightest chance?

Not to mention the lives destroyed. In his years on the force, he had seen any number of families torn apart, wives and children abused and beaten, and otherwise good men gone bad from their weakness.

The writer fellow—Poe—came to mind, the one who'd written for the papers that passing strange poem about the crow. Of course, some said he'd never been a hard drinker or an opium eater at all, claiming it was his critics who had slurred his name, that in fact he'd died of some sort of trouble with his brain. Others, though, insisted it had been the combination of the drink and laudanum that had done him in. They had found him sprawled out senseless, over in Baltimore.

Denny shook his head at the waste. A clever man like that, well-educated and all, dying like a pauper! Something must have obsessed him, sure.

Denny himself, and his da before him, God rest his soul, had taken the pledge before ever coming across. And after close on six years of patrolling places like Five Points, he could only be thankful that the good Lord had so moved him.

The shoulder he'd wrenched tossing the drunk with the broken bottle had begun to ache like a rotten tooth. Days like this, Denny felt twice again his twenty-six years. Rubbing a hand over the back of his neck, he gave a weary sigh and turned onto Mulberry.

He would have one more look about, just on the chance of spying the little Hogan lad. It was worrisome, this situation with the missing boy. The lad's pal, Tom Breen, had finally admitted to Denny that he "wouldn't be a'tall surprised if Billy's uncle didn't thrash him now and then."

But young Tom hadn't been able to offer even a clue as to where his friend might be. So Denny was right back where he had started the night before, he and Mr. Whittaker: in the middle of the Five Points, without a thought as to where to try next.

Still, he would have himself another look. In fact, he decided abruptly, he might just pay a call to Billy's family. With any luck at all, Sorley Dolan wouldn't be at home. When he wasn't too drunk, he usually worked at one of the gambling dens in the Bowery. Perhaps he could pry something out of the two wee boys, or Nell herself, if Sorley wasn't there to scare them dumb.

Picking up his pace, he slid his hand to the butt of his pistol for reassurance. In the Five Points, a policeman might carry no real authority. But he always—*always*—carried a loaded gun.

It took Quinn less than five minutes in Five Points to know she had made a mistake. Not in fleeing the Shelter, she quickly assured herself, but in coming to this place, which must surely be the devil's den—right here, in New York City.

She walked into the midst of a square in which most of the garbage barrels of the city appeared to have been dumped. In equal numbers, pigs and small raggedy children ran wild among the rubbish, animal waste, and broken bottles. The pigs were fat, the children were bones.

Quinn stifled a gag at the putrid odors assailing her. The farther she walked, the worse the stench!

Even in the gloom of gathering darkness, there was no mistaking the squalid ugliness of the place. A number of streets intersected with narrow lanes and alleys diverging every which way—and all of them seemed to be lined with nothing but taverns and bawdy houses!

The noise spilling out onto the streets was unimaginable. Rough, bloated faces—both men's and women's—hurled curses and laughter from broken upstairs windows. From the taverns, loud, tinny music pumped a kind of savage hilarity into the air, competing with the crashing of bottles and the wailing of infants.

There were people everywhere, faces mirroring a multitude of nations and races—but mostly black faces and Irish faces, lined with despair and gaunt with tragedy. Drunks with black eyes stumbled over one another. Hard-looking women stared at Quinn with open hatred. A cacophony of Irish brogue and black prattle warred with the strangely out-of-place merriment of fiddles and tambourines.

Quinn felt as if she had been picked up and plopped down in the midst of a lunatic's nightmare.

Suddenly a hand gripped the back of her neck, jarring her out of her thoughts. Whirling about, she yanked herself free and lashed out with one hand to club her assailant.

The drunk, filthy beyond belief, with not a tooth in his head, stood leering at her. "Eh, lassie, I've got money for a good time, don't I, now? Lookie here!"

As he attempted to turn his pockets inside out, Quinn backed away, then veered and bolted across the square.

At the sight of a dark, cavernous old building, so far gone in decay it appeared diseased, she reversed directions. To her right, outside the wooden paling surrounding the square, hovered a row of taverns—mean in appearance but at least lighted.

She had just reached the wooden fence when a deep, commanding shout stopped her in her tracks.

"Here! Just a minute, now—hold up!"

He was on her in a shake, one huge hand seizing her shoulder and whipping her about. "What—" He reared back, staring at her. "Why, it's the lass from the Bowery!"

Quinn blinked, gaping first at the copper star on the stalwart chest, then at the familiar face illuminated by the lights from the taverns.

He stared at her. "'Tis! I thought so! Quinn O'Shea, isn't it, now?"

The foolish man actually appeared happy to see her! He grinned—the wide, canny grin of the old Celtic sin-eater himself. And after what he had brought on her!

Quinn stared at his copper badge, her insides burning with fury. *Blast!* It was him, all right, the copper who had saved her hide in the Bowery that night back in July. An age ago, it seemed.

Sergeant Price. He had rescued her from the two drunken dandies bent on having their way with her, but then he had turned and undone his good deed by sending her off with the sanctimonious Ethelda Crane.

Didn't he have the gall, though? Standing there with his hands on her shoulders, grinning like the village eejit! And himself the cause of her misery all these months!

Quinn shook off his grasp and backed away, scowling at him.

The leprechaun glint in his eyes dimmed. "Whatever would you be doin' in the Five Points, lass? This is a terrible place altogether!"

Quinn merely glared at him, saying nothing. If he found out she had run off from the Shelter, wouldn't he be taking her back?

"Don't you remember me, now? Sergeant Price? Didn't I help you out of a bad spot some months back, in the Bowery?"

"I don't recall," Quinn snapped. She'd not give him the satisfaction of admitting she remembered him at all!

He went on beaming happily, as if he were genuinely pleased to have run onto her. Policeman or not, Quinn speculated, the man might be a bit simple.

"Sure, you must," he insisted. "Two drunks were making things difficult for you, and wasn't I the policeman who got you out of that fix?"

"And marched me into an even hotter pot of trouble!" Quinn spat out before she could stop herself. "Aye, you were the one, right enough!"

The cheeky grin disappeared. "I don't know that I take your meaning." His eyes went over her. "And what's this, now? Isn't that the dress the girls at the Shelter house wear? You wouldn't be staying there after all this time, sure?"

"No, and indeed I am not, no thanks to you!"

He frowned, causing his heavy eyebrows to come together over his nose. "Then why would you still be wearing that sack? Not that it isn't becoming, mind." The frown gave way to another grin, this one a bit smug.

Seething, Quinn clenched her hands at her sides. "And would I be wearing the hateful thing at all if the pious Ethelda Crane had not stolen *my* dress—and it the only one I owned?"

Pocketing his nightstick, the sergeant crossed his arms over his chest and stood appraising her. Quinn had to steel herself not to squirm under his policeman's chicken hawk eye.

"I'm thinking perhaps we need to start over," he finally said, his rugged face now altogether serious. "Supposing you tell me what it is that has you so bothered. And while you're about it," he added, "you might explain your business in the Five Points—which happens to be, if you haven't already discovered as much, the lowest, meanest place in the city."

His clipped brogue had thickened. Quinn placed it as northern, with a taste of the sea: Donegal, more than likely. This gave her slight pause as to the wisdom of sparring with him. Wasn't it common knowledge that Donegal men could be hard and a bit sly? Yet, for the sake of Ivy and the others still trapped in the Shelter, shouldn't she be telling what she knew about the goings-on in that place?

She decided to risk it. If he thought to take her back, she could lose him quick enough. He was set like an oak tree and no doubt would be just as wooden on his feet. Outrunning him shouldn't be much of a task.

Quinn's instincts told her he was not nearly so fierce as he would make out. Despite his sturdy size and deep frowns, he didn't quite fit her notions about policemen. His eyes seemed dusted with laughter, and she thought she might have even sensed a depth of kindness in the man.

So after a slight delay, Quinn allowed him to lead her off to a bench in front of one of the taverns, where she started in with her story. She took no small satisfaction in the surprise that gradually began to register on his face as she told him about her experiences at the Chatham Charity Women's Shelter.

The longer she talked, the more his eyes bugged. Twice he stopped her with an incredulous grunt of outrage, but to give the man his due, he listened to her story with the patience of a priest.

37

The Price of Justice

For Man's grim Justice goes its way,
And will not swerve aside:
It slays the weak, it slays the strong,
It has a deadly stride:
With iron heel it slays the strong,
The monstrous parricide!

OSCAR WILDE (1854–1900)

Discouraged by his failure to find Sergeant Price after nearly an hour of searching, Evan gave up and went back to the buggy. After months of familiarizing himself with the Five Points, he wasn't nearly as fearful of the deadly slum as he had been in the beginning. Still, he was cautious enough not to go roaming about the place after dark, especially alone.

He set out for the police station, hoping that if he didn't find the sergeant there, he could convince one of the other policemen to accompany him. It was pointless to go back to Billy Hogan's flat by himself, he knew. He had no illusions about his effectiveness against a brute like Sorley Dolan. He wouldn't get past the door, and even if he did, what then? No, if he were to make any progress in his search for the boy, he needed someone like Sergeant Price, who looked as if he could easily take on three of the likes of Sorley Dolan.

Riding through the Five Points after dark was a truly harrowing experience. Nearly every house was a tavern that at night shook with the sounds of drunken cursing and laughter, music, and, often, blood-chilling screams. Everywhere the narrow alleyways cut right and left, disgorging an endless parade of rough-looking men with angry eyes and women whose faces bore the evidence of years lived out in pain and defeat. The streets were rutted and slick with mud. In some places children played knee-deep in the mire.

As he drove toward the Hall of Justice, Evan's anxiety gave way to a heaviness of heart at the sight of so many children—"lost children"— trapped in this leprous breeding ground of evil. Most of them had no chance whatsoever of escape, but instead would spend their precious young lives caught up in the squalor, sin, and violence of places like Paradise Square and the Old Brewery.

Five Points wasn't peculiar to America alone, he knew. It was the same throughout Europe. Whether it was London, with its deadly slums teeming with forgotten children, or Ireland, with its homeless, starving little beggars, thousands upon thousands of small souls remembered only by God were being crushed before they ever felt a single touch of love or human kindness.

Evan anguished for the Billy Hogans of the world, the children without hope, without a future. And yet, what could he do? He was only one man, with scarcely any money to speak of, little physical stamina, and frightfully little time. He had a family to provide for, a job to attend to, and a small ministry of sorts with his boys in Five Points. Some days it was all he could do to keep going. What else could he possibly do?

As he pulled up to the Hall of Justice, often referred to as "the Tombs," Evan sat in the dark silence of the buggy for a moment, struggling to regain his composure. Even as he fought for calm, there came a stirring in his spirit—unexpected, unannounced—that took his breath and held him there, waiting.

Shaken, he squeezed his eyes closed, as if to shut out the turbulence of the day, his churning emotions, and the ordeal that awaited him yet this night.

But instead of the peace he sought, the weight upon his heart seemed to grow even heavier, more oppressive. He felt surrounded, submerged in tragedy and need. Nora...Johanna...Billy...the abandoned souls of Five Points...the lost, forgotten children—such need, such desperate, insurmountable need! Like a hand pressing down upon his soul, the burden increased, weighing down on him until he could scarcely breathe.

"Oh, Lord, enough—enough! I cannot bear any more!"

Not knowing whether he spoke aloud or if it had been his spirit crying out in rebellion, Evan shuddered and bowed his head, wanting to pray, *needing* to pray, but so enervated and depleted he could scarcely find the *strength* to pray. And so he merely sat there, letting the silence of the night wash over him until he could bring himself to leave the buggy and go inside.

How much are you willing to do, Evan?

His heart pounding, Evan lifted his head, opened his eyes and looked around, then raised his face to the dark, starless night. "How…how *much*, Lord? Why…whatever I can, of course…b-but…"

Are you willing to trust Me?

His throat tightened. "Why…I've always t-trusted You, Lord."

Will you trust Me with everything? With Nora…your family…your job… your future…your life?

Again Evan closed his eyes, fighting back the tears now threatening to spill over. "I try, Lord…You kn-know, I try…"

Will you trust Me to help Billy Hogan…and the others like him…My lost children?

"Oh, *yes*, Lord…why, You're their only hope!"

You are their hope too, Evan…you, and My church…you are My hands… My feet…you are their hope.

For a long time darkness surrounded Evan. He saw nothing, felt nothing, heard nothing, until at last he sensed a distant glimmer of light slowly rising up in him, growing brighter and clearer, warming him as it filled him.

"What shall I do, Lord? What *can* I do?" he whispered.

Trust Me, Evan…trust Me, and be brave, for I will ask much of you.

Evan opened his eyes. He sat there in the darkness another moment. He tried to steady himself with a long breath of night air, but was seized instead with a fit of coughing. Finally, his legs trembling beneath him, he stepped down from the buggy and started for the entrance doors of the Hall of Justice.

Nearly half an hour later, inside a small office just off the entryway, Michael Burke listened as Evan Whittaker finally ended his explanation about Nora's illness.

Certainly, this wasn't the way Michael had planned for the evening to go. The truth was, Evan's unexpected arrival and distraught condition would mean the cancellation of an important meeting—a meeting Michael had been counting on for some time.

Parlie Cottle, an informant, had finally agreed to open up about Patrick Walsh's protection and prostitution rackets in the Bowery and the Eighth Ward. It had taken months of threats and "persuasion" just short of strong-arm tactics to convince Cottle to talk. And now that he'd finally softened, Michael was going to have to put him off.

Not that any of Cottle's information would be enough to bring Walsh in. There was still a ways to go before that could be accomplished. But every stone added to the pile built the wall around Patrick Walsh that much higher. And some day, Michael had vowed, the wall would be great enough and strong enough to hem him in entirely. Someday, no matter how long it took, he would have that snake's skin.

But tonight, something else took precedence over Patrick Walsh. One look at Evan Whittaker, and Michael had known that everything else would have to wait.

He sat now, stunned and sick at heart to think of Nora being so dangerously ill. He had all he could do to follow the rest of Evan's account. His mind had locked on a memory, and refused to release it: the memory of three children in a small Irish village, in another time that now seemed an age ago—Morgan and himself and the tiny, timid Nora. Had any of them ever imagined that life would turn out so vastly different than it had been then?

They had spent the days of their youth trekking over fields or the rocky seacoast, being foolish and carefree children—as carefree, that is, as a child in Ireland ever dared to be. They had spent their childhood together, worked at their chores about the village together, played their games and had their adventures together.

There was no way they could have known that the future would bring starvation and separation, loss of home and even family. Their worst nightmares had not forewarned them that one would live out his days in a wheelchair; one would lose a wife and be estranged from his only son; and the other...Nora...would endure horror after horror, losing most of her family before finding happiness with the good man who now sat across the desk, trying not to fall apart.

Always...always there had been the awareness that Nora could never be quite as foolish, quite as carefree, as Morgan and himself, Michael remembered. Her slattern of a mother, the unwanted children, the poverty, the appalling conditions of her life—no, Nora had never, ever, been carefree. There had been an unspoken agreement between him and Morgan that Nora was to be cherished and protected, at all costs. She was their lass, and they would have given their lives for her.

Twice he had asked her to marry him. Twice she had refused. He had loved her then…and he loved her now, but as a sister and a friend. She was a part of his past…his youth…his heart.

Oh, Nora…Nora Ellen…you can't be dying…we won't have it…we won't let you die, do you hear? We *won't let you!*

Michael's throat tightened, and his eyes burned with a rush of tears. He got up, turning his back on Evan for a moment until he could regain his composure.

Finally he faced him again. "What can we do to help, Evan? Sara and I—what can we do?"

Evan wiped a hand over his eyes briefly, making an obvious effort to steady himself. "Well…you can p-pray for us, of course. Moreover, if you would speak to Sara about helping m-me to find a girl for the house, I'd greatly appreciate it. We m-must find someone as soon as possible, you understand."

Michael nodded, forcing himself to smile. "It's as good as done, man. You know Sara—she won't rest until she finds the very girl you need. Now, what's this you were saying when you came in, about needing help for the little Hogan lad? What's happened to Billy?"

By the time Evan finished relaying his concern and suspicions about Billy Hogan, rage had emptied into the flood of Michael's other emotions. He was already halfway around the desk before Evan asked for help in finding the missing boy.

"We'll go at once," said Michael. Suddenly alert to Evan's exhausted appearance and ashen skin, he stopped. "Why don't you stay here? I'll take one of the men with me. We'll make Sorley Dolan talk, I'll guarantee it."

Evan shook his head, pushing himself up from the chair. "N-no. I want to go with you. I can't rest until the b-boy is found."

"All right, then," Michael agreed reluctantly. "But we'll be taking another man along. Stay here and rest until I see who's available."

Denny Price, fuming and impatient, approached the Franklin Street entrance of the Hall of Justice, pulling a mulish Quinn O'Shea along beside him.

"Will you let *go?*" she demanded. "I'm not one of your drunks to haul about however you please!"

"I told you, we'll be going to the station so you can tell your story to the captain! A formal complaint is needed before we can get an investigation under way." Denny attempted to tighten his grip on her arm.

"And I told *you*," she snarled, yanking her arm away from him, "that I'll not be talking to anyone else this night! I need a place to stay and a job, before I can go worrying about that sour old Ethelda Crane and her Shelter house!"

Denny turned, hoping to put out her fiery defiance with his sternest glare, but it had no more effect on her than an icicle on a firestorm.

Hardheaded!

"I'll be giving you a place to stay in the lockup if you don't cease your foolishness! And wasn't it yourself who said you wanted justice done? Well, the place to start is with a complaint—in writing."

The blood pounding in his ears, Denny reached again to grab her arm.

Fending him off, she stood her ground. "Perhaps I don't write," she said. Preening like a duchess, she gave her immense mane of hair a toss.

Watching her, Denny tried not to think about how small and young she looked. Just a wee thing, she was, appearing half-starved in that disgraceful sack of a dress. She had hair enough for two lasses—an odd color, like sand—and a thin band of freckles, not much darker than her hair, running across her nose. The enormous brown eyes were flecked with gold, like a cat's, and Denny suddenly realized what she had reminded him of all along: a scrawny, wee kitten, set out in the cold on its own keeping. Now here she was, bravely prowling about in search of the means to survive— too wounded to trust, too proud to beg.

"It strikes me," he said, careful to keep the slightest note of pity out of his voice, "that any *girsha* with such a saucy mouth would be clever enough to write her name. Now, will you come along like a good lass? After we tend to business, I promise I'll help you find a place to stay."

For a moment he saw the flint in her eyes spark, the defiance blaze up. Ah, she didn't like being obligated, that was clear.

Pulling herself up to her full height—which was not all that impressive—she regarded him with a look that took his measure. "And will you promise as well to help me find my friend, Bobby Dempsey?"

A wave of remembrance, followed by sympathy for the girl, hit Denny hard. As if she hadn't had enough, he was now about to increase her troubles. "I'm sorry to have to tell you, lass, but your friend—well, I'm afraid there was an accident. Your friend, Bobby Dempsey, is dead."

She stared at him as if he had struck her. "Bobby? Bobby Dempsey is dead?" she finally choked out. "But, how—"

"'Twas an accident on the docks, lass," Denny said gently. "I doubt he ever knew what hit him."

She stood, unmoving, staring down at the street for a long time. Denny tensed, anticipating a bout of tears, and altogether uncertain as to how he would go about comforting this strange lass with the wounded eyes.

"There's no justice," she said in a low voice. "None at all. Bobby, he never hurt a soul. He would have risked his hide to save a wee bird. He was a good, simple soul, and what does he get for it?"

She looked at Denny, and he flinched at the mixture of pain and anger in those startling eyes. But then she surprised him by motioning to the doors, saying, "Well, then, let's have it done with. Let's be seeing to your formal complaint."

Denny followed after her, trying not to notice the faint slump to her thin shoulders as she walked through the doors of the Hall of Justice.

Inside, Quinn's sorrow for the loss of Bobby Dempsey was quickly crowded out by a fresh wave of apprehension. "The Tombs," as Sergeant Price referred to the place, was a huge, mausoleum of a building, daunting in its very size and stateliness.

Quinn was keenly aware that this was a *police station.* It would have a gaol—a large one, from the looks of the place—where criminal offenders were incarcerated.

She knew an instant of panic. This was the very thing she was running from—first in Ireland, and most recently the Shelter, which to her way of thinking was as much a prison as any gaolhouse.

She had entered of her own volition—but for *what?* Something called *justice?* She was mad entirely! What had she ever known of justice back home? Growing up in Ireland, a body didn't see much in the way of justice, other than the relentless cruel hand of the Brits grinding the Irish into the bogs. Had she really thought to find anything better here in the States?

"Come along, lass. We'll see if the captain's still here."

The sergeant moved as if to take her arm, but Quinn jerked away, shaking her head. "I've changed my mind," she said, still backing off toward the door.

"Ah, no, and you can't!" protested the sergeant. "Now come along. Everything's going to work out all right—"

Quinn darted a glance over her shoulder, gauging the distance to the door. Bitterly, she realized that if she could only have found one of the ladies from the mission society before now, she might not be in such a fix. That Mrs. Burke, for example—the one who claimed to be married to an Irish policeman—had appeared more than kind. If only she had come back!

"There's someone else I want to talk to," she said abruptly, facing the sergeant. "A lady."

He eyed her with suspicion. "A lady, is it? And just how would you be knowin' a lady?"

Quinn stiffened, a queer heaviness settling over her chest at his words. Did he think her such a slattern, then, that a lady would avoid her altogether? Involuntarily, she glanced down over herself, feeling wretched at the sight of the wrinkled brown dress, hanging loose as a horse blanket over her frame.

She shook the feeling away, resisting the wave of shame that threatened to sweep over her. It wasn't her fault, now was it, that she had lost her clothes in the river, and later her one remaining dress to Ethelda Crane's greedy hands!

Lifting her chin, she leveled her frostiest look directly at the policeman. "How I'm knowing her is none of your affair. As I said, I will speak with Mrs. Burke or no one at all."

"Mrs. Burke?" The man stared at her as if she'd said something most peculiar.

Quinn nodded, curious as to what accounted for his startled expression.

"The lady you're asking to speak with is Mrs. *Burke?*"

"Didn't I just say as much?" Quinn snapped, impatient with his thick-headedness.

For a moment the sergeant said nothing, but merely stood there, regarding her with an odd expression. Now that she'd had a long look at him in the light, Quinn grudgingly admitted that perhaps the man didn't appear quite as simple as she'd first thought. His face was pleasant enough, bronzed and wind-whipped, with a slightly arrogant jaw and unusual gray eyes, with lashes as thick as any woman's.

He might have appeared to be a good-natured man if only he wasn't so insolent. But, him being a policeman, no doubt he thought he had a *right* to be insolent.

"I don't suppose you'd happen to know this...Mrs. Burke's...given name?" he asked her abruptly.

"I don't," Quinn replied.

"I see." Still watching her, the sergeant raked a hand over his chin, then glanced back at another policeman coming out of the office across the room. "And what did she look like, your Mrs. Burke?" he asked.

Thoroughly annoyed with him, Quinn frowned. "She looked like a *lady*. She was dressed grand and had kind eyes." She hesitated, then added less sharply, "I believe she limped a bit."

The other policeman walked up to them, and Quinn said no more. She had had more than enough of the sergeant's insolent questions for one night. Besides, it was perfectly obvious he didn't believe anything she had told him about Mrs. Burke.

Ignoring her entirely, Sergeant Price turned to the other policeman. "Mike—Captain," he said with a grin.

The other policeman arched one eyebrow, then nodded. He barely glanced at Quinn. He was a big, handsome man, taller than Sergeant Price, though perhaps not quite so brawny. Dark-haired and dark-eyed, he sported a roguish black mustache. He looked, Quinn decided with a shiver of misgiving, like a man who could be very dangerous. He also looked very angry.

"Evan Whittaker is in my office," he said shortly. "He needs help."

Sergeant Price's expression quickly sobered. "He's still looking for the little Hogan lad, is he?"

The other gave a curt nod. "I'm going back to Five Points with him."

Abruptly, he turned to look at Quinn, then back to the sergeant, as if expecting an explanation.

"Captain Burke," the sergeant said, also turning to eyeball Quinn, "this is Miss Quinn O'Shea. She hails from the Chatham Charity Women's Shelter." He paused. "It would seem that she has urgent business with your wife."

38

Angels Unaware

God's presence surrounds you,
His angels around you,
The light of his love falling soft
On your face...
A heaven above you,
A family to love you,
Sleep, child, in your cradle
of blessing and grace.

OLD LULLABY

It was dark by the time Nora finished nursing Teddy. As she stood waiting for Johanna to light the oil lamp between the changing table and the crib, she tried to shoo Finbar off her skirts.

The wee cat's life seemed to revolve about Johanna and the baby. He liked nothing better than to find them together in the same room—an appreciative audience for his mischief.

After laying the baby on the table for changing, Nora caught Johanna's attention. "Take Finbar out of the room, dear," she said, signing the words as she spoke. "Otherwise, he'll be trying to jump up on the table with Teddy."

Johanna scooped up the cat in her arms and left the room. A moment later Aunt Winnie entered. "Here, Nora, let me do that. You go and sit down, dear."

Invariably, Nora tried to dissuade Evan's meticulously groomed aunt from changing the baby's messy didies—and just as invariably, Aunt Winnie dismissed her protests as utter foolishness.

"How many times have I done this by now? And I haven't swooned yet, have I? Just you sit and rest while I take care of Teddy." Frowning at Nora, she added, "Perhaps you should *lie* down, dear. You look quite exhausted."

"Oh, no, I'm perfectly fine," Nora insisted, sinking down onto the side of the bed as she tried to ignore the weakness that had plagued her all afternoon. "I might be just a bit tired, is all."

Aunt Winnie darted a glance over her shoulder. "Well, there's nothing for you to do in the kitchen. Daniel is being treated to dinner by that nice Dr. Grafton, so he won't be in tonight. I have everything quite in hand. We can eat as soon as Evan comes, though we really don't know when that will be, do we?"

"He thought he would be late. He said we should go ahead without him, but I'd rather not." Nora watched the older woman lift Teddy into her arms. "I do hope he doesn't stay in the Five Points after dark," she went on. "That frightful place. But he's so worried for the little boy, there's no telling what he'll do if he can't find him."

"Well, he was going to ask one of the policemen for help, so I'm sure he'll be quite safe," said Aunt Winnie. She smiled down at Teddy squirming in her arms. "*This* little man seems restless tonight. You don't think he's caught cold?"

Nora attempted to shake off the old familiar lethargy stealing over her. "I hope it's not my milk. Evan says I fret too much about everyone. I do worry about *him*, I confess. He's so very busy of late, and his lungs aren't all that strong. And Johanna—she troubles me as well. She's so unhappy." Her eyes went to Teddy. "Some say worry can turn a mother's milk."

Aunt Winnie's eyes were kind, her voice gentle. "I don't pretend to know much about babies, dear. But perhaps you should take Dr. Grafton's advice and begin to wean Teddy. It might be better for both of you."

Nora gave a reluctant nod. "Perhaps. It's just that he's my last one, don't you see. It might be that I'm altogether selfish, but I find myself wanting to keep the closeness between us as long as possible."

Evan's aunt put Teddy down in his crib and soothed his whimpers of protest. At last he quieted and, with a tiny sigh, lay studying his surroundings.

"I don't think you're being selfish at all," said Aunt Winnie, coming to sit beside Nora on the bed. "I've never been a mother, but I think I understand what you mean. Still, dear, if it would be best for Teddy—and for your health—then perhaps it's time."

She took Nora's hand. "Try not to worry about Evan. I'm sure he'll be home soon. As for Johanna"—she glanced toward the door—"I doubt that anything but time will help her very much. She's still grieving, I'm afraid."

"You've seen her resistance to Teddy?"

Aunt Winnie nodded. "Yes, and it's heartbreaking. But grief can't be rushed, Nora. You know that as well as I do. Some of us simply take longer to heal. Goodness knows, that poor child has suffered enough loss in her young life to destroy a weaker spirit. I really do believe she'll be all right, in time."

"I hope so. I had thought Teddy might make a difference, but I'm beginning to wonder. I know she cares about him—you can *see* the longing in her eyes! You can sense her wanting to touch him, to pick him up—it breaks my heart to watch! I've prayed and prayed for her, but she's still frightened…and in such pain."

Evan's aunt gave an understanding nod. "No doubt the child *is* frightened," she agreed. "Frightened that she might somehow hurt Teddy. Poor dear—she's still blaming herself for what happened to her brother," she said with a sigh. Getting to her feet, she took Nora gently by the shoulders. "Johanna will be all right. She just needs time. And you, dear heart, need to rest. I want you to lie down now," she said, gently pressing Nora back onto the bed and pulling the comforter over her legs. "Just for a little while. And no arguments."

"But Teddy—"

"Teddy will more than likely be fast asleep in no time. But Johanna and I will keep an eye on him, never fear."

Feeling too lightheaded and weak to protest, Nora sank back against the pillows and closed her eyes. She was only vaguely aware when Johanna came back into the room and sat down in the chair beside the crib.

In the kitchen, Winifred made a last, unnecessary inspection of the ham and cornbread. Reassured…again…that all was well, she permitted herself a smile of satisfaction.

She hoped the Lord would forgive her a certain amount of pride where her cooking was concerned. For years, she hadn't been allowed near a kitchen. She had outlived two husbands, both men of means, whose estates had been glutted with servants. Until the death of Neville, her second husband, her culinary abilities had consisted of pouring tea and passing scones.

In the midst of her second widowhood, however, Winifred decided she had had quite enough of being helpless. To the outrage of Neville's family, she departed the drafty, creaking country house and took rooms in London, where she proceeded to teach herself the womanly arts of cooking and keeping house. She now managed both with a certain flair, if she did say so herself.

She had already determined that after she and Lewis were married— the thought brought a smile—she wouldn't allow herself to slip back into uselessness. He had Ginger and plenty of other servants, of course, but she intended to play an active part in managing the household.

Going to the sink, she began to wash up the dishes she had used in preparing the meal, smiling ruefully as the hot, soapy water reddened her hands. She doubted that she'd ever feel any particular domestic satisfaction about washing dishes.

Her thoughts returned to Lewis—a frequent occurrence these days— and it struck her that she might suggest he lend one of his own servants to Nora and Evan, at least temporarily. More and more she saw the need for Nora to have help on a daily basis, certainly more help than Winifred herself could provide.

For a moment she stood, unmoving, her hands still submerged in hot water. Lately, every thought of Nora seemed to bring an accompanying heaviness of heart and a dark shadow of fear. Something was very wrong with Nora; Winifred was sure of it. She thought Evan suspected as much, too, but was doing everything he could to deny it, poor lamb. How could he do otherwise, devoted as he was to her? Nora was his life.

She bit her lip and gave a long sigh, then went on sudsing the bowl in her hands. She wondered if Nora knew about Evan's appointment with Dr. Grafton today. She rather doubted it. Evan would keep his silence rather than worry her.

The fact that the doctor had asked to speak with him was frightening. Surely it hinted at something serious.

How would they ever manage if Nora was indeed, as Winifred had begun to suspect, seriously ill? They would *have* to get domestic help then, perhaps someone to live in. There would be medical bills, perhaps hospital costs.

They had Evan's salary, of course, and she was sure Lewis would increase it in an instant. But Winifred knew from her experience with Neville that a lingering illness most often demanded exorbitant sums of money. Even for the wealthy, prolonged illness could be a terrible drain on finances.

Johanna's uncle in Ireland sent a generous living allowance for her each month, but there was still little Teddy to provide for—and the matter of an education for Daniel John, who hoped to become a physician.

Winifred stood, unmoving, her hands still plunged beneath the dishwater. For some time now, she had been formulating a plan that would ease things considerably for Evan. She'd been uncertain as to how to go about it, for Evan was terribly independent, but she thought she had finally found the answer.

Evan's savings in London were as good as lost to him. In order to prevent that terrible employer of his—Roger Gilpin—from learning his whereabouts, he had found it necessary to forfeit his bank account and leave all his personal belongings behind when he came to the States.

But Winifred had plenty of money, more than she'd ever spend, even if she lived to be a doddering old fool. Besides, as Lewis Farmington's wife, she wouldn't exactly be indigent.

She smiled to herself. Lewis's shrewd financial advice was largely responsible for the investments that were even now fattening her bank account. At least, she thought wryly, no one could accuse her of marrying the man for his money. Of all the reasons she could think of for falling in love with Lewis Farmington, money did not even make the list.

Oh, she *did* hope she would hear from Jeremy Cole soon! If he'd managed to do what she asked, it could make a wonderful difference for Evan and Nora, especially now. She had great faith in Jeremy; there was no more clever solicitor in London. More to the point, however, he had been a good friend to Winifred for years.

Emptying the dishwater, she dried her hands. Jeremy was clever all right, but she could hardly expect him to break the law on her account. Still, if there were any way under God's heaven to free Evan's savings without that awful Roger Gilpin finding out, she knew Jeremy would figure a way to manage it.

She had given him strict instructions that no one—absolutely no one—must ever learn of Evan's whereabouts. And that, of course, was what complicated the whole affair.

Winifred had deliberately kept Evan in the dark about her attempts on his behalf. If Jeremy were successful, it would be a delightful surprise for her troubled nephew. If Jeremy failed, then she intended to transfer a sum from her own funds into an account in Evan's name.

Either way, Evan must be allowed to believe that it was *his* money. She had already stipulated in her newly drawn will—with Lewis's approval—that Evan receive her entire estate. If he happened to receive a share of it while she was still alive, so much the better—she would enjoy watching him use it.

When the dishes were done, she went into the small adjoining dining room to check the place settings and candles. Just inside the door, she stopped. The trouble-making cat—Finbar, of all the presumptuous names!—was perched on Evan's empty chair, eyeing the table.

Winifred flew at him with a hiss, flapping her apron. He leaped screeching from the chair and bolted from the room.

Shaking her head, she dusted off the chair with her hand. She continued to be appalled that Evan, otherwise such a sensible man, actually tolerated that bothersome little creature inside the house. There was no accounting for the way the entire family put up with the cat's mischief.

After straightening the tablecloth, Winifred went to the window and looked out. It was dark outside, but with enough moonlight that she could make out the distant outline of the park. Arms folded, she hugged her body, shuddering. She could scarcely bear the sight of the place, a bleak reminder of Little Tom's untimely death.

In the daylight, she actually avoided looking out this particular window, which faced the park. It was enough to live with the effects of tragedy without being constantly reminded of it. Yet the sorrowful eyes of poor, tragic Johanna never quite allowed anyone to forget what had happened last spring.

Johanna. Whatever was to become of the girl? The death of her little brother seemed to have isolated her even more than her inability to hear or speak. Nora and Evan—and that wonderful boy, Daniel John—had tried everything to break through the wall of silent grief that seemed to surround her. They had all been so hopeful the baby might make a difference, but Johanna continued to avoid little Teddy.

It was no exaggeration to say that everyone in the family had labored in prayer for Johanna, herself included. What Winifred confessed to no one was that it was becoming more and more difficult to pray with any real hope, just as it was increasingly difficult to imagine what kind of future might lie in store for the girl.

Unexpectedly, almost as if in response to her troubled thoughts, one of her favorite portions of Scripture settled over her heart: *"For I know the plans I have for you," says the LORD, "plans for welfare and not for evil, to give you a future and a hope."*

Winifred held her breath, a sense of wonder sweeping through her. For the first time in a very long time, she felt her shadowy concerns and dark dreads about Johanna…and Evan and Nora…begin to recede behind a slowly rising light of divine promise.

She had no idea as to why she should suddenly feel hopeful. She only knew a subtle brightening of her spirit, as if God's loving heart had touched her own with a gentle reminder that He was still in control…He still cared…and there was still hope.

Johanna sat on the chair between the double bed and the crib, keeping watch and occasionally dozing. Aunt Nora was sleeping soundly, but baby Teddy was wide awake. He fidgeted about, shaking his fists with fierce determination or pursing his tiny mouth into a frown, then a grin.

Johanna watched him out of the corner of her eye, trying not to notice his baby antics. She couldn't stop a smile. But when a wave of longing to pick him up and cuddle him seized her, she quickly looked away. Resting her head against the back of the chair, she closed her eyes. Soon he renewed his efforts to get her attention, but Johanna forced herself to ignore him.

In her mind, she began to chant the little nonsense rhyme she had made up, a rhyme Teddy would never hear, but which she had created especially for the angel game:

Oh, Teddy-Dear, don't you fear,
God sent an angel
To guard and watch over you all through the night….
My Teddy-Boy, she'll stay close by,

To love and protect you till night becomes day.

Sometimes Johanna pretended that *she* was baby Teddy's guardian angel, sent from heaven to protect him. She hoped it wasn't a sinful thing, pretending to be an angel. She only did it because she imagined it helped Teddy to understand why she couldn't pick him up, or tickle him under the chin as Aunt Winnie did, or rock him to sleep—or do any of the things she secretly longed to do.

Being an angel she couldn't be an ordinary big sister, as she yearned with all her heart to be. But she could stay near him and watch over him. She could even allow her heart to whisper that she loved him.

Johanna understood that the angel game was only make-believe. In truth, she wasn't entirely certain she still believed in angels any longer. If they were real—as Uncle Evan insisted they were—where had they been the day wee Tom drowned in the pond? Why hadn't the angels saved him?

And yet she could not quite bring herself to give up the game altogether, for it allowed her to pretend, at least for a time, that she was very important to Teddy, that she had a legitimate reason for staying close to him.

Besides, not all of the angel game was make-believe: part of it was real. She *did* love baby Teddy. That much, at least, was entirely true, no matter that it was a secret.

Johanna had another secret, one she didn't quite know what to do with. She had told no one about it, for if anyone knew, she wasn't sure what it might mean to her.

She could make sounds...sounds in her throat. She remembered the night she first discovered the secret. It had been late, long past midnight, on one of the nights after Little Tom's death. She had been lying face-down on her bed, crying for her brother, crying for her loss. Those nights following the drowning, she often wept until daybreak—hard, wracking cries that left her limp as a rag doll afterward.

On this night, she had been seized with an unusually violent fit of weeping. Earlier, she had fallen into an uneasy sleep, only to be startled awake by the memory of seeing wee Tom carried, lifeless, from the pond. Newly assaulted by a vicious storm of guilt and grief, she had felt herself trapped behind a steadily rising wall of stone and mortar. One by one the huge stones hemmed her in, building her prison higher and higher, the dense walls crowding in on her by degrees until she could see no daylight, could breathe in no fresh air, only the cold, dank stench that often came from a dry well.

Wild with terror and anguish, she clutched her head with both hands, burying her face in the pillow. A torrent of violent sobs ripped from her throat, while her mind screamed in agony for release.

Then she had felt the peculiar sensation in her ears, the hot tickling in her throat, like a vibration. She screamed into the pillow again…and grabbed her throat as something seemed to explode from deep inside her.

She had known then that there was sound…a voice…somewhere deep within her, trying to break out.

She had never experienced it again, had deliberately checked any impulse to allow the sound to escape. What had happened that night months ago still frightened her, in some way even threatened her, and so she had kept it secret all this time.

Sometimes Johanna felt as if her entire *life* was a secret…as if the wall of terrors that had surrounded her that night had finally become a reality, and no one could see her trapped behind it.

39

Acts of Desperation

The winter is cold,
the wind is risen....

FROM THE "COLLOQUY OF THE ANCIENTS,"
THE FENIAN CYCLE

Quinn was disgusted with herself for feeling so intimidated. Sitting beside the grim-featured police captain, she set her face straight ahead, avoiding even a sideways glance in his direction. She was determined not to let him see how rattled she was in his presence.

Quinn was realistic enough to concede that she would be fidgety in the company of *any* policeman. Even the younger, good-natured Sergeant Price put her on edge. There was no denying that she had her people's innate distrust of the Law. She also had reasons of her own to *avoid* the Law.

She told herself it was the police wagon that unnerved her so, not the man. A "Black Maria," he had called it, explaining that it was used for transporting prisoners.

That was exactly what she felt like—a prisoner. In the course of the evening she had escaped her cell at the Women's Shelter only to find herself strong-armed by Sergeant Price. In short order the sergeant had handed her off to the custody of his captain, a black Irish warrior-type, who, to Quinn's amazement, turned out to be the *husband* of Mrs. Burke!

After listening to her initial explanation about the Shelter, the captain had proceeded to question Quinn in a blunt, but not unkind, manner about her "business" with his wife. Still somewhat dazed by the reality

311

that the granite-jawed captain was indeed married to Mrs. Burke, Quinn
had found herself tongue-tied for one of the few times in her life.

To give the man his due, Sergeant Price had stepped in to help inject
some order into her story. Apparently, his interpretation had sounded
more plausible, for the captain wasted no time in changing tactics. After
sending Sergeant Price off with the one-armed Britisher—something to
do with a missing little boy—he then informed Quinn that *he,* and not
the sergeant, would be escorting her to his wife.

Quinn could tell he was suspicious of her—and clearly impatient.
However, her hopes were somewhat buoyed when he mentioned something to the sergeant about a "subcommission" and the likelihood of an
"immediate investigation of the Shelter."

Stealing a glance at his stern profile beside her, she wondered what her
situation actually was. What would they do with her, once she had spoken
with Mrs. Burke? The captain seemed a hard man, and she wouldn't put
it past him to try to cart her off to another "shelter" of some sort. Or a cell.

Quinn dug at her skirts with both hands. No matter how the captain
planned to dispose of her, she would be one step ahead of him. For the
first time in months, she was inhaling the air of freedom. It might bear
the stench of garbage and animal droppings, but it smelled of heaven itself
after her lengthy confinement.

"You needn't be afraid, girl," the captain said unexpectedly.

Quinn jumped, snapping her head up to look at him.

"If you're telling the truth," he said, looking over at her, "you've nothing to fear."

"'Tis the truth," she said, out of sorts at the way he continued to question her story. He had already challenged her more than once before they
ever left the police station. "Is that why you're arresting me? Because you
don't think I'm telling the truth?"

He swung around to look at her. "I'm not *arresting* you, girl! Unless I'm
mistaken, *you're* the one who insisted on speaking with my wife!"

Stubbornly, Quinn didn't answer, but kept her gaze fixed straight
ahead. Out of the corner of her eye, she saw him finally turn his attention
back to the street, his jaw set tighter than ever.

Silence hung between them for a long time. As they drove, Quinn
became aware of the gradual change in their surroundings. They had left
behind the rutted streets, the pigs, the ramshackle taverns, and turned

onto a broad, tree-lined avenue, cobbled and well-lighted. Gas lamps flickered on the corners, and the lace-curtained windows of the stately houses glowed from within. The odors were different, too. The sour, yeasty smells and the stench of garbage had been exchanged for the scent of woodsmoke and late-falling leaves.

"We're almost there," the captain said, turning a corner. Quinn took in their surroundings with surprise. Although she remembered Mrs. Burke as being a finely dressed, soft-voiced lady, she would never have thought to find an Irish policeman living in such a grand setting.

The farther into the neighborhood they went, the larger and more elegant the homes appeared. Many were mansions, with three, even four stories, wide, rambling porches, and cone-shaped roofs. Most were surrounded by ornamental iron fences and towering trees.

At the end of the street, they pulled up in front of a sprawling mansion of dark stone, with ivy concealing much of the front. Although there was nothing particularly spectacular about the house, it reminded Quinn for all the world of one of the aging castles back home. Surrounded by enormous old oak trees and gracious landscaping, it looked peaceful and somehow inviting.

She glanced over at the captain. As if aware of her scrutiny, he motioned toward the house and said, "It belongs to my wife's grandmother. We live here with her."

Without another word, he jumped down from the patrol wagon and surprised Quinn by coming around to her side to help her down.

The frigid November wind seemed to go right to the bone as soon as she stepped out of the wagon. Her thin sweater was next to useless, and she couldn't keep from shaking. Even her teeth were chattering.

The captain opened a sturdy iron gate, and they started up the walkway. Quinn gaped at the place, wondering what madness had made her insist on coming here. What sort of a reception could she expect from someone living in such grandeur as this?

She stumbled, and the captain caught her elbow to steady her. For an instant she wondered if she had the slightest chance of outrunning him. As if he'd read her thoughts, he frowned at her, then gestured toward the front door.

Quinn hurried along beside him, bitterly regretting her folly in coming here. But she had brought it on herself, and it would seem she had no choice but to see it through.

Johanna struggled to stay awake. The room was warm, the oil lamp dim, and she couldn't seem to keep from nodding off. Glancing over at the bed, she saw that Aunt Nora was still sound asleep. Teddy, however, was wide awake and playful. Every time he managed to catch her eye, he would flail his fists in the air and grin at her, as if for approval.

Finally she got up and walked to the window. There was just enough light from the moon to see Dulcie's house next door through the trees. As she watched, the tree branches, now stripped of their leaves, bent and swayed with the wind. She hugged her arms to herself, relishing the bedroom's warmth.

The cabin in Killala had always been cold. There had never been enough firewood, and sometimes, especially at night, the wind off the ocean seemed to blow right through the rooms.

One of the things she liked most about America was the warm houses. She had seldom been cold since they arrived. In truth, she liked a great deal about her new country, but she sometimes felt guilty for acknowledging the fact. Both of her parents had died in Ireland, her sister and little brother here in America. She must be wicked entirely, to feel so grateful for her new life. It didn't seem right, somehow, that a new country, a new home—no matter how warm—could even in part make up for all she had lost.

For a long time she stood staring out into the night, thinking about her family. Then a shadow on the drapes caught her eye, and she turned around. The mischievous cat, Finbar, was crouched on top of the lamp table near the crib, vying for Teddy's attention.

Obviously, Teddy found the cat's mischief great fun. His round cheeks were pink, his small fists and feet pummeling the air as Finbar traced a path about the base of the lamp.

Johanna watched them for a moment. She liked to see Teddy laugh. Even if she couldn't hear him, she liked to imagine what he must sound like when he wrinkled his tiny nose and opened his mouth until his eyes almost disappeared.

In truth, she also enjoyed the cat's naughty capers. But Aunt Nora didn't like Finbar about the crib. She had best call a halt to their fun.

Finbar slanted a look at her, and, as if encouraged by her smile, cocked his head to one side, then the other.

Johanna started toward him, wagging her finger. At the same instant, Teddy pushed a hand through the crib, reaching for the cat's tail. Finbar lurched, bumped the oil lamp, and sent it toppling.

Johanna saw it all like a dizzying dream. The cat bolted wildly from the room. The lamp crashed to the floor. The oil flamed. And Teddy's round little face went strangely sober.

The tablecloth ignited instantly, the flames lapping up the material. The fire spread out over the oil like deadly tentacles stealing across the floor—toward the bed on one side, Teddy's crib on the other.

Panic struck her, and Johanna opened her mouth to scream. But no sound came.

She *had* to wake Aunt Nora! She started for the bed, then stopped. A thin finger of flame was already creeping up one leg of the crib.

Without another thought, she lunged toward the crib, grabbing Teddy up into her arms. As she pulled him against her, she turned back toward the bed and saw Nora shift as if she were coming awake.

A ribbon of fire slithered between Johanna and the bed. Smoke burned her eyes, filled her lungs. The baby's small fists clutched at her dress as he stared at the flames in obvious terror.

In desperation, Johanna threw back her head and squeezed her eyes shut, straining, pleading, for the voice to come.

A shuddering vibration ripped from her throat. Her eyes snapped open, and she saw Nora bolt upright in bed, gaping at the scene around her in horror.

Sara was in the sitting room, reading by the fire, when she heard Michael's voice. Surprised but pleased, she jumped up from her chair, calling out to him as she hurried from the room.

"Michael? I thought you said you wouldn't be home until late—"

She stopped dead at the sight of her husband and the young girl at his side. Her mind instantly registered the fact that Michael looked strained and slightly harried, while the girl appeared resentful and even a little frightened. "Michael?"

His expression momentarily brightened at the sight of her. "Sara, I've brought you a visitor."

It took only a moment for recognition to dawn. "Good heavens—it's… Quinn, isn't it? Quinn O'Shea, from the Shelter! Why, my dear, how good to see you! But how did you ever manage to find me?"

Sara broke off, looking at Michael for an explanation, but he merely lifted his brows in an expression of wait-and-see.

Stepping closer, Sara decided she'd been right about the fear in the girl's eyes. Impulsively, she reached for her hand. "Well…it's very nice to see you again, Quinn. I've thought quite a lot about you."

Something flickered in the gold-flecked brown eyes—whether relief or surprise, Sara couldn't tell.

"You…you do remember me, then, ma'am?"

The girl's voice trembled. Sara studied her, wondering at her obvious distress.

"Why, of course, I remember you! Michael, I told you about meeting Quinn at the Shelter?"

He regarded Sara, then the girl, with a slightly puzzled frown. "I'm not sure I recall—"

"Oh, surely you do!" Sara interrupted, smiling at Quinn. "The day I toured the Chatham Women's Shelter with Helen Preston and the others. I told you about talking with one of the young residents. Remember?"

Michael nodded slowly, finally giving a faint smile of recognition. "Aye…I believe I do at that. I expect I'd forgotten the name."

Still holding Quinn's hand, Sara studied her. She had wondered from time to time about what might have become of the slight Irish girl, who had so poignantly reminded her of a trapped and helpless animal. Compassion mingled with curiosity at the sight of those wounded eyes and the thin frame beneath that hideous, shapeless dress.

"Would either of you like to tell me what's going on?" Sara asked, trying not to show her impatience.

"Miss O'Shea here has asked to talk with you," Michael said dryly. "She insists that she will speak with no one else, that it's a matter of some importance."

A corner of his mouth quirked, and after searching his eyes a moment, Sara turned back to Quinn. "Is something wrong, dear? Are you in some sort of trouble?"

The girl seemed highly agitated. She bit her lower lip as her gaze darted around the room. She looked as if she were tempted to turn and run.

Uncertain as to whether she should press, Sara looked to Michael for help.

He hesitated for a moment, regarding the girl with an unreadable expression. "Sara, why don't you show Miss O'Shea where she can freshen up a bit, and then perhaps we could have some supper while we talk. I could do with a bite, and I imagine she could, too."

"Oh, of course! I expect neither of you have eaten, have you?" Tugging gently at Quinn's hand—a painfully thin hand, she noted, Sara said, "Come along, dear. Let's you and I go upstairs. Michael, Mary should still be in the kitchen. Why don't you ask her to set out another meal for you and Quinn? There's potato soup and roast beef—and fresh bread. We won't be long."

Winifred had her head halfway in the oven, checking the ham, when she heard the scream—a primal sound, like that of a wild animal. Straightening, she raced to the door to see the troublesome cat go tearing down the hallway, screeching like a wild thing. She leaned against the doorpost and sighed. How could one tiny cat make such a hideous noise?

And what had the little goblin gotten into now? She wiped her hands on her apron, preparing to do battle with the cat, children's pet or not.

She was on her way down the hall when she heard the baby shriek and begin to cry. She wrinkled her nose against the acrid smell of... *smoke*! Her heart in her throat, she took off running.

At the bedroom door, one sweeping glance took in the terrifying scene: the blazing tablecloth, the flames lapping at one leg of the crib, the fire spreading over the floor. And in the midst of the nightmare—*Johanna*!

With one arm the girl held Teddy tightly to her, while with her free hand she lifted her skirts to avoid the flames snaking past her as she jumped. And Nora—*oh, Lord have mercy*—Nora was stumbling from the bed, trying, in all her weakness, to yank the blankets off, no doubt to cover the fire!

Flying into the room, Winifred grabbed Johanna and pushed her and the baby safely out into the hallway. Then she went back for Nora.

Nora, dazed, was struggling to breathe. Winifred half-carried her from the room, entrusting her to Johanna's care. Running back into the bedroom, she hauled the blankets from the bed in one sweep and began to throw them on the flames.

After a moment, Johanna appeared next to her. They fought the fire side by side, using blankets, then pulling the drapes from the windows for good measure. Though it seemed an eternity, they finally brought the flames under control.

Other than a room filled with smoke and some ruined drapes and bedding, there was little damage. Exhausted, Winifred wiped a hand over her eyes and stood looking at Johanna. The girl's thin, lightly freckled face was smudged, her eyes red-rimmed from the smoke. They were both coughing, and Winifred knew if her hair was even half as smoke-dusted as Johanna's, she was a sight.

But they were safe.

Putting an arm around the girl's slender shoulders, Winifred led her from the room, where Nora stood with the baby whimpering in her arms.

Taking Johanna by her shoulders, Winifred slowly turned her around so the girl could read her lips. "I want to be sure you realize what you did tonight, Johanna," she said, speaking slowly and deliberately, her eyes going over the thin, smudged face.

Johanna's eyes widened, and Winifred hurried to reassure her. "You are a very brave girl, dear," Winifred said, squeezing her shoulders. "You saved your baby brother's life tonight. Quite possibly, you saved *all* our lives tonight."

Johanna flushed, but Winifred held her gaze, going on. "It's true, dear. And when Teddy is old enough to understand, we will tell him about the night his big sister saved him from the fire!"

She hesitated, then gently put a hand to Johanna's smoke-tracked cheek. "Child…did you know you have a voice?" Lightly, she touched the girl's throat. "I heard you cry out." Winifred touched her own ear, then Johanna's throat once more. "I heard you, dear."

Johanna put her own hand to her throat and, her eyes wide, nodded. A trace of a smile stole over her smoke-grimed face.

Reaching then to take the baby, Winifred stood by as Nora and Johanna embraced. When they released each other, Johanna turned, her gaze going to Teddy. Winifred smiled and without hesitation handed him over.

"Aren't you a lucky baby," she said, making sure Johanna could read her lips, "having such a brave big sister to take care of you?"

40

The Sound of Singing

Thou, and Thou only, first in my heart,
High king of Heaven, my treasure Thou art.
Heart of my own heart, whatever befall,
Still be my vision, O Ruler of all.

ANONYMOUS (IRISH, EIGHTH CENTURY)

On the other side of the door, they could hear a man's voice raised in anger, followed by the low tones of a woman and children. The sergeant pounded three times. After a moment they heard the thud of heavy footsteps stumbling over the floor.

"Uh-oh," muttered Sergeant Price. "It sounds as if Sorley is at home, blast the luck. Do you mind holding this for a bit, Mr. Whittaker?" he asked, passing Evan the lantern he'd brought with him from the patrol wagon.

Watching the door, Evan tensed. Like the sergeant, he had hoped Sorley Dolan would be away. Although it was reassuring to have the strapping policeman at his side—armed with a nightstick and a pistol—he dreaded a second confrontation with Billy's drunken "uncle." Drawing himself up, he pulled in a deep breath, waiting.

The door flew open, crashing back against the inside wall. Sorley Dolan loomed in the doorway. His bloodshot eyes narrowed when he saw Evan and Sergeant Price.

"G'd evening to you, Sorley," said the sergeant. His tone was cheerful as he stood tapping the palm of one hand with his nightstick. "Having a night off from the job, are we?"

"What is it you want?" snapped Dolan. Turning his attention to Evan, he eyed him as he might have an ugly insect. "And what're *you* doin' here again?"

"Now, Sorley, is that any way to be greeting an officer of the law—not to mention a gentleman like Mr. Whittaker?" The sergeant's fixed smile stopped short of his eyes, Evan noticed, and the nightstick was still very much in evidence as he slapped it against his hand with a little more vigor.

"I thought I told you the boy don't live here anymore!" Dolan snarled, glaring at Evan.

Sergeant Price gave Evan no chance to reply. "But weren't we just thinking that Billy might have come home by now? Sure, a boy his age isn't likely to favor life in the street to his own warm bed, now is he? Especially with the winter upon us."

"Well, he hasn't come back, and I don't look for him to!"

Dolan made a move as if to slam the door shut, but the sergeant stopped him by wedging one large foot in the doorway. "If you've no objection, Sorley, I believe we will have a look about the flat, all the same."

Evan heard the subtle change in the policeman's voice as his tone took on a note of warning.

The sergeant shoved his way past Dolan, saying over his shoulder, "Come on in, Mr. Whittaker. Sorley doesn't mind."

Holding his breath, Evan followed the sergeant inside to one of the most sparely furnished, dismal rooms he had ever seen. The floor was bare wood, splintered and stained. There were no curtains at the window, no rugs on the floor—no sign of even the slightest attempt at homemaking, except for a cookstove, thick with grease, and a rickety table crowded with bottles and dirty dishes.

Four rough, unmatched chairs, two of them broken, were pulled up to the table. In one of them sat a dull-eyed, sallow-faced woman of indeterminate age. She looked up as they entered but said nothing. Two small boys in the corner near the window stopped their play to watch Evan and the policeman with wary expressions. After a moment, they both scurried over and plopped down on the floor at the woman's feet.

Evan shuddered at the thought that this cold, desolate room was home to Billy Hogan. No doubt the worn-looking woman was his mother, the nervous little boys her sons by Dolan.

Sorley Dolan stood in the middle of the room, his meaty shoulders hunched as if in self-defense. His face was flushed and set in a dark, malignant scowl.

"You got no call breaking into me house, Price!" he exploded. "I done told the Brit that the boy is gone, and he won't be back!"

The sergeant paused in his inspection of the room to face Dolan. "Why, Sorley, I didn't break into your house! The door was wide open, didn't you see?"

Abruptly, his forced good humor disappeared, giving way to a cold, hard look of challenge and a thickening of the brogue. He stepped closer to Dolan. "Tell me, though, Sorley, what is it that makes you so sure young Billy won't be coming home? You wouldn't be keeping any secrets from us, now would you?"

Not waiting for a reply, the sergeant pointed with his nightstick to a thin blanket strung over a doorway. "That's the bedroom, is it? We'll just have a look."

"There's no one in there!" Dolan thundered, feinting as if to charge the policeman. The sight of the sergeant's hand going to his gun stopped him.

Finally, the woman spoke. "'Tis the truth," she said woodenly. "Billy ain't been home for days."

Sergeant Price studied her with a skeptical eye. "Where is the lad, then, Nell? Sure, you must know the whereabouts of your own boy."

She shook her head. Watching her slow movements, the dejected, slightly glazed expression, Evan thought she must either be slow-witted or in her cups, he couldn't tell which.

"Nell?" prompted the sergeant.

Before she answered, the woman slanted a quick look at Dolan, who twisted his mouth into an ugly sneer but said nothing.

The woman dropped her eyes to the table. "Billy run off," she said, her voice so low it was barely audible. "I don't know where."

The sergeant regarded her with a look of disgust, then motioned to Evan that he should follow him into the bedroom.

Evan raised the lantern to light their way into the dark room. There was virtually no furniture, except for two large pallets in one corner and a sagging iron bed at the opposite end of the room. Raggedy blankets had been tossed over the pallets and the bed. Dirty clothes littered the floor.

A feeling of great sadness settled over Evan as he stood looking about the cold, cheerless room. Once more he was overwhelmed by the realization that Billy Hogan had lived and slept in these dreary, disheartening surroundings.

"Could there b-be another room?" he asked the sergeant. "We can't simply give up on the b-boy!" Desperation seized his heart. There was not even the slightest sign that Billy had ever lived in this wretched place. For all the evidence of his presence, one could almost imagine the child had never existed at all. And yet Evan could not shake the feeling that something of Billy was still here…if not the boy himself, then at least some part of the anguish or loneliness he might have suffered in these rooms.

Suddenly realizing that the policeman had spoken to him, he turned. "I'm sorry, Sergeant?" he said, blinking.

"I was just saying, in answer to your question, Mr. Whittaker, that these two rooms are it. There's nowhere else to look, I'm afraid."

Evan nodded, still unable to shake the nagging sensation that Billy was near. On one level, he understood that his concern and anxiety for the boy might be clouding his reason. There was also the fact that he had gone for two days with scarcely any sleep or nourishment. That alone was enough to impair his judgment.

Aware that the sergeant was watching him, Evan expelled a long breath. "Yes…well, then, I suppose there's really n-nothing else we can do here, is there?"

"Sorry, Mr. Whittaker." The policeman motioned toward the makeshift curtain that divided the dreary bedroom from the main living space. "I'll have another go at Dolan before we leave, though I don't think he's likely to tell us any more than he already has."

"I'd n-not want to see you provoke the m-man, Sergeant. He's obviously bad-tempered—and drunk. There's no telling what he m-might do."

"Oh, I can handle Sorley well enough, sir," the sergeant answered with a grim smile. "You needn't worry yourself about that."

In the outer room, Dolan stood at the open door, his face a thunderhead. The woman and little boys were just as they had left them.

Evan followed Sergeant Price to the door. The policeman shot a nasty grin at Dolan, whose mottled face darkened even more. "I'll be back, Sorley," said the policeman. "I'm sure you must be worried about the boy, but we'll keep up the search, don't you fret. And I'll be stopping by now and again to let you know of any developments."

He paused, and Evan saw his eyes go hard. "And, Sorley, should I find out that you've not been entirely truthful with us—" He broke off. Again he began to tap the nightstick against the palm of his hand, saying nothing more but merely shaking his head as his eyes raked Dolan one last time.

Sorley Dolan made a low, growling sound in his throat and lunged forward, but the policeman was quicker. In a movement so fast Evan almost missed it, the hand with the nightstick swung upward, catching Dolan under the throat. At the same time, the sergeant threw himself against the man, driving him against the wall, pinning him in place with the nightstick wedged under his chin.

The sergeant pushed his face into Dolan's, his teeth bared in a terrible rictus of a smile. "You don't want to be trying my patience like that, Sorley."

His eyes blazed as he shoved the nightstick even harder against the man's throat, but he never raised his voice from its quiet, menacing tone. "Now, I'll be back, Sorley. One way or the other, I'll be back. And you had best be hoping that before I come, I find young Billy, safe and sound."

In the storage closet off the coal cellar, Billy Hogan came awake with a moan. The sound of his own voice and the sharpness of still another new pain had roused him from his twilight sleep.

He lay on his side, listening to his labored breathing. He tried to pull in a deep gulp of air, but the pain in his chest squeezed off the attempt. Every part of his body hurt, even his teeth.

He lifted a hand to make sure he could still see, for his right eye was almost swollen shut, and his left burned and watered all the time. He could just make out the outline of his fingers in the darkness. Relieved, he dropped his hand back to his side.

From a nearby corner came the familiar, dread rustling sounds. *The rats were waiting....*

Their noises were louder than Billy remembered. He thought he heard a squeal, but his ears rang so fiercely of late that he couldn't be sure.

He put a hand to his belly. He couldn't imagine why it was so big when he hadn't eaten for such a long time. He felt swollen and sore. For some reason, he found himself remembering the starving Hayes children back home, before they died in the snow. Their bellies had been swollen, every one of them, though their arms and legs had been nothing much but sticks.

Was he starving? It didn't seem likely, since he wasn't even hungry. He couldn't remember how long it had been since he had last eaten, but if he were starving, he would be hungry, wouldn't he?

He squeezed his eyes shut and tried to go back to sleep. He slept most of the time now, when the pain didn't keep him awake. He no longer listened for the door to open, no longer strained to hear Uncle Sorley's voice saying he could come out.

Uncle Sorley wasn't coming back for him this time.

Billy tried not to think of his uncle; instead, he turned his thoughts to his da. He thought about his da a lot lately. It was peculiar, how he could still remember Da's face, the sound of his voice, after so long a time. He had often awakened him on cold winter mornings by wrapping him up tight in the covers and lifting him out of the bed, blankets and all. Da would hold him on his lap then, the two of them perched on the side of the bed, until Billy came awake, still drowsy and warm in his father's arms.

Here in the cellar, when the cold gnawed at his bones and the pain wracked his body, Billy would pull himself up into a tight ball, pretending that he was back in his own bed at home, and Da was holding him, keeping him warm. Sometimes he even fell asleep that way, imagining the feel of his da's strong arms wrapped about him.

Billy's eyes came open as the scratching sounds grew closer. He shivered, gritting his teeth.

Staring into the darkness, Billy struggled to remember…something…

The song…he had to find the song…the song about the light…Mr. Evan said the Light would keep the things of darkness away….

Someone whispered in the darkness. Billy smiled, thinking it might be his da, after all, come to let him out.

Sing, Billy…sing. Sing away the darkness…sing about the Light….
Keep on singing, Billy…keep on singing….

Inside the small dark entryway downstairs, Evan and Sergeant Price stood talking in hushed tones. Still sensing the same peculiar restraint he had felt in the apartment, Evan found himself deliberately putting off leaving the building.

"I don't quite know what to do n-next, Sergeant," he said, "but I'm m-most grateful for your help. And your patience."

The policeman waved away his thanks. "I want to find the little lad as much as you do, Mr. Whittaker. Billy's a fine boy. As for what to do next, I've already passed the word to the other men. We'll all be keeping an eye out for him, you can be sure."

"Thank you, Sergeant." Evan hesitated, weary beyond measure, yet unwilling to give up. "I don't suppose…we could walk around a bit m-more."

"We can do that, if you like. But if you don't mind my saying so, Mr. Whittaker, you look as if you could do with a good night's rest. Are you all right, sir?"

"Oh…yes, I'm…"

Evan was totally unprepared for the sudden tightening of his throat, the stinging of his eyes. His voice caught, and, dismayed by his own weakness, he slumped against the wall, his body trembling. "I'm sorry…"

Sergeant Price moved to take the lantern. "Mr. Whittaker," he said kindly, putting a hand to Evan's shoulder, "why don't I just see you to the ferry? My word on it, I'll not give up the search for the little fellow."

Evan nodded, wiping his hand across his eyes. "Yes, perhaps you're right. I should g-go home. I don't want to worry N-Nora any more than—"

He broke off, holding his breath as he listened. *It couldn't be…yet, that voice…*

He knew that voice!

The sergeant frowned, still holding on to him as if he feared Evan might fall where he stood. "What is it, sir?"

"D-did you hear something?" Evan asked him, moving away from the wall. For a moment, he'd thought he heard a child's voice. Billy's voice. But he must have imagined it….

And then he heard it again. "There! Did you hear that?"

He strained to listen above the other muffled sounds echoing through the building—a baby crying, voices raised in an argument, children shouting at one another.

"Perhaps I was wrong," he said uncertainly. "I thought…it sounded like someone…singing."

They both stood, tensed and expectant. Scarcely breathing, Evan sorted out the sounds, one at a time, dismissing one, then going on to the next, much as he did when he was listening for a sour note among the boys in the choir.

There! He put a hand to Sergeant Price's arm. "Do you hear?"

Slowly, the sergeant nodded, regarding Evan with a questioning expression. "Aye, there would seem to be someone singing, right enough." His puzzled frown hinted at his unspoken question: *what of it?*

Evan turned to stare at the narrow, boarded door in the shadows. He moved toward it, leaned and pressed his ear against the scaling wood.

> "*...Be Thou my vision, O Lord of my heart,*
> *Naught be all else to me, save that Thou art,*
> *Thou my best thought by day and by night..."*

"*Waking or sleeping, Thy presence my light.*" Evan finished the words, barely able to choke out the last. "That's *him*! That's *Billy*!" He turned to the sergeant. "I'd know that voice anywhere!"

The policeman stared at him. Then, holding the lantern with one hand, he released the wooden bar across the door.

The door opened onto a dark, steep stairway. "Must go to the coal cellar," said Sergeant Price. "Looks black as the pit down there." Holding the lantern out, over the stairway, he started down. "Hold on tight, sir. These steps are in bad shape."

The singing was still faint, but sounded closer now. Evan's heart hammered. It was Billy, all right! There was no mistaking that bell-like voice, though it sounded fearfully weak and tremulous.

He was singing the same words over and over again, words to the old Gaelic hymn "Be Thou My Vision."

Evan thought his heart would explode as they descended the rickety stairway.

Sergeant Price ducked his head as they entered a dark, filthy cellar. Inside, he raised the lantern, passing it slowly from side to side. They could see nothing but a coal bin and some empty crates.

"Listen..." Evan whispered. In the eerie glow from the lantern, their eyes met. The singing had stopped.

Seized by a spasm of coughing as the coal dust filled his lungs, Evan fumbled for his handkerchief. When he could again catch his breath, he watched the sergeant explore each corner of the cellar, then shake his head.

"But he *must* be here somewhere!" Evan insisted. "We *heard* him!"

Suddenly, the policeman whipped around, raising a hand for Evan to listen. "There! It's coming from the other side!"

The sound was faint, like the whimper of a wounded animal.

Sergeant Price motioned for Evan to follow him. "Over here," he said. He lowered the lantern, revealing another door in the shadows behind the steps.

"Blast! It's locked!" muttered the sergeant as he shook the handle. Handing the lantern to Evan, he threw his shoulder against the door, but it held.

"Stand back, sir."

Evan stood aside while Sergeant Price took a step back from the door. One good kick was all it took; the shabby door broke free from its frame and slammed inward against the wall. Retrieving the lantern from Evan, the policeman drew his gun. As they entered, he tracked the sound of the soft moaning with the beam of the lantern.

Evan's heart hammered, and a wave of dizziness swept over him. He knew he was on the verge of passing out. He stopped for just an instant, willing his head to clear, forcing himself to breathe deeply.

Sergeant Price trained the lantern on the far corner of the closet, following its beam until he suddenly stopped. *"Lord, have mercy!"*

A moan of horror ripped from Evan's throat as he stared at the nightmare scene before them. Billy Hogan lay, facing them, curled up like an infant. His face was a mass of bruises and cuts, his eyes swollen shut. Dried blood streaked his face. His knees were drawn up almost to his chin, but Evan could see that the child was emaciated. Despite his protruding abdomen—no doubt the effect of starvation—his arms looked pitifully thin.

The boy moaned, and Evan went weak with relief. *He was still alive!*

Sergeant Price stepped forward, and gave a cry. Evan moved closer. His eyes followed the swaying light from the lantern—the sergeant's hand was trembling—and saw a sight that threatened to take his sanity.

A band of large brown rats hovered malevolently near the prostrate child's feet, as if poised in some macabre death watch.

Evan threw a hand over his mouth and gagged. The sergeant roared in rage and rushed at them, sending them squealing and scurrying back to their nest.

"*Devils!*" the policeman thundered as they ran. Pocketing his gun, he turned to Evan. "Why don't you let me take care of this, Mr. Whittaker?"

But Evan was already on his knees beside Billy. "I'm all right," he insisted. For a moment he was afraid to touch the poor, bruised body, fearful of inflicting still more pain. Finally, he was able to bring himself to put his hand to the wheat-colored hair, now matted with dirt and blood. The boy was shaking, his entire body jerking violently, as if in the throes of a seizure.

"Poor lad is freezing," muttered the sergeant, throwing off his coat and tucking it carefully around the small body.

"Oh, Billy...*Billy!*" The boy's name tore from Evan's throat like a sob. "What have they d-done to you?"

Billy moaned but didn't open his eyes. Evan went on stroking the boy's hair and calling his name, moving to make room for the sergeant when he knelt beside him.

"Let's have a look at the little fellow," he said softly. The policeman's large square hands moved as gently and as confidently as those of a surgeon over Billy Hogan's small body. Evan could almost sense the man fighting to keep his anger under control as he appraised the evidence of such unthinkable cruelty.

"He's taken a terrible fierce beating, poor little lad. And he's half-starved as well."

"Sergeant..." Hearing the tremor in his voice, Evan stopped to draw in a steadying breath. "The rats..."

"It wouldn't appear that the filthy creatures got a chance at him, Mr. Whittaker." Putting his ear to the boy's chest, he listened. "But he's in a bad way, poor lad. It's the hospital for him, but I'd not want to move him yet."

He got to his feet, saying, "If you'll stay with him for a bit, I'll go for Doc Hilman—he's just up the street. And I'll need to get one or two of my *boyos* down here to help out. We'll be locking Sorley Dolan up yet tonight."

With the sergeant's help, Evan sat down on the floor, bracing his back against the wall so he could cradle the boy's head in his lap. The child mumbled something incoherent, his body still shaking. Evan tried as best he could to soothe him, stroking his hair, murmuring words of comfort. The sergeant stood, watching the boy with compassionate eyes.

Suddenly, Billy twisted, then gave a sharp moan as if the effort had sent fresh pain shooting through him. "Da?"

Evan bent lower over the boy. "Billy...Billy...can you hear m-me?"

The boy turned his face up toward Evan, but his eyes remained closed. "Da...is it you, Da?"

Over Billy Hogan's small body, Evan looked up and met the gaze of Sergeant Price. Shaken, he saw that the eyes of the big, rugged police sergeant were glazed with tears, as were his own.

"He thinks you're his daddy, Mr. Whittaker," said the policeman with a faint, sad smile for Evan. "His real da died some years back, before they came across."

Looking down at the boy Evan murmured, "Your...your Father is here, B-Billy. He's right here with you." *Oh, Lord, You are here... You've been here all along, haven't You?*

With a last look at the boy, the sergeant said, "I'd best be going after the doc and my men, Mr. Whittaker. You'll be all right till I get back?"

Evan nodded, never taking his eyes off the small, battered face. His hand trembled as he continued to stroke and smooth the boy's hair. Again Billy twisted and moaned. "Da? Is it morning yet?"

Evan's breath caught in his throat. He nearly strangled on his words as he strained to answer. "Soon, B-Billy. Soon, it will be...m-morning...."

Slowly, as if the very act were an agony, Billy opened his eyes. He stared up at Evan through narrow slits. "Mr. Evan? Is that you?"

Somehow Evan found the strength to smile. "Yes, Billy. It's...M-Mr. Evan."

The child's swollen mouth actually curved in a vain attempt at a smile. "You were right...about the singing, Mr. Evan."

Evan leaned closer. "What's that, son? What about the singing?"

Billy's eyes closed again, but the ghost of a smile remained. "I remembered what you told us, Mr. Evan...about the singing...how it would build a fort round about us to keep away the things of the darkness—"

Billy gave a gasp beneath the sergeant's heavy coat. "It worked, Mr. Evan. It worked...just like you said it would. Did you hear me? Did you hear me singing?"

The tears Evan had struggled to control now fell free, streaming down his face. "Oh, yes, Billy...I heard you singing," he choked out. "I heard you, son...and so did your heavenly Father and all His angels."

41

The Ways of Women

May God be praised for woman
That gives up all her mind,
A man may find in no man
A friendship of her kind.

W. B. YEATS (1865–1939)

N ot long before midnight, Evan finally arrived home. Two of Sergeant Price's men brought him across from the hospital on a small boat sometimes used for searching the harbor.

He practically stumbled the last few steps up the walk. He could not remember ever being this weary in his life. But at least he had the comfort of knowing that Billy Hogan was safe in a hospital bed at Bellevue, and he expected that by now the brute responsible for his injuries was in a cell. There had been no mistaking Sergeant Price's resolve to lock up Sorley Dolan before the night was over.

Aunt Winnie opened the door before he could insert his key in the lock. "Evan...dear boy, you look absolutely exhausted!"

Inside, he allowed her to take his coat for him. His weary mind reached to identify the odor in the house. "Aunt Winnie? Is something b-burning?"

She turned to face him, and he saw for the first time that she looked uncharacteristically disheveled. Her hair was mussed; her dress appeared wrinkled and—stained. He stared at her, feeling the beginning of alarm. "Aunt Winnie, is something wrong?"

She took him by the arm. "Everything is under control, dear. You needn't worry. We had a minor fire, but no one was hurt."

"A *fire!*" His stomach knotted with dread. "Nora—"

Holding him firmly in tow, Aunt Winnie steered him toward the parlor. "Now, dear, everything is perfectly all right, I promise you. Nora is fine. So are Teddy and Johanna. Come along, you can see for yourself."

As she led him across the hall, Evan knew one irrational instant of denial. He was exhausted, famished, and slightly ill. He simply could not deal with another crisis yet tonight.

"In here, dear. We'll explain."

He stopped just inside the doorway of the parlor, vastly relieved to see Nora on the small settee in front of the fireplace, smiling rather wanly at him. A thrill of surprise shot through him at the sight of Johanna in the rocking chair by the window, with Teddy sound asleep in her arms! She, too, looked up and smiled as he entered.

For a moment Evan simply stood, staring at the scene in front of him. But his relief and pleasure quickly gave way to renewed concern as he became even more keenly aware of the smell of smoke.

Before he could ask anything else, Aunt Winnie urged him into the room. "I must warn you, dear, that the bedroom is a bit of a disaster. I've tidied up as best I can, but we'll have to replace the drapes and the bedding."

Evan gawked. "Whatever are you t-talking about? What happened?"

Aunt Winnie shushed him. "The baby's sleeping, dear. Do keep your voice down." Leading him over to the settee, she went on, her tone characteristically cheerful. "There. You just sit right here with Nora, and I'll explain. Then we'll get you something to eat. A cold supper will have to do, though, dear. I forgot all about your dinner while we were putting out the fire in the bedroom." She paused, catching a breath. "I'm afraid I burned the ham."

It was nearly midnight by the time Sara had seen Quinn O'Shea safely to bed, then sat listening in dismay to Michael's bleak news about Nora.

They talked quietly in the sitting room, Sara curled up in the armchair by the hearth, while Michael stood with his back to the fire, warming his hands.

Still shaken by the events of the evening and her fear for Nora, Sara was beginning to feel the effects of the long day. She could think of little to say, other than the question that had lodged in her mind since first hearing about the seriousness of Nora's condition. "She *will* be all right?" she asked anxiously. "With proper treatment and the right care…she can get well?"

"I'm not…certain that's the case," Michael said after a noticeable hesitation. "But if not altogether well, at least she should see some improvement. That's how Evan put it."

"Poor Evan. How is he?"

Michael shrugged. "Pretty much as you'd expect. Frightened. Distressed. But…managing, I'd say. You know how he is."

Sara nodded, her heart aching for the steadfast, devoted Englishman they had all grown to love and admire. "We must help them, Michael. However we can. I'm sure Father…and Grandy…will want to help, too."

He nodded. "Of course, we'll help. Apparently, Evan and Dr. Grafton intend to explain things to Nora the first of the week. Once Nora knows, we'll talk with them and see just what we can do."

After a moment, he came to her and, lifting her out of the chair, took her place, then settled her onto his lap. "In the meantime, though, Sara *a gra*," he said, wrapping her tightly in his arms, "what, exactly, are you intending to do with your wayward girl upstairs? Hmm?"

"I don't quite know," Sara admitted with a sigh. "She can stay here for the time being, until we think of something."

He stroked her hair, saying nothing for a moment. "Sara, I hope you won't be too hasty in involving yourself with this girl. We don't know her at all, remember."

Sara pulled back enough to look at him. "We know she needs help. And we know she's bright and brave and seems quite resourceful." She paused, then added almost angrily, "And we know a terrible injustice has been done to her."

"Indeed. But I still think you need to be cautious. It's my observation that Quinn O'Shea might be running from more than Ethelda Crane."

She frowned. "I suppose you can't help thinking like a policeman, Michael, but do keep in mind that the girl has only come across recently. Obviously, she's frightened and unsure of herself. But that doesn't have to mean she's *running* from something, does it?"

He studied her for a moment. "Perhaps not. But there's a look about her I've seen too many times before, Sara. If you asked me to define it, I'd not know how. But—"

He broke off, and Sara knew she hadn't convinced him.

"Surely you've noticed how skittish she is around me?" he said. "She acts as if she half expects me to haul her off to jail at any moment."

Sara shrugged off his skepticism. "You've told me yourself the Irish are often suspicious of policemen. And the truth is, darling," she added, "that you *can* be rather intimidating. Especially when you're wearing your grim expression."

"Indeed?" He cuffed her lightly on the chin, then pulled her back into his arms. "Well, at any rate, we'll have to be making some arrangements for her soon. She seems willing enough to work, but she's had no chance to go looking for a position as yet. Being Irish is going to severely limit her chances. You'd best warn her about the way things are for the Irish in New York."

"I'll help her find something," Sara said, brushing off his concern. "Michael," she said, burying her head against his shoulder, "you *are* going to launch an investigation of that dreadful Women's Shelter, aren't you?"

"Oh, you can count on it. I'll set my best men to it, first thing Monday. And I intend to ask for a subcommission investigation as well. We'll do whatever it takes to clean house at that place, including closing it down, if need be."

"I want to help," Sara announced, again rearing back to look at him.

"I think the police can handle it, love," Michael said teasingly.

"But I *want* to help," she repeated, all seriousness. "And I think I can. Ethelda Crane is used to members of the mission societies visiting the Shelter now and then. She'd have no reason to be suspicious if I made an unexpected call." She paused, then added, "Michael, I mean it. Please, let me have a part in this."

Taking her by the shoulders, he searched her eyes. "The woman really got to you, didn't she?"

Sara bristled. "I sensed Ethelda Crane was an unqualified phony the day I met her. Not to mention the fact that she's a bigot."

Even now, months later, Sara became incensed at the memory. She could still see the pious Ethelda Crane, standing in the midst of the group of women from the church, her tight, thin lips wagging on and on about the "filthy, diseased" Irish.

She should have confronted the woman right then and there, Sara thought, still angry with herself for walking away. And she should have demanded a thorough investigation of the Shelter—and its administrator—at the same time. There was no telling how much grief she might have spared Quinn O'Shea and the other residents if she had only followed her instincts.

With a long sigh, she sank against Michael, grateful for his warm strength and his patience. "I'm so thankful for you, Michael. You can't imagine."

He brushed his chin over the top of her head. "Because I tolerate your propensity for stray animals and wandering girls?"

She heard the smile in his voice, knew he was trying to lighten her mood. "That, too. But mostly for being yourself...for being all the things I'm not."

"Such as?"

"Oh...practical. Sensible. Steady. Dependable."

"You make me sound deadly dull, love."

"Hardly. I can't think of a man *less* dull than you. But certainly I'm not quite as prudent or rational as I need to be at times."

He chuckled softly as Sara went on. "And I suppose I need to heed your caution about Quinn. I'll admit that I find myself admiring the girl's grit. I do like her, Michael, but it's true that we don't know her—even if she is upstairs, sleeping in our best guest room."

Still stroking her head with his chin, Michael uttered a small sound of approval. "I know you only want to help the lass, Sara. And so do I. It's just that, at present, I think Nora and Evan should be our first concern. That doesn't mean the girl can't stay here for a time, if your grandmother doesn't object. We'll speak with her in the morning, and—"

"Michael?" Sara jerked upright and looked at him instantly. "Didn't Evan tell you that what would help most...is a girl to take over the house-work and look after Teddy?"

"Aye, he did."

"They'd be looking for an immigrant girl, more than likely. Someone who wouldn't be expecting an exorbitant wage, perhaps someone who would be satisfied with a small salary in addition to room and board?"

Michael nodded. "Yes, she'd have to be reasonable about her earnings. They don't have all that much to spare, but Evan said they'd manage somehow."

"Michael?" Her voice was muted, muffled against his shoulder. "What about Quinn?"

Michael grew still. "*Quinn?*"

With one hand on his chest, Sara pushed herself back and looked at him. "Yes, Quinn! She's recently immigrated. She's young, she seems healthy—and I doubt she'd be expecting an unreasonable wage, not for her first position in a new country. Oh, Michael, she might be just the one—"

"Now, Sara, just slow down a bit." He caught her hand in his. "I don't think Quinn O'Shea is necessarily the best choice for Evan and Nora."

"Why not?" Suddenly impatient with the sensible nature she had been praising only a moment ago, Sara frowned at him.

"For the same reason I told you not to be too quick to get involved with the girl. We know nothing about her! You're suggesting that Evan and Nora take a complete stranger into their home, to help look after Nora and the baby—"

"Michael—you told me once that you trusted my instincts about people. Remember?"

He admitted, grudgingly, that he had told her exactly that.

"And didn't you just say that Nora and Evan should be our first concern?"

He clamped his jaw and nodded.

"But you also agreed that we should try to help *Quinn*, too."

"All right, Sara, that's true. But it wasn't my intention to drop them all in the pot together to see if they can make soup! Quinn O'Shea is but a slip of a girl, and a stranger at that. We haven't even a notion as to whether she knows how to keep house or cook or tend a baby." He stopped. "And don't forget," he said pointedly, "that Evan and Nora are our friends."

"It seems to me that's exactly why we should be trying to help them. Michael—couldn't we at least *talk* with Quinn?"

Michael frowned. "Talk with her?"

Sara nodded eagerly. "Yes, couldn't we talk with Quinn and find out if she has the necessary qualifications for such a position? Don't you see, Michael? If Quinn *is* qualified…and if she's interested…we'd be helping *her* as well as Nora and Evan! Quinn would have a job and a place to live—and Nora would have the help she needs. It could be an ideal arrangement."

In the end, he agreed that, no, it wouldn't hurt to talk with the girl. He was quick to remind her, though, that talking would not obligate them. And, yes, she did have a point: It might turn out to be a good thing for the girl as well as for Nora and Evan. He said all this, and then he smiled as Sara threw her arms around his neck and told him, not for the first time, that he was really quite wonderful.

42

I Have Brought
You to This Place

My heart is the seed of time, my veins are star-dust,
My spirit is the axle of God's dream.

T.D. O'BOLGER

Late the next morning at the hospital, Evan said a final goodbye to Billy Hogan, reassuring him that he would be back to visit the next day. "Right after Sunday m-morning worship," he promised. "Perhaps Daniel John will come with m-me. Would you like that, Billy?"

The boy managed a faint smile. His forehead was bandaged, as was his left eye. His cuts had been cleaned and dressed, and due to a fractured shoulder, his right arm was in a sling. But he was alert and able to communicate with Evan and Michael Burke, who had walked into the children's ward not long after Evan arrived.

"Mr. Evan?" The boy's voice was little more than a whisper. Obviously, he was still in great pain. It occurred to Evan again that, given Billy's grave physical condition, it was nothing short of miraculous that his voice had reached beyond the coal cellar the night before to attract their attention.

"Yes, Billy?" Evan bent lower to hear him.

The child glanced at Michael Burke, standing at the foot of the bed with his arms over his chest, then lowered his voice even more. "Am I in trouble?"

"Trouble?" Evan stared at him. "Why, of course, you're n-not in trouble, Billy! What would make you think such a thing?"

The boy's gaze slid back to Michael Burke, who obviously had heard

337

his question. Smiling, the policeman came around the bed to stand next to Evan. "I'm here strictly as a friend, Billy. You helped me out in a tight place a couple of years past. Do you recall?"

Billy frowned, shaking his head. "No, sir."

"In the Five Points, when the strikers jumped me and Sergeant Price? You ran for help. If it hadn't been for you, we'd have been in a bad way for certain."

The boy's expression cleared, and he gave a brief nod.

"Am I going to get well, Mr. Evan?"

"Oh *yes*, Billy!" Evan rushed to assure him. "Why, you're going to be as good as n-new in no time. I have the word of two physicians on that. But you m-must do exactly as the doctors and nurses tell you while you're here."

The boy looked away, and Evan thought he was drifting off to sleep. But after a moment, he asked quietly, "Do I have to go back home when I'm well?"

Evan swallowed against the knot in his throat. He turned to look at Michael. The policeman's expression was grim as he gave a curt shake of his head.

"N-no, Billy," Evan said quietly. "You don't."

After another silence, the boy turned back to face Evan. "Then where *will* I go?"

Evan drew a deep breath, let it out again, still not answering. An urge overwhelmed him to gather the broken boy against his heart and tell him he would take him home with *him*. But with Nora so ill and the house already crowded, how could he even think of it?

Instead, he sank down on the side of the bed and took Billy's hand in his. "It's too soon to m-make plans just yet, Billy. For a while, you're going to b-be right here, getting strong and well. B-but I promise you, when the time comes for you to leave, we will find you a good...*safe* place to live. Please promise m-me you won't fret about this for now, that you'll concentrate on getting well."

"Aye, Mr. Evan," Billy said after only the slightest hesitation. "I promise."

Seeing that he was growing drowsy again, Evan rose. "Captain Burke and I m-must go now, Billy. You rest. And be sure to eat everything the nurses b-bring you. I'll come again tomorrow."

On the way out, Evan could not help but notice the crowded

conditions of the ward. Every bed was taken, many with children much younger than Billy Hogan. Some lay sobbing, in obvious pain. Others bore bruises and injuries all too similar to Billy's. The scars of abuse.

Unable to restrain himself, Evan stopped several times to visit with a youngster who looked unhappy or lonely. By the time he and Michael reached the exit of the hospital, his heart felt almost as heavy as it had the night before.

Outside, they stopped to talk before going their separate ways. "I came in a patrol wagon," Michael said. "Why don't I take you to the ferry?"

Evan shook his head. "Thank you, Michael, but I think I'd like to walk a ways. I think b-best when I walk, and...well, I have a fair amount of thinking to d-do."

"About Nora, I expect."

Evan nodded, drawing his muffler more tightly about his throat. "And Billy. About a lot of things, actually."

They both stood looking out over the East River, choppy in the brisk November wind. As always, the river was dotted with a variety of ships, largely immigrant vessels. They kept coming by the thousands, week after week, month after month, bringing their sorrows and their dreams to America.

"Have you talked with Nora yet, about your visit with Dr. Grafton?" Michael asked, still staring at the river.

"No. Dr. Grafton is coming by Monday evening. He thought it m-might be best for him to be there when I tell her. It's just as well. It was too late last n-night. I was exhausted, and with everything else—well, it will be best to wait, I think."

He explained about the fire, went on to tell Michael his Aunt Winnie's observation: that God's purpose had been accomplished in the fire, that He had turned it to good use for Johanna. "Ever the optimist, Aunt Winnie," Evan said with a faint smile. "And as Nora would say, I'd not b-be the one to argue with her."

After a long silence, Michael turned to him. "Sara and I want to help, Evan. However we can. You and Nora—well, I expect you know—we feel that you're family."

"Thank you, Michael," Evan responded, pleased by his words. "I'm sure Sara will be a great help in finding us a girl to live in." He turned to look at Michael. "I think it's absolutely vital that I find someone as soon as p-possible. N-not just anyone, of course, but someone Nora will feel comfortable with, someone qualified."

Evan paused and gave a rueful smile, "It should be a very simple m-matter, don't you think: finding a girl who's willing to take on the responsibility of keeping house, as well as providing care for an infant— and Nora? A very small, crowded house with a g-great deal of work. And all at an af-affordable wage, of course. I can't think why I'd have any difficulty finding the person we need."

Michael folded his arms over his chest, regarding him with a studying look. "Well, Evan, as it happens, you may *not* have all that much trouble finding someone. In fact, we may have already found her—if you're agreeable, that is."

Evan stared at him. He was unable to suppress the surge of hope that began to rise in him as Michael explained the situation with the young woman named Quinn O'Shea.

Michael ended his story with a word of caution. "Sara says I'm too much the policeman, but I'd not feel right if I didn't tell you I have misgivings about the girl. I can't shake the feeling that she's not being altogether candid with us."

"You think she's lying?"

Michael hesitated. "Perhaps not *lying* so much as…withholding something. I know you're anxious to find a girl right away—but with Nora and the children, I also know you're not wanting to take any chances. I just thought I should mention what I suspect."

Evan thought about it for a moment. "You say the girl has n-nowhere to go?"

"She has nothing but the clothes on her back, and that's the truth. Sara was going to enlist her grandmother's help this morning in altering a few things for her. She's absolutely destitute." Michael's eyes darkened. "Apparently, she never saw the first penny of a wage, though she worked several hours a day at the Shelter."

"You indicated that she's had experience, m-managing a household?" Evan asked thoughtfully.

"So she claims, and Sara seems to think the lass is knowledgeable."

Trying not to feel too eager, Evan chose his words carefully. "Perhaps it wouldn't hurt to at least talk with her. It would seem that an arrangement m-might be as beneficial to the girl as to us."

"Sara said as much last night. She likes the lass."

"What about the girl? D-does she seem interested in the position at all?" Evan asked, feeling more hopeful still.

Michael lifted an eyebrow. "Let's just say she seemed a bit dubious at first, that the English and the Irish could manage to live under the same roof without starting a war." He grinned. "But Sara seems to think you and Nora can settle her doubts about that particular issue."

Evan walked for a long time. He walked, and he prayed, letting his thoughts wander where they would.

He thought about Nora and the shadow that had recently fallen upon their life together, and he wondered if he would ever sleep an entire night through again, without waking up in fear for her.

Yet on the heels of that somber thought came the reminder of every-thing Nora had survived up until now. The famine in Ireland. The loss of her entire family, except for Daniel. The nightmare of the Atlantic cross-ing. The scarlet fever. Teddy's difficult birth.

Not to mention the fire last night, he thought with a sigh.

He could not help but remember how she had looked the first time he ever saw her: a small, weary, half-starved woman with a world of sorrow in her eyes. God had brought her from that seemingly hopeless life all the way across the ocean, through danger and illness and threat of death, to meet the challenge of a new life in a new land with a new family.

Didn't Nora herself maintain that the Lord had been with her, at her side, through the very worst times in her life, through all the pain and the suffering she had endured?

What was it she had told him the night Teddy was born?... *"This much I do know and believe...I am closer to our Lord during those times than at any other moment of my life."*

Considering what God had done for Nora...for all of them...in the past, Evan felt he could do no less than trust His faithfulness for the future. His father's exhortation echoed in his mind: *"Be brave, and trust God."*

He walked on, only vaguely aware of the sharpness of the wind. As he walked, he seemed to feel the very heartbeat of the city, sensing its energy and agony all about him. He passed among people of countless nations, people of unknown tongues and exotic dress. America was rapidly becoming a nation of immigrants, a nation virtually built upon the dreams and sweat and suffering of all those coming to her shores in search of refuge.

It seemed a wonder and a glory to Evan that the God who had sustained Nora…and himself…through the shadowed valleys of their lives was also the God of all the thousands of immigrants who even now were building this new nation. How He could be in the midst of so many people, yet abide in the hearts of each, was a miracle that never ceased to amaze Evan.

For while it was true that there was suspicion and division, in some cases even hatred, among the peoples of these various nations, there was also a common bond of faith joining them all: faith in the same God upon whom the early colonists had founded their nation.

Thousands had already begun to push west, lured by the fortunes to be made in gold…and to the north, to the security of factories and industry…or to the heartland, where land was vast and rich and fertile. And they were taking their faith with them.

For over seventy years, God had been at the heart of the growing, struggling United States. And now, as they were about to enter a new decade—the 1850s—God was still at the heart of a surging, dynamic America, whose boundaries seemed limitless…and whose destiny appeared to be greatness.

For as long as God was at the heart of America, could America be anything *less* than great?

Walking more slowly now, Evan looked about at the omnibuses, the police wagons, the hackney cabs, the carriages. He wound his way among merchants and street vendors, organ grinders, businessmen and beggars.

And all along the way, the ever-present, often homeless, children darted in and out of alleys, playing their games or plying their trades, peddling paper flowers or candy, shining shoes or picking pockets. They were everywhere. Children with dirty faces and hungry eyes, timid smiles and tear-tracked cheeks. Clothed in rags or paper shoes, their bodies were often bruised, their gazes furtive. Some orphaned by circumstance, others discarded, like dirty rags…abandoned, forgotten, and alone.

America's children.

And it dawned upon Evan as he walked that something must be done for these little ones if America was to have a future. The country, this wonderful new nation, was failing her children! And if the country failed her children, her children would eventually fail the country.

The hope…the future…of any nation was its children. Something had to be done for the Billy Hogans of the United States. They needed a place to *go*, these outcast, abused little ones: a place where they could be safe and grow up knowing the peace and love of God and a family.

But where? Evan slowed his pace. A sense of desperation, a fathomless kind of *yearning*, like nothing he had ever known, swept over him. He was still dimly aware of his surroundings, but it was as though nothing existed except the swelling urgency inside him. He was no longer tuned to the clamor or the heartbreak of the city.

In that moment, even as he continued walking, he felt himself seized and held captive. He felt the cold, but not its sting—as if the Father had wrapped His arms about him and was holding him, carrying him…all the while whispering to him…

I will take care of Nora, Evan. Trust Me.

Heartened beyond measure, Evan pressed his muffler closer to his throat. "I know, Lord…I know You will."

I will take care of Nora's needs…and yours. I will sustain you and your family, Evan. Trust Me.

It no longer mattered that he was in the middle of a busy city. Evan walked on, his steps lighter, his heart lighter, too, as he murmured a silent prayer of thanksgiving.

Trust Me, Evan, to take care of you and those you love. And I will trust you to take care of My children.

Evan caught a breath and held it, his heart racing.

I have brought you to this place for a reason, Evan. I have blessed you along the way with family and friends. I have put people in this city for you, people to love you and encourage you and affirm you…and I have put you in the city for My people. For my children. I told you I would ask much of you….

Evan stumbled, then stopped where he was, waiting. "Yes, Lord?"

As you entrust your loved ones to Me, I now entrust My children to you. Save the children, Evan. Trust Me…and save My children.

Trembling, Evan looked around. He was astonished to realize he had walked all the way to the Bowery. He was on Elizabeth Street, near Grand, in the midst of one of the largest German settlements in the city.

He stared out into the street, at shoppers and merchants making their

way between the horse-drawn buggies and wagons coming and going.
Turning, he scanned the buildings lining the street, most of them familiar.
The bakery, the cooper shop, the sign maker's. Not an entirely disreputa-
ble neighborhood, by New York standards.

Unexpectedly, the sun came out, struggling through the low dense
clouds of the November sky, casting a faint silver spray across the rooftops,
illuminating one building just to his right.

Three stories high, it was a wide, sturdy-looking structure of dark brick
that, although obviously not new, looked to have been reasonably well
maintained. It appeared to be vacant—unusual in this neighborhood.

Evan started to walk away—he had already been gone from home far
longer than he'd intended—but he found himself hesitating. As he stood
there, his gaze traveling the length and breadth of the building as the sun
hovered just overhead, he thought he heard…just for a moment…the
sound of laughter and singing.

Children's laughter. Children's voices.

He glanced around. There were no children in sight.

His eyes went back to the building that had taken on a strangely cheerful, friendly appearance in the warm glow from the sun. He stood there a
long time, staring at the vacant building.

At last he turned once more to leave.

And again, he heard the children. Happy, carefree, countless children.

I have brought you to this place, Evan…for the children….

As if caught in a dream, Evan found himself approaching the building.
Slowly, he walked up the stone steps to the massive double doors, where a
sign had been posted: *For Sale or Lease. Inquire at Gartner's Bakery.*

Evan stared at the sign for a long time before retracing his steps. In the
street, he turned for one last lingering look at the stalwart brick building.
Familiar, somehow, like an old friend.

As he stood there, he felt something stir, like a whisper, a murmuring
in his spirit.

Whittaker House.

A place for the children.

Then, with the distant voices of children ringing in his heart and the
early afternoon sun shining golden upon his back, Evan Whittaker turned
away and started down the street, toward Gartner's Bakery.

43

In Search of
an Ancient Glory

The country's history and our own
Lie just beyond the portals of the Past.
Here we confront ourselves
In the echoing footsteps
Of all those who have gone before.

ANONYMOUS

Dublin
Early December

The sky at noon was startlingly clear. December had made an unseasonably mild entrance, with a succession of almost balmy days and
crisp nights.

Outside the Gypsy wagon, Sandemon, in his shirtsleeves, felt himself gripped by a restless, indefinable yearning more often associated with
young hearts in the springtime of the year. He had been too long confined:
almost five weeks in this wagon with the two youths. Five weeks of critical illness and the relentless strain of nursing. Five weeks of fending off the
impatience and peevishness occasioned by such confinement.

Soon it would be over—a great relief! He threw the last of the con-
taminated cloths on the fire and stood watching the smoke wind its way
slowly upward. He was missing Nelson Hall and the household, missing
them grievously: the mercurial humor and companionship of the young

master, the delight of the children, the shy kindness of Mistress Finola—
and, of course, the peppery wit and wry good will of Sister Louisa.

His family.

Poking at the fire with a stick, his thoughts roamed to each of them,
wondering how they had fared this past month. What sort of new mischief might young Annie have involved herself in by now? And the baby—
ah, the golden son of Nelson Hall—he would be rounder still, and more
alert. And the *Seanchai*...

His mood sobered. He fretted much about the young giant, so very
needful, yet so determined in his quest for independence—and so poignantly obvious in his love for his wife.

Sandemon knew, whether anyone else in the household did or not,
that the two still lived as friends, not as intimates. They were clearly
devoted to each other; only a blind man would not be sensitive to the
affection that flowed between them. But they lived apart—entrapped, he
suspected, by their individual fear of rejection and, perhaps, by a lack of
awareness of each other's feelings.

Yet he held high hopes, indeed had given much prayer to those hopes,
that in his absence the two would finally acknowledge their love...and
their need...for each other. If the *Seanchai* once perceived the depth of
feeling in his young wife's eyes, perhaps he would at last be able to throw
his restraint to the wind and open his arms to her...just as he had already
opened his home and his heart to her.

But he was a proud man, the *Seanchai*—proud, and possessed of
uncommon self-control. Sandemon had long sensed the conflict of emotions in the young poet. His fierce resolve to place no demands, no obliga-
tion, on the tragic young woman he had married must surely do continual
battle with his love for her.

As for Mistress Finola, although she could not look at her husband
without her heart rising in her eyes, she appeared equally determined to
expect nothing from the marriage.

Sandemon sighed and shook his head. He did not fancy himself to be
a matchmaker. All he could do was pray for them, these two young lovers
who loved only at a distance. He would continue to pray, and continue
to hope that by now, at least one of them might have realized the gift they
were meant to be to each other—and taken steps to break down the wall
keeping them apart.

He expelled a long breath, staring into the fire at the smoldering remnants of his long, arduous battle against the cholera. With a rueful smile,
he thought perhaps he should also be praying for patience—patience
enough for just one more day. For tomorrow—ah, tomorrow—they
would be leaving the wagon at last! Tomorrow he would be free to return
to the family!

But the thought of tomorrow brought to mind the disturbing question
of what tomorrow might mean for the young Gypsy inside the wagon. Just
this morning, he had confided to Sandemon and Tierney Burke that he no
longer had a home to go to. When questioned, he had explained the concept of *marhime*—banishment from his family and the entire Gypsy camp.

Tierney had tried to persuade him that he was wrong, that surely his
people would welcome him back. But Jan Martova had simply turned
his mournful black eyes on his friend, saying, "You do not understand
our ways. I assure you. By now, I have been banished from the *kumpania*."

Sandemon turned to glance at the open windows of the wagon. From
the sound of the conversation inside, it seemed the argument was still
going on. He could not help but overhear the youths' exchange, and what
he heard troubled him greatly—not only for Jan Martova, but for Tierney Burke as well.

"But that's crazy!" Seated on the floor of the wagon, Tierney leaned
against the wall. He had to make a determined effort to keep his contempt
for the absurd Gypsy customs out of his voice. "You didn't do anything
wrong! Why would they banish you for trying to help a friend?"

Opposite him, also on the floor, Jan Martova sat, rosining the bow of
his violin. "I told you, you cannot hope to understand our ways. You are
Gorgio. Our laws are ancient and logical only to the *Rom*."

"Your laws are *unfair*, if you ask me," muttered Tierney. He went on,
giving Jan no opportunity to respond. "As for keeping your wagon here,
on the grounds, I don't know whether Morgan would allow it or not. But
I'm not the one to ask. I'll have no say in it, especially now."

Jan nodded. "I understand. The decision has to be the *Seanchai*'s. I
merely thought perhaps, if you were to speak with him first..."

Tierney let out a short, self-mocking laugh. "Morgan isn't going to let

me back inside Nelson Hall! Not after what I did. By now, I've been banished, just like you."

Jan Martova studied him. "Will he really be that angry, do you think?"

Tierney gave another humorless laugh. "I think he may very well wring
my neck!" He cracked his knuckles. "If he even gets that close to me."

For a long time Jan said nothing. One forefinger traced the neck of
the violin. Tierney noted the gentleness with which his friend handled the
instrument, as if it were made of marble or gold, rather than old, battered-
looking wood.

"So, then, what will you do?" Jan asked. "Where will you go?"

Tierney shrugged. "I don't know. I'll get a job, I suppose. Find a place
in Dublin for a while."

Jan shook his head. "I cannot think it will come to that. I believe you
misjudge your *Seanchai*."

Tierney made no reply. Although he had witnessed only fleeting
glimpses of Morgan's temper, he had seen enough to convince him he
would no longer be welcome at Nelson Hall.

He supposed he really couldn't blame Morgan. The man had opened
up his home to him, practically made him one of the family, taking him
in on short notice, with no questions asked. In repayment, Tierney had
lied to him and willfully defied his authority.

He thought Morgan might have eventually forgiven the deceit. The
man could be surprisingly tolerant at times. But Tierney imagined the
chances of his forgiving anyone who endangered his family were slim
indeed. And there was no denying the fact that his recklessness had put
the entire household at risk.

He leaned his head back against the wall and closed his eyes. A gnawing sense of guilt had kept him awake most of the night. He was thoroughly disgusted at the way he had botched everything. The mess he'd
created for himself was bad enough, but to realize what his foolishness
was likely to cost Jan Martova made it worse. He was beginning to think
he should have stayed in New York and taken his chances with Patrick
Walsh.

"I regret that I won't be able to keep my wagon here," Jan said. "I had
hoped to stay close, for the sake of our friendship."

Tierney opened his eyes. "We can still be friends," he said awkwardly,
not quite knowing how to voice his own feelings.

The other gave a brief nod. "That's true. We can maintain our friendship wherever we are. But I would like to stay because of Sandemon as well."

Tierney shifted and stretched, impatient with the weakness that still
swept over him with even the slightest movement. "You like him a lot,
don't you?"

"Sandemon?" Jan nodded. "I think he is a noble man, yes. A great man.
But even more than that, I am hungry for his teaching."

Tierney thought about his own feelings toward Sandemon. "I didn't
care much for him at first, I admit. Back home, the Irish and the blacks
don't get along."

Jan Martova looked surprised. "But why not?"

Tierney shrugged. "There aren't enough jobs to go around, and the
blacks will work for lower wages. It causes a lot of bad feelings."

"But surely you must respect Sandemon?"

Tierney hesitated, then nodded. "I suppose I do. He risked his life for
us, after all. Yeah, I owe him."

Jan Martova nodded. "He has changed my life, I think."

Tierney regarded him skeptically. "Changed your life?"

Jan smiled and laid the violin aside. "Yes, I would say he has done just
that. All the more reason I had hoped to stay close to him. I want to continue to learn from him, about your—my—God."

Always ill at ease in any discussion about faith, Tierney remained silent.

"Are you a believer?" Jan asked abrupdy.

The question made Tierney squirm. Avoiding the other's gaze, he
delayed his answer. But the memory of the fever-dream he'd had during
the cholera wasn't as easy to avoid. The dark tunnel, the faceless shadows
that had groped at him, the whispering, the lake of fire...

No matter how hard he tried to forget what he had seen that night—
or *thought* he had seen—it wouldn't go away. Not completely. Like some
kind of dread specter, it lurked, just below the surface of his mind, rising
to haunt him when he least expected it.

"I don't know what I believe," he finally answered. And he spoke the
truth. He couldn't remember a time when he hadn't been confused and at
odds with himself about what he believed. He wasn't like his da, who never
seemed to question or doubt matters of faith. With Da, it had always been
a case of absolutes. Right is right, and wrong is wrong. No compromise.

But for Tierney, it had never been that simple. He had never actually thought through what he believed, had never really confronted his feelings or tried to articulate them. At some level he knew he believed in God, and certainly he believed in evil. He supposed he believed in heaven and hell, though what constituted each had never been clearly defined in his thinking—another difference between him and Da.

He had listened to the long exchanges at night between Sandemon and Jan Martova, had pondered a number of the Gypsy's questions.

But did he believe Sandemon's answers?

Did he really believe that a world in which injustice seemed the norm—a world in which hatred, suffering, and violence seemed to reign unchecked—was the creation of a merciful God, an all-powerful God? Did he really believe that the madness which seemed to grip the entire universe was the result of sin, that this same deadly universe would one day be redeemed by its Creator? Did he really believe that God had a Son who allowed Himself to be nailed on a tree between two common criminals… a Son who willingly gave up His life for the sin of the world?

He wasn't sure. No matter how many times he raked it through his mind, he ended up back where he started: He simply did not know what he believed.

He had, of course, felt a tug toward the faith of his Irish Catholic friends in the city. But that attraction might have been no more than his boyish desire to be like his friends. To be Irish in the neighborhoods of lower New York was to be Catholic. And fulfilling his Irishness was the most important thing in Tierney's life—had been ever since he was a boy.

Wasn't that the real reason this trip to Ireland had meant so much to him? Even if it had come about because he'd gotten himself into a jam in New York, it was still the attainment of a dream: to see the land of his roots, to walk the ground of his ancestors, to finally become the son of Ireland he had always believed himself to be.

Years ago, Tierney had set his heart on discovering for himself the ancient glory of Ireland and its people…*his* people. This was the distant star he meant to follow, the dream he would pursue.

But with his careless deceit and rebellious ways he had tarnished the dream, and the star somehow seemed more distant than ever.

He had disappointed Morgan, betrayed his trust—and the stark reality of his failure hurt more than he could ever have imagined.

Morgan Fitzgerald was the one man he respected and idolized more than any other—including his own father. Growing up, long before he ever met Morgan, Tierney had dreamed of one day sitting at the great poet-patriot's feet, to learn from him—to become *like* him.

Like Morgan, he would wed himself to Ireland. He would become so much a part of the Irish nation that his very heart would merge with the land until they were one. He would spend his life for the country and its freedom.

His initial disappointment, upon discovering that the legendary rebel had become more poet than warrior, had soon given way to renewed respect. For he had come to realize that, even confined to a wheelchair, Morgan Fitzgerald was still a giant of a man, still altogether worthy of his admiration—and still, in all the ways that really mattered, the embodiment of the Irish spirit to which Tierney aspired.

He understood now, with some surprise, that he very much wanted Morgan's respect, his approval. The realization that he would never have either was a bitter taste that wouldn't quite go away.

Before the cholera, he had been so sure of himself. He had come to Ireland to pursue his dream, to search out his past, to find his soul. He had known exactly what he was doing, where he was going, where he belonged.

But now, for the first time in his life, he seemed to have nowhere to go. Separated from his father, he had no family to speak of. Alienated from Morgan by his own waywardness, he had no place to go.

In the land his heart had long named as home, Tierney Burke had become an exile.

44

Folly or Grace?

I have squandered the splendid years
That the Lord God gave to my youth
In attempting impossible things,
Deeming them alone worth the toil
Was it folly or grace?
Not men shall judge me, but God.

PADRAIC PEARSE (1879-1916)

Morgan made the announcement over supper that evening. "Sandemon and his patients will be leaving the wagon tomorrow," he said.

He had anticipated Annie's reaction. She bounced out of her chair, her dark eyes dancing, almost sending the tumbler in her hand flying. "Truly, *Seanchai*? Oh, at last!"

Morgan gave a nod, darting a smile at Finola and Sister Louisa. "The Gypsy lad brought word. Sandemon says the risk of contagion has passed, and though his patients are not yet strong, they no longer require his care."

"How weary poor Sandemon must be!" said Finola.

"Indeed," said Sister Louisa. "We must all be thoughtful enough not to tire him with endless questions his first day back." She directed a meaningful look at Annie. "No doubt he will be in need of much rest and renewal after such an ordeal."

Ignoring her, Annie gave a precarious wave of the crystal tumbler. "I shall make Sand-Man a gift!" she declared. "A coming-home gift. Perhaps an ink sketch."

Morgan eyed the tumbler as she chattered on, her Belfast accent launching the words like arrows. "Or perhaps I should make three sketches—one for Sand-Man, and one each for Tierney Burke and the Gypsy. Will you help me, please, Sister?"

Not waiting for a reply, she plunked the tumbler down on the table with a thud. "I'll go and collect my sketchbook," she said, banging into the chair leg.

"Annie…" Morgan stopped her. "I'm afraid there will be no opportunity for you to speak with either Tierney or the Gypsy."

Already on her way to the door, Annie whirled around, frowning. "But Sand-Man said the danger of contagion is past."

Morgan drew in a long breath. "Contagion isn't the issue," he said bluntly. "The Gypsy will be leaving. And so will Tierney Burke."

Annie looked at him in obvious bewilderment. "Leaving? But where would they be going after being so ill?"

Avoiding her eyes, as well as the questioning looks of both Finola and Sister Louisa, Morgan laid down his fork, carefully aligning it with his plate. "Where they go is none of our concern. But they will be leaving Nelson Hall. That doesn't mean you cannot make a sketch for them, if you like," he added, softening his tone.

Looking up, he met Annie's eyes. She stood very still, as if holding her breath. "You're sending them away, aren't you? You mean to punish Tierney Burke for his deceit." Her voice was quiet and noticeably strained.

Somewhat noisily, Sister Louisa rose from her chair. "If you will excuse me," she said, "I have papers to mark."

Finola, too, stirred in her chair as if to get up. But Morgan shook his head, gesturing that she should stay.

Turning to Annie, he studied her, groping for the words that might help her understand. "You're right. I *am* going to ask them to leave, immediately. But not by way of punishment, *alannah*."

Annie said nothing. Her back was straight, her eyes accusing. "The Gypsy would be leaving anyway," Morgan went on. "He will go back to his people. As for Tierney, you must see that I could never trust him after what he did. His behavior was thoughtless and inexcusable. He deceived me. He deceived us all. And his treachery could have cost us our lives. I cannot condone his deceit."

Annie shifted from one foot to the other, her gaze fixed on the floor.

"Perhaps he's sorry. Perhaps he will ask your forgiveness, once he has the opportunity."

"He can ask all he likes," Morgan snapped, "but I'll give him no quarter. I'll not have him under my roof again. He will leave Nelson Hall tomorrow—he and his heathen Gypsy friend."

Morgan felt the force of Annie's disappointment as she slowly lifted her face and searched his eyes. Discomfited by her unwavering scrutiny, he had to resist the urge to defend himself.

"Sand-Man says we must always be willing to forgive." The dark eyes held a glint of challenge.

"Sandemon also says we must live by the Truth," Morgan shot back, suddenly annoyed that she would question his judgment. "Tierney Burke is a stranger to the truth."

Annie continued to study him for another moment. Where Morgan would have expected the customary flare of temper or childish stubbornness, there was only a steady gaze, a faint hint of reproach.

"May I be excused, please, *Seanchai*?" she finally asked, her words clipped.

Morgan was reluctant to let her go. He felt an unreasonable need to explain himself, yet sensed it would be best to wait. At his brief nod of dismissal, the girl whipped about and walked stiffly from the room.

Alone with Finola, Morgan avoided her gaze. Annie's odd behavior had unsettled him. Half-expecting a fit of temper or even outright defiance, he didn't quite know what to make of her silent censure. He realized now that he had hoped for her understanding and felt strangely wounded by the lack of it.

Finola's chair was pulled close to his. He could have easily reached out to take her hand. Instead, he gripped the arms of the wheelchair, feeling uncertain and awkward.

Finally he looked at her. "And do you also disagree with my judgment?"

"'Tis not for me to agree or disagree, Morgan," she replied softly.

"That's not true. You know I value your opinion." What he did not say, of course, was that he coveted her *good* opinion—of himself. "What you think is very important to me, Finola. Sure, you must know that by now. Please...speak your mind."

She smiled, the faint, shy smile he had come to cherish. Leaning toward him a little, she lifted her hand as if to touch his arm, then seemed to reconsider. "I think...perhaps...you are being too hasty." She spoke slowly, obviously choosing her words with care. "I wonder if you shouldn't take more time before making such a decision."

So Finola, too, thought him unreasonable! Morgan stiffened, looking away. "I mean only to protect you and the rest of the household," he said tightly. "I can't think why you and Annie are so quick to condemn me for guarding your safety."

Now she *did* put a hand to his arm. He turned to look at her and was caught off guard by the tenderness in her eyes. "Oh, Morgan, I don't *condemn* you! How could I..." She released his arm, for a moment turning away, as if she had spoken out of turn.

Finally she looked at him. "I think I understand why you feel you should send Tierney away. May I speak frankly?"

"I would never have you speak any other way to me," he told her, meaning it.

His eyes went to her hands, the long, slim fingers now laced tightly together in her lap, as if whatever she was about to say disturbed her.

But she looked directly at him when she spoke, and her voice was strong and steady. "Perhaps you mean to discipline Tierney for his thoughtless behavior. I'll not deny he acted carelessly—"

"He *deceived* me!" Morgan bit out, his tone much sharper than he'd intended.

"Yes, he did. He betrayed your trust." She paused, but her gaze never wavered. "I think he also frightened you. He exposed all of us to the cholera, and that was a terrifying thing."

Morgan nodded, trying to anticipate her argument.

"Yet I can't help but think that you care deeply for Tierney, and not simply because he's the son of a friend. I believe you care about him as a person."

She looked to him for confirmation, and again Morgan nodded, grudgingly. "I had developed a certain amount of fondness for the young fool, that's true. But the boy should pay for his deceit, Finola! It was no small thing he did!"

She drew back, staring at him. "Morgan—he almost *died* with the cholera! He has been deathly ill for weeks. Do you not think that payment *enough*? What must he do to earn your forgiveness?"

Morgan's ears rang with her words. Abruptly, he whipped the chair around, wheeling himself over to the window, where he turned his back on her and sat, staring outside.

"He might have been responsible for all our deaths," he said woodenly. "I could have lost you...Gabriel...Annie...because of his waywardness. How do I forgive him for that?"

He heard the rustle of her skirts as she rose and came to stand behind him, but he did not turn around. After a moment he felt her hands rest lightly on his shoulders. He shuddered under her touch, his pulse racing wildly, foolishly, at her nearness.

"Morgan, you've remarked more than once how very much Tierney reminds you of yourself when you were younger. 'Poured from the same mold,' I believe you said." She paused. "You've also admitted that, like Tierney, you committed your share of thoughtless deeds. I can't help wondering...were any of your own youthful escapades irresponsible or dangerous? Perhaps even treacherous?"

Morgan's shoulders tensed. "No doubt," he said shortly. The truth was, his own wanton past would make Tierney's behavior appear almost harmless. "I told you the rogue I used to be. And who can say that if it weren't for the infernal bullet in my back, I might not still be making the grandmothers wag their tongues. But I cannot recall ever endangering an entire household simply to indulge myself, and that's the truth!"

He was almost certain he detected a smile in her voice when she responded. But he deliberately didn't turn to see, for fear she would drop her hands away.

"I'm sure you didn't," she replied. "But Tierney had no way of knowing he had been exposed to the cholera."

"More to the point," Morgan countered, "if he hadn't defied me in the first place, he would *not* have been exposed."

Her hands tightened on his shoulders, and he felt somewhat reassured that at least she wasn't angry with him.

"You told me once that the good priest, Father Mahon, helped to save you from yourself," she said, her voice thoughtful. "What did you mean?"

He sighed, reluctant to bare such a sordid part of his past. Yet he had never tried to mislead her or appear to be anything other than what he was—a forgiven fool.

"You might say that Joseph Mahon epitomized to me the biblical example of the Prodigal Son's father. Apparently the good man spent a great deal of time on his knees for my unworthy soul, and when I finally came to my senses, he opened his arms to me without so much as a word of rebuke."

Joseph...ah, Joseph, I will never cease to be grateful for your faithfulness....

Morgan's throat tightened and his eyes stung at the memory of the priest he had loved like a father. "I've never doubted that I owe my redemption to Joseph's relentless prayers on my behalf." He smiled wryly to himself. "And did I happen to mention that he also saved my stubborn neck from the noose?"

Her hands increased their pressure on his shoulders. "You did, yes. And you also told me that it was Father Mahon who reunited you with your grandfather."

Morgan nodded. "Aye, he did. I didn't even know I *had* a grandfather until Joseph went searching for him."

As the silence stretched out between them, Morgan's thoughts roamed to the priest who had played such a significant role in his life. "I don't suppose a day ever passes," he said, more to himself than to Finola, "that I don't give thanks for Joseph Mahon."

Her voice was infinitely soft behind him. "And do you ever wonder where you would be now, had it not been for Father Mahon's presence in your life?"

Her quiet words jolted Morgan. He sat, numbed by the significance of her question.

"I expect your life might have been much different if your compassionate priest had denounced you, rather than forgiven you." The gentleness of her tone in no way lessened the impact of her words. "How many times have we heard Sister Louisa say that 'grace begets grace'? It almost sounds as if the forgiveness Father Mahon demonstrated to you...might have helped you to extend forgiveness to your grandfather."

Morgan felt as if a burning coal had been dropped into his heart. Silence hung between them, a silence so intense Morgan could hear her soft breathing in counterpoint to the loud hammering of his heart.

"I'm sorry, Morgan." He heard the note of dismay in her voice. Her hands left his shoulders, and Morgan felt suddenly chilled. "I had no right to say that to you. I'm sorry..."

Morgan shook his head, trying to dispel the thunderous pounding in his ears. "No...no, don't apologize," he said, lifting a hand. "I asked you to have your say."

"No, it's not my place—"

He wheeled the chair around to face her. "Of course, it is your place, Finola," he said, wishing she could accept the fact that he welcomed her candor, even if he did find himself temporarily taken aback by it. "You're my wife, after all."

Silence fell. As Morgan watched, a look of despair came over her features. Concerned, he reached for her, but she stepped back, then turned and fled the room.

He watched the empty doorway for a long time, trying to understand what he had said or done to cause her to run away from him. He had been about to tell her that she had reached him, after all, with her painfully accurate insights about Joseph Mahon and his grandfather. He wanted to tell her that he would always listen to what she had to say, that indeed he thought she, more than anyone else in his world, would always be able to reach inside him and touch his soul and turn him toward light instead of darkness.

For a moment, before she left him, he had come within a heartbeat of pulling her into his arms and begging her to love him. And for one wild, irrational instant, he had almost thought she would welcome him.

Madness.

He had almost forgotten all the promises he had made to himself about her: promises to cherish her, to protect her—and to expect nothing from her. In his loneliness, he would have made the great fool of himself, possibly creating an irreparable breach in their already fragile relationship.

He could not remember when he had felt so lonely, so isolated. He had somehow managed to drive them all away from him: Annie and Sister Louisa...and, God help him, Finola. With his hardheaded tactics and utter lack of sensitivity, he had alienated himself from those he needed most.

At least tomorrow Sandemon would return. But in the meantime, he faced another long night; he could hardly expect Finola to make her usual appearance after putting Gabriel to bed. Disappointment swept over him at the thought, for he had come to anticipate with great eagerness her nightly visits to help him lay out his clothing for the following day.

In truth, he was entirely capable of handling this mundane procedure himself, but he wouldn't for the world have let on. Always, she would stay awhile. They would talk, or play long games of chess. Sometimes she would ask him to play the harp while she sat listening. Occasionally, he managed to coax her into singing, but she was still obviously shy about doing so.

The thought that tonight she would not come to him was almost more than he could endure. Feeling infinitely weary and seized with an aching coldness, he wheeled himself back to the table. Spying Finola's delicate lace handkerchief on her chair, he picked it up. With a sad smile, he brought it to his cheek, savoring her faint scent before tucking the delicate item into his shirt pocket, next to his heart.

Later that night, after nursing Gabriel and leaving him to Lucy's attentions, Finola went through the motions of changing into her nightdress and dressing gown, scarcely aware of what she was doing.

She was appalled at the way she had spoken to Morgan. That she had dared to admonish him still dismayed her. It wasn't so much that she feared his displeasure. He hadn't seemed in the least angry with her for speaking her mind—indeed, had encouraged her to do so.

What troubled her most was the pain she had seen in his eyes when he turned to look at her. She had wounded him. She would rather drive a dagger through her own heart than hurt him, but there had been no mistaking the anguish that had looked out at her. In her attempt to save Tierney Burke from banishment, she had hurt *Morgan!*

She sank down on the side of the bed, hugging her arms to herself. She could not forget the way he had looked at her, the way his voice had faltered when he spoke.

"You're my wife...."

With a broken sob, she threw herself across the bed and let the tears come. All these months of living under the same roof...coming to love him more and more...listening for the sound of his voice...cherishing the smallest things—the touch of his hand on hers, the low sound in his throat that marked the beginning of his wonderful laugh, the lilt and cadence of his speech...the smile that drew her into his eyes—oh, how she loved him, yearned to belong to him, dreamed of being a *real* wife to him!

The past few weeks had been like a banquet to her starving heart. The time alone with him morning and evening, helping him with the small, ordinary, yet intimate, things…putting on his·shoes for him, laying out his clothing, trimming his hair…she had clung to every moment like a gift. A part of her had even begun to hope….

What had she hoped? That he would begin to think of her as a woman, rather than a simple-minded younger sister? That he would finally respond to her love for him and love her in return? That the world would stop its turning and the sky would fall? What?

When he had turned the chair about to face her, his wounded eyes accusing her as he called her his wife, something inside her had shattered. She had known at that instant that if she did not turn and run, she would disgrace herself entirely, would fling herself into his arms and *beg* him… to love her!

She felt as if all her dreams had broken to pieces, and each shard was driving itself slowly into her heart.

What else had she expected, with her mad, foolish longing for the impossible?

She had actually begun to pretend that he needed her, that he might even be falling in love with her a little. In her delusions about him, she had almost been able to believe that she could be *good* for him…could make him happy and fulfilled, could even help him not to mind so much the loss of his legs.

Yet in all her longing to help him and make him happy, she had only managed to offend him and hurt him. The sobs rose up in her—harder, more intense. Rolling onto her side, Finola pressed a fist to her mouth to silence the sounds of her loneliness, and wept.

45

The Glory of Love

This is the mystery, the glory of love:
That in bringing our hearts to each other,
We gain more than we thought to give....
And in giving ourselves to each other,
We become more than we hoped to be.

MORGAN FITZGERALD (1849)

Sister Louisa knocked softly once, then again. When no one answered, she put an ear to the door, listening. At the sound of muffled weeping, she took it upon herself to enter.

She stopped just inside the door, stunned by the sight of Finola, curled up in the middle of the bed like a child, sobbing her heart out.

"Faith, child, what is it?" Louisa thought at once of the baby, and the thought struck fear in her. "Finola—is it Gabriel? Has something happened to the babe?"

The girl shook her head, her shoulders still heaving.

Sister Louisa sat down beside her, reaching to pat her awkwardly on the back. "Here, now.... surely nothing can be so terrible as this!"

Gently, she raised the girl, gathering her close and trying to soothe her with one hand, wiping away the torrent of tears with the other.

"Our Gabriel is quite all right, then?" Louisa asked again.

Finola nodded between sobs.

"Well...are you ill, child?"

Finola shook her head.

"Then, what, *alannah*? Please, tell me what it is."

After a moment, Finola managed a strangled whisper. "Morgan..."

Louisa's mouth thinned, and she gathered the girl still closer. "What *has* the man done now? I suppose he's still determined to throw young Tierney to the wolves, not that the thoughtless *gorsoon* doesn't deserve whatever he gets. Oh, I shouldn't fret about it, dear. Once he has time to think things through, perhaps he'll have a change of heart."

"It's not that."

Louisa lifted an eyebrow, and sighed—a thoroughly Irish, long-suffering sigh. "I suppose he's said something or done something harsh, and you've been hurt. Is that it, dear?"

Finola pulled away, frowning. "Oh...no. No, that's not it at all. I think...I hurt *him*. I disagreed with him about Tierney Burke, don't you see? He said I had a right, that I was his *wife*, but—"

She broke off, looking at Louisa as if she could not go on.

Louisa studied her. "I see," she said quietly. "I expect what you mean is that you...ah...love him as a woman loves a man."

Finola nodded, still looking perfectly miserable.

"And you would like to be his wife...in the, ah, truest sense of the word."

Finola nodded again, attempting to blink away the tears. "I could be a comfort to him, Sister. I could at least help to ease his loneliness. He's had so much pain...and sometimes he seems so alone, and unhappy."

Louisa's mind raced. "He doesn't know how you feel, however, does he?"

Finola shook her head. "Of course not."

"Well, then—perhaps you should tell him," Louisa said practically.

Finola stared at her as if she'd taken leave of her senses. "I could never do that!"

"Why not?" Louisa asked patiently. "He is your husband, after all."

One trembling hand moved to wipe her eyes. "But he doesn't think of me as his *wife*. Not really. He regards me only as a rather dim-witted little sister, don't you see?"

Struggling to keep a straight face, Louisa replied, "That has not been my observation, I confess."

"He doesn't want me," Finola said dejectedly.

"Doesn't *want* you?" Louisa reared back in astonishment. "Good heavens, child, the man *adores* you!"

Finola's chin came up. Ignoring the girl's stunned expression, Louisa groped for the wisdom the situation seemed to call for. Given the poor child's state, there seemed nothing for it but to be direct.

She had seen how things were for quite some time now, of course: the furtive glances that passed between them, the longing gazes when one thought the other wasn't looking, the way his entire countenance brightened when she entered a room, and the way his smile could reduce the girl to utter speechlessness.

Louisa drew a long breath, thinking, not for the first time, that convent life did not always adequately prepare one for dealing with the real world.

Louisa took one of the girl's hands, enfolding it between both her own. "I want you to listen very carefully to what I'm going to tell you, Finola. In a way, I'm breaking a confidence, but I believe the moment calls for it. I think you have a right to know about a conversation that took place between the *Seanchai* and me before you were married."

Finola's eyes grew wider and more incredulous by the minute as Louisa, mincing no words, recounted the discussion that had occurred between her and Morgan Fitzgerald the night he had asked Finola to marry him.

Louisa couldn't quite suppress a smile as she recalled how she had brashly challenged the *Seanchai*'s motives that night. Still clear in her memory was the fiery response her forwardness had evoked.

"Not that it's any of your affair," he had raged, *"but I happen to love Finola…very much!"*

Upon hearing of this exchange, Finola clamped a hand to her mouth. Thinking she finally detected a faint glimmer of hope in those marvelous blue eyes, Louisa pressed on.

"I had questioned him, you see, on his right to bind you to a marriage in which there could be no real union. With his customary forthrightness," Louisa said dryly, "he gave me to understand that he was indeed altogether capable of a real union. I believe his exact words were: 'My legs may be paralyzed, but I am still a man.'"

Finola's hand slipped away from her mouth. Her eyes were enormous. "Then it's not that he can't…I wasn't sure…" She turned crimson and quickly looked away.

"Oh, he was quite…assertive about that particular point," Louisa said, her mouth quirking. Then she grew serious, for she knew the rest of her story was of the utmost importance to the girl. Gently, she explained how the *Seanchai* had assured her that he would never "force himself" on Finola, that he would expect nothing from the marriage: He only wanted to protect her and take care of her.

Gripping Finola's hand even more tightly, Louisa's eyes met hers. "I shall never forget the way he looked at me at the end, or what he said: 'In *my* mind, Sister Louisa, this is not a marriage of convenience, nor is it a lie or a sham. I will be a true husband to her, as long as I live—or as long as she desires it.'"

Louisa paused, expelling a long breath. "Oh, child—your husband loves you with all his huge heart! But he will never, never touch you unless you let him know it's what you want. It's up to you, don't you see? Beyond all doubt, the man will open his arms to you in a moment, once he knows how you really feel."

Louisa stopped. Suddenly she realized that she might be encouraging this fragile young creature to bolt headlong into a relationship she was ill prepared for. What if Finola was not yet strong enough to handle all the implications and demands of marriage—especially marriage to a man as complex as Morgan Fitzgerald?

Louisa sighed, reluctant to voice her doubts, yet for Finola's sake, unwilling to ignore them. "Certainly, you can rest assured he loves you. But, Finola...*alannah*...you have been through a great deal in your young life. You say the *Seanchai* has had much pain...but so have you, dear. And although I have witnessed enormous healing and great strength in you these past months, I can't help but wonder—"

Louisa broke off. Did she really have the right to try to influence Finola's judgment? Although she often thought of her as a child, she was *not*. She was a woman, had given birth to a son—and she loved a man. Loved him deeply, so it would seem.

"Finola...are you quite sure that you are ready...that you are *able*...to give yourself to a man, even the *Seanchai*? Oh, child, be *sure*! Be sure that you are prepared to give your all, for I suspect a man like Morgan Fitzgerald will settle for nothing less than everything."

For a long time they sat, Louisa holding Finola's hand, as the girl stared down at the bed, scarcely breathing. When she finally looked up, Louisa saw there were new tears glistening in her eyes.

"Can we ever truly be sure of anything, Sister?" she asked softly. "I know only this: that I love Morgan more than everything, more than life itself. I know that I want to be so close with him that we are as one person. I want to spend the rest of my life in his presence, if possible. I want to take away his loneliness, and make him laugh, and give him back as much of his manhood as a woman can ever give a man."

For an instant her voice faltered. But her face was radiant in the candle-light as she seemed to gather the strength to go on. "I want to have Morgan's children. I want to make a home for him, a home of peace and light and love. And, yes, I believe I am able to give whatever may be required of me in order to be the wife he needs and deserves."

Louisa struggled to still the trembling of her lip. Unable to restrain herself, she clasped Finola by the shoulders. Through her own tears, she studied the clear, blue gaze that seemed to reflect a new strength and assurance.

"Then go to him," she said, her voice none too steady as she once more gathered Finola into her embrace. "And tell him how you feel."

Finola's heart hammered with a mixture of hope and dread as she stood at the closed door that connected her bedroom with Morgan's. With her hand on the doorknob, she hesitated, suddenly seized by uncertainty.

What if Sister Louisa were mistaken? What if she had read something into Morgan's feelings that wasn't there at all?

She stood very still, scarcely able to breathe with the tension. Her hand gripped, then released, the doorknob, then grasped it again. Rapping lightly on the door, she waited. When there was no response, she turned the knob and stepped cautiously into the room.

Flames dancing in the fireplace and the oil lamp by the bed provided the only light in the room. Morgan was propped up in bed, asleep.

Finola advanced quietly, on tiptoe, to stand beside the bed. His eye-glasses had slid part of the way down the bridge of his nose. A deep wave of copper hair fell idly across his forehead. In his nightshirt, with one massive fist curled against his chest, the other hand covering the book he'd been reading, he looked years younger, like a boy caught up in his dreams. A very large boy, blessedly unaware of his vulnerability.

For a moment, Finola stood watching him, listening to his even breathing, savoring this rare opportunity to study him unobserved. His hair and beard were burnished copper in the glow from the firelight. The strong, almost arrogant set of his jaw was softened by sleep, and the faint lines that webbed outward from his eyes were less pronounced than usual.

Standing there, drinking in the sight of him, Finola could almost catch a glimpse of the boy he might have been. The image was bittersweet and wrenched her heart. She wished she could have known him then, before his tragedy…and her own.

But she had not come here to mourn the boy she had never known. She had come to offer herself to the man he had become.

Her heart pounded, her pulse raced. Stepping closer, she gently removed his eyeglasses and placed them on the bedside table. Carefully she slipped the open book from under his hand.

Then she saw what he had been reading, and she felt as if she would die for the love of him. Her eyes traveled to his face, then back to the Scriptures, marked at the parable of the Prodigal Son.

Tears rose to her eyes—tears of joy, and love as she placed the Bible next to his eyeglasses. Bending over him, she tenderly brushed the wave of hair off his brow. He flinched, the hand on his chest jerking. His eyes came open slowly, and as Finola watched, his gaze cleared and came to rest on her. He blinked, then again.

"Finola?" His voice was thick and husky with sleep. "Is something wrong?"

Finola shook her head, saw his eyes follow the movement of her hair, which she had left unbraided.

He lifted a hand to his face as if to remove his eyeglasses.

"I put them on the table," she told him, smiling.

He studied her. "Gabriel…is he all right?"

"He's been asleep for hours."

He nodded, still watching her with an uncertain expression as he pushed himself up a little in the bed. When Finola sat down beside him, he drew back as if he'd been struck.

"Well," he finally said, a little too loudly, "this is…a pleasant surprise. I was afraid you wouldn't visit me tonight, after the great oaf I made of myself in the dining room."

"I was lonely," Finola said quietly. "I wanted to be with you."

Something glinted in his eyes, just the flicker of a question.

"My bedroom is cold," Finola said with a fleeting glance at the robust fire across the room. "I'm afraid I've never quite learned to build a proper fire."

His eyes went to the fire, then came back to Finola. She could see the reflection of the flames burning out at her.

The blood pounded in Finola's head as she leaned toward him, taking his hand. "May I stay with you tonight, Morgan?" she asked simply, holding his gaze.

His eyes darkened, lingering for a moment on her face, dropping to the satin ribbon at the throat of her dressing gown. For an instant, he appeared stricken. "I'm not sure I understand…" he said softly, his voice still husky.

Finola drew in a deep, ragged breath. "Morgan, do you love me?"

"What?" He sounded as if he were strangling.

"Do you *love* me?" Finola repeated, clinging to his hand. "As a woman?"

He looked everywhere but at her, the fire in his eyes leaping higher. "Must you ask?" He gave a short, choked attempt at a laugh. "I seem unable to appear anything but foolish in your presence. What sort of affliction could it be but that of a man in love?"

He paused, fixing his gaze upon her. "Yes, Finola *aroon*, I love you— with all my heart and soul, I do love you."

His hand trembled violently in hers. The strength of his emotion startled her. "Morgan…look at me. I want to tell you something, and I want you to look at me when I say it."

Slowly, he dragged his gaze to her face. She saw it then—the sweet, reluctant admission of love in his eyes, mingled with an old hurt and perhaps the beginning of a faint light of hope.

Briefly, Finola pressed her fingers against his hand, then released it and stood up. Swept up in the thrill and relief of hearing his confession of love at last, she felt her own hands tremble now as she slipped her fingers beneath the ribbons of her dressing gown.

Her eyes never left his face…his beloved face…as softly, speaking in the Irish, she told him the secrets of her heart, her love for him, her desire to belong to him. As she spoke, she slipped the dressing gown from her shoulders to stand before him in the ivory satin nightdress she had chosen just for tonight.

Morgan caught his breath, and his head sank back against the pillow.

"I love you, Morgan," she said again, reaching out toward him. "And I am asking you to make me your wife…."

At first he made no move, but simply bathed her in the glow of his love-softened gaze. Then, he rose up on one elbow and reached for her hand, pressing her palm to his lips in a gentle, lingering kiss. "Are you sure, Finola *aroon*? Please, be very, very sure, for once you are truly mine, you will be mine forever. I would die before I let you go."

Finola freed her hands just long enough to extinguish the lamp, then turned back to him. As she slipped into the bed beside him, the ivory swan pendant he had given her as a wedding gift escaped her nightdress. Clasping it in one hand and putting her other hand to Morgan's heart, she brought her face close to his and began to repeat, again in the Irish...

"*I, Finola, take thee, Morgan, to be my wedded husband, for now and forever....*"

Framing her face with his hands, he held her, searching her eyes as if trying to look into her heart. Finally, he smiled...a glory of a smile that fell over Finola's face like stardust. At last he added his voice, unsteady as it was, to hers. Speaking in the ancient language of their people, he drew her into the warm, safe haven of his arms...

"*I pledge to thee my love...my fidelity...and life...for now and forever....*"

And to the Prodigal...Grace

The son said to him,
"Father, I have sinned against heaven and against you.
I am no longer worthy to be called your son." But the father said
to his servants, "Quick! Bring the best robe and put it on him. Put
a ring on his finger and sandals on his feet. Bring the fattened
calf and kill it. Let's have a feast and celebrate. For this son of
mine was dead and is alive again; he was lost and is found."

LUKE 15:21-24

The next morning, Morgan Fitzgerald sat by the window in his bed-chamber, watching the dawn of yet another mild, sun-touched December morn. He had cracked the window, relishing the sweet-scented air. He knew that all too soon December's flirtation with springlike temperatures would end, giving way to winter. But in the meantime, he meant to absorb every precious moment of warmth he could before the cold set in.

Glancing across the room, he smiled at the scene revealed in the first light of dawn. Finola still lay abed, but not alone. Well before daybreak, she had gone to collect Gabriel for his early morning nursing, and now the two of them lay snuggled together, warm and dozing in Morgan's enormous bed.

He watched them for a moment, drinking in the sight of his wife's golden hair falling like a curtain of sunshine over the babe cuddled to her heart. *If a man could die from happiness,* Morgan thought, *his time might be near.*

Unexpectedly, a sound filtered through the haze of his content. Faint, indistinct, and elusive, the music caught his attention, and he reached to open the window a little more.

He sat listening with growing wonder and appreciation as the strains of a violin came wafting across the grounds from the Gypsy wagon. It could only be Jan Martova. Although the Gypsy seemed to carry his fiddle with him wherever he went, this was the first time Morgan had actually heard him play.

The music was exquisite: achingly melodic, tormentingly lovely. Morgan had never heard anything quite like it. It seemed composed of both the ancient Celtic and the Romany, a haunting blend that carried with it the wailing of the wind across the mountains and the mystery of secrets whispered around the campfire.

He realized at once that he was hearing an exceptional talent, a brilliant gift. The boy played like a master! And yet Morgan sensed the unrestrained joy, the wildness and spontaneity of one who plays freely, whose spirit soars, unencumbered by the boundaries of form and method.

Hearing Finola stir, he motioned her to the window. She left the babe, still sleeping, and came to stand beside him.

"Listen," he said softly. "It's the Gypsy. He plays as if inspired, don't you think?"

"'Tis beautiful," she agreed, putting a hand to his shoulder. "Morgan, what will happen to him now? You said you feared he might no longer be welcomed among his people, after all that has happened."

Morgan nodded. "The lad risked his life to help a *Gorgio*—an outsider. Worse yet, an outsider who exposed the entire camp to the cholera. From the little I know about the Romany, Jan Martova will be an outcast from now on."

"Are they really so harsh?"

"It's their way," Morgan said. "I've been thinking...if you agree, that is, that I might allow him to keep his wagon where it is. At least for now. Until he's stronger and can make some plans."

"Oh, I'm *glad*, Morgan!" She stopped. "But a bit surprised, perhaps."

He smiled at her tact. "It has occurred to me that a soul which holds such exquisite music cannot be all that dark. Besides," he said, "who knows what wonders the mighty Sandemon may have wrought in these past weeks, eh? It's difficult to imagine anyone being altogether unchanged after so long a time in his presence."

"And Tierney?" she asked after a moment. "What of your young prodigal?"

Still smiling ruefully to himself, Morgan covered her hand on his shoulder with his own. "Ah, yes, my prodigal. I have done much thinking about the young rogue. And I find that I keep coming back to myself." He sighed. "It would seem that the very least one prodigal can do for another is to extend grace as he has received it. And since this prodigal has been given grace in great abundance, I can hardly deny a measure to Tierney Burke, now can I?"

Morgan turned to look up at her, and she bent to kiss him, her hair falling free to veil his face. His heart swelled with love and an overwhelming awareness of how greatly he had been blessed, and he clung to her, whispering a tender Gaelic endearment.

For several minutes Finola stood quietly beside him, listening to the music from the Gypsy wagon. "His music sounds…so joyful," she said softly. "His heart must be happy, in spite of all he has endured."

Morgan nodded, bringing her hand to his heart. "And can you hear *my* joy, Finola *aroon*? Can you hear the music of my heart?"

Finola dropped to her knees beside him and pressed her cheek next to his heart, as if listening. Morgan could hear the smile in her voice when she answered him. "Let me see…ah, yes…I hear it! Can it be? It would seem that the great *Seanchai*'s heart is playing a love song!"

Gently, he tipped her face to his and smiled into her eyes. "*You* are the song of my heart, *macushla*. You are the joy, the music of my life…and you will always be."

Be sure and read the final book in The Emerald Ballad,
Dawn of the Golden Promise...

In the fifth and concluding volume of her bestselling The
Emerald Ballad Series, BJ Hoff brings the exciting Irish-
American historical drama to a climax with all the passion
and power readers have come to expect from her.

The saga finds Morgan Fitzgerald adapting to life in a
wheelchair as a result of an assailant's bullet to his spine.
Meanwhile, his wife, Finola, must face the dark memories
and guarded secrets of her past. In New York City, policeman Michael Burke is caught in a conflict between his
faith and his determination to bring a dangerous enemy
to justice.

This unforgettable series began with the promise of an
epic love story and an inspiring journey of faith. The finale
delivers on that promise.

A Note from the Author

When I first began to research the idea for the first book in this series, *Song of the Silent Harp*, I discovered a strong religious thread throughout the history of Ireland. I hope I have communicated to my readers a clearer understanding of how Christianity influenced the lives of some of America's Irish ancestors.

During those years of study and writing, I became aware that it is virtually impossible to separate the past from the present. The struggles and successes, the trials and triumphs of our forebears, make up not only a rich heritage but also contribute in immeasurable ways to what we—and our world—are today. Like young Daniel Kavanagh, I believe that, from God's perspective, yesterday, today, and tomorrow are one vast *panorama*, a continuing epic that our Creator views in its entirety, from the dawn of time through the present to eternity.

Further, history *does*, indeed, repeat itself. Most experiences of the past continue to happen. The horrors of famine and hopelessness that surround many characters in The Emerald Ballad still exist. Month after month, year after year, the innocent victims of war, disaster, political indifference, and oppression go on suffering and dying, just as they did in Ireland during the Great Famine.

Government programs and private charities cannot begin to meet the escalating demand for worldwide assistance. I believe the Christian church should be at the very front of international rescue operations, for it is the *church* that bears the responsibility—and the privilege—of giving love to a world that needs it.

I invite you to join me in finding practical ways to help through your church or favorite charity. There are many organizations that provide an opportunity to put faith and love into action. One person *does* make a difference.

BJ Hoff

Rachel's Secret

Bestselling author BJ Hoff delights with her compelling series The Riverhaven Years. With the first book, *Rachel's Secret,* you'll discover a community of unforgettable characters, a tender love story, the faith journeys of people you'll grow to know and love, and enough suspense to keep the pages turning quickly.

When wounded Irish American riverboat captain Jeremiah Gant bursts into the rural Amish setting of Riverhaven, he brings chaos and conflict to the community—especially for young widow Rachel Brenneman. The unwelcome "outsider" needs a safe place to recuperate before continuing his secret role as an Underground Railroad conductor. Neither he nor Rachel is prepared for the forbidden love that threatens to endanger a man's mission, a woman's heart, and a way of life for an entire people.

Where Grace Abides

In this compelling second book in the The Riverhaven Years series, you'll get an even closer look at the Amish community of Riverhaven and the people who live and love and work there. Secrets, treachery, and persecution are a few of the challenges that test Rachel's faith and her love for the forbidden "outsider," while Gant's own hopes and dreams are dealt a life-changing blow, rendering the vow he made to Rachel seemingly impossible to honor.

The Amish community finds their gentle, unassuming lives of faith jeopardized by a malicious outside influence. At the same time, those striving to help runaway slaves escape to freedom through the Underground Railroad face deception and the danger of discovery.

SONG OF ERIN

The mysteries of the past confront the secrets of the present in bestselling author BJ Hoff's magnificent *Song of Erin* saga.

You'll be intrigued by this panoramic story that crosses the ocean from Ireland to America. In this tale of struggle and love and uncompromising faith, Jack Kane, the always charming but sometimes ruthless titan of New York's most powerful publishing empire, is torn between the conflict of his own heart and the grace and light of Samantha Harte, the woman he loves, whose troubled past continues to haunt her.

AMERICAN ANTHEM

At the entrance to the city, an Irish governess climbs into a carriage and sets out to confront the man who destroyed her sister's life—a blind musician who hears music no one else can hear…

On a congested city street, a lonely Scot physician with a devastating secret meets a woman doctor with the capacity to heal not only the sick…but also his heart…

In a tumbledown shack among hundreds of others like it, an immigrant family struggles to survive, and a ragged street singer old beyond her years appoints herself an unlikely guardian…

So begins *American Anthem*, a story set in 1870s New York that lets you step into another time to share the hopes and dreams and triumphant faith of a people you'll grow to love.

> "An eloquently told story that weaves
> history, music, faith and intrigue…
> an absolute pleasure."
> CHRISTIAN RETAILING

> "The story gently unfolds with intriguing characters,
> and the sound of music, which Hoff manages to make fly off
> the pages with her glorious and passionate descriptions."
> —CHRISTIAN LIBRARY JOURNAL

GREAT REVIEWS FOR BJ HOFF'S MOUNTAIN SONG LEGACY TRILOGY

BOOK ONE, *A DISTANT MUSIC*

"BJ Hoff always delights readers with her warm stories and characters who become part of your 'circle of special friends.'"

JANETTE OKE,
BESTSELLING AUTHOR OF *LOVE COMES SOFTLY*

"For this Kentucky woman, reading *A Distant Music* was like driving through the eastern hills and hollers on a perfect autumn day, with the scent of wood smoke in the air and the trees ablaze with color. BJ Hoff's lyrical prose brings to life this gentle, moving story of a beloved teacher and his students, who learn far more than the three Rs. I brushed away tears at several tender points in the story and held my breath when it seemed all might be lost. Yet, even in the darkest moments, hope shines on every page. A lovely novel by one of historical fiction's finest wordsmiths."

LIZ CURTIS HIGGS, BESTSELLING AUTHOR OF *THORN IN MY HEART*

"As always when I open BJ's books I'm drawn into a place that is both distant and at home...as I tell my husband, I wish I could create the kinds of characters BJ does because I fall in love with them and want them always as my friends."

JANE KIRKPATRICK, AUTHOR OF *LOOK FOR A CLEARING IN THE WILD*

"In some ways, *A Distant Music* is reminiscent of the 'Little House' series. Each chapter recalls the details of an event or some character's dilemma. Eventually, though, Hoff connects all the threads into a solid story whose ending will deeply touch readers. *A Distant Music* should find an eager audience."

ASPIRING RETAIL MAGAZINE

BOOK TWO, *THE WIND HARP*

"BJ always does a great job of drawing her readers into the lives of her characters. I'm sure that there will be many who will be eagerly pleading to know 'what happens next.' I will be among them."

JANETTE OKE, BESTSELLING AUTHOR
OF *LOVE COMES SOFTLY*

"BJ Hoff continues the story of Maggie and Jonathan, who must endure their share of trials before reaping their reward. Though this novel is historical, BJ Hoff deals with issues that are completely contemporary...Kudos to the author for charming us again!"

ANGELA HUNT, BESTSELLING AUTHOR OF *THE NOVELIST*

BOOK THREE, *THE SONG WEAVER*

"Like a warm visit with a good friend over a hot cup of tea, *The Song Weaver* offers comfort and satisfaction... and you don't want the visit to come to an end."

CINDY SWANSON

"BJ Hoff is a master at characterization, and her stories are rich with insight. I love the historical setting and learned something new about the role of women in that society."

JILL E. SMITH

"*The Song Weaver* is the last book in the Mountain Song Legacy story, and I hate to see it end. I'll miss Maggie and Jonathan and all the others...A very satisfying end to a special series. She never disappoints."

BARBARA WARREN